Penny Dreadful
and the Poisonberry Fortune

Carl Paolino

Carl Paolino Studios, Inc.

Copyright © 2015 by Carl Paolino.

All rights reserved. Printed in Canada. No part of this book may be used or reproduced in any manner whatsoever without written permission except in the case of brief quotations embodied in critical articles and reviews.

Second Printing

ISBN-13: 978-1492872115
ISBN-10: 1492872113

Carl Paolino Studios, Inc.
53-121 63 Street, Maspeth, NY 11378
www.WhoIsPennyD.com

To Charles Salvatore and Josephine Angelina Paolino,
you are dearly missed.

Index

Chapter 1
The Gothic Kingdom

There is a place called the Gothic Kingdom and it truly exists. Some would argue that it doesn't because you can't locate it on a map. But if you set out to find it you would see that it does not lie between here and there, but resides comfortably between your own imagination and the hum drum world we now live in called home.

I will draw you an example; if you were out for a walk and found yourself in an unknown place, you would be thinking to yourself that you were "lost" by our definition of that word.

However, in truth you would not really be lost, because you would be somewhere. You may not know where that somewhere was or how to get home from that very place at that very moment, but by using your five senses you may confirm that you are definitely somewhere. You could see things, feel things and hear things, therefore your only wise conclusion is that you are not lost. What you would really be is confused.

And that brings us right back to the Gothic Kingdom. If you were a confused sort of person, as most people are, there could only be one of two outcomes when seeking this place.

One, you may never find it. Even if it were directly under

your toes and you were to step on it, trip over it, or walk around it every day of your life you still may never see it.

Or two, you may have been summoned there because of some unusually bad deed that you found you were compelled to commit, and thus you may never find your way back home. Home being where you came from, that is. The Gothic Kingdom, would be your new home for an unknown-unknown amount of time.

Now aside from the rules that govern the entrance to this place, for those of you who were not originally born there, there are people who are born there and may never see the place where you come from. So that makes us all even.

Now about those who were born here and those who were not, there are some very particular people who have lived in both worlds, yours and theirs. One such "crossing over", from the Gothic Kingdom to your world was initiated by one particular individual as an opportunity to find love; a force so strong that no single world could contain it. Therefore, no one can blame him for that.

Ultimately, he returned to the Kingdom since he was of Goth origin and brought with him the love of his life to live in harmony with him for forever and a moment.

But that moment was shattered when it became an absolute necessity for this particular person, of Goth origin and another, from our world to live in harmony as they planned; as their very lives were at stake.

But I am getting ahead of myself. So before I go on and on about these two very extraordinary people who crossed over from their own world to the other's to find love, I would like to say a little something about this particular place in general; the Kingdom itself.

As one might imagine the landscape of the Gothic Kingdom to be, it has a very old look about it. Hard to put a finger on it exactly, but it definitely has a European flavor. The shops look as though they belong in the Middle Ages, and the cobblestone streets look from just about that same time. And everything appears grey.

There is some color of course, but there is that darn dreary thing going on all the time that makes everything look dull, as if the sky is in a perpetual overcast mode.

Situated at the far end of town, practically in the next county, there is a castle made of natural stone as tall as a forty story building. It has spires and a flying buttress or two and a tower that could easily hide a princess or a mother-in-law or an ogre inside.

Since no one has gone up to that tower for any reason or for so many years, I will suggest we believe that an ogre is up there and not a mother-in-law, who as we all know get very bad reputations. I will leave the validity of that last statement up to your imagination.

This castle is the product of great artisans, architects and construction workers from many years ago, but today it declines from decades of decay. Way, way back when the castle was new, it was the home for many animals and there were humans living there as well. It was common knowledge that they all got along just fine because they all spoke English. Speaking English, as insisted by the humans who lived there, was the key to civilized cohabitation.

All of the animals disagreed with this, of course. Their incessant arguing on this issue with the humans forced everyone to simply speak his own language and not pay any attention to what either humans or animals were saying. Strangely enough, this seemed to work.

Now, there is one more misconception that may need to be cleared up. If you are imagining a happy colorful castle filled with unicorns, forest pixies and dancing fungus, then you are in the wrong kingdom. Especially now, because the dark times have come and it looks like they are here to stay.

Having said that, we get on with the story.

The extraordinary young couple I spoke about above were very much in love, and lived in this castle. The gentleman's name was Natty Dreadful.

He came from a very old and well-respected family, who were part of the Poisonberry Clan and he had lived in the

Kingdom his whole life. He was a Goth aristocrat by any other distinction, and a fancy dresser as most Goths are. His clothes were trimmed with frills and lace, delicate, yet very masculine. His goatee was always well groomed and his hair was black and slicked back. Around his neck he wore a silver locket containing a picture of his love and a memento she gave him on the very first day they met.

His young bride, the woman in the picture, secured in the silver locket around Natty's neck was known only as Lucinda.

Her origin is unclear at this time, but it was suspected that she did not originate from the Gothic Kingdom but from the world you call home. Gossipers, rumor spreaders and people with small minds in general, who were not unlike the writers of the tabloids in your local supermarkets made her a target of their craft. They insisted that she must have been from Long Island, China or possibly one of the outer planets such as Mars.

This, they claimed was the source of her magic, a magic so powerful that she was able to enchant a Goth aristocrat.

But rest assured, Lucinda was not an alien. She was as much a human as Natty was. The point is that she was not of Goth origin. How she came to live there exactly is still a mystery and will remain one until further notice.

So, this young bride known only as Lucinda was so pretty that she made single men sweat. Sometimes they even threw up when she looked at them and hid from her after doing so. Her platinum blonde hair may have been to blame for that but it was never confirmed.

Like her hair, her conversation was short and to the point, as was the way she did business in the marketplace that was located just outside the castle. This market was held there every other day, yet always managed to be open for business four times a week.

Lucinda always wore a dress with delicate stitching that was almost always in purple and black. Sometimes she wore black and purple just to throw people off.

She was also pregnant as anyone could plainly see. She

looked about eight plus months or so, and she was careful in every sense of the word, including watching what she ate and limiting her exercise routine to walking. (Sometimes, for a great distance.)

Natty was often heard attempting to limit Lucinda's work habits, while Lucinda was always trying to increase them.

"Lucinda, remember what the midwife said," Natty would say.

"I do," Lucinda would reply. "She said I may exercise all I want, but cliff repelling is definitely out."

"No, she said the cliff repelling is just fine," Natty would retort. "But carrying too heavy a package in your arms is a no no."

"She said nothing of the sort," Lucinda would answer. "She said I can do all the work I want to as long as I have a good stiff drink afterwards at the saloon with the guys. And I should limit the drinking songs to twenty."

"Okay, then, but as long as we limit your drinking to no more than two shots per song," Natty would respond. "And the bungee jumping lessons for tomorrow are definitely out. I have spoken."

"You never let me have any fun," Lucinda in mock anger, would pout.

Then she would stamp her foot down hard to lend credence to the statement.

Or was it real anger? Natty could never tell.

And so it would go on like this all day as Natty and Lucinda, worked at the castle, nearly seven days a week. Only Lucinda not so much since she was with child, regardless of what she said.

All of this may appear hard to believe since Natty sprang from a wealthy lineage, but it is true. The Poisonberry Clan had fallen on hard times, and their wealth was nearly depleted, not spent, but mysteriously misplaced. (Or stolen maybe.)

Anywho, Natty chose to leave the Clan to marry and raise a family, or was it to seek his fortune again? We are not sure and neither was he.

While in school Natty studied engineering and he was very good at it indeed. Thus he was chosen by the master of this castle among many applicants to look after the repairs. Not every repair, just the ones necessary to prevent the castle from falling apart. What good would a castle be if it fell apart?

"I believe in doing the work put before me," Natty would say when asked by a townsperson why an aristocrat would dirty his hands as a laborer. "And if there is no work put before me, then I will invent some. That will teach the work a lesson!"

Lucinda was also a valuable asset to the well-being of the castle. She was schooled in metaphysical-medicinals and was put in charge of the livestock that was used for trade. She kept them healthy and strong. It could not be proven but it was commonly believed that it was her singing to the animals that calmed their nerves and allowed them to heal from any illness.

If this all sounds like a fairy tale come true, then get ready for some very bad news.

Their employer, who was the Lord of the Castle, was a Count. He was also a shape-shifter. Or, a skin-walker, if you prefer. Some use the word vampire but it is so over-used in literature today, so why even go there? But the result is generally the same, so skin-walker it is.

He was not like the ones you may have read about in novels or those that you see on television or in the movies, but a true mimic of any animal it pleases. And like said true mimics he would suck blood for sustenance when in the form of a vampire bat, or hunt and eat his neighbors' sheep when in the form of a wolf. Then, like most mimics, he would deny the deed (never trust a skin-walker, they are all such liars).

When he transformed he usually chose to become creatures of the carnivorous nocturnal type, because they tend to be strong and ferocious. He shied away from the smaller creatures of the pleasant daytime since they were so low on the food chain and thus often became food themselves. It was something he tried to avoid.

But most importantly, he never forgot that when he was in his non-human form that he was at his most vulnerable. Animals are simply that, animals, and can be lured into a trap, caught and well, perhaps we shouldn't go there just yet.

The point is, once caught, he lost his transformation abilities and had to stay as said animal for as long as he was caged. (Or to the end of the natural life of that animal.) This is another reason never to become a fly. If you got stuck on flypaper for more than a day or two, it would all end there.

The Count had been known to transform into a smaller creature, but only on special occasions. So why then would any shape-shifter shift into a grass hopper, for example, if it was so risky?

Simple. As a tiny creature he could easily go unnoticed and find his way under a barn door or hide in the pocket of his foes. Imagine their surprise when they saw him materialize right behind them in the safety of their own home?

Surprise has many advantages. This is one valuable lesson that Natty was very familiar with. He knew his Goth history and it was plagued with wars and the study of strategies and tactics was something he understood quite well. Unbeknownst to Lucinda, these were also part of his plan; a plan he would very soon put into effect.

Now getting back to our Count, it is further unclear how such a strange and unwelcome creature ever came to live in the Gothic Kingdom. Not that it is so hard to believe, unexplained things happen here all the time. But since he showed up, all who lived around the castle were on their guard, for he was real and apparently here to stay. His name, was Count Longtooth. And he lives up to that name.

As for his appearance, you may expect him to be dressed in a tuxedo, like most Counts, but not so. He always dressed in black, and wore a long cloak and cape. His hands, when exposed were long and gnarled. His fingernails were longer still and sharp like daggers. His face looked stretched and narrow and his teeth were longer than normal. Getting a smile out of him would be a practical impossibility.

The commonwealth of the Gothic Kingdom once thrived on a delicate balance between the people, the animals and their commerce. When Count Longtooth came into the picture this balance was disrupted. He was greedy to say the least and had no respect at all for his fellow neighbors both human and animal. He stole, he cheated and he lied. Sadly to report, he was not well-liked.

The Goths, who were the ruling occupants of this world, or so the animals had led them to believe, secretly held meetings to devise a plan to rid the kingdom of Longtooth. But that didn't last long. The Count would foil any plan to be overthrown before it even got started, sometimes with devastating results.

Thus the expression, "careful what you say, for even a fly on the wall may be the Count," was heard frequently.

As for the animals, most of them refused to comment on this matter and to talk in public altogether. They feared for their lives.

What you may next be thinking is, why would Natty and Lucinda, who appear to be hard working, good natured and pleasant folk work for such a man?

There was an ulterior motive afoot and this was the consequence that comes with doing what is right and just. You see, Count Longtooth needed to be stood up against and Natty Dreadful of the Poisonberry Clan was just the man to do it.

Chapter 2
The Great Escape

Natty made sure that he and Lucinda had worked for the Count for as long as they could in order to gain a certain level of his confidence. The Count had begun to trust Natty and Lucinda more and more with responsibilities, which allowed Natty to carry out a plan that he had been hatching for some time now.

For all of his life Natty was a person who planned out everything that he did. He had planned his education, and his employment and he was successful at both. What he didn't plan was meeting a girl like Lucinda in, of all of the strangest places in the universe, your world, and falling madly in love with her. He also hadn't planned to become a father so soon after their marriage.

"Life is full of unplanned things," Natty had thought to himself. "However, since my ultimate plan was to be happy, I guess I planned on meeting Lucinda, who makes me so very happy, after all and didn't know it."

One could say that since everything in his life was working out in his favor; he had educated himself at what he enjoyed doing most and found the woman of his dreams. So perhaps he deserved a credit of merit for an almost perfect plan to see that his life was as fulfilled as he could make it.

You could also argue that Natty was very bad at planning his life out. Not the final outcome of his plans, just the stuff that gets him there.

This kind of argument could go on all day, and if it did this story would have to end right here. But there was more pressing business ahead since this was the very day that Natty decided to end his employment with the Count. If all went according to his plan he would also end the Count's reign of terror over the Gothic Kingdom.

On a very average day not unlike any other, when the sky was as gray as one would expect in a place called the Gothic Kingdom, Natty made sure that Lucinda was out of the castle and far enough away so that if what he planned didn't go as he expected, she would still be safe.

He had also planned her escape from the Kingdom altogether. Detailed instructions were planted in her purse and he planned for friends to "unexpectedly" cross paths with her at her intended location. He did this to be sure that she would not be around the castle to see (what she would consider) the foolishness he was about to attempt.

Natty thought he knew the whereabouts of the Count, but as we have learned already, Natty was not very good at planning. He thought the Count was in a neighboring land on business, and that Lucinda was on her way to a market in the opposite direction. When in fact, they were not.

This was not a good thing, because Natty was about to do something very foolish indeed and get caught doing it. For the moment his plan was simple; he would lure the Count away from the castle on phony business using a document written on the wrong type of paper.

The type of paper he should have used, that would avoid any suspicion would have been parchment but he used a sheet of loose-leaf paper from Lucinda's notebook instead. This would surely tip off the Count that Natty was up to something and he would pretend to leave the castle but remain here instead to see what Natty was planning.

Further, Natty believed, that the Count would assume the physical equivalent of a smaller animal so that he could spy on Natty until his entire plan was completely visible.

When the Count was sure that he understood all of Natty's plan he would suddenly materialize into his human form and say something clever like, "Ah-ha!," or even, "So!". He might say some other things, but it is hard to tell since it didn't turn out that way.

Natty also didn't know that the Count, was not really a Count. If he were a real Count he would have been educated enough to notice that the document from a "land owner" was on a piece of paper that did not come from anywhere in the Gothic Kingdom. In fact it was written on a sheet of loose leaf paper from a page of a notebook purchased at Waldbum's Department Store.

He pretended to go about his business all day, believing that he was being watched by the Count.

He accumulated odd items in the castle that made no sense to collect and piled them up in one hall of the castle. He laughed fiendishly for no apparent reason and then went back to his strange work. Surely the Count would hold off any retaliation until he thought he understood what Natty was up to. He knew that like most animals, the Count was a curious creature and so this became Natty's stalling tactic.

In order for the Count to witness these odd events unnoticed by Natty, he would have to transform himself into a small animal like an insect. A grasshopper, perhaps, then watch Natty for a while believing he was safe because Natty thought that he, the Count, was far away on business.

Natty's real plan was to bait the Count until he could locate him as a smaller creature, knowing full well that he was nearby.

So all the while Natty is going about doing these strange chores in the castle, he is secretly looking out for the Count in the form of an insect. Not just any insect, but one that appeared to show up in every room he entered. One that could be watching him.

When Natty spotted him, he would capture him in a container of some sort, like a large glass jar. He would put him on display for all of the Kingdom to see, and this act would restore his family as caretaker of the Kingdom and everyone would be happy.

But, as already stated, the plan didn't work out that way.

The Count never left the castle since he was not a true Count (as we all now know) and had not been educated enough to read, let alone to know the difference between parchment and a sheet of loose leaf paper. So when the Count approached Natty to not only ask him what this paper said, but to ask him why he was collecting so many strange objects in the castle hall and carrying a large glass jar around, the jig was practically up.

This is not to say that the Count was completely ignorant, but he was not human. As a skin-walker he had just as much use for reading as he would for ballroom dancing. So he pondered over the paper for a long while, before he went looking for Natty to ask him what it said.

Eventually he found him and followed him through several rooms of the castle unnoticed because the rooms were large and cluttered. And Natty never noticed him because he was so deep in concentration, watching out for a small insect that may be following him from room to room and not a person.

Finally, the Count walked into a room at precisely the moment Natty captured a grasshopper on the table in the big glass jar he had been carrying around with him all day.

What came next was even more revealing. Natty didn't notice the Count in the doorway behind him right away. He was overjoyed with his capture of what he thought was the Count, and began to berate the poor grasshopper who was looked very frightened indeed.

The Count was not the sharpest tooth in the lion's mouth, but it was obvious, even to him that Natty had planned to trick him somehow and capture him at some point as well, quite possibly that very day.

He still didn't know how Natty's plan could have worked. But by this time, it didn't matter.

Now here is where the story gets complicated.

The Count had not yet worked up his anger, for if he had he may have transformed into a razorback wild hog and finished Natty right there on the spot. Actually, he was amused. He watched and waited, and eventually Natty heard the Count's heavy breathing in the room and turned around to see that he made an awful mistake, or miscalculation as it were.

Natty needed to lie and lie quickly. His life depended upon it.

"So what do you think?" said Natty after he turned around to face the Count. "It is a new play I am working on."

"I see," said the Count. "Please, tell me more."

"Yes," said Natty. "The farmers have a saying, a funny one indeed. Perhaps you have heard it?"

"I don't think that I have," said the Count.

"They say, hee hee, you're going to laugh when you hear this one," said Natty. "They say that even a fly on the wall, or a grasshopper, could be the Count."

"And what does that mean?" asked the Count.

"Exactly," said Natty. "That's what makes it so funny. It means, that they love you so much, they wish you could be everywhere all the time."

"Do tell," said the Count.

"Yes," said Natty.

"I wonder if the Count is buying this," thought Natty. "How could it possibly be this easy?"

He started to realize that the Count was not an educated creature, but would have to be a complete ass to buy this one. And, what in blazes is he doing here, in the form of himself in the first place? For that matter, why is he still holding onto that paper and who is this grasshopper I just captured? He must have some business of his own and be wondering why I called him all of those foul names just a moment ago.

Natty opened the jar and freed the grasshopper.

"Remember to come and see the show," said Natty to the grasshopper.

The Count transformed his tongue into that of a frog. It shot out of his mouth and snagged the grasshopper in mid-flight as it headed for the window. He then sucked it back into his mouth, chewed it and swallowed.

Yes, things were not looking very good right about now for Natty. He was no fool, he was a kind-hearted person and always thinking of the greater good. This time around he was trying to compete with a truly evil being and on his deceitful level at that.

Nattys' intentions were righteous but he was on the wrong side of the road. This road was occupied by a skin-walker and all of his manifestations.

Just when he thought it couldn't get any worse, Lucinda appeared in the doorway behind the Count.

"Oh, you have got to be kidding!" said Natty as soon as he saw her.

"How nice," said the Count. "You saved me the trouble of looking for you. Now I can destroy you both at the same time."

Lucinda was panting for her breath. Then she brandished a sword from behind her back.

"Your cutlass, my dear," said Lucinda, tossing Natty the sword.

Lucinda wasted no time in fleeing the room once Natty had caught his sword. For a pregnant woman, she could run like the wind and was down the hall before the Count even considered her a threat.

As you may have guessed, earlier that day Lucinda never reached her destination where she was thought to be. She detected that she was being followed and decided to ambush her stalker. She was shocked to see it was Freddy the Barista. When it came to making a good strong cup of Joe, Freddy was down right terrible, but the average Goth didn't know the difference. As long as the coffee was dark and muddy, they liked it.

In the city where Lucinda grew up, however, brewing a quality cup of coffee was an art. She fashioned her coffee much better than his but never spread a word about it. She didn't want to hurt his feelings.

Freddy always smelled of coffee and out on the open road with a wind at Lucinda's back, a strong scent of crushed roasted coffee beans and body odor was easy to detect. She waited for the road to narrow and bend and used that moment to hide behind a thick oak tree. Freddy was inexperienced at being stealthy, so he walked right into her trap.

Lucinda was one of five children, the other four being boys. They were all strapping lads who played football and other manly sports. She was the baby in the family and allowed, under careful supervision, to play with them. She was taught to be rough with her brothers, and they allowed it.

As time went on and they all grew older, Lucinda got stronger and the games they played together got rougher. Eventually all four of her brothers regretted teaching her how to play tackle football and allowing her to play with them. Basically, the stronger she got, the more they got hurt.

Lucinda suspected that Natty put Freddy up to following her but she didn't know why until she threatened him and, let us just say that Freddy the Barista, spilled all his beans at once.

If there was one thing that the Count knew, it was when to attack. Lucinda posed no threat so he didn't bother to follow her, but a man with a sword was a different story. He transformed his clawed hands into large eagle's talons just as Natty came at him. The Count fought off every attack as if it were an easy game for him to win.

Natty wasn't usually a person to attack anyone or anything, including that grasshopper a few minutes ago. But in this case, Lucinda's life was in peril, and he knew his entire plan was foiled, so it was attack first or suffer the consequences.

He was a skilled swordsman, but the Count was a trained killer.

As any one of the many carnivorous animals the Count so

often used to manifesting himself into, he knew just as many ways to fight and to kill.

He was a down right killing machine.

Lucinda made it clear out of the castle and met with many townspeople who gathered to lend support (to her, not Natty.) They were willing to hide her if she would allow them, but for Natty, the writing was already on the wall. This was a fight he could not win.

Never one to give up or give in, Natty utilized all his skills. When he passed a fireplace, he stole the log poker with his free hand and struck at the Count repeatedly with both weapons.

Natty utilized the heavy wooden table in the room as a shield, though it did little to fend off the Count, who transformed the top half of his body into a grizzly bear and smashed the heavy wooden furniture with one mighty pounce.

When Natty ascended a narrow passage of steps, the Count transformed his arms and cape into bat wings and flew upwards to meet him at the top of the flying buttress before he even got there.

At one point as they battled, Natty thought he had the talons of the Count pinned between his crossed sword and fireplace poker until the Count transformed his arms into those of a German Shepard.

The skinny yet muscular canine legs slipped through the cutlass and fireplace poker and kicked repeatedly at Natty's midsection.

Natty managed to retreat but this was no more than a ploy to stall for time.

His once elegant purple shirt and black jacket were torn to pieces. The deep gashes across his abdomen dripped with his blood as he paused to catch his breath.

"Natty," shouted Lucinda from below. "Be careful."

Lucinda knew where this was going. She knew her husband was no match for the evil Count. She pleaded with the townspeople to help him, but their already forlorn faces said it all. They would harbor her if need be until she could evacuate the Kingdom, but in no way could they challenge the Count. They had families, farms, there was so much at stake. This was Natty's foolish doing. And so he would have to answer for it, alone.

In their delusion they thought that once this ordeal was over with, life would get back to normal. Well, as normal as things could be if they believed living under the Count's tyranny was a good thing. Actually, they hated it completely, but it was tolerable. And so this became their norm.

"Natty, be careful," mocked the Count, then he laughed like a hyena.

"You imitate a woman well," said Natty. "Have you had much practice?"

"Oddly enough," said the Count. "I am only able to manifest into the male of any species. I don't know why, but it is so."

Natty grinned and the Count suddenly realized that he was being made a mockery of.

The Count transformed his arms into rows of porcupine quills. He crouched down on all fours and lunged forward at Natty.

The low attack caught Natty by surprise and he dropped the fireplace poker trying to defend himself. His cutlass was then cornered between the quills of the Count's right arm and when he slashed at Natty with his left, he let go of his sword to prevent himself from being cut again.

The cutlass skidded along the ground and fell off the edge of the flying buttress. It plunged down into the dark waters of the moat below.

The alligators fought ferociously with one another at what they thought was their dinner, dropping in from above.

"That didn't take long'" said the Count.

Both Natty and the Count took a moment to pause, reflect and to catch their breaths.

"And now, Natty Dreadful, we come to the conclusion of your employment with me. Unless, you are willing to tell me where you hid my fortune?"

The look on Natty's face may have been surprise, but the pain coursing through his body at the time prevented it from being obvious.

The Count was an animal in many ways but not nearly as foolish as Natty thought he was. When it came to greed, the Count was as sharp as a barbed wire fence.

"Evil is to evil," said Natty. "I should have known better."

"Your answer?" said the Count. "And state it in the form of a plea for your life."

Natty just shook his head.

"I will not," said Natty. "The Poisonberry Fortune belonged to my family and it always will. You stole it from us, and I stole it back. So that makes us even. You will never have it."

"No?" said the Count.

The Count was still stuck on the semantics of the last thought.

"If I stole it from you, then you stole it back from me, that makes us both thieves," said the Count, sure that he was correct. "Anyway, this will be your last chance Natty, am I going to spare your life? Or, do you prefer to swim with the gators?"

Some of the townspeople below were getting restless waiting for the end of Natty to arrive. Time worked in Natty's favor. It gave them, the Townspeople, time to think about the choice they had made and to make a wiser choice instead.

They began to wonder how they could live with themselves if they allowed this dreadful thing to happen. They wondered how they could ever look Lucinda in the eye ever again, or at their own faces in the mirror. Then, their passion called forth the wisdom to do right and they made a new choice.

"We must help Natty," shouted one of the men.

"Storm the gates!" shouted an old woman with her cane raised in the air.

Several townspeople armed with metal rakes and clubs raced across the drawbridge and into the castle. Their broken shoes, torn clothing, and empty stomachs no longer mattered. They would save him or die trying, and then beg for

Lucinda's forgiveness if they were too late.

Natty knew it was over. One way or the other. He released his fear completely and told the Count exactly what he thought of him.

"You know," said Natty, fully aware that he was making the final point of his life. "You are reprehensible in every way. You are evil to the core and your promise means nothing to me. I have lived under your roof and watched you slaughter and steal from those around you. I will no longer give in to your threats and stand by watching you do evil. You will not have my family's fortune and you no longer have any power over me. I defy you."

"Oh, that's too bad," said the Count. "Then I no longer need you. You're fired."

The Count transformed his hand into a large praying mantis claw and swung it across Natty's throat.

It surprised the Count to see that Natty hadn't moved a muscle. It was as if Natty knew the Count's first strike would be a bluff. But how could he, thought the Count? Perhaps he was just frozen from fear. Yes, that was it, the Count thought. After all, everyone, both human and animal is afraid of me.

The tip of his claw caught the small leather string that held up the silver locket that hung around Natty's neck and severed it. The items from inside the locket fell out when the locket hit the ground and opened; a coin, a feather and a tiny picture.

"Humph," said the Count. "I'm impressed. Not even a flinch. I guess you aren't afraid to die."

He then raised his clawed arm for a second time to deliver the final blow that would put an end to Natty for certain.

"Say, bye bye, Natty," said the Count.

The Count stepped forward and just as he did, the coin that had spilled from the opened locket rolled right under his advancing foot.

In a comical fashion unparalleled by any modern day comedian, the Count missed Natty completely with what would have been a deadly strike, and slipped over to the very edge of the precipice.

The townspeople were just stepping onto the highest level of the castle where Natty and the Count were battling. As soon as they entered the flying buttress, they froze at what they saw, still panting to catch their breaths.

It was not the horror show that they had expected. Instead, what they saw would make a great tale to be retold hundreds, if not thousands of times in their local pubs for years to come.

The Count was balancing at the very edge of an enormous drop, swinging his arms furiously to regain his balance. It was obvious that he was about to transform again, but Natty wasted no time in hauling back and gave the Count a swift kick in the back of his pants that sent him tumbling off the edge.

I know what you are thinking. You are thinking why doesn't the Count transform into a bird or a gnat and fly away? Well, because a transformation of any kind under normal conditions takes a lot of mental focus and energy. But under duress, like if the one about to transform were hurtling towards certain death, there would be practically no time, to consider what kind of animal to transform into.

Further, the question would arise of whether or not that animal could even react fast enough to fight for its own life, or have time to flap its wings fast enough to prevent itself from hitting the ground?

This became the plight of the Count as he had but a second or two to transform and escape the meat-starved alligators that resided in his own castle moat.

So transform he did and into a water moccasin, at that. He was small enough to slip between the powerful jaws of the alligators in the moat and fast enough to escape. This was his solution and for the time being it worked.

The feeding frenzy was a quick one. The rapid splashing of water soon calmed and it was unclear if the Count escaped or became a quick snack. It was months before the townspeople ever found out what became of the Count.

The battle was considered a victory for Natty Dreadful and an important lesson was learned by the townspeople that day. In short; it was learned that evil can be fought and conquered.

Natty was led down the hundreds of steps to the edge of the castle moat where Lucinda was waiting for him. They embraced and the townspeople cheered. Although they were all pleased by the outcome, they knew in their hearts that the Count may still be alive and they must all take certain precautions from now on.

The local apothecary bandaged up Natty's wounds whilst others stood guard at the edge of the moat in case the Count surfaced as a half-shark, enraged platypus or some other dangerous animal.

"You've done it, Natty," said Lucinda. "You've defeated the Count."

"I am not so sure, Lucinda," said Natty. "The Count is a resourceful creature. I suspect he will return one day."

More than just one of the townspeople answered his statement with an outcry that echoed off the walls of Castle Longtooth itself.

"Over my dead body, he will," said the townsfolk, and that opinion was met with cheers.

They, the townspeople, were united. They lost their fear. They found a new power in believing in themselves.

"It looked awfully bad from down here, Natty," said Lucinda. "How did you defeat him?"

Natty held out the one tiny coin that the Count had slipped on. It was a penny. Not just any penny, but the same penny that Natty had kept with him since the day he met Lucinda.

"It was this," said Natty. "Your lucky penny from my locket, the one..."

"...yes, the same one you offered to me on the day we met," said Lucinda. "The one cent I was short while making a purchase at the market."

Lucinda caressed her belly.

"Our, lucky Penny," said Lucinda.

"Penny, yes, a brilliant name, is it not?" said Natty. "And it is for her that we must protect the Poisonberry Fortune. She will discover it on her own one day. But until then we must not forget that the Count is vindictive. His soul, as diseased as it is, will never rest until he gets it."

"We will hide you, come live with us," said more than just one of the townspeople.

"It would be unfair to put any of you in further jeopardy for us," said Natty.

Natty turned away and spoke quickly and quietly to Lucinda so that no other person could hear. Miss Davendish listened closely as if it were her business anyway. She plodded closer so she could hear, but Natty turned Lucinda and began to walk away.

"We will flee," said Natty. "It is time for you to go home, Lucinda."

"But we will only be safe there for a short while," said Lucinda. "One day she may need to return here."

"You know this all too well," said Natty. "She has her birthright to protect. But this will give us time to prepare her. And when it is her turn to discover her heritage, she will be ready to reclaim the family fortune for her own. After all, she will be a Dreadful."

Chapter 3
The New House on the Block, Literally

It may sound like a cliché but there was a full moon that night in the tiny hamlet of Terracotta, when a rather larger than normal size moving van raced through the streets. This was unusual for the sleepy town but what made it down right bizarre was the fact that this van didn't make the grinding, clanging, huffing and puffing noises one often associates with the engine of a van of this size.

Although the engine didn't make any sound at all, the rubber tires on the wet pavement were another story: they squealed like a baby pot belly pig as the driver made several sharp turns down the narrow streets. If you happened to be awake at that late hour, you may have mistaken these sounds for a rusty gate swinging in the wind or some other unknown nightly source.

The headlights of the van sharply illuminated what little nocturnal life was present that night. An alley cat was caught in these beams of brightness as it balanced atop a picket fence, then leapt from one well-groomed fenced-in front yard to the next. Even an opossum stopped rummaging through a trash can and sat up to watch the van pass.

This was suburbia at its finest. Garden gnomes, pink flamingos, drunks with lanterns and the like gleefully stood at attention at every home ready to greet any visitor. But not that night. That night, there was a plan afoot. Nay, a secret mission.

Appearing almost lost or disoriented at the very least, the moving van made a sharp turn off of Underdonk Street and swerved right and left down Pleasant Avenue before coming to an abrupt halt. The sound of the brake-locked rubber tires sliding across the pavement was all that was heard.

The house that the van stopped in front of was a two-story, tudor style home, with a large "For Sale" sign posted in the front yard facing the van's front cab. The occupants inside the cab began to move about, appearing as nothing more than shadowy figures. Then, the doors sprang open.

With grace and inhuman speed three characters dressed in long dark robes with hoods, opened the side doors to the van. Ramps were automatically deployed from underneath the van and the hooded figures raced up inside.

In true silent cinema fashion, these pixilated figures managed to carry out of the van several large wooden crates as if they weighed nothing at all.

The door to the vacant house automatically swung open and the hooded figures whisked the large creates inside. There must have been thirty oddly shaped crates in all. A task that would take an ordinary moving crew hours to complete, these hooded figures accomplished in under a minute.

The van's ramps folded back up and the doors closed tightly. The hooded figures leapt back into the cab and as quickly and as quietly as the van had entered this street, it vanished into the dark night. The sound of the squealing tires on the wet pavement was quickly replaced by the clicking sounds of crickets.

The wind began to kick up with a sudden ferocity. It tossed the "For Sale" sign to and fro, until it resembled a metronome. The entire sign was uprooted and flew away completely. Then something totally unexpected happened.

The house that stood behind the sign, the house that had looked abandoned for many months, the house that was nothing more than an ordinary house, began to transform.

It started slowly at first. All that could be heard were the sounds of wood, metal, and glass, splintering, bending, shattering. The second story of the house was the first to go. With one mighty heave it became completely askew from the bottom half.

What one would think to be architecturally impossible, appeared common place. The windows began to stretch to their new odd shapes and the walls began to peel away to reveal a new façade of brick and mortar and tar shingle underneath.

The house number on the front door that once proudly displayed a lucky number eight, is split in half. Not the door, but the number eight itself.

A deep crack appeared in the wood right next to that number forming a perfect number one. When the left half of the number eight fell away the new number on the door now reads the commonly believed unlucky number thirteen.

The street sign on the corner was also affected. A strong wind belted the signpost and spun the Pleasant Avenue sign around like a top. The sign slipped down the pole and became stuck, covering over most of the Underdonk Street sign below it. The street sign then read; UnPleasant Avenue.

The house bore little resemblance to what it had looked like only moments before. It was completely out of place now on the street, and stood out from all the others on the block. Not only because it appeared old and unkempt, but because no two walls of this house remained at a right angle.

The steps leading up to the front door appeared flat up against the side of the house. The windows were contorted and the wood shingles and brick work were lopsided. What was holding this house up, and for that matter what was keeping it together at all?

It looked uninviting and was probably meant to. Those people, who had just moved in, whoever they were, expected to be left alone. There was no doubt about that.

There were questions. So many questions, that the neighbors on this block would soon be asking themselves. Imagine the surprise they would have when they woke up the next morning to fetch their morning papers, or to go for their early morning run or to wander over to the local donut shop for a coffee and found out they had a new neighbor. Or to be more precise, a new house on their block entirely.

Imagine the hysteria the Terracotta Home Owners Association would contribute to with their picket signs and protests in front of this house, what their signs would read, what the write ups in the local papers would say. Imagine the petitions that neighbors would write to make the homeowners conform to their ideal of normality, their endless suggestions and their incessant demands. Imagine it!

There would be pandemonium on this block come morning. It would last for many months. It would not be pretty, but, this too would come to an end.

All of this would go unaddressed by the owners of this house. You would think they didn't notice or even care.

A Pagan holiday would pass every year and malicious children would throw rotten fruit and possibly vegetables at this house. Sometimes eggs. But by the next morning, the residue and smell from the destruction they had unleashed would be gone. The house would look as if it were never defaced at all.

Time would pass and soon everyone on the block would forget about the strange house that suddenly appeared on their block on a warm Fall evening. New rumors would surface, new stories would be told, but all in all it would be ignored completely.

And then, there would be quiet for many years.

For the next thirteen years the house remained unchanged. It was still lopsided and a source of bitter conversation for everyone who passed by. The only change, if any, was in the front yard. It became even more of an eye-sore.

The weeds were as tall as people and small trees had

overgrown and split apart the wooden fence that lined the sidewalk. They nearly covered the first floor of the house from view, and the front door had almost completely disappeared.

The neighbors could be overheard saying that they couldn't wait for the trees and shrubs to cover it up completely, or for the crazy owners to move away. This house was hated and its occupants as well. But if asked why, and if you were persistent, no one could rationalize a logical answer. They would say that they just hated it. And hated them. And then you would be told not to ask again.

How could so much hate have come to roost here in the pleasant town of Terracotta so easily?

It would be a sure bet that the kind and spiritual folks of this neighborhood had never even bothered to make their acquaintance or try to befriend the occupants of this house, not even to borrow a cup of sugar, or bake them an apple pie as a welcoming gesture. Isn't that what good folk do? Isn't that what we should all do before casting doubt and labeling someone as wrong who doesn't conform to our personal sensibilities? Or did they? No one knew. They'd never asked.

Someone must have at one time, right, since there is that one rumored story floating about that begs to differ? Some of it must be true since all gossip starts with some truth. But like all stories the truth lies between the two extremes of what was made up and what is pure fiction.

Incidentally, that rumored story goes like this. It concerns one neighbor, no more than two houses away, one Miss Magilicutty. She claimed to have attempted to borrow a cup of sugar from them, those strange people who lived in that awful house. She claimed that she was in the middle of baking and ran out of said item. She claimed that she got as far as their front door and after ringing the bell, she was greeted by a man holding a live rat. She claimed that he was petting it like a cat and feeding it a cookie when he said to her that he would gladly provide her with that cup of sugar. She claimed that he asked her if she would like to come inside while he checked the pantry and, in fact, if she would mind holding the rat for him whilst he did so.

Miss Magilicutty had been known to overreact on more than one such occasion. Thus the rest of the story, as you will soon see, could simply be a fabrication of her mind.

For instance, every Fourth of July, Miss Magilicutty, claimed that the sounds of the rockets exploding in the sky at the fair three miles away from her house prevented her cat from defecating for a week. And at another time she claimed that the water from her tap was poisoned with unusual minerals, and that they were the cause of her angel food cake sinking in her baking tray before she removed it from the oven, rather than swelling up like a good angel food cake should.

Consequently, she lost the baking contest at the fair that year and tried to sue the town for the amount of the prize money she believed she should have won.

Getting back to the story at hand, Miss Magilicutty had begun to hyperventilate at the thought of holding a live rat and dare I add, never went inside of the house at the strange man's request. So needless to say this didn't end well.

The paramedics were summoned by an anonymous caller and had arrived just before the local news reporters had. It was a colorful story just asking to be written.

So you see there must have been some truth to her story. After all, there is some documentation from this whole drama. Miss Magilicutty had gone to the Emergency Room that day. She had received treatment for her drama queen reaction to whatever happened on the front lawn of that creepy house two doors down from her. And her stomach had been pumped for good measure.

However, these incidences had been few and far between over the last decade. So most of the story above could have been a product of the hyperactive mind of a nosy house wife, and never really happened at all. No one knows for sure.

Now getting back to our story, on one particular morning, thirteen years later, there was something unusual happening.

And this time we had credible witnesses to prove it.

Standing on the opposite side of the worn out wooden fence that separated the normal people who walk on the sidewalk, from the eccentric people who live in this house were two children and one young adult. They paused for a moment to look over the old house on their way to school.

For no reason at all, these three had made it their habit to stop here on their way to school every day and make up a different story about the inhabitants. Like most stories that have been handed down or repeated over and over again, there was a thread of truth within them. But since there was no one to keep track, the line between fact and fiction had definitely blurred.

The oldest of the three was High School level and the two younger children were in Elementary School. They stopped here to entertain themselves, nothing more, nothing less.

The oldest of the three was the primary instigator and the creator of the tall tale she was about to spin. The two younger children, one boy and one girl, devoted their full attention to her. They were her audience.

"I still say it's haunted," said the older girl. "No one ever sees anyone ever go in or come out."

The younger boy looked over the house while picking his nose. "It just ain't normal," he added.

A slight breeze blew across the older girl's hair until it covered her eyes. She looks down at the two younger children.

"Stranger still, little ones," she said menacingly, "my mother says they have a daughter, about your age in fact. And they never allow her out of the house to play. She hasn't any friends at all and she was, home schooled."

"That's crazy!" said the younger girl. "Bad enough we have to go to school all day, but to have it at home too!"

"Look, someone is coming out," said the younger boy.

This was a rare sight indeed, there were but a handful of people in this neighborhood who claimed to have seen any of the owners of this house. The three school children suddenly felt privileged.

The front door opened wide and a middle-aged man, who they recognized as Mr. Gluteus, the truant officer from their school, slowly backed out of the house.

"Yes, yes, of course," said Mr. Gluteus. "It is for her own good, you know? I really don't care one bit about how you choose to raise your child in your own home Mr. Dre-Dre-Dreadful. But rules are rules and she did fail the last state-wide test. I said this several times now."

He wagged his finger furiously at the person he was addressing, someone in the doorway whom they were still unable to see. And then he began to run rather quickly for an overweight middle aged man.

Mr. Gluteus hopped and jumped over the tall weeds, nearly falling on his face, then turned again to complete his thoughts.

"So-so-so don't make me come back here again," said Mr. Gluteus. "I'm a very busy man. Good day to you sir."

And with that he leapt between two broken fence posts and ran clear down the street.

The three children craned their necks to see if they could finally see what every neighbor on this block would pay good money for, a close up look at the owner of the house. There were so few sightings of said owner that they knew that this would fuel the fire of gossip and be worth the special attention they would get at school and at home that day. They would become famous.

Then, not at all sheepishly, but instead quite boldly, Natty Dreadful stepped into the doorway and into the morning light. He looked much the way he always had, but perhaps a little bit more mature and distinguished. A shock of grey hair circled over his left ear.

When he noticed the three little faces of the children looking back at him from behind the wooden fence and weeds of his front yard, he began to quiver with pain. His arms, face and body contorted as he shielded his eyes from the sunlight. He was in pain.

"It burns!" shouted Natty.

He gripped his throat and slunk back inside the house.

The older girl was the first to scream out loud, then the two younger children screamed as well. Their fright may or may not have been real, but let's face it, this is fun to do. They panicked and collided into one another as panicked people often do and as quickly as they could ran off down the block.

Natty peeked outside from his doorway. He looked both ways and when he was sure the coast was clear, he stepped out again into the morning light with an amused smirk on his face.

He leaned up against the side of the door jam and took a sip of his tea.

"I never get tired of doing that," said Natty.

Chapter 4
The Little Goth Girl

Smack in the middle of Terracotta sat their one and only Junior High School. The building was only one story tall and there were only two classes per grade. Most of the students had known each other since pre-K, although there were some who would pretend otherwise.

It was early morning and the hallways were filled with students colliding into one another, dropping their books, emptying their lockers, stuffing their faces with the last bit of their Egg-Mc-Stuff'n breakfast, forgetting why they were there, complaining to anyone who would listen and wondering why they had to go to school in the first place. There were probably two students in this entire fray who were actually thinking about school work. We will meet one of them later on.

When the late bell rang with the most annoying pitch one could imagine, the students held their ears: it was their way of coping. Then one by one they magically disappeared into their classrooms and this very long hallway suddenly became empty. That is, aside from the paper trash on the floor they had left in their wake.

The two front doors to the school were at the far end of this very long hallway. They continued to swing back and forth from the last of the students who came in. Slowly they came to a stop. Those who made it to school on time were there. All others may, just may have gotten caught in the storm that was brewing up outside.

Through the large windows on the front doors at the end of the very long hallway, the sky was darkening rapidly. After only one flash of lightning outside, the hall suddenly appeared darker. A gust of wind pushed the front doors at the end of the very long hallway wide open. The paper trash quickly glided across the floor and settled under the lockers that lined the walls.

The sky darkened further outside and there were silent shimmers of light in the clouds above. The storm was getting closer.

There was a strange silence. Then rising up from the steps outside the front doors at the end of the very long hallway was a dark and shadowy figure about to enter the school.

***

The classrooms looked as bland as one would expect. They boasted twenty desks or so in each room. One wall was lined with windows and there were a front and rear classroom door. Although hard to find in this day and age, there was a good old fashioned chalkboard across one wall. There were no wall decorations or graded papers tacked up for display, the semester had just begun.

On this unassuming morning, not unlike any other, the most exciting moment came when a crash of thunder from the impending storm outside startled the students who had slipped into their after-breakfast coma which made them leap in their seats and then giggle at their foolishness. After all, what was there to be afraid of?

One student, Penny Social, was standing at her desk and doing what she found most appealing to her: talking about herself. She was addressing the teacher as if she were the only student in the room and the rise and fall of all mankind could depend upon her next few words.

Penny Social was dressed to impress. She was the classroom trend setter and prima donna. Her haircut and clothes were styled right up to the fashion minute. She knew it and she flaunted it.

The approaching thunder storm attempted to distract her from flattering herself further, competing for the class's attention with intermittent flashes of lightning and a low rumble of thunder.

It failed once or twice, but with the third and loudest crash of thunder, her illusion that she was the center of attention was shattered. The crash even made one student scream out loud.

In gross retaliation, Penny Social smirked at the students who shivered and stared wide eyed at the dark skies out the window.

"Serves you right," she muttered under her breath. There was an uncontrollable meanness within her slowly boiling to the top.

Penny Social cut into the pause and redirected their attention to the teacher by adding, "If I may be allowed to continue, Miss. Novella?"

There was no doubt of who was in charge of this classroom and it was not the teacher. Penny Social was one bad seed.

Sitting around Penny on either side of her were her two minions, (children actually, barely teens really, or pawns, if you prefer) or as they liked to think of themselves, her BFF's. Britney Britanica sat on her right and Olivia Smothers was on her left.

Britney was a poseur of sorts, a reflection of all that was wrong with Penny Social times ten. She mimicked her clothes, copied her facial expressions and repeated, as often as she could, the last few words of every sentence Penny Social would say. There is not much else to add here. She was a bad seed "wannabe."

Olivia, on the other hand, was, well, different. The lights were on inside, but the occupants were on vacation. She was like a toy train set without an engine, a BLT sandwich without the bread, a song without rhythm, or a mathematical equation illustrated in a schoolbook without a picture of that old guy who looks like Einstein ready to explain it. She dressed like Penny and Britney, more often than anyone should, and reflected their attitude as well.

But Olivia was not really like them. She was a mystery wrapped up in another mystery. But enough about them, since this moment was all about Penny Social anyway.

"Of course, my dear," said Miss Novella their seventh grade classroom teacher. "Continue. Class? Penny is speaking. Show her the proper respect"

Now here is an exceptional piece-of-work. The monarch of this microcosmic organization (AKA, the classroom) was Miss Novella. She was the Head Mistress of this seventh grade, or as she liked to refer to herself, the Queen Bee.

She was middle aged and looked as though she were shot from a cannon. She had pencils jutting out of her screwed up hair and wore thick, thick glasses. It was a small miracle she can see out of them at all.

Her clothes were not at all old, but that sweater, when did she find that? It was full of holes, like she had been wearing it since year one. In short, she looked like a librarian gone bad and was as unpleasant as her looks suggested.

"Thank you, Miss Novella," said Penny Social. "As I was saying, I have in my hands an authorized, autographed and signed copy of the latest Julius Kilowatt CD/DVD before it appears in fine stores anywhere."

Penny Social continued to brag.

"It was a little parting gift from Julius to me while attending the filming of his new music video this past summer," said Penny Social.

She then stroked the jewel case between her fingers admiring it further. Her lips began to move to a song that only she could hear in her head. Her coolness to herself was beyond description.

One boy was very impressed. We know this because an image of Julius Kilowatt was on his shirt. He reached out to touch the coveted gift in Penny's hand.

"Awesome, can I see it?" he gently asks.

Penny Social pulled it away with deliberate speed.

"Nuh-uh,loser!" said Penny Social. "Julius would freak if he found out I let just anyone see this."

Britney smiled to herself. Olivia saw her smile and smiled, too.

The rear door to the classroom unexpectedly swung open and hit the wall with a bang. The lights in the classroom went out and a clap of thunder echoed through the room. A flash of lightning danced across the faces of the entire class of startled students and they all jumped in their seats at the pure coincidence of it all.

With the second clap of thunder and the second flash of lightning, the lights of the fluorescent lamps overhead quivered back up to their full brightness. The temporary brown out was simply that, temporary.

The floor boards of the room creaked to suggest that they were not as alone as they had been a moment before. Then one-by-one the students' heads turned around to see who had entered the classroom from the rear.

Standing in the open doorway was a girl about twelve plus years in age, their age. This girl was Penny Dreadful.

She was a little thing, not as tall as most of the children in the room and not at all as menacing as her entrance may have suggested. She was wearing a black skirt with rows of buckles down the sides. Her blouse was similar and her pointed shoes had a buckle or two as well. Her socks were pin striped. Her hair was long and straight and black and she was wearing a silver locket around her neck, and even from a distance one could tell that her eyes were an unusual shade of green.

The students didn't quite know what to make of her. She could be a Goth some thought, but there was a little more to it than that.

Other thoughts raced across their minds like; "…this is the town of Terracotta, we don't have that kind around here. So where did she come from?" Or, "…she must have moved here from the city where everyone is a socialist and crazy." Or, "I wonder what we are having for lunch today? I hope it's not mystery meat again," was what most people would call a hamburger by any other name, and was clearly on the minds of most of the students.

Penny Social, Britney and Olivia slunk up next to one another, sharing the same devilish smirk.

"Whose broom did she fly in on?" quipped Britney, just audibly enough for those around her to hear.

"Huh, what broom?" said Olivia.

"It's a witch joke, Olivia," explained Britney.

Penny Social said nothing, but she looked over Penny Dreadful as if she were fresh meat.

As soon as the whispering began, Miss Novella detected a chink in her wall of discipline and clapped her hands together.

"Now, now, class, let me see who we have here," said Miss Novella.

She took a few steps forward and stared down her nose through her thick, thick glasses as one would inspect an insect. She looked over Penny Dreadful carefully.

"Your name, dear," demanded Miss Novella impatiently. "Come come, I haven't all day."

A gust of wind slipped in through the slightly opened window and blew a paper off of Miss Novella's desk and right into her hand.

"Oh, my," said Miss Novella, for she was easily startled and then surprised as she glanced down at the paper. "Penny?"

She then did a double take at the possible concurrence of the name on the paper belonging to the young girl standing before her.

"Penny Dreadful, is that correct?" said Miss Novella. "Speak up, dear. I can't hear you."

Penny Dreadful simply nodded.

Miss Novella exhaled deeply as if a great burden had been put upon her. Her eyes raced around the room and she mumbled as she thought to herself.

"What am I supposed to do with another child in my class?" said Miss Novella. "This is just great. Bad enough you're starting a grade in the middle of the school year...."

Miss Novella was suddenly interrupted by one of her students, Anthony, a rather astute looking young lad who had the habit of speaking up any time he wanted to.

"But Miss Novella, school only started a week ago," said Anthony.

"Quiet Anthony," said Miss Novella who then fired back at him with one of her stock put-downs. "And stop picking your nose."

Anthony hung his head in shame. Not because he was picking his noses, but because he wanted to. He strangely believed that Miss Novella was a mind reader. What he didn't know was that most of the children in the room were thinking about picking their nose at that very minute.

"Well just don't stand there like a construction worker on his lunch break, take a seat, young lady," said Miss Novella, pointing with her gnarly forefinger. "Right, over, there."

The seat she addressed was nearly at the rear of the room.

Penny Dreadful removed her backpack and slowly crossed the room to take her seat. Most of the students stared at her while some begin to whisper even before her back was turned.

Ignoring them, Penny Dreadful placed her backpack over the back of a chair that was way too large for her, then scooted in to sit at a desk that was way too tall for her as well.

Penny Social seized the moment.

"Miss Novella," said Penny Social who then smiled as she began. "As you know this class already has one Penny, me, and since I was here first I motion to give the new kid a new name. Like, ah, Broomhilda, or Witchy-poo, or something trite like that."

Some of the students laughed. They mistook her passive aggression for wit.

Britney didn't waste even a second to take a ride on her coat tails by adding to the insults.

"I second the motion," said Britney.

Olivia appeared to be daydreaming, but her Pavlovian response kicked in and she jumped in as well.

"I third the motion," said Olivia. "Motion passed."

She then slammed her fist down on her desk like a hammer on a gavel. She was well trained.

"Motion denied," said Miss Novella. "That may be against the law. I'm not sure."

"But that's not fair," whines Penny Social. "What will happen the next time you call on me and she answers? What then?"

"You do have a point there, Penny," said Miss Novella to Penny Social. "Not you…," said Miss Novella to Penny Dreadful. "…her," said Miss Novella correcting herself. "The solution to this is that I will call you Penny S, and the new kid, ah, Penny Dreadful, that is, Penny D."

Penny S spun her finger around her temple to her friends as soon as Miss Novella turned her back to return to the front of the room. Britney and Olivia found it amusing and covered their smiles.

One precocious pre-teen, Malcolm Waxenburg, fancied himself the class clown. He was never the jock type and as a larger child than most boys his age, he was hardly ever picked on and that suited him just fine. He was never destined to be a rhode scholar and he knew it. His interests lied elsewhere other than in his studies.

Malcolm found his true calling in life, it was his talent to make himself laugh at even the oddest and most trivial thing. For example; his failing grades, his disheveled appearance and his ability to finish his lunch in class right under the nose of Miss Novella, were on his short list of things to laugh at.

Today, Malcolm assigned himself a new goal. He would test the new kid and see what she was made of. Not out of malice, he would never mean her any harm, he was not a mean child by far. But, ah, what he wouldn't do for a good laugh. Thus, he quickly formulated a plan.

Slowly, methodically, Malcolm lifted his desk off the ground an inch with his knees. He shimmied himself a few inches closer to Penny D before putting it back down. He had mastered this action after months of careful training and repeated it like a ballet. He could even do it to the rhythm of the quickest head turns of any teacher, least of all Miss Novella.

So as she turned away from his general direction to write on the board, Malcolm moved his desk closer and closer still to Penny D.

Within arms' reach, Malcolm proceeded with step two of his spontaneous plan. Still unseen by Miss Novella, he lifted a silicone spider out of his pocket and reached forward with his opposite hand to lift open the flap of Penny D's backpack. His eyes glowed with what he knew would be a memorable moment at lunchtime when she discovered the spider lurking next to her lunch bag, and thought it real.

The backpack flap was lifted, the fake spider dangling in Malcolm's hand, he paused to savor the moment. Then much to his surprise the head of an over-sized tarantula, viscous pincers poised ready to strike out at him, emerged from beneath the backpack flap. They snapped shut nearly missing Malcolm's fingers.

He heard the serrated edges of the pincers close tightly together as they squeezed the silicone spider they had snatched from his hand. Just as quickly as it had advanced from her backpack, it retreated from whence it had come.

Malcolm screamed out, lost his balance and fell back off his chair.

"Someone, help me!" panicked Malcolm loudly.

Miss Novella, a drama queen to the bitter end marched down the aisle in a huff and stopped right at Penny D's desk.

"Malcolm," barked Miss Novella. "What in blazes are you up to now?"

"It's not me this time, Miss Novella," said Malcolm.

He pointed to Penny D's backpack, his hand still quivering.

"It's in there, a huge hairy bug," said Malcolm.

Miss Novella had fallen for Malcolm's pranks before. She knew that she should know better but her eyes were drawn to Malcolm like a dieter is drawn to the dessert menu and as an addict of such fare, she played right into it.

"Penny D, you better let me have a look inside there," said Miss Novella. "It may be poisonous."

Quite innocently and without any fear of discovery Penny D offered up her backpack to Miss Novella to inspect. She then spoke for the very first time. Her voice was sweet and her tone non-threatening. Confidently, she made her point.

"Although most theraphosidae are venomous and can cause extreme discomfort over several days if bitten," said Penny D, "none have yet to be connected with a human fatality."

To wit Miss Novella quickly replied, "Huh?"

Malcolm didn't even hear the exchange, he was still in panic mode.

"Don't open it, Miss Novella," warned Malcolm. "It's huge and hairy and had two big teeth and almost took my fingers off."

Miss Novella closed one eye and stared down at Malcolm.

"Big teeth, you say?" said Miss Novella, baiting him. "Like a dog or a raccoon? Just how stupid do you think I am, Malcolm?"

She quickly turned her attention back to Penny D.

"It looks as though we have another practical joker in the class," said Miss Novella. "As if one were not enough."

And with that she walked away.

Penny D glanced over her shoulder at Malcolm who was still on the floor and mouthed the word "sorry", looking quite sincere as she said it.

Malcolm's face transformed from one of fear to one of understanding as he climbed back up onto his chair. The joke was on him and he got it good. He leaned back on his chair and winked, pointed his finger at her and made a click sound with his tongue.

This incident did little to calm the uneasiness in the room that had all begun with the storm outside. The children slid their desks further away from Penny D.

Miss Novella clapped her hands together to get the classes attention.

"Let's get back to work," said Miss Novella. "This is a good time for me to remind you that your first project of the semester is due in two weeks. But since Penny D has joined us after I assigned it, I have no choice but to go over the material again from the very beginning."

The students moaned.

Penny S's hand shot up.

"Miss Novella," commanded Penny S.

"Yes, Penny. I mean, Penny S?" said Miss Novella correcting herself.

Penny S prepared her first all-out attack on the new kid in the room.

"Perhaps I could explain our assignment to our new visitor?" said Penny S. "Thus spare the entire class the misery of hearing it again simply because she wasn't in attendance last week?"

"I don't see any reason why not," said Miss Novella. "Proceed."

With arms akimbo, Penny S composed her thoughts and began.

"Our first class project assignment is to perform a speech accompanied by a demonstration about what your family, assuming you have one, admires most about you, provided there is anything at all," said Penny S. "You are welcome to bring in a visual tool. For example, if gardening is your forte, a noble interest praised by many parentals, you may bring in a flowering plant to display the excellent quality of your handiwork."

"Nailed, it!" said Miss Novella, punctuating Penny S's speech in a high voice tone.

Penny D slouched in her chair, looking even smaller than she had first appeared and feeling more isolated then she ever thought she could be.

Malcolm didn't bother to move his desk away from Penny D as the other children did. Still undecided if this little Goth girl could be of any threat to him, he defiantly held his ground.

"That's right, I'm cool," thought Malcolm to himself. "I am not afraid of little Goth girls."

What sounded like a tiny belch emerged from Penny D's backpack. The silicone spider sprung out and landed on top of Malcolm's head.

Chapter 5
Strange Friend Fellows

In a normal town like Terracotta, and when I say normal I mean average, children on their lunch break at school would be shouting and running and talking and laughing and playing and eating their very special lunches prepared for them by their mothers or, bought from the deli the night before or, purchased from their grocer's freezer far in advance. But in this case, on this very special day, the very first day of school for one Penny Dreadful, there was none of that.

On this very special day the school yard was instead very quiet. There was no shouting, or running, or talking (I think you get the idea). There was some whispering going on, and the piddle-paddle of little feet against the wet cement tiles as a student scurried from one pack of youngsters to another. It was as though secret messages were being sent via human courier from one foxhole to another to deliver the latest whereabouts of the enemy in time of war. But for the most part, it was quiet.

The rumors in the digital world on the other hand, were spreading with lightning speed. A Twister account was set up and there were already thirty seven followers. The word on the street was that there was a new student in town, or at least in this school, since she was in town all her life, even though no one had ever seen her or even spoken to her. It said she had mysteriously appeared in Miss Novella's seventh grade classroom under some very strange circumstances that very morning.

That much was true, there was no denying it, but there were a host of lies that followed. Lies like; "she and her family were here in Terracotta hiding out from organized crime", "she was part of a cult that worshiped an ancient god", and the most bizarre of all, "Penny D was an undercover police officer".

Little did they realize, that the very first "Twist" was not that far from the truth.

Overall, it was nothing but a lot of conjecture based on ignorance, and that brought on fear. Small minds fed on fear and like a fire, and it burned out-of-control at Terracotta Junior High.

Gossip has a way of taking on a life all its own. By the end of lunch period the story had grown to the point where it hardly resembled what really had happened at all. The one and only unusual incident that did occur in Miss Novella's class, was retold so many times it ended up sounding something like this; that one student heard that another student was bitten by a rabid squirrel that the new girl kept in her backpack. The student was rushed off to the hospital and was not expected to live. Further it was reported that the new kid claimed she was a sorceress and dabbled in the black arts.

It was no longer about the truth. It had become a popularity contest instead. Even though the stories were all negative, Penny Dreadful had become the talk of the school. Every student wanted to know her in some way and eventually to despise her to show solidarity to their friends.

This madness had to stop. The new kid had no right to demand all this attention. Someone had to call a halt to this insanity and set things straight. And Penny Social considered herself the person to do it.

As Penny D sat all by herself on one of the benches opposite the playground eating her sandwich, she tried to divert her eyes from the cold little stares of the students who were still on their lunch break. She felt more alone than she could ever remember feeling in her life.

If she were home she would have the company of her family and her pets, but she was not home, she was here.

If it were not for the one friend she had found in her backpack this morning, still hidden from view, she would have just picked up and run home. Still, she wondered, how he had slipped in there when she wasn't looking.

As the crowd of students slowly dispersed, Penny D noticed one boy, the boy who sat near her, the only pre-teen in the class who didn't move his desk away from her, not contributing to the school yard hysteria. When he, Malcolm, and Penny D made eye contact, he gave her the age appropriate most awesome sign of approval, the upwards head nod.

She looked around to be sure that he meant this cultural and iconic sign of greeting toward her and not to someone else who had just come up behind her, someone on the other side of the metal fence perhaps. Since there was no one there, on the other side of the metal fence, she concluded that he meant it for her. So she kindly nodded back.

It was a little awkward for sure, she thought to herself, but perhaps this is what it is like to make a friend. She really had no idea since she didn't have any. No human ones at least.

This wonderful moment of contact, even if it were nothing more than that of the first kind, was suddenly shattered by a visitor of the third kind. And like they say, bad news comes in threes.

Penny S, Britney and Olivia marched right up to Penny D, all sporting the same mean look on their faces.

"I don't believe that story about a spider or a raccoon or whatever they say is in your backpack," said Penny S. "I should just take it and look inside for myself."

Penny D offered over her backpack for inspection.

"Oh, puh-leeze," said Penny S. "You think I was born a decade ago?"

The after lunch bell rang with the same annoying tone as the morning one. The few students who still remained in the yard began to file back into the building. This included Malcolm, who was watching the confrontation from afar, shaking his head to himself as he left the yard. The wheels of ingenuity in his head were seriously at work. Penny S and Britney were two people he had no patience for. But they did give him pause to stop and think about how he might prank them.

Olivia, on the other hand was a case all her own. Her expression suddenly changed to one of delight as soon as the bell rang.

"Time to get back to class," said Olivia and she ran off before anyone could stop her.

Britney obediently turned to leave as well, but before she could do so Penny S grabbed her by the arm and stops her short.

"Keep your training bra on," said Penny S. "I just need to get one thing straight with our new guest here."

Penny S leaned in so that Penny D could not miss a single word she was about to say. However, Penny D found herself focusing on the little twitch in Penny S's left eye. It made her think to herself that Penny S may have a food allergy to something she ate. Or perhaps being mean was the cause. She was always taught that meanness can cause all manners of illness, so why not an eye twitch? These were just one of the many useful lessons she learned from her Uncle Caligari, on how to live a healthy and creative life, but we will hear more about him later.

"You don't scare me one bit, Pinky Dreadlocks, or whatever your name is," said Penny S, knowing full well who she was talking to. "And I'm just itching to tell you why. It's because I...don't...like...you."

The backpack on the bench jumped a few inches all by itself and almost went unnoticed. Britney caught the bags movement in the corner of her eye.

"It just moved," said Britney. "Did you see it? The pack-back, I mean the backpack"

Penny S turned to Britney, more fed up than annoyed.

"Will you stop it already," said Penny S. "There is nothing inside that bag. And do you think you could at least look at me when I am talking to you?"

The wholesome peaches and cream complexion of a twelve plus year old girl suddenly drained from Britney's face. Still unbeknownst to Penny S, Britney was watching the backpack open up all by itself, and a large hairy tarantula leg unfold from inside. And then another. And then another.

Giving up on Britney, Penny S turned to face Penny D. At that very same moment the tarantula that so efficiently startled Malcolm, sprang from the backpack and landed on Britney's head.

Britney managed to shriek out two little words before running off in a frenzy, her arms flailing like a cartoon character.

"It's alive!" shouted Britney.

Penny S did a triple take, she wasn't sure where to look. She knew something had happened and also knew that she missed it entirely. After all, it was not about her, so why should she care.

"Pathetic," said Penny S in complete deadpan.

She was not going to play along and provide any attention to anyone that could have anything to do with derailing her agenda. She had come over to give Penny D a beat down and she was not going to be distracted.

Then a dark shadow rose up and covered over her. How strange, Penny S thought to herself. The rain was gone, and it was only midday but it was getting dark already. Her narrow focus began to widen, and slowly, cautiously, the nasty expression on Penny S's face, that had become her trademark in class, began to melt away.

Just behind Penny D, draped over the metal fence like a feather boa, was an enormous python. Unlike any baby snake Penny S may have seen in her science class, this one had a face that was unusually expressive. It looked as though it were very happy to see her, or, perhaps to find its next meal.

It licked its lips and appeared to smile. But that was probably nothing more than her perception of the python's very large mouth from her very low angle.

Before Penny S could let out a scream, the python lunged forward.

Penny S was quick on her feet. She didn't have a smart comment this time, she simply took off like a rocket; a loose rocket in a meteor shower. She first headed for the monkey bars. She thought to herself that she could lose whatever was following her in there. As she bent and twisted through the tiny openings in the bars first to the left then to the right, she felt confident that she had already lost him.

When Penny S turned around she found that the python was still coming. It, too, went into the monkey bars with the same dexterity that she had and bent and twisted through the tiny openings of the bars. And it was almost upon her.

Penny S shot over to the sliding pond and scaled the ladder like an insect. When she reached the top she glanced over her shoulder and saw that the python was all tangled up in the monkey bars and she thought to herself how clever she was that she made a clean get away.

She was getting ready to slide down when she noticed that although the body of the python was over at the monkey bars, its head was at the bottom of the slide waiting for her, mouth wide open. Startled, Penny S slipped and slid down the slide head first. The python swallowed up half of her body, her tiny legs still kicking out of its mouth.

The python bucked and quivered as it tried to swallow her up whole. Her legs were suddenly sucked in all the way and her compressed little body began to slowly travel down its throat.

Penny D leapt onto the python, her feet and her arms wrapped around its midsection. She was determined to prevent it from completely digesting that bad little girl.

"Rebecca!" screamed Penny D. "Let her go, Bronte got me into enough trouble as it is. Now, spit her up!"

Rebecca the python, or Becka as Penny D affectionately called her, closed her eyes, pursed her lips together and stuck her nose up into the air. She was not going to give in.

"Becka," demanded Penny D. "You mind me this instant."

But Rebecca slowly shook her head "no" in defiance. It appeared that she was going to eat Penny S for sure.

Britney wobbled past them as all of this was happening, she was near exhaustion. "Bronte, the tarantula," was still holding fast to her head and menacing her with heavy breathing sounds.

Britney had run clear around the school perimeter and she never noticed that Penny S had been swallowed up by the python.

Frustrated, Penny D resorted to plan B. She began to tickle Rebecca and there was an immediate response. Rebecca began to convulse from holding in her laughter, her body coiled in circles as if in pain. Then in one mighty heave, Penny S came sliding out of her mouth and onto the pavement.

She appeared to be alive and awake but not quite sure what had even happened. She was drenched with python saliva from head to toe and shivering a bit from the experience. She looked over her body, counted her fingers, yeah, they were all there. Then she slowly climbed to her feet.

Penny D was standing up on the bench she had once sat on. Her arms were folded and she looked furious. Just then Britney came wandering by again, completely tuckered out. She came to a complete stop in front of Penny D.

The tarantula was still on her head and it was menacing her with its pincers by snapping them in the air, like one would snap their fingers.

"Bronte, down!" Penny commanded to the tarantula through her clenched teeth.

Bronte, leapt off of Britney's head and landed next to Penny D on the bench. He knew he was in trouble and quickly rested his head on her feet.

Rebecca also anticipated a lecture from Penny D, so she coiled affectionately around her and snuggled her head just under Penny's arms, then blinked her eyes up at her.

"Oh, don't you guys try to make up," said Penny D. "I am so very mad at you right now."

Britney took Penny S by the hand and quietly lead her away.

"Well, what do you have to say for yourselves?" said Penny D.

What happened next cannot be explained. It would appear that Penny D could talk to her two animal friends and that they could talk with her as well. Rebecca was the first to respond, and quickly make light of the incident.

"Why Penny, it looks like you are off to an exciting first day of school," said Rebecca, in what sounded like an Australian accent.

"If screaming is any indication," said Bronte in a hoarse male voice, "I think they like you."

Penny D looked confused and forgot for a moment what she had been so angry about.

"I'm not so sure, Bronte," said Penny D. "The other children keep running away from me, too."

"Why dear, that's how humans play," said Rebecca. "They run away from me all the time. I enjoy it immensely. They run. I catch them. I let them go, they run again. And a good time is had by all."

"Hmmm, I thought I told you two to stay home until I return?" said Penny D.

"You did, but I got this idea, see," said Bronte, "from an old book I found in our library. It was called, Mary Had a Little Lamb."

"And the really strange part was, that she didn't eat it," added Rebecca. "The little darling kept it as a pet. How crazy is that?"

"Then, it followed her to school one day," said Bronte. "You dig?"

"And that's where you got the idea from, yeah, I get it," said Penny D. "Listen, we'll sort this all out when I get home, as for now, you better get going. The guano is about to hit the fan."

The yard door squeaked as it slowly opened. Miss Novella peeked out into the yard armed with a broom. Several children were piled up behind her.

But the school yard playground was quiet and empty. All that was left was Penny D sitting alone on the bench, her sandwich still in her hand.

Chapter 6
What Little Girls Are Made Of

On her way home from school that afternoon, Penny D simply couldn't shake the feeling that she was being followed. That feeling, and the whispers she heard behind her were a dead give-away.

She didn't know how long she would be able to stand it. It had been an entire day of whispers and fingers pointing at her when no one thought or cared if she saw them or not. The entire school appeared to be obsessed with her. There were no name callings per say, with the exception of the prize winning comments from Penny S earlier that day, but she did overhear a few choice words like; witch, Goth, socialist, and pagan.

She knew what all of those words meant, well, the encyclopedia definitions of course and she didn't find them as a whole insulting. If there were any new definitions of these words that she was unaware of, then that would be an entirely different case.

What bothered her most was that there was all of this talk about her and not a word spoken to her. What were they afraid of? Did they think she would bite them if they spoke to her? Or perhaps not her, but that little creature in her backpack might.

So Penny D walked home by herself and dreamt of making a new friend. Her mother told her that there would be many children her age at school and making friends would be very easy. She told Penny D that she had grown up in a town just like this and had gone to a school just like hers and that she had never had any problems making new friends.

It had made sense to her at the time but after a day like this one, it was hard to imagine it be true. Nonetheless she was never one to dwell on what was challenging her patience. She instead chose to imagine what kind of new friend she would make tomorrow and how that would come about.

Penny D remembered a daydream she had once. She had imagined herself climbing a tree one day and right before her eyes a boy would appear. He too was out for an afternoon swing. Climbing trees was an acceptable form of exercise so why not an acceptable form of meeting nice people?

Anyway, she thought, she would break the ice and be the first to say something clever like, "It is a fine day for tree climbing, is it not?" She had imagined the boy would smile and answer, "Why yes, and did you know you have the most exquisite green eyes?" To wit she would answer, "Oh, thank you. They are emerald to be more precise."

This always brought a smile to her face as it did this very moment. Then the whispers behind her began again and shattered the daydream to pieces.

The long day at school was an unhealthy dose of reality. It proved to be much different than what she had been told by her mother.

All day she had been patient. But that was all about to end. Penny D stopped and allowed her backpack to drop as she turned around. She was not angry but certainly fed up and the expression on her face clearly showed that.

The children who were following her, not unlike most adults, once caught doing something wrong reverted to that basic instinct of survival. They ran for it.

One girl, tall and lanky, darted across a lawn. She hopped, skipped and jumped over the garden hose and sprinkler oscillator that were left out that day. The water suddenly began to flow through the hose with an elevated level of pressure and the grass lawn became an obstacle course full of dangerous traps.

The hose became her first challenge. The loops of plastic hose whipped around her like a jump rope gone mad, whirled around by invisible children.

Artfully the tall girl jumped over and then ducked under the rings before she tripped and fell flat on her face. She quickly became tangled in the coils of hose. The water oscillator sprayed a fine mist around the perimeter of the yard, as it was supposed to. But when it reached the tall girl it became stuck in a permanent washing-over position.

As the tall girl fought to untangle herself from the hose, she found herself sitting in a large puddle of mud.

The second child running to avoid a confrontation with Penny D met his fate in a more humiliating way. It began when he hid behind a large oak tree at the edge of the curb. He believed he was safe until several birds began to poop on his head and shoulders from above. It looked as if every bird in the neighborhood found him as their target.

The boy panicked and tried to make a run for it without looking exactly where he was going and fell over some nicely stacked trash bags at the curb for sanitation pick up.

One of the plastic trash bags burst when the boy landed on it and discarded scraps of food shot into the air like a geyser. He had but a second to glance upwards to see the left over TV dinners and dog food from the unknown neighbor's house as they came plummeting back to Earth and landed on top of him.

The third and last child, who had been abandoned by the first two, had an oddly shaped head. He didn't run or hide like they did. He just stood there looking at Penny D. His odd shaped head had nothing to do with this fact.

Penny D marched right up to him, the boy with the odd shaped head and spoke her mind.

"Go ahead and stare," said Penny D. "So I'm strange. So what? I have a python and a tarantula for pets and I talk with them too. I also like rats, bats and my hobbies are taxidermy and kendo. If that makes me a weirdo, because I'm different than you, then fine. I admit it. There. Are you satisfied now?"

The boy with the oddly shaped head didn't know what to say or where to look. He could tell that Penny D was annoyed but he didn't know why. He also believed that this must have been his fault somehow because incidences like this happened to him all the time. And when I say incidences I mean unknown people yelling at him for unknown reasons.

What Penny D didn't know was that he was not one of the children whispering behind her. The tall girl in the mud and the boy in the trash had been talking to each other. This lad was there for an entirely different reason.

So the boy with the oddly shaped head tried to process what was happening. He glanced over at the tall girl who was struggling to stand: she was still slipping and sliding in the mud. The water had now stopped flowing through the hose and her face and body were completely brown. As she tried to walk away from the over-saturated lawn, her feet became stuck. One-by-one the grass swallowed up her sneakers, pulling them clean off her feet.

She was past the point of caring and when she reached the sidewalk she just left barefoot.

The boy with the oddly shaped head then looked over at the boy who was the victim of a bird poop attack. Almost naked now, he slowly tore off his infected clothing while sporting a disgusted look on his face.

Then, quite unexpectedly, the boy with the oddly shaped head looked Penny D right in the eye and explained himself.

"I'm Harold,.. Milquetoast," said Harold, as if that explained everything.

It may have done just that because Penny D no longer felt threatened in any way and quickly composed herself. She pursed her lips, realizing she may have made a mistake and misjudged why Harold was with those two other children.

She could tell that Harold was not the type of boy that would make fun of anyone, but instead the type of boy who others may make fun of.

However, the day had been a long one and she was still fed up. She wanted it to finally end so she gave Harold the opportunity to clear his name.

"So, Milquetoast," said Penny D, "you go home this way?"

Harold pointed in the opposite direction.

"No," said Harold. "I believe I live in that direction."

"Then stop following me, stalker boy."

"I wasn't following you, honest," said Harold. "I was following them, I mean, stalking them, no wait. I don't know what I mean."

It was obvious that Harold was a bit confused. Not by his stance on this issue but by life in general.

"I'm probably bothering you," said Harold. "I should go."

Unbeknownst to either of them there was a friendship brewing. They had a common ground. They were both misunderstood.

"Aren't you afraid of me and my pets?" said Penny D. "Haven't you heard in school about what a spooky little girl I am?"

"No, I'm not afraid," said Harold. "Of you. And I like animals. I have a pet worm. Would you like to see it?"

Harold reached deep into his pants pockets and fished around for something.

"No, I pass," said Penny D. "Whatever you have in your pants pocket just leave it there. See you in school tomorrow, Milquetoast."

Penny D turned and left. She picked up her backpack and continued on her way home. Harold called out from behind her, holding up a worm in his hand.

"I found it!" said Harold.

Chapter 7
The Dreadful Mansion, Or Home As Penny Calls It

Penny Dreadful collapsed onto a very strangely shaped couch. It succumbed to her body weight and the edges of the foam in the cushion cuddled around her. She looked very forlorn and the couch appeared to sense it.

A big comfy couch in the middle of the living room is usually the most sought after item in the house, home, apartment or livable dwelling. It is used for all sorts of recreation, like a dining spot, a sleeping place, the library alternative, their TV companion and last but not least the trampoline.

Depending upon your age it could also be used as a safe house. By removing the cushions and building a fort, or magical transport to worlds unknown, one could pretend it was a vehicle of some sort. But in Penny D's home, it served a different purpose. It empathized.

It was in the center of her living room in the the Dreadful Mansion, and drew everyone (family members and visitors alike) to it. If you had a bad day, or you were troubled about something in general you knew that all you had to do was allow the couch to accept you.

You would simply sit, flop down on it, leap into its waiting arms or just collapse into it as Penny D did. The couch would do the rest. But for the very first time, the couch didn't deliver what she expected.

Sure, the couch was as comfy as ever, like so comfy that she would never ever want to get up, but the point was that she didn't feel better. Perhaps that was why the couch began to envelope her, to share her pain even more.

But enough about the couch, we have a whole room to explore.

As for the rest of the room, it was out-of-sync with the rest of the world as far as Penny D could now see. After only one day at school she saw life a little differently. She started to see things not as how they are, or as she would have them be, but as her Uncle would encourage her to see them. That is as they saw them. They, being the hundreds or so students, teachers and administrators of the school she now had to attend. A student body she was now part of.

Anyway, all of the furniture in the living room looked like it came from two different landscapes from two different paintings that had suddenly melted together.

For example; there was a grandfather clock in the corner of the room that Salvador Dali would be proud of and a wind up record player sitting on a table. You may be asking yourself, what is a wind up record player anyway and why would you have one? Let us just say that it is a very, very old way to listen to music. It is an item that is still cool to look at and if you were a person who frequented museums it would get you very, very excited.

There was a staircase to the upper floors that emptied into this room as well. It appears narrow and flat against the wall, as if no one could possibly ascend it if they tried. Not without mountain climbing gear, anyway.

The ceiling and all four walls met at strange angles and the windows were impossible to see through. The glass was discolored and must have been so old that it simply gave up trying to be glass and began to run downhill. Then it suddenly froze in time for us to look at and think about how impossible it must be to look out of.

The walls proudly displayed some hanging portraits of some very strange looking people. They may be relatives, but no one was sure. These portraits were old and were left here by the movers, so they may even have been leftovers from a previous move, because one good look at them would tell you that they would probably never be missed.

As for the pictures themselves, they appeared flat and obviously painted. However, the expressions on their faces appeared to change depending upon the mood in room. Right now they all looked sad. One of them was crying.

Lucinda Dreadful glided into the room in an almost unnatural fashion. She was obviously moving her feet, but she was a delicate woman and very graceful.

She appeared a bit more mature since we had last spoken of her, but still elegantly dressed in purple and black, her platinum blond hair was no longer short and draped down her back. She was like a ray of sunshine in a rather drab dimly lit room.

"Hello dear," said Lucinda. "How was your first day at school?"

Penny D's mood didn't change. The couch sensed it and provided a space for Lucinda to sit next to her. When she did, it squeezed them closer together.

"Awful," said Penny D.

"Dear," said Lucinda. "Did you make any new friends?"

"No," said Penny D. "Not that it matters. I don't have any old friends."

Lucinda swung one arm around her daughter. Penny D struggled to release an envelope from beneath her body, she had been sitting on it. She handed it to her mother.

"Here," said Penny D. "And before you read it, it is only right that I tell you that I don't care."

"What is it?" asked Lucinda as she opened the envelope.

She read it over carefully.

"Oh, this is good news," said Lucinda. "Your teacher wants you to join a club. That makes perfect sense. She believes it would help to ease your transition."

Penny D had been holding back but she could no longer control her frustration. The couch sensed her hostility and spat her up to the surface, into the middle of the living room floor. In a flash her mother was right alongside her.

"Mother, why am I so different?" Penny D demanded.

"What . . . different?" asked Lucinda, pretending not to understand. "How do you mean?"

Lucinda was never good at lying. She pulled on her fingers when she does so. She believed and practiced in truth above all things and a few other values that most people carry on about but rarely practice.

For example; Lucinda believed in love at first sight, that food didn't really make you fat, all people are good deep down inside, the egg came before the chicken, red licorice was better than black, and in one mindset that had given her the most opposition from all of her family members, the belief that everyone can change their life, no matter the circumstances!

She didn't know why she was right, but she believed with all her heart that she was.

Natty had a slightly different point of view. He believed in the laws of quantum physics and he applied them to his daily life, his love for his family and especially when he shaved.

His engineering skills were well-honed over the years. He could invent almost anything he put his mind to now. His theories and the practical application of said theories were an integral part of his life. He believed that a home should reflect its owner's sensibilities and, conform to his needs instantly, and in the Dreadful Mansion, they did just that.

He called this, "Reductive Engineering." It was the practice through any mechanical means both physical and metaphysical, to reduce effort and waste in the creation of anything that may assist in living a better life for one's self and all his loved ones.

Now getting back to Penny D who knew that if she simply spoke her mind, her mother would listen. As she began to walk, her mother was instantly along with her, because if she didn't she would miss what Penny D had to say.

They entered a hallway together that appeared to turn for them as they traveled through their house. The walls, the floor and the ceiling all appeared to move and line up, leading them to some unknown location, or perhaps to exactly where they intended to go.

Lucinda was determined to tackle the problem and nothing was going to stop her. Her daughter meant the world to her.

"What exactly do you mean, by different?" said Lucinda, and then she squinted her eyes.

"Don't say that I'm not, because I know that I am," said Penny D. "Everyone can see it except you, father and Uncle Caligari. Everyone at school can see it and as a matter of fact, just about everyone on your side of the family. They don't say anything to my face . . . but I know what they are thinking."

A set of double doors opened wide and Penny D and Lucinda found themselves walking through their kitchen. Never one to waste an opportune moment, Lucinda leaned over to taste a spoonful of a thick soup as she passed a big boiling pot.

Penny D put on a face and mimicked her relatives.

"Oh, that Penny has scary pets," said Penny D. "Oh, the last time I went near Penny I was struck by lightning." Then she looked up at the sky to be sure she was safe.

Lucinda tries to console her by petting her head.

"Penny," pleads Lucinda.

"Don't stop me, Mother," said Penny D. "I'm on a roll."

Lucinda stopped with the baby pat. Her daughter was being serious and so Lucinda respected it. The walls closed around them and the floor beneath Penny D's feet turned her around as well. She had little choice it seemed but to face her mother. It was as if the house knew all along that this was the moment they confront their problems.

Penny D was still trying to look away, but she was actually

thinking of bolting out the door. In almost all of the classic books she read, it appeared to be what all teenagers did in time of crisis.

Then, her better judgment kicked in and she remembered that she was always taught to face the issue at hand and never back down!

She figured it this way: if she were in the right then the truth will present itself. If she were in the wrong then she would have to face the consequences. Either way she owed it to her mother to hear her out. Penny D looked up at Lucinda.

"My lucky Penny," said Lucinda. "I do have something to tell you. And, I guess I should have told you this a long, long time ago, and I'm sorry for that. But you see, it was not that we ever lied to you. We would never do that. But there was something we left out. Oh, I guess that is like lying. But that is over now. We were waiting for just the right time to tell you. And, well, I guess now is that time."

Lucinda searched for the words. And then she remembered how Natty had put it. She didn't completely understand his reasoning, but it was all she could think of at that moment.

"You wouldn't discuss hydraulics with a toddler would you? Or, molecular cohesion with a monkey, would you?" said Lucinda.

Lucinda suddenly realized how stupid she sounded.

"Okay, that sounded ridiculous," said Lucinda.

Lucinda closed her eyes and took a deep breath.

"It's like this," said Lucinda.

Another room suddenly unfolded, and standing right in front of them both was, Natty Dreadful. Perhaps it was the house that was bent on keeping certain secrets or the will of Natty. It was hard to tell, but either way he managed to show up at just the right time to spoil the spoiler.

Natty looked Lucinda directly in the eye, pointed to his wristwatch, and shook his head no.

"Oh, Natt!" said Lucinda as if she could read his mind. "She is practically a young woman. When then? Well I disagree.

And what if I do it anyway? What then? That's what you say. Talk to the pinky."

Lucinda appeared to be having an argument all by herself because Natty wasn't saying a word. Or perhaps she had had this same argument with Natty so many times, that she knew what his stock replies would be, and she was playing out the entire scenario that was in her head. Or, not.

Not only did Natty refrain from answering Lucinda, he was also sure never to make a face or roll his eyes when she looked away or make any crude gestures of any kind. He was a good man and would never disrespect his wife for anything. However, he did know how to make a point.

Penny D seized the moment and followed her nose because this explanation, or argument, or whatever it was supposed to be wasn't going anywhere.

"There must be something delightful baking in the oven," she thought, and she wandered away from the one sided conversation.

When Penny D opened the oven she was delighted to see newly baked oatmeal cookies in the shape of bats. She quickly scooped one up and juggled it until it cooled down. She then popped it into her mouth and stuffed her skirt pocket with another two.

Finally there was quiet. Lucinda was not angered, or if she was she hid it very well.

"All right then," said Lucinda and stamped her foot.

Perhaps she was a bit miffed after all. She took a moment to compose herself and sighed.

"It's not easy being Dreadful," said Lucinda out loud.

Natty appeared to slip away along with the room he had entered from. Lucinda and Penny D were alone again.

Lucinda pulled a hung chain next to a paneled wall. The wall opened to reveal a hidden elevator. Penny D and Lucinda stepped inside and she handed her mother a cookie as the wall swallowed them up.

"I promised you an explanation, but at this time I do not have one," said Lucinda. "I am asking you to trust me and that all of your questions will be answered soon enough."

"Okay, mother," said Penny D.

It was not the answer she had wanted to hear, but she was grateful that her mother and father cared enough about her to address her concern and not ignore it completely. Penny D trusted in her mother that her question would be answered at the appropriate time. In teen-speak, that meant Penny D would bring it up again in a week or so.

Inside of the open carriage elevator Lucinda leaned over to talk into a metal cone at the end of a metal hose that hung down from the ceiling.

"Ascend," commanded Lucinda.

The elevator rattled as it began to move. We should assume that it was traveling upwards, but judging from the way their bodies were jolted, it could have been in any direction at all.

Lucinda became very excited all of a sudden.

"Let's talk about your birthday," said Lucinda. "Your father, uncle and I believe that thirteen is a very special year. Did you have anything in mind that you would like to do?"

As the elevator passed an upper floor, Bronte leapt inside and onto Penny D's shoulder. He rallied for her attention by doing a little dance from one shoulder to the other. She gave him a pet on top of his head as tears swelled up in her eyes. It would appear that her frustration has returned.

"I want some human friends," said Penny D. "No offense, Bronte. You know I love you."

Bronte lowered his head.

"I want to do something normal," said Penny D. "Like normal kids do."

She wiped her eyes with her sleeves then stuffed the last of her cookie into her mouth as the elevator came to an abrupt stop. Lucinda leaned forward to direct all of her attention to Penny D so that when she was ready to speak, she would hear every word. The cookie now spent, she continued.

"It's my birthday, right?" said Penny D. "I should have whatever I want, right? And what I want is to be normal."

The elevator started again and Bronte leaped off into a crawlspace as it passed between floors. Within that same space was an unusual man in mid nineteenth century clothing. He was on his hands and knees carrying a butterfly net. He was stalking a rather large creepy insect. The man was her Uncle Calagari. He smiled to Penny D as they passed him.

"Hello, Uncle," said Penny D.

"Normal, you say?" said Lucinda. "I thought you were normal. Hmmm, let me think about this. When I was a little girl growing up in New Jersey we used to have sleep-overs. That's as normal as you get, I suppose."

The elevator stopped again. A wall opened up allowing Natty to step inside. This time he used words to express his thoughts and the look on his face clearly showed that he wished he didn't have to address this at all.

"I don't think so, Lucinda," said Natty.

He began to make strange faces like a child who just ate some raw spinach.

"Think of the loud noise, the mess and the cold little stares," said Natty, and then he shivered a little bit just to drive home his point.

Lucinda's voice changed and became raspy.

"Do you mean like this one?" said Lucinda, her voice louder and her stare cold.

Natty was taken aback by her look.

"Point well taken, dear," said Natty.

"A party with a few of your friends it is then," said Lucinda. "Even a sleep-over if you like. Isn't that right, Natty?"

"Quite," said Natty.

The elevator door opened again. Lucinda and Penny stepped out into their observatory. Natty remained on board as the walls swallowed him up.

The tiny room was decorated all Gothpunk, it looked like a cross between a 1950's sci-fi space opera and a haunted house. In the center of the room was a very large telescope. But instead of it being focused upwards at the heavens, it was pointed downwards at a small petri dish.

Penny D practically danced around the room she was so excited.

"This is great!" said Penny D. "My very own party. May I show my guests my mummy collection?"

"Of course you may," said Lucinda.

Penny D pulled back on a large brass lever. It activated a viewing screen. She adjusted a knob on the telescope and the image on the screen came into sharp focus. It showed two strange insects fighting, perhaps using Kung Fu.

"May we play party games?" asked Penny D.

"There is nothing stopping you," answered Lucinda.

Uncle Calagari, the peculiar gentleman from a few moments ago who had been crawling through the walls with a butterfly net, suddenly appeared and stood right next to Penny D.

"Dear Uncle," said Lucinda, "Guess what?"

"I don't think that I can," said Uncle Calagari.

"We plan to throw a party for Penny right here at the house," said Lucinda.

"Capital idea," said Uncle Calagari. "I could make you a gargoyle piñata, if you like, and fill it with all sorts of slimy treats for your friends?"

"That would be lovely," said Penny D.

"This will be a birthday to remember," says Lucinda.

"In more ways than you know," said Uncle Calagari.

Penny D threw one arm around her mother and another around her Uncle.

"Thank you, thank you, thank you," said Penny D. "Now all I have to do is make a few friends."

Chapter 8
The Night Terrors

Penny D went to bed that night with a myriad of images spinning through her mind. She would flip flop from her conversation with her mother and the birthday party she was going to have at her house to the very bad events that happened at school that day. Need I list those?

She knew what she was supposed to be thinking. From early on she had been taught to believe in 'right thought thinking'. She had read all the great masters who believed in this, practiced their preachings and so far, it appeared that everything had worked out for her because of this.

Penny D was also an energetic pre-teen who knew how to fight and defend herself using sticks and ordinary house-hold objects. Her Uncle Calagari had taught her well and no one ever got hurt. Well, she didn't at least. It was a game to them with no winner or loser. Her uncle had taught her to believe in cooperation and never in competition. She played along because it was fun, nothing more, nothing less.

She also found enjoyment in the simple things like cooking and gardening. She loved to talk and play with her pets, only two of which you have met. Her mother taught her to follow her heart and never listen to the good opinions of other people. Lucinda had also taught her that the right answer to any question comes from within you, not from without.

Her father reinforced these ideals to always do what was right. If there were a steep price to pay for being virtuous then it was a penance she should happily pay back, for it meant she had messed up in some way earlier.

Although Penny D was satisfied with the way things were in her life at the present time, both consciously and subconsciously she knew that something was amiss. She still had so many questions. Questions about her father's past, and more recently about why they had resisted sending her to public school until now.

She was often asked by her mother's side of the family if she could attend the neighborhood school rather than be schooled at home, would she? Her answer was always steadfast, that she would not. The love and attention she got from her family and pets was more than they could imagine.

Yet, there was that great big fat pink elephant in her room. She tried not to look at it, but it was always there. Staring at her day and night. It was not a real elephant of course, but an imaginary one, a concept in her mind. It was an itch she couldn't scratch. It was, well, something that she could not describe. And so, Penny D called it the pink elephant in her room.

That was what she really wanted to know about and what she was sure her mother had been about to tell her until her father stopped her. She believed in them both, so if she was told that she needed to wait a little longer to hear all about it, then she was willing to do so.

But still, there it was.

To amuse herself, she made up a game about it. She pretended it was a relative from New Jersey. It was a lot like the cousins, aunts and uncles she had there anyway. She met them all over the years, so she had little to compare it to but the idea was the same and it amused her. Neither she nor her parents felt comfortable around any of them. It was as though they were always holding something back. Like they were not telling her something, or speaking their true minds. She believed that they never really meant what they said, or said what they meant.

For example, when they would say, "Hello. How are you, little Penny?," it was obvious to her that they didn't really care how she was. Because before she could answer them and begin a discussion about her health, oceanic whaling in the Eighteenth century, or the latest archeological find in Kenya (these were only some of her interests at that time), their attention was off in another direction. To her, this was proof positive that they didn't really care.

And so, as it was with her relatives and so many of the adults in the town where she lived, it didn't take much to distract them. They were a stage magician's dream, Penny D thought.

But what bothered her most about her relatives was that their minds were so focused on criticizing her. Not to her face, but certainly to her mother.

They criticized the way she was dressed, and questioned why she wasn't allowed to go to a 'real school' instead of being home schooled. They also harped on asking what country her father came from and a boat load of other nonsense as far as she was concerned.

Lucinda politely addressed their concerns more than a handful of times and in the kindest words. She was more than patient with her own kin until finally one day she snapped.

This was none of their business and once and for all she let her long platinum blond hair down and gave them more than an earful. She stopped short of telling them all how dismissive, insulting and unappreciative they were of Natty, for no reason other than how he loved her so dearly.

Getting Lucinda angry was always a mistake and they knew it. Although it was not easy to do, since she was so even tempered and loving, like all humans she could be pushed too far.

The last time Lucinda was asked by her tons of cousins,

aunts and uncles about her personal life, and I do mean the last time, since she has not seen or spoken to any of them since the last family gathering, she opened up the dreaded Pandora's Box of family secrets.

In front of all her family and strangers present at that picnic to hear, she asked Aunt Thelma when her daughter Lizzy would finally be paroled. The ghastly look on Aunt Thelma's face should have been enough to end what would later be referred to as Lucinda's Tirade, but no, it didn't stop there. Lucinda then asked Uncle Jazzy why he was always embarrassing the children by talking about their complexion since his was nothing special, her cousin Dana if he knew he had a girl's name and did he expect to ever get a girlfriend since he was now middle aged, and lived in his mom's basement. It appeared that everyone attending was up for grabs, or everyone who had found a special interest in embarrassing her in the past. Lucinda made sure not to leave anyone out. She even included the long-time family neighbor, Escobar, asking if his neighbors knew what he was growing in his basement?

Well, they all got the hint and the Dreadful family was never invited back to New Jersey ever again. For a family get-together in New Jersey, that is. The state of New Jersey itself had no grudge against Lucinda, so far as we are aware of.

Anyway, Penny D found a creative way to deal with this unknown issue in her life. She created an imaginary place where she could store all of this stuff that she knew she had no current use for. It was in the trunk at the end of her bed.

Whenever she found herself wrapped up in a dilemma, obsessing over something that didn't make her feel good, she would shake herself and say, "Enough of that, into the trunk with you!" Sometimes she would hold up an object and blame it for what was bothering her, and give it a scolding and toss it into the trunk as well.

She would then turn her attention to something that did make her feel good; like her pets, her books, her charcoal drawings, her plants, her mother, her father, her uncle, and feel good about that, and never look back. It was what she was taught; to embrace the good and to let go of what bothered her. It worked every time for her. Life was good.

But not tonight.

The cause of her discomfort was what she wanted most, to have something she had never had; some human friends. And in order to have human friends, or so she believed, she would have to deal with all these new issues.

First, there was the issue of finding another student in her class with compatible likes and dislikes, she thought. Then she would have to learn their lingo and talk like them and share in their social rituals. She was aware that she knew so very little of this. It was a concern of inadequacy on her part and that was something she didn't like. Something she had never faced before.

Penny D was always taught to be herself. But in order to be part of this school she would have to be something more than just that. She would have to be something she was always taught she should never be. Perhaps that was the reason her mother and father had home schooled her, to spare her this misery, she thought further.

Wait, was it misery? But the very notion of having a sleepover party excited her. Suddenly she found herself delighted by how much fun it would be to have friends. Maybe she was over thinking this. Perhaps it was all too easy. Just how hard could it possibly be to make friends anyway?

Penny S had lots of friends and she was no winner by any stretch of the imagination. And what of Olivia? It would appear she didn't have any imagination at all, for if she did, why would she be following Penny S and Britney around?

It was getting very late and by now Penny D had convinced herself that making friends was as easy as Exploding Pie, one of Uncle Calagari's favorite desserts to bake and probably just as much fun to eat.

After all, she may already have one friend, that sloppy boy, Malcolm, who believed that girls could be afraid of spiders. How preposterous was that? "Everyone knows that spiders are our friends and how important they are to our ecosystem," Penny D rationalized.

Needless to say these were the issues swimming around in Penny Ds' head as she lay in her bed. She knew she was wrong for thinking them just before sleep. Her Uncle had taught her to focus on the good events of the day in her last moments before sleep and nothing else. And if there were some events that hadn't gone her way, she should imagine them happening differently; more in alignment with the way she would like to have had them go. This always put her in a calm state and she always had a good night of sleep.

But not tonight, tonight she would toss and turn in a Mobius Strip of consciousness. Her thoughts would go round and round and there was no end in sight. Complete exhaustion eventually overtook her and she slipped into a deep sleep-coma accompanied by some very unusual dreams. (For Penny D, anyway.)

***

In her dream Penny D found herself in an ordinary clothing store, the kind of place she would never go. She was staring into a full length mirror and saw herself as she was, but unusually sad.

The store around her was bright and colorful. There were signs that advertised how awesome she would look in every item that clothed the mannequins. It was a cheerful place and better yet, everything was at half price.

Penny D was suddenly confronted by Penny S, Britney and Olivia. They were standing to the right of the mirror and they were all that she could see. She looked them over hungrily, they looked happy and satisfied to be who they were. For three twelve year old girls, they were dressed to kill.

Their clothing was sweet and they didn't look so young in their tight jeans, face make up and recently color streaked hair.

"I know you guys don't like me very much," said Penny D. "But I want you to know how hard I am willing to work to become your friend."

"I don't know, we have very high standards," said Britney.

"Very high standards," repeated Olivia, completely unsure of what those standards could possibly be.

Penny S looked over her newest victim.

"However, we are ready to make an exception," said Penny S. "But that would mean you will have to make a few changes."

"Changes," said Penny D. "What kind of changes?"

"To begin with, the black dress has got to go, it's so five minutes ago," Penny S replied.

Penny S reached over and with one mighty pull the black dress that Penny D was wearing was torn away and flung into the air. Like most dreams, there was that awkward moment when something like having your clothes disappear should bother you but doesn't. Perhaps this was because Penny D cannot see herself, she was too focused on her mentors.

"But I like my dress," said Penny D. "I don't like to wear pants.

She was ignored completely by her new fashion designers.

"And where did you get that hair?" adds Britney.

"My hair?" said Penny D. "What's wrong with it?"

"Sweetie, you look like Elvis," said Britney. "Lucky for you he's dead. That goes too."

Britney held up a can of hair color spray and shot it right at Penny D. For a moment everything got foggy and Penny D could no longer see. She coughed but didn't complain.

"Oh, oh, oh!" said Olivia "I have an idea."

"Careful, don't hurt yourself," said Britney.

"What she really needs is an attitude," said Olivia.

"Good one, O," said Britney and gave her a thumbs up.

Penny D's sight was returning and she once again gave all of her attention to the mean girls before her.

"An attitude?" said Penny D. "I don't understand, what kind of attitude and how could that possibly be a good thing?"

"Without the right attitude, honey," said Britney, "you will never be one of us."

Like a drill Sargent, Penny S threw a list of orders at Penny D.

"Drop that hip like you forgot how to stand straight, raise that shoulder as if it were broken, put that hand in your pocket, open your mouth and show your teeth like you just ate something nasty, and for goodness sake, stop looking me in the eye when I'm talking to you!" said Penny S. "Now roll your eyes like you couldn't care less about what I just said. There. Now that's an attitude."

Suddenly Britney became all girly-girly. You would think she was playing dress-up with her younger sister.

"Okay, you're ready for a look-see," said Britney. "Turn around and look in the mirror."

"She might even pass for human now," adds Penny S.

"Ditto," said Olivia.

Penny D slowly turned to look at herself in the full length mirror. The first thing she noticed was her pierced belly button ring peeking out between her low rider jeans and her tight belly shirt. Her breathing became heavy as she looked up at her face. She was wearing glossy lip stick and her eyes had more mascara than anyone should be allowed to have. The glitter over her eyes didn't make it any better. Her hair was no longer black, it was a rainbow of colors instead. She reached up to her face with her hands and saw long fingernails with cute animal heads painted on each one.

Penny D could hear the three girls behind her laughing at her, at what they had convinced her to do. And then she screamed.

***

Penny D was lying in her bed, still screaming in her sleep. Her room was as misshapen and ghastly as one might expect by now. She looked as though she were trying to pull off her fingers, all the while muttering to herself words that were completely inaudible.

The door to her room suddenly burst open and a very large rat hopped up on the bed. With its tiny hands in a manner not believed possible by a rat or any other vermin, it took Penny D by the collar of her striped pajamas and sat her up. Then it repeatedly slapped her face. (Delicately, of course. Or perhaps, as delicately as a rat on a mission could possibly be.)

Through a thick English accent, the rat spoke to her.

"Penny?" demanded Hawthorne. "Penny, are you all right? Please wake up, dear Penny."

Penny D was still half asleep even though her eyes were open wide.

"I don't want to be like you anymore," said Penny D looking around the room for people who weren't there. "I changed my mind. I want my old clothes back. And my old hair too."

She suddenly realized where she was and who she was with and what had just happened. She took Hawthorne into her arms and hugged him.

"Hawthorne!" said Penny D. "I don't want to be like them. They're mean and selfish. And their taste in fashion is abysmal. If that's what it takes to be liked, then I don't want to be liked. I don't want to be normal and have normal friends anymore."

"Can't…breath…," said Hawthorne.

Penny D let up on the bear-hug and Hawthorne wobbled around on the bed for a moment from a lack of oxygen.

Penny D wrapped her arms around her legs and hung her head.

Hawthorne came around and assessed the situation. He slowly approached her and petted her head sympathetically.

"There, there, darling," said Hawthorne. "Being popular ain't what it's cracked up to be. Take it from me, I ain't exactly welcome everywhere I go. Now lie back down. Come on."

Penny D laid back down. She held a straight face but Hawthorne could tell that she was still sobbing on the inside.

"We can talk about all of this popularity stuff in the morning," said Hawthorne. "Now close your eyes and think about your birthday in a few weeks and you will be fast asleep in no time. That a girl."

As Hawthorne shushed her, her eyes slowly closed.

Suddenly there was a blood curdling scream coming from down the hall. Penny D appeared unaffected.

"There you are love," said Hawthorne. "Even Uncle Calagari is sound asleep."

Chapter 9
The Pranksta

Malcolm Waxenburg, was the sloppy boy that Penny D told her mother about who thought that girls were afraid of spiders and probably worms and other night crawling critters. Perhaps the origin of his belief came from his older sister who kept telling him so. He also believed in a good laugh. No one knew where that came from.

Thus he was willing to do anything to get a good laugh. Not just for himself, oh no, no, no. He wanted to share them with everyone. Little did he know just how important that would really become later in his life.

He plotted and planned and schemed and hoped he wouldn't get caught in his constant preparation for that big laugh. Because if he did get caught just one more time, it would mean his expulsion from Terracotta Junior High School.

Just last year he was caught with his pants down, so to speak. Well, actually, his pants were down, he was in the Boys' Wash Room taping plastic tubes to his underwear.

It's a long story. You see, it all began when he found a link on the internet that explained how a Hollywood special effects movie magician created the blood gushing effect of a person who was suddenly attacked by a werewolf. This was the highlight of his favorite movie of all time, "Werewolf-Zombie-Mummy Apocalypse", and it intrigued him.

Using the mechanical skills that his mother always told him he had, he wasted no time in attempting to recreate that same effect and planned to take it a few steps further.

In his mind he thought this would be a great joke to play in front of the entire school. And the end-of-year Step Up Program Ceremony would be a perfect time to do it.

Or so he thought. But thinking things through was never part of what a teenager did best. It has something to do with the synapses in their adolescent brains not firing enough or firing too much. I forget which, and I don't think anyone knows for sure. The short story was that he thought it was a good idea at the time. And yes, Malcolm may have been only twelve and a half years old but he was certainly ahead of his time.

So the plan was for Malcolm to make a complete fool of himself at the Step Up Program Ceremony and in true dramatic fashion fake his own death, because he thought that this would be funny.

Perhaps what really intrigued him was the idea that just when everyone believed he was a goner, beyond any help, he would show that it was all a joke and that he was not bleeding at all. That he was perfectly fine.

The more he thought about this the more he liked it. No one was going to get hurt, he thought to himself, and who doesn't like a good fright just before a good laugh? After all, isn't that why we watch horror films in the first place?

Beginning with nothing more than the story vice of his favorite films, Malcolm planned to reconstruct the scenes as a live event. He reviewed them in his head and they were almost all the same. The killer quietly stalked the helpless female heroine. Then just before he stabbed her in the back the first time, she moved out of the way and the killer fell over something and got hurt himself in some odd Hollywood nonsensical fashion.

Although the audience was scared when the killer first stalked his helpless victim, they laughed twice as hard when he repeatedly missed her. Said formula was repeated continuously throughout the film until this sad excuse for a film came to a predictable end. He loved every second of it.

Malcolm's plan was a simple one. He would spend his allowance on the supplies he needed, all purchases from a nearby supermarket and a tropical fish store. He would mix up his own blood recipe from corn syrup and food coloring and pour it into a cake decorating syringe secured in his pant's pocket.

Attached to the cake decorating syringe would be a plastic fish tank tube. He would run the tube up under his shirt and into his hair from behind his head. When the right moment arrived he would pretend to be hurt, put his hand in his pocket and squeeze the trigger on the cake decorating syringe. Blood would flow up the tube that was duct taped to his underwear and into his hair. Blood would then pour down his forehead. Malcolm would scream in pain and fall over and die he figured.

Then, miraculously, he would stand up on his feet, show the audience that he was unharmed and the crowd would go wild as he took a bow. People would throw flowers at him and young girls would throw kisses. He would be their hero that day. Or so he figured.

After a dry run in his dad's garage using the device he kit-bashed together, just when he thought he had perfected the trick he got another idea to improve it. But to execute this new idea properly he needed an unsuspecting stooge to go along with the gag until he produced what filmmakers call the 'money shot'; that glorious moment when the cake decorating syringe trigger would be pulled and the sweet corn syrup would cascade down his face appearing to be blood.

There was a boy in his sixth grade class who didn't talk much. He was just a little over weight for his age, a little too tall for his grade, a little too slow for his own good and as if that were not enough, he stuttered as well. His name was Vincent.

Malcolm had no intention of making Vincent look foolish, he was not a mean child. (That special malevolent trait was already cornered by Penny Social.) Malcolm simply felt that he needed an accomplice who would not ask questions and who would do as he was told. All geniuses feel this way, or at least that's how they are portrayed in cartoons. Igor do this. Igor do that. Igor was always so stupid or needy that he did as he was told and never asked why. On the rare occasion he did, he was told to shut up and that was that.

Anyway, Malcolm thought that if he had a second person pretend to kill him with a plastic sword by hitting him on the head, it would only add to the drama of the moment when the blood began to pour. So they met after school and rehearsed the action.

Surprisingly to Malcolm, Vincent was a natural with the plastic sword, and perhaps much better than he thought he would be. In fact, Vincent told Malcolm a secret that he had never told anyone at the school before.

First he swore Malcolm to secrecy, then, he told Malcolm that he was a Sedi Master. Not a full blown Sedi Master, but a Junior Sedi Master. Or a master-in-training.

Malcolm didn't know what that was outside of the movie reference from a sci-fi film franchise that was created a decade before he was born. Vincent further told Malcolm that he and his father traveled the country on holidays dressed up in authentic-looking movie costumes and armed with very realistic looking plastic swords.

They were accompanied by Vincent's father's friend, a superhero in his own right, known only as Mr. Protoplasma. They put on a stage-combat show together at comic book and Sci-Fi conventions and the like.

Who knew? The mild mannered, slow witted, over weight tall kid, with a stutter that Malcolm randomly picked to assist him was living a double life. And, he was not a stooge at all.

Quickly rethinking his plan he decided to leave out the

part about the blood flowing from his head when divulging the finale of the stage show to Vincent. This way it would be just as much of a surprise to him as it would be to the audience on the day of the event. Or so he figured.

Confidentially, he was afraid that if he did divulge the secret plan, Vincent would back out. Vincent kept repeating Sedi Master proverbs while they practiced the sword routine and it was beginning to make Malcolm nervous.

So that was his plan. But it didn't work out that way.

While practicing the blood effect on his own one last time, Malcolm suspected that the blood was not flowing fast enough through the tube and needed a boost. The sword duel was so fast paced that he felt the culmination of this great drama should happen much more quickly.

His solution to this problem was to attach a helium filled balloon to the plastic tube 'pipeline' to force the blood to flow faster. He would hold the balloon from a string in his hand. The plastic tubing ran out of the balloon and down the string and into the cake decorating syringe in his pocket. This he believed, made him look inconspicuous.

The eventful day arrived and Malcolm was in the process of rigging the entire ingenious device under his clothing in the Boy's Wash Room when Vincent marched in and resigned from participating.

Malcolm was beside himself with disappointment. When he asked why the dimwitted Sedi Master-in-training was quitting, the dimwitted Sedi Master-in-training replied without even the hint of a stutter,

"You were trying to deceive me," said Vincent. "Even a Junior Sedi Master can tell when evil is afoot. And I will not be part of your scheme to embarrass yourself."

And with that Vincent turned on the heels of his Junior Sedi Master boots and walked out of the Boy's Wash Room.

Malcolm began to display signs of what one might call the teenage version of a conniption. His arms flailed about as he shouted out words he had only seen written in magic marker on the walls of the public rest room in the train station.

The blood tubes and the cake decorating syringe dangled down around his ankles with his pants. The plastic stopper in the helium balloon started to come loose. Malcolm, who was still in the middle of his fit, also didn't notice that three people; the assistant principal, Mr. Goldenthorp, his son and his son's best friend had entered the Boys' Wash Room.

Mr. Goldenthorp was an unusually tall man and his son, who was also unusually tall for a ten year old, stood there watching this spectacle with the son's best friend who was unusually short for his age.

Looking back on what had happened that day it was no surprise to Malcolm that, as they stood watching him have his childish temper tantrum, they would have noticed that the helium balloon he was holding was beginning to shrink.

He believed that it was impolite for them to stay and that they should have left him to finish whatever it was that he was doing. But, they didn't. They stayed.

Bored from the speeches that day, the two boys had folded their programs into paper planes and flew them at Malcolm in mid-fit. One boy had held up his MyPhone and had taken a picture of Malcolm as well.

So in Malcolm's mind what had happened, was their own fault, and he was not to blame for it in any way. If there was an ounce of respect in that wash room that day, the worst that would have happened was that Malcolm would have made a big mess all over himself.

But no, Mr. Goldenthorp, his son and his son's best friend had stayed to watch.

The helium balloon gas shot down through the tube at an alarming rate and forced the fake blood that was in the cake decorating syringe to travel up through another tube in Malcolm's hair. But instead of dripping down his forehead as planned it sprayed out like a geyser all over Mr. Goldenthorp who was the tallest object in the room. And just when you'd have thought there was no more fake blood left in the cake decorating syringe, two shorter bursts shot out quite low and squared both the assistant principal's son and his best friend in the face.

It ruined all their new clothes and their day as well.

Malcolm's parents were called into the school and they didn't like that one bit. They were forced to sit in tiny chairs at tiny desks in a tiny classroom and watch the Assistant Principal go into what only could be described as an adult version of a conniption.

They, Malcolm's parents, were told that Mr. Goldenthorp had wanted Malcolm expelled for this horrible prank but his request was denied.

The principal was a much wiser man than the assistant principal and didn't believe in such severe punishments for a minor lavatory mess like this. But he did agree that Mr. and Mrs. Waxenburg had to pay for damages and that if there was just one more incident like this, Malcolm would be thrown out of the school. Malcolm had been on thin ice ever since.

This didn't sit well with his parents. If he was expelled, Malcolm would have to take a bus to school in the next town. It was a sixty minute trip in each way. So basically that meant more distance between him and authority figures and more time to get into trouble.

Needless to say, he was warned and threatened by his parents all the way home and told how embarrassed they were by his behavior. Further, they said that if he were to ever even consider such a foolish idea again, there would be severe consequences. His father had repeated the word, "severe" several times for good measure.

Later that night, Malcolm's father had entered his bedroom and asked Malcolm if he took any pictures with his MyPhone of the Assistant Principal when the deed previously described had first happened. When he replied that he had not, it was obvious that his father was disappointed.

Even more strange, his mother packed two snacks in his lunch bag for school the following day and every day for the next week. They never spoke of the incident ever again.

Malcolm was a bit more cautious now when conceiving a new prank, or so he thought. He never figured that the silicone spider bit with the new student could possibly have gone awry. Nevertheless, Malcolm felt motivated to continue his life's work and his passion.

If there was one given in a crowd of people it would be that almost anyone could do almost anything unusual without being noticed.

Malcolm called this his, "hide-in-plain sight," theory and he understood this principle very well. With this in mind he leaned into a school hall locker that wasn't his own. He nonchalantly looked over his shoulder at the many students who passed him in droves, talking to one another and minding their own business. Or so he figured.

Like a cat burglar in training, he went back to his work. Once it was completed, he closed the locker, but ever so gently.

Standing right behind the open locker door, who up till that very moment had gone unseen, was Penny D.

Without missing a beat Malcolm began a conversation.

"So, you can really talk to snakes?" said Malcolm.

"She's a python," said Penny D.

"Ah, your python and your spider?"

"He's a tarantula."

"Right."

Penny D still felt a little uneasy talking to children her own age, she had so little practice. She felt more comfortable talking to adults. But she was on a mission and so she sucked in her courage and went for it.

"Yes I can talk to them," said Penny D. "My pets. Does that sound weird to you?"

"No," said Malcolm. "You're a tarantula and python whisperer. I saw a movie about that on cable. Can you tell my dog to stop pooping on my bed?"

Penny D pondered over the strange request.

"Why don't you tell him yourself?" said Penny D.

"I can't talk to dogs," said Malcolm.

"Neither can I," said Penny D.

"Ohhhhhhh . . . ," said Malcolm, and this time it made a

little more sense to him then before.

They smiled at each other and Penny D finally discovered the connection between people her age that most understood already. Here was someone who was willing to accept her for who she was without any judgment. That made them peers.

Malcolm motioned with his head that they should walk to their next class together. As they did the students around them suddenly began to take notice. Malcolm who already had a reputation for doing, well, crazy things, had been lurking in an unknown student's locker for ten minutes or so, and went unnoticed. But as soon as it looked like the new girl in school, the only Goth girl in their entire school, who had a reputation of her own had a new friend, they all took notice.

It didn't take long. There were texts, "twists," and some other new forms of unidentified digital media invisibly streaming through the air in the hall that day. This was big news. The Goth chick had a friend. How strange was that? And, it was Malcolm. How insane was that?

Penny D was still so new to the pleasantness of this situation that it had not completely sunk in yet. She rattled her mind to come up with a subject to lengthen their conversation, then she remembered where she had found Malcolm mere moments before.

"That wasn't your locker," said Penny D. "What were you doing in there?"

"Ah, right," said Malcolm. "It's Britney's."

He owned up to it and cupped one hand around his mouth to prevent any passerby from overhearing him.

"Can you say, booby trap?" said Malcolm, in whispered tone.

He followed that up with a wink and pointed his finger at her.

"Watch," said Malcolm.

Malcolm stopped and turned around to look back at where he had been standing just seconds before. Penny D did the same.

They saw Penny S, Britney and Olivia walking over to their lockers, all located against the same school wall. They were all so busy chatting about their usual nonsense that they never noticed that almost everyone in the hall had stopped what they were doing or from going where they were going and even took a few steps back.

It would appear that the students had seen Malcolm after all and were simply minding their own business. Or, they had suspected what he was doing and secretly approved. In either case, a few of the students shielded their faces with their books.

In perfect synchronization Penny S, Britney and Olivia all dialed their combination locks.

Malcolm remained cool. And Penny D, who was not in on the gag or had no point of reference to what might happen when it came to anything that Malcolm did, remained the same.

"Do you belong to any clubs?" said Penny D.

She felt herself becoming comfortable with Malcolm and the change of subject came easily.

"Me, nah," said Malcolm. "They don't have a club for what I do. I wish they did."

"My Mom says I have to join a club," said Penny D.

"Harsh," said Malcolm.

One by one Penny S, Britney and Olivia began to open their lockers. Penny S was first and when the door of her locker swung open a "can of snakes" sprang out at her. Penny S spun around, startled, with one of the snakes wrapped around her head.

Malcolm had glued Velcro to the snakes, so they would be sure to attach to her long hair. Penny S ran off screaming, the snakes trailing behind her like a Chinese Dragon at a Chinese New Year's parade.

Britney was easily distracted by the obvious prank that was successfully perpetrated on Penny S. Without thinking, as she most often acted, she opened her own locker. She was immediately sprayed from within by three cans of Silly

Web. Her arms became tangled as she tried to stop the constant flow of plastic webbing coming at her from inside of the locker.

She tried to close the door but it became jammed open. Malcolm had fixed the door to the locker so it would hold the position until the cans were empty. Britney's hair became so tangled that she eventually just gave up. When the cans finally ran out of juice and the bombardment ended, Britney just walked away.

You would think that Olivia would think twice before opening up her locker, but let's face it, by now we have learned that Olivia hardly even thinks once. She opened up her locker anyway and peeked inside. Like really peeked inside, with her whole head. There were no explosions or an evil Jack-in-the-Crate leaping out at her to frighten her.

Instead she removed an envelope from inside with her name on it. She opened it, and removed a card from inside the envelope. She read it. She blushed. She closed her locker and walked away.

As much as the students in the hall had enjoyed the show, they were at least respectful enough to allow all three girls to leave the hall before bursting out into semi-silent controlled laughter.

There were more than just a few students present who still considered Penny S a friend, but that was only to her face. In some secret way they probably just feared her.

There were a few high fives between students and twice as many texts, "twists" and other unknown digital messages immediately being posted on numerous social pages following that incident.

Penny D remained calm, while Malcolm looked mysteriously content. Actually, he felt absolutely victorious.

"The first two I get," said Penny D. "But what exactly was that last one about? What was in that letter to Olivia?"

"I'm conducting an experiment," said Malcolm, who then smiled.

"I see," said Penny D, and she smiled back.

Penny D suddenly thought to herself how easy it was to make a friend. That is, if Malcolm was a friend. In theory it would appear so.

She knew enough about science to know that in order for a theory to be proven it must first be tested. Penny D took a deep breath and went for it.

"I'm having a birthday party next week," said Penny D. "It's no big thing. Maybe you would like to come?"

The next two seconds were probably the longest two seconds of Penny D's life, or so it appeared. Her entire life passed before her, a cold sweat broke out across her forehead. Her throat became very, very dry. She told herself that she should just walk away now and spare herself the agony of hearing Malcolm tell her that he couldn't because he had to go fishing to feed his family. Or, that he was involved in a marble tournament, or that he simply didn't want to because he really didn't think she was his friend. But she didn't. She decided that she would face the music and stand her ground. She would wait for his reply and accept it no matter the outcome.

"Sure," said Malcolm. "Sounds like fun."

"It does?" said Penny D. "Ah, yeah, it will be. Lots of fun. I promise. I don't really have a theme yet, or an itinerary, but I was thinking it may be a sleep-over. Not that you have to, but if you wanted to, you could. My mom said so."

"Pajama Party!" said Malcolm, most excitedly. "Whoa. I've heard about those ancient rituals from my parental units. But I never dreamed that I would live long enough to participate in one."

Malcolm's mind was still racing from the very notion of a pajama party, or was it racing from the very notion that any student in this school would want him at their party, one will never know. Then a new idea hit him. And as it is with Malcolm, he had to up the ante.

"Maybe, you could invite Olivia?" Malcolm sheepishly asks.

"Oh?" said Penny D. "Oh."

It was all Penny D could think of to say for the moment.

Then without skipping a beat she answered.

"Sure," said Penny D. "Why not?"

And she said it whole heartedly. Penny D was never one to hold a grudge, and Olivia had never really done anything mean to her. It was not that she felt that Olivia was a victim of sorts, she firmly believed that we all made our own decisions and we should take responsibility for the outcome of those decisions.

If Olivia decided to placate to the selfish whims of Penny S, then she would have to answer for those acts one day. It was not her place to punish Olivia for her poor choice in friends and certainly not her place to judge her either. So when she said she would invite her, she meant it.

Malcolm was ecstatic.

"Co-ed pajama party," said Malcolm. "How insane is that? Oh, I have to think up some new gags."

Penny D didn't know how to answer him, but the smile on her face said it for her.

And a new friendship was born.

Chapter 10
Club Dread

The school bulletin board looked menacing to Penny Dreadful. When did life get so complicated? When she was home schooled she would wake up in the morning, have breakfast and begin to read from the teachings of Plato or Socrates. Then just before she broke for lunch she would have enough time for a quick fencing session with her Uncle Calagari.

After lunch her afternoon lessons would begin with twenty minutes of meditation followed by a free-style interpretation of a Shakespearian play of her choosing.

Her average school day at home usually covered the entire day. It would have been shorter if not for the minor distractions. For example; her friends, Bronte, Rebecca and Hawthorne would horse around while she were trying to concentrate on her work until she dropped what she was doing and chased them all around the house.

When the home studies became too intense, Uncle Calagari would show Penny D how to do card tricks, or her mother would demonstrate how to create origami, or her father would break out his unicycle, juggle and play the harmonica for her (not necessarily at the same time). What more could a girl want?

But here, in these organized halls of education, it was so distracting. "Just look at this stuff," Penny D thought to herself. She was told that she had to pick one of these clubs to join and there were so many to choose from. It was not a lack of choices, but the lack of substance that left her dumbstruck.

Being the girl she was, and always out to do what was right, Penny D was determined to follow through and join a club, even though she didn't want to. She began to scan down the long list on the bulletin board.

There were clubs for all kinds of sports like baseball, basketball and football, but Penny D had no idea what those could possibly be. Then there were some social clubs like; the Occupy the Lunch Room Club. It appeared there was an ongoing protest by the students in the cafeteria. They wanted better food in general, but they were willing to settle for better desserts. Fig and prune pudding wasn't going to cut it. More than one student had claimed that it gave them a bad case of the runs.

This week they were protesting the spinach and artichoke sauce that was spread on the meat loaf. They claimed that it was actually worse than it sounded.

Moving on.

Below that was the Halloween Club. Now that sounded interesting to Penny D. She had no idea that there were any Pagans in Terracotta, let alone any in her school. Penny D thought to herself that it may be fun to dance naked around a barn fire at night and sing songs. At least that was her basic understanding of some pagan practices.

Since she knew she didn't really know what it was like to be a pagan she decided to research it further before making that decision. She would do her homework first, so to speak and if she found it peaceful, creative and informative, she would consider it for next year.

Another social club was listed for the students who played a board game called, "Bridges and Trolls." This game was loaded with magic spells and trickery. It sounded very creative. The only drawback she saw was that they requested you bring a skilled partner and the notice clearly said that no novice players were welcome. So that one was out.

Penny D knew that her new school was not that large and there were not enough students here to possibly occupy this many clubs. Perhaps this is what pre-teens her age did after school, join clubs. More than one, even. Several, perhaps. How interesting.

Finally, at the very bottom of the list, there were the clubs for The Arts. Now there was something she believed that she knew enough about to fit in. So she read them all over carefully.

The first of these to catch her attention was the Drama Club. She knew what drama was all about, she read Christopher Marlowe and Tennessee Williams. Admittedly she didn't catch all of their innuendoes, but the rhythm of the sonnets sounded like a song. She would sing them to herself from time to time, the ones she had memorized that is.

On the flip side of Drama was comedy and Penny D knew this all too well. Her pets kept her laughing with their daily antics. For example; one time Bronte had climbed inside of a large Mason jar to eat the grape-banana jam at the bottom and he couldn't get out. He loved Uncle Calagari's special recipes and ate so much of the jam while he was inside of the jar that he couldn't fit through the opening in the lid that he had climbed in from.

Penny D knew he was told by her uncle to stay clean away from the new jam jars. She asked her uncle what she should do.

"Serves him right," said Uncle Calagari. "He should stay in there until he loses a few extra pounds. That would teach him a lesson."

But tarantulas don't like captivity and he was starting to freak out. Never one to inflict a cruel punishment on anyone or anything, even if they deserved it, Penny D rolled him off of the table and smashed the glass in order to free him. It gave

Bronte a headache, but he at least said he learned his lesson. (Or so she thought.)

Comedy and tragedy aside, Penny D knew how to act. The stage was one of her father's passions and she was inspired by his love for it. She often heard him say that if he hadn't studied engineering, he would have become an actor. To this statement her mother would always roll her eyes.

"On the other hand," Natty would add. "Lucinda was a much finer actress than I could ever be an actor. Look, she even mastered the elusive eye roll."

This very thought brought a smile to Penny D's face as she reached up and signed her name to join the Drama Club.

That afternoon, Penny D found herself in the school auditorium. There were a few boys already up on stage brandishing wooden swords and listening to the director. Or so the director thought.

The truth was that most of them just wanted to be in a play that had a sword fight so that they would get to die on stage. For this they were willing to put up with hours of rehearsals and memorizing some dialogue.

As Penny D timidly entered the stage, all eyes were upon her.

"Excuse me," asked Penny D. "Is this where the Drama Club meets?"

"You're new here, aren't you?" said the Director.

She, the Director, was a wee bit younger than Penny D and the authority of her position in the play had already gone to her head. So much so, that she spoke openly and into the air as if the theater itself could actually understand her, and for that matter, empathize with her. In truth, the theater didn't care what she thought.

"How am I supposed to successfully direct a play when they keep sending me inexperienced talent?" said the Director. "Okay new girl, we'll try you out."

"My name is Penny and I already have acting experience," said Penny D. "So I will not require any special attention."

"Whatever," said the Director. "You can be the MacGuffin

in this scene."

One of the boys, who appeared to be playing with his sword and not listening at all, suddenly woke up. He then did something that is usually taboo in real theater: he interrupted the director.

"The Ma-gufferin?" said the boy. "What's that?"

"The MacGuffin was a cinematic term coined by film director Alfred Hitchcock," said Penny D. "He used it to describe the object of desire that the protagonists were after in his films. It rarely needed to be defined, it was simply a tool of his trade to move his story forward."

"I see we have a smarty-pants on stage," said the Director.

Then she clapped her hands twice ignoring Penny D entirely.

"Let's get right to it, shall we?" said the Director. "Here is how the scene goes down. Hamlet must defend the new girl's honor against the three men who are threatening her."

Then she pointed to a metal chair as if the world were at her command.

"New girl," said the Director. "Sit on that rock and look scared."

"That's ridiculous," said Penny D. "I don't need a boy to defend my honor."

"Of course you do," said the Director. "You're a girl."

Then she smiled at one of the boys on stage and he in turn smiled back.

"Besides, I'm pretty sure that's the way things were done back then," said the Director.

"Shakespeare wrote those words over four hundred years ago," said Penny D. "We've come a long way baby."

"And your point is, you're going to defend yourself?" asked the Director.

The boys on stage didn't even bother to cover their mouths when they laughed at the comment that Penny D just made.

Penny D used the tip of her shoe to flip a sword up from the floor high enough so that she could catch it with her hand. Then, with lightning speed, she spun around the stage like a top, smacking the wooden swords out of each of the three boys' hands with her own. All four boys were taken by surprise and backed away, one made a run for it and left the stage completely.

"Yes, I, am," said Penny D.

If one look was truly worth a thousand words, then the look on the Director's face must have been an encyclopedia. It was obvious that Penny D would not fit in here at all.

And that was the end of Penny Dreadful's Drama Club experience.

Moments later Penny D was standing at that same bulletin board she had been earlier. She crossed out her name from the line under The Drama Club where she had written it.

Suddenly another club caught her eye. It was called, the Sci-Fi Club. Penny D found the laws of physics interesting. She studied Newton's Law and was so impressed that a man who lived so long ago could create a law of physics that was still part of science today. She reached up and signed her name.

Penny D soon found herself sitting in a classroom with four other students who were dressed up in strange looking costumes. I guess, by the normal standards set forth in this school, she fit right in. But they, the other students, were aliens all. Not the out-of-this-country kind, but the out-of-this-world kind. And they were a colorful bunch.

One child was dressed like a giant cockroach, a costume sewn together by his mother. It was very cute actually. He had several arms and there were some sequins sewn on his wings that made them shimmer like a real roach. He was very proud of it.

A second student wore several mop heads glued to a long robe. Even his friends didn't know what he was supposed to be but I guess you could say, he looked like a spaghetti monster.

The third student in the room wore a costume made completely of cardboard boxes. A large box covered his torso and several shoe boxes were slipped around his arms and legs. The boxes had wires and buttons glued onto them. He may have figured they made him look futuristic or high tech.

The fourth and final alien costumed student in the room had made use of a lot of tin foil. He was completely covered in it. It must have been very hot in there. Penny D wondered to herself how he could breathe.

The next thought that crossed her mind while she sat there waiting to be acknowledged, was how she felt on her very first day of Junior High School. She was dressed a little different than the other students and all they did was stare at her.

Now it was her turn to stare at them. The only difference was that she was not judging them negatively by what she saw. She rather liked what she saw and thought that they were a creative bunch, and probably enjoying themselves. But she couldn't understand what any of this had to do with science-based fiction.

One student, the cardboard robot, who was obviously Vincent, saluted Penny D with two fingers to his forehead.

"Greetings, Earthling," said Vincent in a strange voice. "We mean you no harm."

"Greetings," all the students repeated at the same time. "We mean you no harm."

They saluted Penny D as well.

"Who me?" said Penny D.

"You are the only human here," said Vincent.

"Not too many students in this school who would agree with that," said Penny D.

She attempted to make a joke and although it was a good one she didn't get the response she figured she would.

Vincent looked over to his other club members. He made a buzzing and clicking sound as he moved. He was a robot, after all.

"We should laugh at her joke to make her feel comfortable," said Vincent.

All the students in the room began to laugh, but in their own alien language of course.

"Listen, Vincent," said Penny D. "What exactly is this club all about?"

"I am not Vincent," said Vincent. "Vincent is my Earthly projection. I am Krank-Ok from the eighth planet in the Labrodor system. But you may call me, Krank for short."

"Right," said Penny D. "My bad. So, Krank, what do you guys do in this club?"

"We discuss matters of great cosmic and scientific importance," said Krank-Ok.

"Like. . . ?"

"Like, what sci-fi movie we would like to see made, and video games we plan to invent one day."

"I see. So basically you dress up in unusual costumes, talk about things that no one has ever heard of and try to fit into a social setting that cannot understand you."

"Ah, yeah, that pretty much sums it up."

"So how different is that than my life right now?"

The aliens in the room went into a huddle. In their own strange languages they began to discuss the matter at hand. It sounded like gibberish to Penny D, mainly because it was.

Krank-Ok came out of the huddle and turned to Penny D.

"We make cupcakes, too," said Krank-Ok.

"What flavors?" said Penny D.

"Stratosphere Strawberry and Gravity Grape," said Krank-Ok.

Needless to say, this was the end of Penny's dreadful Sci-Fi Club experience.

For a third time Penny D stood at that same bulletin board and crossed her name out on the line below the SciFi Club.

Her level of enthusiasm, as low as it already was, had dropped considerably but she was still determined. She pulled at the pencil that was hanging from the string and signed her name one last time. The line above where she signed it read; the Heavy Metal Club.

Something clicked.

Perhaps it was the very large latex apron that Penny D was now wearing, or the thick leather gloves that barely fit her hands. Or perhaps it was the dark glasses that covered her eyes, but here in the deep bowels of the Terracotta Junior

High School basement, Penny D attended a club located in the metal shop.

There was a teacher standing over her. He was a jolly man, he even looked a little like Santa Claus supervising the production of toys in his super toy factory. He, too, was wearing the gear that Penny D was. His beard reached the middle of his shirt and was mostly white. The very tip of it was singed black.

He talked to Penny D as loudly as he could but his voice still could not be heard because the room was extremely noisy. The other students in the room, mostly boys, were hammering away at pieces of metal, punishing them for their flatness. They each dreamed of creating something new and different, something they never knew was possible. That and the heavy metal music the teacher had playing over his desk speakers filled the air.

The teacher's name was, Mr. Kindle and there was an immediate bond between Penny D and him.

Through the loud music and hammering and sanding and grinding, Penny D understood him just fine. He gestured to her with his hands various detailed instructions. She nodded her head, pointed to a few places on a large scrap of metal in front of her and then looked up to him for approval.

When Penny D committed herself to something, she wanted to get it right. She waited anxiously for his authorization.

Mr. Kindle answered her with another series of hand gestures. She nodded. He nodded back. They were communicating!

Penny D gave Mr. Kindle a thumbs-up, lowered her dark glasses over her eyes and began to disc-sand the metal piece that was trapped in a steel vice with her electric sander.

Sparks lit up the room and reflected in the dark glasses that Penny D was wearing. It was like the Fourth of July. A moment later she stopped sanding. There was a big smile on her face. She removed one glove to give Mr. Kindle the okay sign.

Thus Penny Dreadful found a new club experience that was to her liking.

Chapter 11
Mystery Meat

It is a little known and even less believed fact that the one place in most Junior High schools that is the most frightening of all (and that demands your attendance) is the one you would least suspect. It is not the vacant smoky washrooms, the stressed out principal's office, or the scary nurse's station. No, it is the school's dreaded cafeteria.

Do not make light of this. There are unseen dangers lurking in every corner of that place. In fact, there is so much that does not meet the eye, one hardly knows where to start.

So to begin with, let us start with the excruciating level of noise that emanates from that place. It is deafening. The sounds of everyone and anyone talking, screaming and walking which bounce off the high ceiling, the bare walls and the tiled floor are intolerable. This room is an architect's nightmare come to life.

The choice of furniture also contributes to the chaos. The metal pipe legs of the tables and chairs are in a constant state of flux and trumpet like wild elephants as they slide across the floor. Even the shuffling feet of the students sound like a stampede.

Students cringe at the very thought that they have little choice but to eat here on the poorly washed tables where traces of food left over from days or weeks past, mixed with the smell of the detergents used to clean them.

The food is all together another issue. It is vile. It is mysterious. It could not be identified on most days. But perhaps the one most redeeming quality of the food is that it has inspired several students over the years to become microbiologists. The mystery of the food that is served here on a regular basis is perhaps the catalyst some bright young minds need to discover a cure for an unnamed disease one day.

On a typical day in the cafeteria at Terracotta Junior High School, the following would occur and in the following order. The students would come in, wait on line for their food, sit down to eat it and as they left, they would clear their places on the table where they sat.

Simple, right? Doesn't take much thought. And on a good day that was all that would occur. On a bad day, a food fight could erupt, a social bully could make an under classmate cry, someone's lunch money may be "misplaced," shall we say, and vomit figures into the scenario at least once a week.

On special occasions, select students would risk their social status for an opportunity to right a wrong. And physical injury would result.

As for the students of Miss Novella's class, they had their lunch break about half way through the period. They usually entered the cafeteria in an orderly fashion long before Penny D. She was usually last in line.

It was not that her goal was to be last and their goal to be first, but she never saw any reason to be first or second or third. As stated before, she was taught not to believe in competition. There was plenty of food for everyone as far as Penny D was concerned and if by some fluke of nature they ran out of something before she got there, she would be no less happy.

In her mind she was not meant to have those peas or potatoes or the mystery meat of the day, as Malcolm labeled the hamburgers, and that is all there was to it. She would not go hungry. She would not starve. There would still be ample food to eat.

Just yesterday all the canned fruit was gone from the dessert tray when Penny D had arrived at the end of the food line. It was also at that very moment she remembered that her Uncle was making one of his exploding pies for her and that it would be ready for her when she got home. This was all the more reason why she shouldn't eat any dessert.

So the absence of canned fruit on the dessert tray on that day, she believed, was a reminder to herself that she should save some room in her belly for something better. And there was nothing better, as far as Penny D was concerned, than exploding pie.

Needless to say the pie was great that afternoon. And yes, it did in fact explode. After she ate it, not before. With flavor, that is.

So as you see, it all worked itself out.

Getting back to today, as the students of Miss Novella's class filed into the cafeteria, they made it their first order of business to leap over, walk around and in some cases fall over the Occupy the Cafeteria Club members. They, the club members, parked themselves on the floor between the cafeteria entrance and the line for food.

This was a fire hazard and would not be tolerated by the school administration, but the leader of said club was very clever and planned their every movement carefully. There were few who knew when a "sit-in" was going to occur and where. Actually the where part was easy. It was always in the cafeteria.

Athena was the leader of this occupy movement, but that was not her official status. She claimed to be a bystander, but everyone in the group knew to look to her for orders through a series of head nods and eye blinks. They feared that the establishment, AKA, the Principal's office, may attempt a coup d'etat to remove her. The official unofficial leader of this club was little Paulie. Granted, this didn't fool anyone, but every movement must protect its leader or the group would fall.

Demonstrations aside, the next order of business was for the students to pick up a tray and enter the food line. One by one they traveled down the narrow path between the food dispenser carts and the seated students of the school.

Food was slung at them by the kitchen staff from the opposite side of the cart. Experience had taught them to hold a napkin up across their faces each time they paused in the line to have their food thrown onto their plates. Splashing had been known to occur.

But this was all commonplace.

However, today a new jeopardy was percolating.

It all began with a lot of plotting and planning by Penny S, the master mind of the operation. The plan spread like wild fire first to her absent-minded followers via the electronic digital media, then throughout the entire school.

On a normal day, in an institution of this size, more than one grade could attend this feeding fray at any given time, but never the whole student body at once. On this particular day it appeared that everyone from Terracotta High School was in attendance, they just kept filing in. Slowly, but steadily.

They were like a hungry audience waiting for a show to begin or like the common people who attended the coliseum in ancient Rome to wait for the slaughter.

The main difference was that only a few of these students came to see blood. Most were simply there regardless, and Penny S took full advantage of it. She loved an audience.

In her bright orange jeans and orange striped shirt, Penny S strutted across the room as if she were the leader of inmates in a penitentiary. She wanted everyone to notice her. She was making an appearance.

The look on her face confirmed her intentions, her mind was made up. Today was going to be her first act of revenge on Penny D and it would come in the form of humiliation in front of the entire school.

Penny S and her minions were impatiently waiting at the

end of the line for Penny D to arrive. They knew she would eventually show up and when she did they had one unexpected surprise; Malcolm was with her. This did nothing to alter their plans.

Malcolm was in a very talkative mood that day and delighted with himself at the days / weeks earlier events. Moreover, he had an audience all to himself to share one of his latest ideas with. It concerned a prank, of course, and involved some bologna and a skunk.

Never one to be rude, Penny D listened for as long as she could and then pointed out a fatal flaw in his plan. This flaw would have resulted in Malcolm getting caught with a live skunk in school and even though it was a well-trained and de-scented pet borrowed from a pet store, it would also mean his expulsion.

Malcolm was blown away. He wondered why he hadn't seen it coming.

"Thanks, Penny D," said Malcolm. "It looks like I should bounce all of my ideas off of you while I still have them in the Beta testing stage."

"No, you don't need to do that," said Penny D.

"Yes, I think I should," said Malcolm. "You always see something in my plan that could have tripped me up. Unless you don't want me to?"

"Oh, no, that's okay," said Penny D. "I don't mind. Bring it on."

Penny D made a funny gesture with her fingers that may have made sense if she paid more attention to her fellow students who did that sort of thing all the time. It may have been something about the fingers or the position of her hands or that odd look on her face, but it didn't matter to Malcolm, he understood anyway. She was trying to look cool.

"That's what I like about you," said Malcolm. "You're not all girlie-girlie."

Penny D wasn't quite sure what that meant. She knew what girlie meant, that she was like a girl. She also knew that Malcolm knew she was a girl. She had no gender confusion issues.

She believed she did everything a girl should do; she cooked, she cleaned, she dissected dead frogs, she wrestled with a deadly python and she was even pretty good at spitting across her yard and hitting the fence. Her uncle taught her that one.

But what exactly did Malcolm mean when he used the girlie word twice? Could it mean she wasn't girl-like? She couldn't see why not, she knew how to speak her mind on any subject she knew about and she was beginning to understand boys. What else was there?

Malcolm was a treasure-trove of bizarreness for her to analyze. He was constantly offering up tid-bits of information about a pop culture she knew nothing about.

Only once had her mother told her about boys. She said, "Ah…boys are very different than us. And at the same time just like us girls. And that is why we like them. It's a welcome paradox, really." Even more oddly, Penny D understood exactly what her mother meant. Or so she thought.

Regardless of her mother's wisdom, she still didn't know what Malcolm meant so she just played along. She figured that in time it would all become clear. And at that point she would adopt the phrase as her own and use it daily.

Just a few steps ahead of them there was trouble brewing. Penny S was thinking over the traps that she had planned for Penny D that day. She made sure that she, Olivia and Britney entered the food line just ahead of Penny D because Marvin was put in charge of executing the first of many said traps and Penny S wanted to be close enough to take a picture with her MyPhone.

Marvin, was an average kid by every means. Maybe he was even less than that since he didn't have any friends in school at all. He was two years older than Penny S and had a very, very big crush on her. He had carried it with him since third grade. It was so much of a crush in fact that he would probably even rob a bank for her if she asked him to.

Anyway, Marvin was the kind of boy who knew how to

keep busy. Fully aware of his social ineptness he had a ton of time on his hands. So much time in fact that he had joined six school clubs. None of them were sports related and they appeared to have no common ground between them.

They included; the School Bus Washing Club, the Thesaurus Club, the Envelope Stuffing Club and the Body Building Club. The last of which, he never attended. Muscular teenagers made him nervous.

He also worked in the school cafeteria in the spare time he had during the lunch break. He had a nervous stomach most of the day and couldn't eat around people his age so this was time well spent, he thought. He ate very well at home though, he lived with his grandmother and she fed him just fine. Actually, grandma was a marvelous cook.

Marvin was good at following orders and so he got along well with the kitchen staff. So well in fact that he was recently promoted to chief food slinger at the hot food cart.

When Penny S found out about his newly appointed position, she used all of her feminine charms to suddenly "notice" him.

Her first attempt to "break the ice" with Marvin, happened quite accidentally. She was ducking out of her last class five minutes before the bell. Miss Novella was always so distracted, Penny S could literally walk out of class while Miss Novella was fixing one of her drooping stockings.

When Penny S realized that Marvin had caught her red handed wandering the halls, her survival instinct kicked in. All she had to say was, "hello, big guy," say it like she meant it, and Marvin was hooked.

He turned red from excitement, then white from fear, now if he could only stop breathing and turn blue, he would have resembled an American flag.

His face pigment issues aside, Marvin was a hall monitor and he knew he had a duty to report Penny S for this breach of school policy. But he didn't. He kept it to himself and Penny S remembered him for it.

It was not that she felt grateful for what Marvin did, or

didn't do for her, like report her to the Assistant Principal's office as he was supposed to. What she came away from the experience with was that she could take advantage of him if she needed to and get clean away with it.

A short time ago Penny S had approached Marvin with the first step of her plans to humiliate Penny D. She didn't quite put it that way of course, but Marvin was not stupid, he knew where her story was going.

At first he didn't want anything to do with it, but he eventually agreed. Penny S could be very convincing to a distracted mind if she chose to be.

You would think that her tall tale about Penny D who once kicked a small puppy down a flight of stairs would have swayed Marvin to break a few more school rules for her. But no, it didn't. It was the pathetic lie of verbal abuse that Penny S made up about Penny D that won him over.

She told Marvin that Penny D bragged incessantly how she verbally abused her poor, helpless, invalid grandmother that was the lie that did the trick. It apparently hit home with him. This lie he believed.

The food line was where it was all supposed to begin.

Penny S addressed her troops just loudly enough for everyone around her to hear. She and Britney cut the line just ahead of Penny D so they could lead the charge. Britney stood ready with her MyPhone on camera mode and Olivia was supposed to act as back up, but something shiny caught her eye and she wandered off.

It all began as an innocent and nonchalant conversation. But don't let that fool you, there were trigger words in her sentence, carefully placed there to cue a chain reaction of events.

"So, what season is it, Brit?" said Penny S.

"Fall, of course," said Britney. "What ditz wouldn't know that?"

"And what colors do we wear in the Fall?" said Penny S.

"Duh, like Fall colors, of course," said Britney.

"Like, black?" said Penny S.

"Like, no, never," said Britney. "Earth tones, like if you have any brains at all."

"Like what is so wrong with wearing black?" said Penny S.

"It shows all the dirt," said Britney.

"Dirt, or food?" said Penny S.

"For sure," said Britney.

So sure that their master plan was going to work, both Penny S and Britney telegraphed their expectation of what was about to happen next. They both quickly unfolded their napkins and held them up in front of their faces.

This was Marvin's cue. Both Penny S and Britney were about to get their daily dose of slop slapped down on their plates.

With the perfect precision and aim that Marvin had cultivated, he hit his marks in the center of Penny S and Britney's plates without even trying. Penny D was up next.

If you looked closely, you can see the anger built up inside of Marvin. With revenge in his eyes, he spooned up an extra heavy load of mashed potatoes and garlic on his spoon. He dipped it in gravy and just before he slung it in Penny D's general direction, Malcolm had something to say.

"Hey Dude, how is your grandma?" said Malcolm.

"Huh?" said Marvin, completely taken off guard.

Malcolm had used the same trigger word that Penny S had used to get Marvin involved in her crazy nut scheme in the first place. It was all that he had to hear and his well-focused attack was derailed like a supermarket shopping cart losing a wheel in the middle of the frozen food section.

"She used to be on my candy drive route until the school forbid me from selling anything to anyone in the community," said Malcolm. "She was always my best customer."

"That's so sweet," said Penny D. "It would be nice to meet her one day."

Marvin's face soured, there was something not right here. Penny D smiled at him and all the hatred he had for her disappeared. And then the questions came.

How could it be that if Penny D were such a horrid person,

why would Malcolm, who he knew from their stint in detention together, be her friend? It didn't add up.

But the die was cast and Marvin's automated response kicked in.

Britney lowered her napkin and cut a hole right through the conversation with a brilliant expletive, in hungry anticipation for what was coming.

"Ha!" said Britney. "Serves you right!"

Marvin's hand sprung into action. The large spoon of mashed potatoes and garlic dipped in gravy was moving up and towards Penny D. But as it is with any action brought on by anger, it was unbalanced.

The large spoon of mashed potatoes and garlic dipped in gravy got caught en route to Penny D's plate. Marvin's sleeve, although rolled up, had slipped down and got hooked on the edge of the metal food tray. The contents of the spoon flung in the wrong direction and hit a new target instead. It hit Britney.

"You moron!" said Britney. "How is that even possible? Look at me. Look at what you did."

Martin tried to wipe Britney's blouse with his latex glove.

"Whoa!" said Britney. "You did not just try to just touch me there, did you?"

There was an extreme look of fright on Marvin's face. He shook his head furiously. He was simply trying to help and wasn't thinking.

"No, no, no I didn't," said Marvin.

Penny S was almost as humiliated as Britney, not because anything had happened to her, or because she felt bad for her friend, but because her first plan was foiled. She took Britney by the arm and moved her off the line.

The students who had been watching the fiasco parted for them like Moses had parted the Red Sea, then led Penny S and Britney right to their waiting table. This did little to shut Britney up, and she continued to rant like a crazy cat woman.

Britney was never shy about speaking her mind. The entire cafeteria continued to hear about what a Doofus Marvin was and she even added that he should be on that animated TV series about the two stupid kids who make fun of everyone all the time.

"Right on, brother," said Malcolm to Marvin. "You did all humanity a great service."

"Sorry," said Penny D. "Don't take it personally. She's angry all the time."

It was too late. The damage was done. Marvin swore to himself that he would never talk to a girl ever again. They just didn't like him. They all thought he was a jerk and a complete waste. He was thinking that he should quit the volunteer kitchen staff right now. Throw down the latex gloves and leave in total shame.

"We've not been introduced," said Penny D. "You must be in a higher grade. I'm Penny D. I just started school here. I'm in Miss Novella's class. What is your name?"

Penny D held up what was left of the line to wait for an answer. Malcolm waited as well. He nodded to Marvin. This meant that it was okay to answer. Or, that she, Penny D, was okay in his book.

"Ah, Marvin," said Marvin. "I'm in the ah, ninth. Grade."

"It is nice to meet you Marvin," said Penny D, and she smiled at him.

As Penny D moved on Marvin realized that he just broken his oath to himself. Perhaps he could talk to girls after all, he thought. "They may even like me one day. When I'm rich and powerful and own my own company I may even marry one. We will live together in a great big mansion overlooking the water. Our dogs, Barney and Rasputin will play in the front yard together."

Yes, Marvin was stuck in a time loop. Until, Dim arrived.

"Hey stupid," said Dim. "Gimme foods."

Marvin was shocked back to reality by Dim, a co-grader. Dim was dim for sure and downright angry from the time he woke in the morning until he went to sleep that night. Dim being dim in every sense of the word, was the first and last born child of Stumpy and Dipsy, his parents. Just imagine if you can what they must be like.

Then, without any hesitation, Marvin gave Dim a double helping of 'foods,' as Dim often demanded, slapping it hard on his plate. Once done he moved on and did not think about how to make Marvin's life any more miserable than it was.

By the time Dim arrived at the cold drinks cart, Marvin was visiting his future self again at his mansion by the shore and playing with his dogs.

What happened next will need some careful explanation. To Penny D the following events were simple, since this was how she saw most of her life unfold. But to those around her, those who do not share her particular point of view, it was something that the school would buzz about for some time after.

You see, most attached their personal spin to what they saw and altered it. They either blew it way out of proportion or they tailored it to include themselves when they in fact had nothing to do with it at all. The common colloquial term for those people was the "Drama Queens." To them, everything was an event or a production. And nothing in life was simple.

There were also the Refusalists. No matter what they experienced, be it proven by science and logic, it could not have really happened or taken place. They still saw what they preferred to see even if it was never there, or if it even hurt them.

But thanks to hand-held digital technology there was an overwhelming evidence that the following scenario did take place in the cafeteria and Penny S regreted every last moment of it.

To Penny D, who didn't own a MyPhone and couldn't differentiate an App from an apple pie, the following is all that she remembered happening in the cafeteria on that fateful afternoon.

That is, she, Penny D, had just sat down with her tray of food. There was no mystery meat on her plate since she never ate anything that could not immediately be identified. She chose to go with the sure bet that those green things were vegetables and took a healthy helping of them. Then she chose to sit at the only empty table, the one by the cafeteria door. It was the table that most students avoided since there was a hall monitor standing just outside in the hall.

This made little difference to her and Malcolm, who was used to sitting by himself anyway. It was not that he was disliked by any of the students, they just didn't know when he was going to pop-a-gag causing something to blow up in their faces. So they played it safe and steered clear of him when he was eating.

No sooner had Penny and Malcolm sat down to eat, that Penny D dropped her fork. She pardoned herself from the table and dove underneath to fetch it.

The fork had landed square under her seat so she had to turn to face the wall behind the table and slip down under the table to reach it. As soon as she did, she realized that she was not alone. Harold was under the table with her.

"Hello Harold," said Penny D.

"What?" said Harold.

"I said, hello," said Penny D in a louder tone.

Even under the table the noise in the room was so distracting, that it was easier to hear someone on the other side of the room than the person staring right at you under the table.

"Oh, hello Penny D," said Harold.

"I was wondering why you hadn't shown up at lunch," said Penny D.

"I did," said Harold. "I just chose to remain incognito."

"I see," said Penny D. "No, actually I don't. Why not come up topside and join me and Malcolm? There is plenty of room at our table."

"No," said Harold. "I'm fine right here."

"Are you planning to go without lunch today?" said Penny D.

"There are worse things in Terracotta Junior High School, Penny Dreadful, than are dreamt of in your philosophy," said Harold.

"Good reference," said Penny D.

Suddenly another fork dropped down from above and landed next to Harold.

"Besides," said Harold. "I have forks to pick up."

"I see," said Penny D. "If you will not join us, then may I bring you the donut I took for dessert? It has chocolate on it."

"If it is still there when you return to your seat, sure, send it on down," said Harold.

What a peculiar thing to say, Penny D thought to herself. But then again almost everything Harold did was a bit odd in general.

"I didn't understand that as well, but you have a deal," said Penny D.

Penny D gave Harold a little wave and slowly climbed back up to her seat.

The noise in the room, as chaotic as it had been only a moment before, was near silent when she turned in her seat and sat upright.

The first thing she noticed was that her entire tray of food was also gone. She then noticed that Malcolm was gone too. There were fresh traces of food on the table in front of her where she was going to eat, but the whereabouts of her tray was a mystery. Finally, she noticed that most of the students sitting at most of the tables were all staring at her. Some were even standing and nervously holding their fingers to their lips.

Penny D knew that there was more here than met the eye; that something had happened, but she didn't know what. She quickly looked under the table to ask Harold what he knew. But when she did so, he was also gone.

"Rumble Fish Steak," Penny D kept thinking to herself. Her uncle simply must be cooking something up as awesome as Rumble Fish Steak for dinner tonight. Because after a strange day like this, she would need it by the time she got home.

Penny D got up from her seat. She walked around the table and left the cafeteria.

If Penny D were not Penny D but another student in the

cafeteria at that time on that day, a student who was up on the latest digital media social blitz from Terracotta Junior High School, she would have read the warning. It was simple and to the point. It stated that something that should-not-be-missed was going to happen in the cafeteria on this day. That was what she would have seen if she were not Penny D but another student.

So let us start again from the moment after Britney had gotten accidentally splashed with food by Marvin and she and Penny S were heading for their table to begin their next diabolical scheme.

As the plotting continued Penny D and Malcolm were just arriving at their table.

Dim was just joining Penny S at her table when Olivia appeared from nowhere. Penny S stopped her short.

"Olivia, go sit at their table," said Penny S, pointing to Penny D.

"Okay," said Olivia and picked up her food tray to leave.

"Be sure you sit in front of Penny D and distract her," said Britney.

"Distract her how?" said Olivia.

"It doesn't matter," said Penny S. "Just talk to her. She'll listen. She hasn't learned to ignore you yet. And remember to get her to stand up when I give you the signal. Drop your fork on the floor and ask her to get it for you."

"Okay," said Olivia. "What is the signal."

"Just go sit down there and keep an eye on me," said Penny S. "I'll make it real obvious so you can't miss it."

"Okey-dokey," said Olivia.

"Dim?" said Penny S. "Do you know what to do?"

"What am I stupid?" said Dim. "I go sit next to her and when she gets up to get the fork I slip the chocolate pudding under her butt. She sits in it and then everyone thinks she did it in her pants."

Then Dim began to laugh uncontrollably. It was uncomfortable even to watch it.

"Brit?" said Penny S.

"Camera ready," said Britney. "StoogeTube, here we come. We're going to make viewer status history with this one. It's going viral, baby!"

This was probably the worst plan for revenge that anyone could ever possibly conceive of. There were so many flaws in it that it resembled Miss Novella's sweater.

Uncle Calagari often recited to Penny D that any plan driven by revenge, must have a disastrous outcome and if Penny D were not under the table to witness the event, she would have been made proud of her uncle. That is not to say that she wasn't already.

Penny S was so bent on her lust for getting even with Penny D for what she herself had instigated, that she was desperate enough to ask Dim to be her ringer. She knew what Dim was like. She knew he was as angry at the world as she was. But what she didn't know was why he was so angry and she didn't care.

This already put her plan in jeopardy. Dim became a wild card, a loose cannon on the deck of a wooden ship in the middle of a raging storm at sea. Therefore, there was no way this could end well.

But Penny S didn't care. She pulled the trigger and lit the fuse. Olivia was given her marching orders.

Now here was where the plan fell apart even before it got started. Before Olivia reached the table where Penny D was sitting, Penny D dropped her own fork and excused herself to retrieve it. So when Olivia arrived at the table she stopped to wonder to herself if she had come to the wrong table. She knew it was only a few feet away from where she was sitting with Penny S, so it was inconceivable to her that she had gotten lost. So, all she did was stand there with a look of constipation on her face wondering how this all had come to pass.

Dim on the other hand was like a locomotive that left the rail road station and was already doing about one hundred miles an hour. There was no stopping him.

He walked over to where he once saw Penny D was sitting and plopped down his food tray with so much force that the food on the tray splattered all around. Under normal circumstances this would only have made a tiny splash, but since the kitchen help feared him so, his extra, extra helpings erupted on his tray like tiny volcanoes.

Little did he realize or care that Penny D was no longer sitting where he sat himself down. She was of course under the table at the time but she may just as well have been invisible since Dim was, well, dim.

Further, Dim didn't realize, or care, that Olivia had gotten tired of standing and holding her food tray and sat down at precisely when he did. So the food on Dim's tray, that was already piled high, splashed Olivia.

This didn't appear to bother her much, but when it happened, she mistakenly took it for the signal that Penny S had said she would be sending her.

"Oh," was all that Olivia could say and immediately threw her fork on the floor and looked for Penny D to ask her to retrieve it for her. Since Penny D was no longer there, Olivia decided to improvise.

"Excuse me Mr. Dim," said Olivia. "When Penny D returns, will you tell her that I dropped my fork and ask her if she will pick it up for me?"

At that very same time Malcolm who was sitting across from Dim was dumfounded by the careless act that Dim had just created. He, too, had gotten some of Dim's food on his shirt and when he stood up in disgust, he noticed that Olivia was picking out the food from her hair.

"You stupid clod," said Malcolm.

Dim may have been dim, but he became fully aware of everyone around him when he was being criticized. It was as if his battery power had suddenly been fully charged. He stood up and was a whole head taller than Malcolm.

Malcolm didn't back down. He pointed at Olivia and made his case.

"Look what you did," said Malcolm, pointing at Olivia. "Now apologize."

A case had been made thousands of years ago that love

made one strong; that the force of love could make one do amazing things. Or, in this case, make one say some very stupid things that may just get one very, very hurt.

"It is a bad idea that you talked to me that way," said Dim. "Now I have to hit you."

With one mighty swipe from one of his arms, Dim cleared the table of all the food trays as if this were his way of punctuating his statement.

"Bulk, crush!" said Malcolm, in a mock superhero voice. "I ain't running. Come get some."

Let's face it, to be a "pranksta" you have to be tough. Your path is pitted with all sorts of dangers. Not Dim tough, but tough enough to stand your ground.

Malcolm stood there and put up his fists, he was determined to prevent Dim from hitting him in the face. If he was lucky one of the hall monitors would arrive just in time with the assistant principal and prevent him from getting killed.

Dim went right in for the kill. He may have been dim, but he was also very fast and strong. Malcolm put up both of his fists to block the oncoming mallet Dim called his fist and intercepted the punch. However, the punch was so powerful that it sent Malcolm's own hands right into his face.

The entire cafeteria of students rose to their feet. Not so much cheering for anyone in particular but praying that Malcolm didn't get hurt too badly. Dim may have been the favorite to win this fight but he was not the favorite in any other way.

As Penny S stood up on her feet and cheered Dim on, a mysterious hand appeared behind her. It held a plate of chocolate pudding and slipped it onto her seat right below her bright orange pants.

Dim went into transformer mode and began to cascade his punches, one after the other at Malcolm.

He managed to fend off most of them, but a few made contact. The last of the punches sent Malcolm right off his feet and into a trash barrel.

Dim was just about to go in for another round of what he

called, "punch-the-dope," when a mysterious foot slid in front of Dim and tripped him as he advanced. He landed right in the arms of the assistant principal who had stepped right in front of him.

It could have been an odd coincidence that Mr. Goldenthorp was so good at breaking up fights, but the fact that his arms were long enough to keep two high school students separate from one another no matter their reach, surely worked in his favor.

With one great hand he took Malcolm by the collar and looked him right in the eye.

"Waxenburg, we meet again," said Mr. Goldenthorp. "It looks like the three of us are going to take a little visit to the principal's office."

"Hold on, Mr. Goldenthorp, sir," said Athena. I recorded the whole incident on MyPhone. Malcolm is innocent and I can prove it."

"Give me that," said Mr. Goldenthorp, as he let go of Malcolm and confiscated the MyPhone.

"Don't bother to erase the file, I already uploaded it to my social page," said Athena.

Malcolm gave Athena a thumbs up and a friendly nod. He was then ushered out of the room along with Dim by Mr. Goldenthorp. Athena chased after them.

The excitement was all over in a flash. There was a crowd all around Penny S since she had the best spot for viewing the fight, she was right in front. She quickly retreated, pushing her way back to her table through the thick body of students.

"Get away from me, you morons," said Penny S.

Then Penny S sat back down directly onto the plate of chocolate pudding and it made a very distinct squishing sound when she did. Not anyone, least of all Penny S knew what had happened, but they all knew where to look. They had all read the posting.

Penny S slowly got up and glanced over her shoulder to see the thick brown stain on the back of her pants as did everyone else in the room. It may have been just as funny to see but no one was laughing.

"If anyone at all takes a picture of this, so help me, I will hunt you down," warned Penny S.

Most of the students in the room diverted their eyes from Penny S who slowly backed out of the cafeteria.

The noise in the room, as chaotic as it had been only minutes before, was near dead silent when Penny D slowly climbed out from under the table.

Low and behold, her entire tray of food was gone. Malcolm was gone. There were fresh traces of food on the table where she was going to eat and the students sitting at most of the tables were all looking at her.

Penny D knew that there was more here than met the eye; that something had happened, but she didn't know what. She quickly looked under the table to ask Harold if he knew something more, but when she did, he was gone as well.

"Rumble Fish Steak," Penny D kept thinking to herself. Her uncle simply must be cooking something up as awesome as Rumble Fish Steak for dinner tonight. Because after a strange day like this, she would need it.

Penny D got up from her seat. She walked around the table and left the cafeteria.

Chapter 12
Let's Get This Party Started

Just a short while ago Penny D didn't have any human friends at all. But as of today she had one more than she expected.

Walking home from school was no longer a lonely activity. She knew for sure that there was someone not far behind her. She may not have known who it was or if he, in fact, wanted to be her friend, but she knew he was there. It was kind of comforting.

She trusted that he was there for a very specific reason. Perhaps it was just curiosity. She was now well aware of the fact that she was just more than a little bit different from everyone she met. But what was mostly on her mind was whether he, that unknown person around her age from her school would in fact like to be her friend. He must want to. Why else follow her then?

Penny D tried to image what that would be like and she drew a blank. Maybe she was just too tired of trying. This whole school thing was so new as was the whole being out in-the-daylight-thing.

She missed her long walks at night or at dusk. She was now

on a regimen that got her to bed hours earlier than what she was used to. Occasionally she started to think about the summer and how she would be able to go to bed much later again and sleep later as well.

But for now, she was finding the change soothing. The sunlight on her whitish skin also felt good. So new to her. And nice.

Without even turning around Penny D suddenly knew who it was that was behind her.

"Harold," said Penny D, calling out. "Come over here."

An average person may have looked behind Penny D and seen nothing at all but she was trained in the art of tracking, American Indian style. This was just one of the many survival techniques her Uncle Calagari covered in their daily lessons.

When one was well schooled in this very unique practice, he also became attuned to the opposite. He became fully aware of when he was being followed. It could have been by an unusual scent in the air, a change in the way the animals flew or in their singing, or it could be the overwhelming quiet. Something was amiss (or perhaps it was inherent, her mother was a great tracker and we know how that turned out).

Penny D turns to face her stalker.

"I'll wait," said Penny D.

She heard a tree branch snap and Harold fell out of a tree not more than thirty paces behind her. Penny D winced from the pain that Harold must have felt at that very moment. It could not have been pleasant.

"We've been through this before," said Penny D, in a very sweet way. "I don't like being followed and I don't want to see any more worms. I dig them and all that, Harold, but you need a better reason for hiding in a tree and waiting for me to pass."

Harold may have looked a little more disheveled than usual. There was no telling how long he had been up in that tree. He got up and plucked the leaves from his hair and checked for broken bones. None found, he tried to bring up the nerve to address Penny D on an urgent issue.

"Come on, spit it out," said Penny D. "You owe me at least that."

"Malcolm said you invited him to your awesome big birthday bash and sleep over party," said Harold.

Suddenly Harold felt a sigh of relief and the pent up feeling of holding all that in was completely gone. He was not a person who spoke openly to anyone. And that was a very long sentence with lots of information in it. He opened the top button on his collared shirt. If it were possible for steam to rise out from underneath his clothing it would have.

"I, he did?" said Penny D. "He really said all that?"

For just a moment it was Penny D's turn to be put on the spot. Sure, she felt flattered that for the first time she was in this school she was the subject of positive gossip. There were some immediate butterflies doing their thing in her stomach and she was not so sure why.

Maybe this was a turning point in her new school career, she thought. She liked it and wondered how she could keep this going.

"Wow," said Penny D. "I mean, maybe you would like to come, too?"

Harold looked as if he had just swallowed an insect. Or was hit with a hammer, or maybe it was as simple as being told that his pants were on fire. Yes, he had that kind of look on his face.

"You're inviting me?" said Harold, as he began to hyperventilate. "I've never been invited to a birthday slash sleep over party before."

Harold turned on his heels and walked away very, very fast.

"Where are you going?" asked Penny D.

"I have to prepare," shouted Harold over his shoulder.

"But it's not till next week."

"That soon?" said Harold and he began to walk a little faster.

Harold did that all the way home for the very first time in his entire life without anyone chasing him.

Penny D found herself all alone on that street corner wondering if all boys were as strange as Malcolm and Harold. And if so, was it a mistake making their friendship in the first place, let alone inviting them to her house?

***

Penny D threw herself across her bed and stared up at the ceiling. She appeared down right elated. As if taking her lead Bronte, Rebecca and Hawthorne did the same. Perhaps it was a strange thing for a tarantula, a python and a rat to do, but Penny D's bed was so comfortable you would do the same, given half the chance. It moved a little just like the comfy couch in the middle of her living room and propped up their heads making them all that much more comfortable.

"Something is very different about you tonight, dear'" said Rebecca. "But I can't quite put my tail on it."

"I feel different," said Penny D.

"There is a glow all around you," said Bronte.

Hawthorne hopped up on top of Penny D's belly for a closer look. He sniffed her face.

"I don't sense anything different," said Hawthorne.

Being the only other woman in the group, Rebecca knew from the get go what it was.

"It's a boy isn't it?" asked Rebecca.

"No," said Penny D. "Well, yeah. Two in fact."

All four of them sat up on the bed at the same time. It was an easy feat since the bed assisted them. Hawthorne scooted off of Penny D to the side to avoid being tossed by the sudden reposition.

"Young lady, you have some explaining to do," said Bronte in his most fatherly tone.

"I actually have two boys who want to come to my birthday party," said Penny D. "I can't believe it. Somebody pinch me."

Excited all, they leapt to their feet (belly in Becka's case). As best they could, baring the lack of arms or human ones at least, Penny D's pets took turns congratulating her. Bronte sprang back up and off of Penny D's bed and belly bumped her. Hawthorne hopped up on her shoulder then onto her head and mussed up her hair. Rebecca coiled around her and gave her a great big hug.

"Me loves some parties," said Bronte.

Penny D's pets began to sing together. "Par-ty, par-ty, par-ty!"

"Guys?" said Penny D. "There is one little problem. I need to ask a little favor from all of you. You see..."

Penny D knew what she was about to ask of her friends was a lot. But she also knew that her friends were true friends. And to a true friend you could ask anything. They may not agree or even do what you ask, but they would never hold it against you.

"My new friends might be afraid of you," said Penny D. "Actually, I know they will be down right scared to death of you. Except maybe for Harold. He doesn't appear to display much common sense. Anyway, what I need for you to all to do, in order to help make this party, my very first party ever, with my new friends from school…is well…"

"Spit it out already, darling, I'm getting acid indigestion just listening to you," said Rebecca.

"Could you all stay out of sight?" said Penny D. "Just for this one night? Until they all go home the next day since it's a sleep over party?"

Penny D bit her lip. She knew she had just crashed their dreams.

"No worries there, darling," said Rebecca. "It would be our pleasure to help you to prepare for the party and then stay out of sight until all of those delicious little darlings go home. Isn't that right, gents?"

If you have never heard a rat and a tarantula grumble under their breath before then you may never want to. It was terrible.

"Gentlemen!" demanded Rebecca.

"No worries, baby," said Bronte. "Like always, we got your

back."

"Count me in too," said Hawthorne.

"You guys," said Penny D, as tears built up in her eyes.

What followed was a group hug of the strangest sort.

Chapter 13
The Mystery That is Olivia and Other Children Her Age

Obviously, Penny D had ventured out of her home more than just once in her thirteen years, although she preferred to do so in the evenings when it was dark and the creatures of the night flew and lurked about. Like them, she was altogether hardly even noticed, and she was fine with that.

She had never felt like the target of any ridicule or malice. Her nose was almost always buried in a book to and from her destination, be it the grocery store, the library or the junk yard (these were her most frequented places to visit).

The grocery store was a curious place for her. She often thought to herself about how everyone who went there seemed to be under the impression that it would run out of food at any second. She always expected the store manager to make some kind of announcement as soon as she arrived saying that the all the food was now gone so everyone should go home.

What prompted this thinking was how everyone shopping there was in so much of a hurry. They were in a hurry to load up their carts, a hurry to pay for their food and a hurry to get out of that store as if they were being chased by someone who didn't get enough of what they wanted and were going to ask for some of theirs.

To Penny D this was nothing more than a place that her parents sent her, to purchase some of the raw goods that would allow them to bake, broil, or barbecue. Absolutely nothing more.

So, what was all this rush-around and hurry thing all about? She believed that this mystery would resolve itself at some point so she would simply file it away for now and deal with it later on.

The library was not much different from the grocery store in the same respect that she was hardly noticed by the other people who were there, and in the fact that everyone, barring the elderly, were in a hurry again.

Mothers with children and the students who used this free facility were in a hurry to drop off the books that they had borrowed a week ago, a hurry to find a new book, a hurry to pick up the one that they left a request for and, most of all, in a hurry to check said book out as quick as possible.

Penny D immediately thought that they must be on their way to the grocery store to do their shopping, before they ran out of food.

The elderly were a different breed. They were in no hurry at all and actually looked like they enjoyed reading like she did. Some of them even noticed her. The elderly men nodded their heads to her and the elderly women told her she had lovely hair, and that she needed to get out in the sun more.

It was only after a few years of watching the people of Terracotta race to be the first ones to do everything that Penny D began to conclude that the people who lived here were not living in the fear she suspected; a fear that the general grocery store would run out of food and the public library would run out of books.

The newest place on her list of most rushed to places in Terracotta was the gym. This place fascinated Penny D because she couldn't understand it at all. The machines in the gym were not going anywhere so there was nothing for it, the gym, to run out of. Yet the people of Terracotta rushed in and out of there anyway.

It was a fun place to visit, none the less. Not really visit, since Penny D didn't go inside, but she would cup her hands around her eyes as she looked in through the outside glass window. There she would watch as the same good town folk rushed from one exercise machine to another to work out.

If one machine were busy, the one that one good town's folk wanted to use, they would wait impatiently nearby to use it. They would tap their feet, run their fingers through their sweaty hair, talk to themselves, play with their towels and drink from the bottle of water they kept with them at all times.

And what was up with that bottle anyway? Penny D wondered if the bottle they carried did in fact contain water and not some special elixir to keep them running for hours. Could something that potent actually exist, she wondered, that would allow them, the nice people of Terracotta, to run to the library and then to the grocery store after the gym? Then she wondered, that if it did exist, would she want some?

All conjecture aside, there was one thing that Penny D did know for sure: it was that the daytime hours were just too darn busy to be enjoyed. She knew that when she arrived at the grocery store, what she had been sent there to buy would always be there and when she paid a visit to the library, the book she was looking for was always there as well.

What was wrong with these people, she thought? What horror were they expecting? Even if the book at the library they wanted was not there, and it had been taken out by someone else, couldn't they find another book to read among the half million other books?

Penny D was an avid reader and so she further concluded that the nice people of Terracotta were uber-avid readers and must consume books like she could devour a slice of Uncle Calagari's exploding pie. And, that they were remarkably strong; they must eat a lot of red meat, since that was the busiest aisle at the grocery store and clearly exercised for hours on end at the gym since it was so busy.

She was actually wrong on both accounts, and discovered this on her own in uncommon hours.

There was also one last place that Penny D frequented, the junk yard. The owner and proprietor was Professor Linkage. He was the last in a long line of junk yard owners before him. His father performed the same service for a living (buying and selling old parts of tools, machines and such) and his father before him as well. His family lineage and their association wth this line of work may have gone further back than that but there was no way of knowing.

Penny D was usually sent there by her father to find a precision made gear, have him mill a specially designed mechanical part or to fetch a Rasputin-slider, whatever that might be.

When she arrived, Penny would always meet Professor Linkage and he was never in a hurry. He always welcomed the girl to sit down and listen to his stories of the wonderous machines of today and what he dreamed to invent tomorrow.

There was one story in particular that he liked more than any other because he told it to her once a month. It concerned the proper method of manufacturing a light bulb and how it had changed over the decades. He swore that light bulb manufacturing is different today and that they were not created to last, but to burn out after delivering a very select number of hours of light. This way, he explained, the consumer would have to by a new light bulb once a year or so.

He cited a firehouse in Livermore California, where a light bulb was still burning and had been for over one hundred years. "Go look it up," he would say, not just after this one story in particular, but after every story he told her.

He was like an encyclopedia. His stories were amazing and when Penny D checked on them in the library, she found out that they were indeed accurate. He knew about anything mechanical and chemical in precise detail, and he was good at explaining them in terms anyone could understand.

Out of sheer curiosity, Penny D once asked him about how a laptop computer worked. She had seen one in the window of an electronics store.

Professor Linkage made an unusual face at her, gave her the intermittent mechanical part that Natty had sent her there for and told her it was time for his nap.

She knew she hadn't done anything wrong and was not being punished for asking, but she also learned that Professor Linkage preferred the old technology to the new. She also learned that she should never ask him such a question ever again. And she didn't.

Penny D found it so much easier to observe the more interesting things in her town after sunset. There were far less people out and far less traffic on the streets as well. The people who were out were moving at a much slower rate, so she didn't feel as if she were in a race of some sort.

Sometimes she would cross through the park, since it was well lit and she believed it to be safe. She saw all sorts of people doing all sorts of things there. None of them involved her so she went unnoticed as she stopped to watch them.

There were young couples sitting on benches staring up at the stars who looked as if they were in love, bats chasing moths because they tasted so delectable, chipmunks doing, well, she had no idea what chipmunks do. But they looked so busy all the time so it must have been something very important.

She tried to talk with them, but they either didn't have the time to discuss their agenda with her or they couldn't understand her.

"Hello Mr. Chipmunk, my name is Penny, what's yours?" said Penny D.

She imagined that if the chipmunk had bothered to answer her it would have said something like, "Are you nuts? Can't you see I'm busy?"

Then she laughed to herself since she found the nut and chipmunk reference so amusing.

This caught the attention of the young couple sitting on

the bench together. They wondered what was wrong with the girl who was talking to the chipmunks and laughing to herself. Or perhaps, they may have thought, even worse yet, talking and laughing at no one at all since the chipmunks were nowhere to be seen from where they were sitting.

Sometimes Penny D watched an old timer who played chess all by himself under a park lamp. He was the most interesting to her. She wondered if she could beat him at the game.

It was at this time that she detected that a strange phenomenon occurred when her attention was fixed on what she enjoyed most: it was as if nothing in the world mattered or even existed. Time would stand still and she felt at home. She thought she would study this phenomenon one day and unlock its mystery. But until then, being lost in her daydreams was fun and she did it often. She included it into her house chores to make that time pass more quickly.

I guess the point is, that Penny D was in a different place right now. She was actually interacting in the world she used to watch from afar. She was interacting with other children her age and found them undisciplined, rude, selfish and always hungry.

She believed they were very lucky to live in an area that was pleasant and in an economy that was stable, regardless of what naysayers wanted her to believe. And she didn't believe that the world was coming to an end any time soon.

She didn't know what other children were taught by their parents, teachers, their friends and the social media that was so strongly influential in their lives. But she assumed, most erroneously, that they were taught to be good, patient, hard-working, well focused and grateful people as she was.

So to her the whole school experience was an eye opener. Just about everything that she was taught to be, to feel, to think was frowned upon. Individuality was something you feel, inside you, and not something you purchased in a store.

Once Penny D wandered past an electronics store and a television was on in the window. She had told herself it was a silly gadget and never paid it much attention.

While at her cousin's house one day, they, her cousins, aunts and uncles were all of course glued to the living room couch, watching everything that came on that machine in reverent silence. Even the commercials!

Heaven forbid if Penny D opened up her mouth to ask a question. She was always taught to ask questions if there was anything she didn't understand, so she did. Her cousins just ignored her or shushed her. Their mother, her aunt, may even gently scold her on an issue of manners. The mysteries of television went unexplained to her. It was a good thing she brought a book with her everywhere she went.

Anyway, at this particular time while standing in front of the electronics store Penny D suddenly felt that she had been too judgmental on the subject of watching television. Since she suddenly came upon this one operating in a store window, the sound completely audible from outside, she thought that she should stop and give it a fair shake. So for the next twenty minutes or so Penny D stood there watching the big flat screen.

There was an attractive glow around it from behind the glass in the window and since it was dark outside, she did feel herself drawn into its open arms.

However, that was where the attraction ended.

The first image she saw was of a demonstration of some sort; people were screaming at a marching crowd and in one case throwing things at them. She didn't know why, and it wasn't explained. The feeble anchor person attempted to explain what was going on but failed miserably.

A man who worked within the store, noticed her watching the television outside and changed the channel. He did it with a smile and it was obvious that he wanted to put something on that he felt she would enjoy more than the news.

The show that he chose for her to watch was perhaps the strangest thing Penny D had ever seen. She could tell that it was animated since it resembled two very crudely drawn boys, badly colored in and stranger still, they hardly moved.

She could also tell that they were supposed to look about her age and had speaking impediments. So she gave them her very best attention so that she would not miss the higher meaning to this telecast. In short, she gave them her respect.

What she soon found out was that they were discussing girls, perhaps her age, maybe older and not in a very flattering way. They made fun of a particular girl that they apparently knew. They ridiculed her hair, her clothes, her weight issues and the choice of celebrities she idolized. Just about everything was up for scrutiny, even her undeveloped female figure.

"What is this?" said Penny D out loud.

At that exact moment the man who had changed the channel for her only moments ago stepped out of the store to smoke a cigarette. He was on his break. He couldn't help but hear her question.

"It's 'The Jerky and Doofus Show,' said the man. "They are so funny."

"You think this is funny?" asked Penny D, who was not laughing.

"I mean, if you like that kind of stuff," said the man. "Yes."

"Let me see," said Penny D. "You are asking me if I like the idea of watching two boys disrespect other people their age and laugh at it? Hmmm, that is a hard question to answer. May I ask you a question, sir?"

"Sure," the man answered cautiously.

"Are you married, do you have a daughter?" said Penny D.

"I am married, yes," he answered. "No kids, but I have a younger sister."

"I see," said Penny D. "How would you feel if these two boys were making fun of your little sister? What would you say then?"

The man laughed out loud. Not at Penny D, but in a playful way, as if she were the one who didn't understand.

"Young lady," said the man, "these are only cartoons. They ain't real."

There was no sense in taking that conversation any further. So Penny D simply went home. She did however take with her a part of the conversation to think about. The keyword there was real.

Someone created that TV show and they were real, so how could the show be any less real? It wasn't imaginary. She, Penny D, had seen it and found it on a fundamental level very insulting.

Where does real live, she thought to herself as she walked down the street to school this morning? Was it on that TV, or in the classroom, here on the street or in her own home? Perhaps it was all in her head.

She knew she needed to give this more thought. She wondered if she were part of a different reality all together and was somehow born here by accident. She didn't see eye to eye with most of the adults she ever met and none of the children in her class. Except for Malcolm. He was noticeably different.

Penny D needed a sign. Something to tell her which way to go.

Then, Olivia Smothers appeared.

Penny D studied her for a moment and then easily caught up to her, Olivia was not a fast walker. She was not even a slow walker. Olivia walked at a speed that was somewhere in between and then for no reason she would stop and appear to contemplate something. Anyone could guess what that was about, because it was never obvious.

Actually, it didn't take much to distract her. A fallen leaf, a crack in the sidewalk or a whiff of burnt wood in the air from a fireplace or a barbecue caused Olivia to stop and wonder. Sometimes, for way too long. It was a small miracle she made it to school at all.

Penny D started to daydream on her own and wondered how early Olivia would have to leave her house in order to get to school on time.

The "Olivia Effect," as Harold coined the phrase, actually did have an effect on those around her. It was a very calming effect like that of a food coma.

Penny D shook her head and brought herself back to the present. She summoned a burst of ambition, and prepared an opening line in her head. She had some business with Olivia and she was going to attend to it right now.

Before she could spit it out, a new thought crossed her mind; how long did she think it would take for Olivia to realize that she had someone walking alongside her?

"Stop that, Penny," said Penny D to herself. "It is just the Olivia Effect again. Fight it. Stay in the now."

Her overwhelming determination to face Olivia with what she knew she had to ask her told her that her experiment was over. She would start up a conversation and do it now. She wished herself good luck first.

"Good morning, Olivia," said Penny D.

There was no response. For a fleeting moment the "Olivia Effect" kicked in again and Penny D found it interesting to see how long Olivia could keep her eyes open without blinking. Then she remembered that the school was just down the street and so she was running out of time. She had to speed things up so it was now or never.

"I said, good morning," said Penny D.

"I heard you the first time," said Olivia. "I was trying to decide if it was or not."

"Oh," said Penny D. "Right. You may not be aware of this, since we don't talk very much and that is not because I don't like you or anything. In fact, I have no opinion about you at all. But I am turning thirteen next week and I am going to celebrate it with a party at my house. Do you think you would you like to come? To my birthday party that is. We'll be doing, you know, fun things." said Penny D biting her lip.

She knew she had said way too much and probably lost Olivia after good morning.

"Fine," said Olivia. "When?"

"Here, I have an invitation for you," said Penny D.

This was a lot easier than Penny D had expected it to be. She now had three school friends coming to her birthday party, and she knew that at least two of them were actually people who wanted to be her friends.

Penny D took out an invitation and held it out to her. The card was hand made on parchment paper, the delicate writing on it clearly told the where and when of the occasion.

Life suddenly went into slow motion. Before Olivia was able to grab the invitation from Penny D, a third hand entered the scene and snatched that invitation right out of her own.

"Let me see that," said Penny S.

It was as if that angry little girl knew exactly when to come out of nowhere with no intention other than to ruin Penny D's morning. She was like a nightmare that just kept returning

"You're having a birthday party?" said Penny S. "Shut up!"

Britney took the invitation away from Penny S and stared at it like she couldn't believe her eyes. Her jaw dropped and her eyes bugged out. You would think that she was told some amazing news, like there was a new sport called Moon-Olympics, or even something stranger. And like just about every situation in her life, Britney reacted to it with anger.

"How come she gets to turn thirteen before me?" said Britney.

As furious as Britney was by what she had just found out, Penny S was delighted.

"I simply cannot miss this," said Penny S.

"No, it's by invitation only," said Penny D.

"You mean, I'm not invited?" said Penny S.

"If Penny S is not invited than I'm not going either," said Britney.

"And if I'm not going, then Olivia isn't going," said Penny S.

It was as if an alarm clock then rang in Olivia's head. Not unlike the "Squidy-Diby-Debbie" alarm clock by her bed. When it rang it was supposed to wake her up in time for school. But instead all it ever did was wake up everyone in the house. Olivia usually slept on. Her pet Puppy, a full grown beagle, would then rush into her room and pounce on her until she got up.

But unlike a real alarm, this one in her head rang and

something clicked. It was as if there was someone at the door actually asking her to come out and play. She felt wanted, probably for the first time in a very long time

"Who, what?" said Olivia. "I'm not? Are you sure? But, I have an invitation?"

Olivia looked around for the invitation. It was no longer in her hand. Britney was still holding it. So Olivia snatched it back from her and put it down her shirt.

Penny S pursed her lips to one side of her face. She was not impressed.

"Oh believe me, I'm sure," said Penny S to Olivia. "You are not going!"

"Oh dog straddle!" said Olivia. "I was so looking forward to it."

"It's all three of us, or none of us," said Penny S. "Deal or no deal?"

Penny D clearly remembered her promise to Malcolm. Making a promise to a friend was something she took very seriously. He had requested that Olivia be invited and she had agreed. To stay true to her word, Penny D felt that she had to make every possible attempt to see that Olivia came to her party. Her mouth went dry but she answered anyway.

"All right," said Penny D. "You may all come."

"I'll check my social schedule and see if I can make it," said Penny S. "My people will get back to your people if I am available."

With a new found confidence from her latest victory over Penny D, Penny S stepped off the curb and right onto Malcolm's skateboard as he hopped off it right in front of her.

Penny S sailed off down the street on the skateboard, shrieking as she did. Britney freaked out and ran after her.

"Hello ladies," said Malcolm, probably unaware of what he had just done.

Malcolm smiled but this did little to hide the bona fide shiner around his left eye. One side of his face looked a little redder than the other as well.

"Oh, don't tell me, did one of your pranks blow up in your

face again?" said Penny D.

"You could say that, but it was worth it," said Malcolm.

He also wore long sleeves that morning to hide the bruises on his arms, yet another souvenir from the beating he took from Dim. Being the master magician he was, Malcolm quickly rubbed his hands together, excitedly to divert Penny D's attention.

"Are you guys ready for the class project report?"

"Like totally," said Penny D, her seventh grade vernacular kicked back in. "I've been rehearsing all night."

"Wait," said Olivia, with a look on her face as if her alarm clock must have gone off again. "Is that due today?"

Chapter 14
Messes in the Afternoon

It was a mixed bag of tricks that afternoon in Miss Novella's seventh grade class. She had each and every student present to the class the culmination of their first school projects of the year. One by one the students took the stage, really the front of the classroom, and stuttered, stammered, mispronounced and speed delivered their projects.

They each took their best shot at telling the class a little about themselves, or way too much about their home life. Take your pick.

All the students had that very same look on their faces like they didn't want to go first. Except for Malcolm. He truly enjoyed giving speeches and getting this much attention.

For most of his school years all the teachers he ever had done their best to squelch his enthusiasm, his ingenuity, his inventiveness, his creativity. But not now. Not here. Not anymore. This would be his moment.

Miss Novella found a seat in the back of the room. She squeezed her oversized body into the tiny seat behind a desk made for a twelve year old. She complained every second of the way but this did little to slow her down. She insisted she had to make this sacrifice in order for her to remain completely objective and view the class projects as they would.

Perhaps without even knowing it, Miss Novella took on the persona of an obnoxious twelve year old. Or regressed to the mental state of a twelve year old as the projects were being presented, take your pick.

In doing so, she made sure to comment during the presentations she didn't like, whispered to other students around her and once she even threw a stick of gum at a nervous student who mispronounced her name.

The childish antics of a mature woman aside, Malcolm got his turn in the spotlight. He was holding up an ordinary bottle of lemon juice in one hand and a plastic container like Flubberwear, in the other.

"Remember to pour the lemon juice in very slowly, not to upset the baking soda," said Malcolm. "Because if you do, the whole thing could blow up in your face and completely ruin your chances of creating the sweetest stink bomb ever."

Malcolm poured the lemon juice into the container and it immediately began to froth over the sides, much faster than he expected. He directed the concoction over the waste pail, but a bigger mess was forthcoming and he knew it. He knew he put too much of one ingredient or the other into the mixture because the pail was suddenly filling up with the foaming material as well.

"That never happened before," said Malcolm. "Perhaps my secret ingredient over powered the others. Anthony, the door."

Anthony was already there holding the door open, as if he knew what was coming. Malcolm picked up the pail and rushed out of the classroom and into the hall.

Miss Novella was clearly unimpressed. She simply cleared her throat and said, "Next."

It was Britney's turn.

It will puzzle the mind if you really stop to think about it and wonder how much time, if any, she spent coming up with this one. She was holding up a hand mirror and looking at herself. Her hair was particularly well styled this day, we give her that. But her whole project appeared to be based upon how beautiful she was to herself.

"You can wear it like this," said Britney. "Or like this."

Britney pushed her hair across her forehead from one side to the other, as if that made any difference in her appearance.

"Either way it works for me," said Britney. "When you have looks like mine, that is. Any questions? Good. There shouldn't be."

One would imagine a shallow presentation like this would unnerve and quite possibly aggravate a real teacher, but as we all well know Miss Novella was something quite different.

"That was very insightful, Britney," was all Miss Novella could say.

Olivia took the floor, or the front of the room as it were. Anthony was standing right next to her, his eyes wide open.

Olivia appeared calm and relaxed. She was doe-eyed, without blinking, nothing new there.

Anthony, on the other hand was struggling to keep his eyes open. Sweat beaded up on his forehead and tears built up in his eyes. Suddenly, he blinked.

The class moaned, Anthony hung his head in shame. He had lost what appeared to have been a contest. Olivia on the other hand continued to stare into space, neither rejoicing in her victory or acknowledging her opponent's honest attempt to dethrone her.

Calmly and without apology Olivia addressed the class.

"As you can see, I could do this all day if I wanted to," said Olivia. "And my eyes never tear up. I win."

Miss Novella was without comment.

A burst of energy hit the classroom. Harold, who we have all come to know as a nerd, a loser, a loner, an anomaly suddenly became much more than just the kid with the strangely shaped head. He was holding up a video game controller and wearing a cap with the logo, "Super X Boy" on it.

With eloquence and precision Harold held the attention

of the entire class as no previous student had done before him.

"Be sure to hold the G button down when executing the double helix move against a fire Wig-Wanna-Bee," said Harold. "Remember, only in, Ninja-Dog Transformer, Part IV: The Paradigm Rulers of Dyslexia, do you have the instant inter-dimensional toaster option. Is everyone getting this?"

The students in the room struggled to keep up with him. They took and compared notes with one another. Some scratched their heads in confusion. In short, they were losing the battle.

Although the students were genuinely interested in what Harold had brought to class, he was rapidly losing Miss Novella's attention. She listens without any interest, her eyes slowly slipping shut.

"Next," said Miss Novella, and yawned loudly.

Penny Social knew full well that it was her turn to stand and proceed to the front of the class. But did she do so? No, she waited for Miss Novella to ask her to. Why? So that she could make an entrance, of course.

She was a manipulator, plain and simple. And she had Miss Novella wrapped around her little finger. Unlike some of her previous classmates, she had completely understood the assignment, and chosen not to do it. Not that this mattered really, it would appear almost everyone in the class knew precisely what he could get away with. Or couldn't.

Whilst some of the students had spent a fair amount of time thinking about and preparing their projects for this day, Penny S had done nothing of the sort. She had put it entirely out of her head secure in the knowledge that she would wing it at the last second and still manage to get an "A" on the assignment. If there was one thing that could be said for her, it would have to be that she was confident when it came to dealing with Miss Novella.

With calculated dramatics, Penny S improvised on the spot. She held up her MyPhone, as if that alone should amaze those watching her. As if there was no one else in the room but her, Penny S opened an app of pictures she took last summer and narrated them to herself as she viewed them. Once in the while, when she felt generous she even answered a question from Miss Novella. That was, if she could hear her over her own annoying voice.

"And here is another picture of me with Julius Kilowatt backstage after his concert," said Penny S. "And one of me and Julius Kilowatt laughing because I told him the funniest joke ever. I made him laugh so hard, he could hardly breathe."

"What was the joke?" asked Paulie, quite timidly.

"You wouldn't get it," said Penny S. "And here is a picture of me and Jules drinking soda. He always laughed when I called him that. I showed him how to make bubble gum flavor. He never did that before. It's so simple, mix equal parts of orange and cream. Bam!"

It may boggle the imagination how a teacher, any teacher could possibly allow this kind of action to take place in her class, let alone accept this subpar level of class project presentations. But as we have already seen, Miss Novella was just one of those teachers who had slipped through the cracks.

The students knew this from day one. And like most children, they took full advantage of it. Some not so much, and some lots.

But students like Penny S, Britney, and most unfortunately Olivia, who needed more structure than most knew they had Miss Novella for whatever reason, wrapped around their sticky little fingers. Not just because they were eating candy when she wasn't looking, but because they knew how incompetent she was and that if they complained the loudest and demanded the most, they could get away with almost anything.

Like it was with all people who are so self-centered, they became so wrapped up in what they were doing that they forget where they were. Or didn't care, as the case may be. The less they cared, the sooner they slipped up.

As Penny S stared into her MyPhone, she began to relive the experience of that summer, forgetting completely that she was in front of a class.

Her father knew some big shot at the record company that represented Julius Kilowatt and pulled some strings. Someone must have owed him a big favor and allowed him and his daughter on the set of a professional music video recording. As if that were not enough, they were actually introduced to Matthew James Baumwall, AKA Julius Kilowatt.

"What is this?" said Penny S to herself. "Oh, that was when I snuck back into his trailer when he wasn't there to look around. And I found his private collection of things that girls throw at him when he is on stage. I took that one there. And I took that one too..."

Even Miss Novella could tell that this had gone too far. She cleared her throat, in almost an apologetic fashion.

Penny S looked up, suddenly remembering where she was.

"I'm done," said Penny S, and went back to her seat.

It was finally Penny Dreadful's turn. She was new at this. She had never done anything like it before (not creating an educational project, she had done that countless time). Uncle Calagari insisted in the use of creative projects to drive home the point behind almost every lesson.

He felt that learning was not really learning unless you had fun doing it and created something new in the process. He would insisted that, "...you didn't learn anything if you simply memorized something, and the only questions you had going into the lesson were answered. For a lesson to be complete, dear Penny, you should have more questions to answer by the end of the lesson, then when it began." Yes, he was ahead of his time.

As for the presenting-it-in-front-of-a-class part, that was all new to Penny D.

From a large brown paper bag placed upon Miss Novella's desk, Penny D began to introduce her visual tools. First she held up a stuffed raven body. It had no head, feet or wings.

She was a little shorter than the average student as we know, so she held it up over her head every once in a while so the entire class could see what she was doing.

"After the raven pelt had soaked for several weeks in formaldehyde," said Penny D.

"For Malba who?" said Anthony.

"Formaldehyde," said Penny D. "It is an embalming fluid. It prevents the organic material from decomposing"

The students pretended to understand and nodded their heads

"It is then rolled onto the plastic form, thus," said Penny D. "This process could take weeks to do properly, so I left the fun part of the process for my presentation. This is where we put all the pieces together."

Penny D lifted the head out of the brown paper bag and begins to screw it onto the body like a corkscrew. This visual was accompanied by a gut wrenching sound.

"Remember not to over tighten the neck," said Penny D. "You could snap it off and then you would have to start all over again."

She then placed the body down on the desk and held up one of the wings.

"As you can see I threaded each wing with aluminum wire," said Penny D. "This way they could be positioned to my liking."

She fanned them out and like magic the wings held their position.

"There, that's a great pose," said Penny D. "Very powerful and confrontational. The final step is to attach the feet. I appear to have forgotten my stapler. Does anyone have one?"

The students in the room had a rather disgusted look on their faces by now. Strangely though, they all wanted to see where this was going. It must have been akin to watching a train wreck.

"No stapler?" said Penny D. "That's okay. I guess I'm done then. Any questions?"

Miss Novella begin to signal her that there would not be a question and answer session, but the words cannot escape her dry mouth.

"I have one," said Anthony. "What happened to all of the guts that were inside the bird, like when it was still alive? The heart, the liver, the kidneys..."

"I fed them to my python," said Penny D.

Little Paulie fainted.

So far this whole day had been one of surprise and one unexpected event after another. What happened next was no less than that.

Although Miss Novella appeared to dismiss her and just about everything of value that Penny D had said, she was still astute enough to reach out with her long arm and catch little Paulie's head as his body tipped over, preventing it from hitting the ground.

"Nurses office," said Miss Novella. "Stat!"

It was as if the students around little Paulie had done this before and knew exactly what to do. Three students managed to pick him up and usher him out the door.

Penny D had to pass Miss Novella as she returned to her desk. She was starting to feel a little guilty, like she should have asked first if anyone in the room was faint of heart before demonstrating taxidermy. But at the time of the presentation it had never occurred to her that anyone could be afraid of dead things. After all, she thought to herself, if it is dead it can't hurt you. And all things die, it is part of living. So what's the big deal?

Apparently not everyone in the class felt that way. Miss Novella reached out and took Penny D by the arm and stopped her.

"I am looking forward to the little chat with your parents at the Parent/Teacher Conference tonight about this," said Miss Novella. "Now put that thing in your locker and never bring it to school ever again. Understood?"

"Yes, Miss Novella," said Penny D.

Penny D figured from the very start that she was going to

ace this project as well as all the others. The work was easy and unchallenging. She followed instructions to the letter and did her homework.

She was not about to criticize any of the other projects that the students had brought to the class, she would never do that. But she was astute enough to know that her presentation was smart, educational, interesting and when she practiced it at home, her pets gave her a standing ovation.

But now she was seeing a very direct correlation between the abbreviation of her last name that Miss Novella had given her on the very first day of class and the letter grade she was most likely to receive for this project.

Chapter 15
Penny Interrupted

In order for life to progress there must be change. Not lateral change, where we do the same things over and over again and end up with the same result. A true change occurs where we learn from the mistakes we make and institute a change. And that could only happen when we begin to think differently.

"When we think differently, we act differently. And when we act differently, our world will change around us," Uncle Calagari would say.

This was the foundation principle for all of Penny Dreadful's home schooling and it worked for her well enough at home. She was well educated by both her parents as well as her uncle. She had a great relationship with them and her pets, and she liked herself well enough. Until now.

Now she was learning a whole new type of schooling. Miss Novella called it social skills. Uncle Calagari called it foolish. Natty Dreadful called it, well, perhaps what Natty called it should not be put in print.

The point is, Penny D was going through a transition and she knew it. She had new friends, a new life in so many ways and she was struggling with it as most pre-teens do. She was still wondering how she was supposed to fit into this whole new world. And if that was not enough, she was at that confusing age where she wanted to be accepted by her peers and wanted them to like her.

One concern Penny D had was that she saw compromise all around her, and this was her greatest challenge at Terracotta Junior High School. She wondered to herself if she was willing to compromise her beliefs in order to be liked? Everything she was taught at home said to do the opposite, and because of that she had reason to pause and think.

And so Penny D took every opportunity she could to do just that. Stop, think and seek wisdom. Her uncle taught her that wisdom was always there, waiting in the wings like the director of a play when an actor forgets his next line, or a reference book on a shelf, forever ready to expand our knowledge.

Her Uncle Calagari would say, "Wisdom is waiting for us to learn from but we fail to see it most of the time because we are distracted. Distracted by exactly what we should be ignoring," is the way he once put it, "we should be laughing at what is distracting us instead of paying any attention to it. Often, it is right in front of our noses."

The middle stall in the girl's washroom was as good a place to contemplate this as any other place in school. You were alone, it was not particularly well lit, it was quiet and it was the only stall in the girl's washroom where the lock on the door was still working.

If Penny D could only resist the urge to read the silly nonsense written on the metal walls around her, she might just find the answers she was seeking.

Too bad these walls are so interesting, she thought. For example, right here it says; "Miss Novella has a secret life, call her at 555-747-8888 to find out more", and, "Malcolm the Pranksta was here on June 13th." That one left her a bit unsettled. What was Malcolm doing in the girl's wash room, she thought.

There was another comment about a friend of hers so she had to read it. She had so few friends at this point that she felt obligated. It said, "What is up with Harold's head?" She had no idea what that meant but the size and shape of Harold's head appeared to be on several student's minds. There were more comments about Harold and Malcolm. Mostly derogatory. So Penny D knew to ignore them because they were her friends and that was that.

As her eyes scrolled down the wall she came upon a comment about someone else she knew. It said, "Penny Social is a goddess." This particular wall-scribbled graffiti mail was the most interesting of all since more than one person had been compelled to voice his opinion on this subject.

The word "goddess" written after Penny Social's name was crossed out and the words "spoiled brat" were written next to it.

"Spoiled brat" was then crossed out and the word "princess" was written next to that, accompanied by an illustration of a crown and a magic wand. Penny D saw no connection between the two but she read on anyway.

The word "princess" and the picture of the crown and wand were crossed out and a colorful vulgar noun was written over it in red. The list went on and on. It was very imaginative.

It would appear that a lot of the people who used this stall had a lot to say on this subject, or about Penny S in general. But to Penny D all it really said was that Penny S was not very well-liked and she was okay with that. She wished it weren't true but it did appear that Penny S deserved all that she had coming to her. In fact, she down right demanded it. She even threatened those around her until she got it.

What confused Penny D the most was why Miss Novella encouraged it. She knew Penny S was troubled in some way. That much was obvious to her. But for Miss Novella to act the same way was inexcusable. She was an adult and should know better. Worse yet, she was put in charge of children.

Who was the genius who thought that was a good idea?

Or perhaps she was the by-product of a faulty system. Penny D had no way of knowing.

Furthermore, she wondered how on Earth could anyone tolerate such horrible things to be said about themselves? It eluded her. She knew that whatever the students thought about Penny S and Miss Novella had nothing to do with her. Or, did it?

She continued to scan the walls for a message. She made up her mind that there had to be one and all she had to do was find it. So far all she could see was the idle gossip of idiots who had lost their way and somehow thought to themselves that writing on a washroom wall would somehow allow their individual voice to be heard. They were wrong.

Penny D didn't know the answers to any of these questions. But there was one thing very clear to her and that was that she had a lot on her mind. Perhaps even too much.

"I have to start from the beginning," Penny D told herself. "I must have missed something. I don't like feeling this way. And I don't even know exactly what is bothering me."

As it was with Penny D so many times in her past, when she reached a point of complete bafflement, she would give up.

Not really give up, but more like give in. Shutdown. Or should I say, let go. And with that an epiphany occurred. The answer to her question just walked in through the front door. Or the Girls' Washroom door, as it may be.

Suddenly, Penny D had company. It came in the form of Britney and Olivia who entered the Girl's Washroom to freshen up.

"She is one sick puppy, I'm telling you," said Britney. "Bringing a dead bird to school. That filthy thing must be full of bird diseases."

She then stuck out her tongue and made a retching sound.

"I love puppies," said Olivia.

Ignoring Olivia completely, as Britney often did, she looked at herself in the mirror and couldn't believe what she saw.

"Oh, no!" said Britney. "This never happened before. I'm

not supposed to get any of these. That Dreadful girl should be getting them."

"Don't be such a drama queen"," said Olivia. "Let me have a look."

From over the top of the middle stall in the Girls' Washroom, Penny D peeked out to see Britney letting Olivia inspect her chin.

"My bad," said Olivia. "It's a zit all right."

"That settles it" said Britney, raising her voice. "I hate that girl! Hate her, hate her, hate her, hate her, hate her, hate her!"

"How do you know it's a girl," said Olivia. "Maybe that pimple is a boy."

"Not the pimple, you brainless moron" said Britney. "Penny Dreadful! I hate Penny Dreadful."

Suddenly the anger on Britney's face overtook her. Her reddened look just got worse as she held her breath and right in front of Olivia's eyes several tiny pimples erupted on Britney's face. It was like watching a nature film where tiny sprouts of vegetables are growing in a garden, and are sped up at a comical rate.

In Britney's case, something that would have taken a day or more to manifest took only a few seconds. Little did she realize that like all children her age she possessed some very special powers.

Something that Penny D was taught at a very young age, is that children have the most active imaginations. Their vision and passion are all they need to experience anything they wish or make magic happen.

It may take a lifetime for that little girl who imagined she would be a scientist one day, to become the person who discovered a cure for a life threatening disease, but eventually, if she held true to her belief, it was bound to happen.

Penny D was sure that this happened to boys as well, but she knew so few boys until recently that she had had no point of reference.

She felt that it was too bad that Britney was wasting all that special talent on her pimples.

"Oh, look," said Olivia. "Let me pop them for you."

"Back off, Dexter," said Britney. "What are you trying to do, scar my face for life? I have to wait this one out."

Penny S burst into the girl's washroom like a staff sergeant.

"What is taking you two Donnas so long?" said Penny S.

Britney covered her face and rushed past Penny S with the speed of a cheetah.

"Brit?" said Penny S. "Like, what happened to your face?"

As she and Olivia followed her out into the hallowed halls of Terracotta Junior High School, Britney let out a scream.

Penny D finally came out of the middle stall of the Girls' Washroom holding her mouth to contain her laughter. She knew she shouldn't be laughing at Britney's misfortune but she was finally given the answer she'd been looking for and she knew it.

This was what she was missing. Her sense of humor.

She was taking it all so seriously; the friendships, the peer pressure, the school, the pre-teen angst, the school assignments, and the teacher who was trapped in the ignorant recesses of her own mind. Penny D had simply forgotten to enjoy the ride.

She should laugh at all the good things that were new to her as well, she thought. That included, but was not limited to, the boys, and, well, that was all she could think of at that moment. None of it was worth getting all stressed out over.

Her job, her new mission in life became clear again; she was to be the best person she could be and not give in to the temptation of self-flattering gratification. She didn't need to dress like Britney to like herself.

Lucinda often told her that she should never pay any attention to the good opinion of other people and what they thought of her. If she had, she would never have met her father and married him. And that would have been a huge mistake.

It was as though a colossal weight had been lifted from Penny D's shoulders. She felt weightless again. Gravity had nothing on her.

This reminded her of a joke that her Uncle Calagari would tell her about a book he was reading on anti-gravity. He would say that he just couldn't put it down.

This made her laugh all the harder.

The late bell suddenly rang with that same annoying sound it always had and broke what brief euphoria Penny D had been feeling. She knew that she had but ninety seconds to arrive at her next destination before the hall monitors came around taking names.

Just earlier today she would have felt a rise in anxiety at the very thought that she would be marked late for anything, but now she simply closed her eyes and composed her thoughts.

Penny D knew the halls were still full of students, thus also full of drama. Students would be running to their classes, or away from their classes as the case may be since most of the day classes were now over.

She also knew that for the next period she was scheduled to attend her metal shop club and it was on the other end of the school, one flight down. Further she knew that if she ran and hadn't run into anyone she could still make it to the workshop before the final bell rang. But running was not her style.

Instead, Penny D decided she would walk. She quickly imagined herself walking briskly through the hall, arms swinging back and forth yet miraculously unaffected by the chaos around her. When she arrived at the East Wing stairwell she would hold the hand rail and descend to the basement. She would exit the stairwell and make it to her club meeting on time.

Penny D opened her eyes and with the focus of a sharpshooter she shot out of the Girls' Washroom and into the hall. As predicted students were rushing everywhere; falling over themselves to get to their final classes of the day or to club meetings.

It was as though Penny D didn't even noticed them. She had made up her mind that she would get to her club elective on time and stress free.

One student suddenly tripped and fell in front of her, the books flew from her arms. Penny D sidestepped the tiny road block and caught the books as they descended. She handed them to another student who was right behind her. The girl on the floor called out, "Thanks!"

Thirty or so feet in front of Penny D was another student in a dizzy rush. He slammed his locker shut without looking and started walking away to his next class. What he didn't notice was that one of the big flappy pockets on his pants was caught in the locker. So as the boy moved his pants tore right down the back. The boy froze after a half a step having heard the tear and was about to become mortified with embarrassment. His entire future flashed in front of him. For the next three years everyone would make fun of him and the tighty-whities he wore. Life as he knew it would become hell.

But Penny D, girl on a mission, ripped a school banner down from the wall that advertised a cake sale and whipped it around the boy's waist like a bath towel.

The boy's dignity was saved.

A few students applauded her but Penny D only had enough time to smile at them over her shoulder before she entered the East wing stairwell.

Racing up the stairs toward Penny D from the basement, were two silly boys. For reasons unknown they hadn't expected anyone else to be in this stairwell but them who wanted to descend the stairs at the same time they wanted to ascend. As strange as this may sound, it was true.

The first boy came to a sudden halt when he saw Penny D and the second boy plowed into him. Books flew and both boys ended up sprawled out on the stairs.

Penny D didn't even lose her momentum and straddled the hand rails on both sides of the steps and sailed over the two silly boys. After she landed she called back, "Are you guys all right?"

One of the boys managed a reply, "We good!"

A fraction of a moment later Penny D was through the exit door at the bottom of the stairs and in her shop class just as the final bell sounded.

Penny D was in her element. Metal shop became her new hobby as well as a great club to join. Mr. Kindle took an immediate liking to her and saw the potential she had to create more than the metal dust pans that most of the students were banging out.

He also saw that her mind was like a sponge. She could take in all that he lectured about and throw it right back at him. She remembered everything.

Just as it was before with the heavy metal music blaring in the background, Penny D found herself hammering away at her metal creation. Mr. Kindle looked over her shoulder and gave her the wildly sought after "thumbs up" of approval. Penny D smiled from ear to ear as she held up her first completed metal work. It was a metal mask.

She placed the metal mask over her face and looked back at Mr. Kindle.

The tinted green protective glass over the eye slots of the metal mask colored everything in the room that same shade of green.

Then unexpectedly, when Mr. Kindle smiled back at Penny D, his one gold tooth, the right of the two front two teeth, shone through the green colored glass. It sparkled brightly back at her in its own natural color. Gold!

Chapter 16
A Novella

The short story here is that it is Parent/Teacher Conference Night at Terracotta Junior High School. If you have ever been to one of these then you know what to expect because it is pretty much the same all over this country.

One of the highlights of the night happens not before the teacher is introduced to the parent or guardian of the child, but when he or she glances at the lineup outside the classroom in the hall. A decent teacher worth her weight in peanuts and pennies should be able to connect the child in her class with the parent or guardian waiting on the line. Sound hard to believe? Consider.

Let us take Miss Novella's class for example. The first motley dressed couple on line, with fear written all over their faces in anticipation of hearing more bad news must have belonged to Malcolm.

By now it was well know that their son had a certain reputation. And this, they feared, may be the night they get the crushing news, the news of what new antic he either attempted or worse, pulled off. This might be the antic that gets him expelled from Terracotta Junior High School.

Next on line was a business man dressed up in his best suit. He frequently checked his watch but not for the time. He continually asked why this whole process was taking so long for no reason other than to justify the need to check his watch.

He planned on this night and had no other appointments scheduled, so what he was really doing was showing off the expensive Bolexx watch on his wrist. As further proof of this all one needed to do was listen to the hints he dropped about how important his job was and therefore how he should not have to wait in line for something of such mediocre importance as this.

Self-importance, material object worship and impatience, were all traits that linked him to his off-spring. He was most likely the father of Penny S.

Next in line was a woman with the doe-eyed look. She repeatedly asked the same question- if this was the correct line for Miss Novella's class. If this was not Olivia's mother, then she should have been.

A bit further down the line we had another woman who couldn't stop texting and shushing her husband at the same time. Her better half, as he referred to himself, was on his cell phone talking way too loudly in the school hall about how awesome his life was in every way. These must be Britney's parents.

At the far end of the line, last but not least there was a couple with odd shaped heads. If it turned out that they didn't belong to Harold, Miss Novella swore to give up teaching and retire.

(Oh please, oh please, let it not be them!)

There were other parents and legal guardians on that line outside of Miss Novella's room. They all came out this night. It was a great turn out. Most of the other teachers only got half of their class represented. Many of her coworkers were jealous that she always got a ninety eight percent turnout.

What was it that drew them out, the parents and legal guardians, to Miss Novella's class? Perhaps they wanted to see the parents of the girl that had generated so many of the bizarre stories their little darlings were telling them at home over dinner. Or maybe they were just interested in how well their own child was doing in school; stranger things have happened.

Not too surprisingly though, there was only one couple missing from the long line outside of Miss Novella's class. She clicked her tongue as she looked them over because she had expected just that. One no-show.

With the precision of a drill sergeant Miss Novella welcomed each and every parent or legal guardian into her room, did her little dance to entertain, then ushered them out the door praying they would never return. But they did. They always came back to see her again. They couldn't help it. The stories they heard at home were just too darn good. They were the fabric that memories were made from.

This was a ritual of sorts in the tiny hamlet of Terracotta. The parents or legal guardians entered Miss Novella's room. They took a seat in a miniature chair behind a miniature desk and looked up at her. They looked ridiculous.

She had her performance down pat. She chose from one of the two speeches she had memorized. She was not spontaneous nor was she versatile. Sometimes her arms flailed uncontrollably as she talked and no one knew why. When it came to the children in her class that she felt were not performing up to her expectations, she was on the attack. It was something that had to be seen to be believed.

Depending upon how much of a push-over she felt the parent or legal guardian was, would determine whether she berated them for having raised a little monster or she simply told them how she was on their side and they would have to work together to correct the problem. It was a crap shoot, really. The dice kind.

On the flip side, she was full of praise and humor when she met a parent or legal guardian of whom she believed to be a perfect student. She even laughed giddily at her own jokes. Just imagine how horrid that must sound.

So one by one Miss Novella blew through the crowd of

parents and legal guardians not remembering what she said to any of them. This was how her fool head worked, it activated her mouth, made it talk without thinking first and swore to the lies later on.

By the time the last parent or legal guardian had left her room, Miss Novella was all strung out. Her clothes were disheveled and her hair looked like it had been put through a blender. She was exhausted. Granted she had stood on her feet for two hours lecturing, but she had said nothing of value. And no one had appeared to notice.

Once the Parent/Teacher Conference night was over, Miss Novella sat back in her chair to rest. She had lived to teach another day. Sometimes she wondered if she could continue. Any sane person could see that she didn't like children. If asked on a full moon night she might even admit to it.

A calmness overtook her. Her mind began to drift. She was thinking about why she took this job in the first place. She had always hated teaching. She wanted to become a lunar botanist, but she couldn't pass the physical to board the international space shuttle, or so she was told.

This world she had created for herself was full of disappointments. Sometimes she wondered to herself what it must be like to actually raise a child, and what could possibly make anyone want to do it?

At quiet times like these she formulated plans of what she would do if she were the President of this country. Then she would wonder why no one even tried to mix beer and wine to create a new party drink. One unrelated topic crossed her feeble mind after another.

Sooner or later she realized that she was off the topic of education disciplines and felt guilty spending her time not thinking about school when she was there. This opened a new kind of crazy in her head and she began to fantasize about mandatory child labor camps in every state. This made her feel better.

It wasn't cruelty, she rationalized, but an important measure given the current state of affairs and it sounded good to her. She felt that her father would be proud of her if she instituted that. He always told her how she would never contribute to society or amount to anything. Secretly, she agreed with him.

All of these wonderful illusions and dreams suddenly burst when she noticed an unusual gentleman in mid-nineteenth century clothing standing right next to her holding a tray of home-made brownies.

Uncle Calagari was soft spoken and slow with his delivery, as if he were careful to choose every word before he spoke.

"Hello, Miss Novella?" said Uncle Calagari. "You are she?"

Miss Novella jumped a little bit when she saw him. She hadn't heard him enter the room. Not that it would have made any difference to her, she jumped at all sorts of things. Ads on TV about deodorant made her jump, dogs barking at squirrels, sneezes and babies laughing as well. She never questioned it and the list went on.

"That is your name, is it not?" asked Uncle Calagari again.

"Well, yes, it is," said Miss Novella. "I'll bet your Penny D's father."

"A bet you would lose, my dear Miss Novella," said Uncle Calagari. "For the lovely child is my niece. I am her Uncle. Calagari is my name. I have come to apologize for her parents who were unable to attend. They were called away on business. Yes. "

"Well," said Miss Novella. "The Parent/Teacher Conference is over, you know? Better luck next time. I was just on my way out."

Secretly, Miss Novella thought that if she counted this queer guy in, she had a perfect attendance tonight.

"Over," said Uncle Calagari. "Yes. I see. Then I apologize for wasting your time. I did so want to meet you. Penny has told us so much about you."

"Well, I, I, . . ", said Miss Novella. She appeared nervous and didn't know why. It was not like she was completely unaware that people talked about her in negative ways behind her back. Sometimes even right in front of her.

She should be used to it by now but instead, like so many people when they are fully aware that they have said or done something wrong to a fellow person, she played dumb and pretended to have no idea what they had said or done.

"She told me so many wonderful things about you," said Uncle Calagari. "Yes."

It had probably been decades since Miss Novella remembered blushing. The last time that comes to mind was when she was ten years old. A boy on her block had made her a paper flower and colored it red like her hair. She never asked him why he did it, but she was thrilled nonetheless. And yes, Miss Novella's hair was red back then. Now, the color defies description.

"Would you care for a brownie?" said Uncle Calagari. "They were made from my own unique recipe. I made them for you."

"Well, yes," said Miss Novella. "I am rather hungry. Thank you."

Miss Novella popped one entire brownie into her large mouth. An almost impossible feat when you take into consideration the massive size of the brownie. But she did it anyway. Obviously she had some hidden talents.

"She is a very difficult child, you know?" said Miss Novella as crumbs from the brownie shot out of her mouth. "Mmmm, these are delish!"

Suddenly from out of nowhere, as if it were planned, a stray cat jumped up on her desk to sniff the brownies.

"Get down, you nasty creature," said Miss Novella. "How did you get in here anyway?"

Miss Novella waved at the cat, but before leaping away and running out of the classroom, it winked at Uncle Calagari.

"Perhaps I may escort you to your mode of transportation?" asked Uncle Calagari. "It is dark outside and some would say that one should exercise caution."

"Well, I don't see why not," said Miss Novella, "And keep those brownies handy, will ya."

"Yes, yes indeed I will," said Uncle Calagari.

He held the tray out ahead of her as if she was a horse and he was leading her with a carrot on a string.

As Uncle Calagari and Miss Novella left the room together and walked down the hall, Miss Novella giggled at something that he had said to her. Her cackle was a higher pitch than the soft tone used by Calagari so it could easily be heard from afar.

"Perhaps, Calagari, perhaps," said Miss Novella, "And please, call me Prudence."

They appeared to hit it off, yet they were quite opposites really. Miss Novella had rarely found herself opening up to anyone before. She began to talk a mile a minute as they continued to walk down the hall and out through the front doors of the school building together.

"As I was saying," said Miss Novella. "That Penny of yours is a strange one. But I imagine everyone in your family already knows that."

The cat that had been atop Miss Novella's desk quickly scurried down the hall. It slipped outside between the closing doors.

"You know, that Penny of yours," said Miss Novella. ". . . she is not the brightest light on the highway, if you know what I mean?"

Chapter 17
A Walk in the Park

Miss Novella considered herself a woman of the world, while in reality she wasn't much more than the sum total of what she thought of the least-liked child she was entrusted to educate. She never felt the need to be part of a family, that is to say get married, or have children of her own, help to raise grandchildren and sit back in her retirement years and marvel at what she created.

Instead Miss Novella felt inspired to become the principle force in her own domain and psychologically torture the children she didn't like in her class. And by "didn't like" I mean children she felt threatened by. And by "threatened by" I mean the children that were smarter, more gifted, wiser, more well-adjusted and just down right more pleasant to be around than she.

It came as no surprise that she fell madly in obsession with Uncle Calagari. And when I say "obsession" I mean in love, or the closest thing to love that Miss Novella could ever feel for someone other than herself.

Calagrai was debonair. He was also handsome, and tall, and a snappy dresser (if you like that nineteenth century clothing look). He was a gentleman around Miss Novella no matter what she said, and he was an adult who knew how to listen. As strangely as that may seem, he listened intensely to her when she spoke.

This was something Miss Novella had never experienced before.

Uncle Calagari was never the man to create a false facade and pretend he liked someone whom he didn't. Although he may give the appearance of someone who is a bit off or out-of-sync with what is going on today, he would never pretend he was someone or something he was not. He believed in the truth and that it was always there right in front of him. For Calagari the truth about Miss Novella was that she was distracted. Plain and simple.

He saw beneath the outer shell, the hardened image, the self-important and very confused exterior of Miss Novella. He saw her as a child who needed to be loved.

Although he knew it impossible to turn back the clock for her and nurture that little girl named Prudence Novella, who was so ignored by the grandparents who raised her and the father she met but a handful of times. He was determined to provide her with the attention she had never gotten. His vision of her was that she had the potential to change herself (despite the lack of that parenting her father, who worked long hours, drank way too much, and searched for his own happiness) could never provide.

As Uncle Calagari escorted Miss Novella to her car that night they first met, they spoke about many things. She quipped about the odd stories of strangers in their town who had been seen wandering around the neighborhood at all odd hours.

These strangers were described as wearing long dark robes with hoods. No one knew where they had come from, what they wanted or where they disappeared to before sunrise. Calagari laughed at the gossip and confessed that he had never seen one, but Miss Novella found the stories imaginative. Although the average resident of Terracotta felt a little bit threatened by these sightings, she instead felt the same excited rush as when she watched a late night horror film all alone on her cable TV.

However, she was not in the comfort of her own home, hidden away and secure behind locked doors. She was out on the street with a gentleman she had just met, probably the first in many years.

How strange. Just a few moments ago he was the manifestation of the imaginary figure that she had made responsible for all the misery she experienced in her classroom. Up untill now, Calagari, the uncle of Penny Dreadful, had been villainized by Miss Novella. He was the source of her vexation, the very person whom she blamed for creating a student that she didn't like from the very moment she'd laid eyes on her. That was, until now.

Then much to their mutual surprise, Uncle Calagari asked Miss Novella if she would like to go for a walk in the park on some cool evening with him and she said yes.

For the following week the students of Miss Novella's seventh grade class at Terracotta Junior High School noticed a change in her personality. She was more spacey than usual, more tolerant than usual, more lenient than usual, and (most unusual of all) she was far less apt to blame Penny D for every little and unimportant thing in her life that made her wig out.

The class as a whole was more complacent. They were thinking that she was ill in some way and took pity on her. Some even spread the rumor that she was possessed. It was not too far from the truth really, she was. She was possessed by her gentleman suitor.

With no more than kind and honest words, Uncle Calagari had transformed the old Miss Novella into the new and improved Miss Novella. She even came to work in better packaging; she appeared to iron her clothes now before putting them on and she started to leave the sweater with all the holes in it at home.

When a leaf fell from a tree outside her window, Miss Novella stopped her lecturing and watched it land. Her students stared out the window trying desperately to find out what she was looking at. But they couldn't. All except, Athena.

Athena knew what was going on. She knew that Miss Novella was in love.

Athena could put two and two together and come up with anything she wanted to; a math equation, jump rope sequencing, military tactical plans, and human relationships. Yes, Athena was appropriately named.

She was good at reconnaissance, too. She had overheard many conversations leading up to the strange and yet very normal way Miss Novella had been acting and had put the pieces together.

The events leading up to said "normal acts" that Miss Novella had recently been reported as committing began immediately after the Parent/Teacher Conference Night at Terracotta Junior High School.

Other reports were filing in from the kind of people whose small minds keep track of such things. They were kept very busy indeed.

You would think that only the old wash women, gossipers and drama queens would find the latest news of Miss Novella interesting, but the Terracotta Block Watch Volunteers, AKA the TBWV, felt that they had an obligation. Or a stake in the claim. Who, incidentally, were also known as the "The Eligible Bachelors of Terracotta who Scope Out Single Women," or the EBTSOSW.

Every evening a small group of them would go on patrol. They, the TBWV for short, claimed they kept the neighborhood safe from burglars and other incorrigibles. But what many believed they were really doing was reporting to their closest friends the current where-abouts of the single eligible women in the area. This included but was not limited to where they shopped, where they stopped for a coffee, when they went out for a run and the like.

As borderline stalking as it may be, they were a harmless bunch and when a single eligible woman would confront them, either out of curiosity or to tell them where to go, they practically played possum. They would freeze up and begin to sneeze as if they were allergic to women. One man was reported to have peed his pants. So you see, they were harmless. Just weird.

The elders of the group, middle-aged men really, did have their eye on one very eligible single woman from the Terracotta district. Her official file classification was; Novella, P / school teacher / high maintenance. The recent activity on her file was growing. Namely, that she was seen accompanied by a strange gentleman of suspicious nature. They were out for a walk in the park late last night and every night this week as well.

And by "late" I mean after nine PM.

Anyway, all of this filtered down to Athena's older brother, Costos, who was an EBTSOSW in training. He was the total opposite of Athena, so that makes him shy, introverted, unkept in appearance and his mouth went dry if he ever had to talk in public. He would quite possible faint if a girl in his class looked at him with big dreamy eyes and asked him a question.

Almost all of the private business of Miss Novella and Calagari had gone public and, for that matter, opened to judgment and scrutiny. Not that it mattered to Calagari, he was above such things. But for the delicate emotional flower known as Miss Novella, it could end up a problem and he knew it. Luckily for them both she was in a place that she had never been in before and too distracted to give the rumors that were circulating via electronic media any credence.

On this particular night Miss Novella and Calagari walked arm in arm down a well lit path in the park. The melodic sounds of crickets and Vextel communicators could be heard all around them. The crickets were doing, well, what crickets do and the short bursts of static from the hand-held battery operated devices clearly told the story that they were being watched.

It was a delightful walk though. They talked. He made her

laugh. They talked some more and laughed some more.

The static clicks suddenly stopped somewhere around that time. It was as if the laughter of two people of the opposite sex activated some kind of deactivation device. Or, from that point forward it was universally understood that they had earned their privacy and they were left alone by the EBT-SOSW. I guess you could say that the bachelors lost interest.

Miss Novella and Calagari came upon a clearing in the park and stopped. While Miss Novella gazed up at the stars for an unusual amount of time, Calagari soon found himself surrounded by four young thug "wannabes."

Calagari was not a man who could ever be followed and not know it. So without any further ado he addressed the situation.

"You intend to persuade me, perhaps through force, yes?" said Calagari to one of the thugs. "Because I appear old and helpless, even at greater disadvantage than most since I am with a woman, you think? To freely supply you with currency, yes?"

"I dun't knows wut you mean, stupid old fart," said Dim.

Yes, it was Dim alright. It would have been nice to think that he had learned something from the cafeteria altercation, but it would appear that he was not a person who learned from his mistakes.

His home schooling was of a different sort than that of Penny D's, one of his many lessons included how to take advantage of people. Like, if someone was old and with female company then they were helpless. Therefore an easy target for quick cash.

"What I mean to say, just so we, you and I do not have any misunderstanding of communication, yes," said Calagari, "is that if you and your cohorts insist on traveling across this very thin sheet of ice. And if so, it will collapse and you find yourself in a very dangerous place indeed, in deep water."

"Where are you from, grandpa, the old freak'n country?" said Dim.

Again Dim was amused by himself and laughed.

The three other young thugs laughed at Calagari's expense as well. They were probably not sure what Dim had said, but when you were stupid, fifteen, and drank a beer you had shoplifted from the local 24/7 Store, you would laugh at almost anything (and probably for far too long).

Once, on a previous 24/7 Store heist of monumental proportions, these teens, cumulatively lifted a six-pack of beer, a whole box of beef jerky sticks and an automobile air freshener. They had then sat on the curb at Factory Square and laughed at their farts and the blinking street light above them until they passed out. Yes, it had been a great night. For idiots.

Luckily for them the Terracotta Block Watch Volunteers had found them before the sheriff. If they hadn't it would have meant a stiff fine for their parents. With what was believed to be the state of the economy today, two of the three teens would have gotten severe beatings and one child would have been thrown out of the house permanently.

Okay, they were hard luck cases, but that doesn't mean we should dismiss out of hand what they were planning to do to Calagari, and Miss Novella who had actually had all four of them in her class at one point. Not that she would have recognized any of them now, she was too busy gazing up at the heavens.

"I see Orion, Cal," said Miss Novella. "Do you see it?"

"I do, Prudence," said Calagari calling out.

He then went back to the business at hand and brandished his walking stick.

"Where did that come from?" said Dim.

"No true gentleman would ever escort a lady out for a walk in the park without coming prepared," said Calagari. "Yes?"

Calagari turned quickly, his back to a different thug to prevent them from thinking through their next move. They countered by repositioning and Calagari, tripped the smallest of the pack, then placed the tip of his walking stick on the back of his neck after the boy hit the ground.

"Stay down, little one, it is the safest place for you, yes," said Calagari. "The night is about to show us something that we have never seen before. A lesson will be taught, the hard way."

As we have seen once before, it didn't take much for Dim to fly into a rage. If there was one thing he knew better than most it was anger. Sadly, once his button was pushed the outcome had to be painful. When in school, it became painful for anyone around him, including his friends. When he was at home it was pretty much the same deal.

They were minors of course, so Calagari had planned not to hurt any of them, even though Dim out-weighed him with twenty pounds of muscle. But as he often told Penny, the larger your opponent, the more force you had to use against them.

Calagari would not be the first to strike, he would never hit a minor even if attacked. Even though he was outnumbered, he would still not break his rule. He would even sacrifice himself if need be to insure safety for Prudence.

"Cal, I saw a shooting star," said Miss Novella as she points to the sky.

"So did I dear Prudence," said Calagari. "And I suspect a second one is not far behind."

Suddenly a trash can toppled over for no apparent reason. Calagari knew it was a well calculated diversion so he did nothing but watch.

But Dim, who could be distracted by a weak gust of wind took the bait and watched the trash scatter across the ground. An apple with one bite taken out of it rolled across the park clearing.

One of the three remaining thugs slowly backed away from the trash and up against a prickly leafed bush. A canvas bag was slipped over his head from behind him and he was pulled bodily into the bush.

His screams of pain mystified Dim and the remaining lad who watched in horror as their friend struggled to remove the bag from his head and fight his enemy. The boy's opponent was nowhere to be seen and so the bush with sharp prickly leaves seemed to attack him instead.

"Someone help me," said the boy. "It hurts, ow, ow, ow, make it stop!"

Dim and the remaining boy just stood there helplessly, watching their friend claw and crawl his way out of the bush on his hands and knees. His clothes were radically torn and there were cuts on his face, arms and hands from the edges of the leaves.

"I'm bleeding," said the young thug. "Look!"

Then with a look of complete failure and humiliation this young thug "wannabe" ran off into the night.

Calagari didn't bother to watch this total embarrassment unfold. He knew better. He scanned the perimeter for what he knew would be another distraction, or another attack.

Like clockwork, the mysterious and masked stranger who had tipped over the trash can, suddenly appeared behind the second thug "wannabe" and tapped him on the shoulder. When the teen turned around to face him, the stranger reached out and squeezed his left nipple and made him cry. It was painful to just watch.

"Go home, little man," said the masked stranger in a deep voice. Then he announced his alter ego to all who were present to hear. Except for Miss Novella who was still busy looking for a second shooting star. "This is my territory and you will not take advantage of the elderly here tonight. For I am, Knight Watch, and I will protect them."

The second thug only whimpered. When Knight Watch let go of his nipple, he tried to run away so quickly, that he fell over the trash can and skinned his knee on the pavement. This did little to stop his retreat, and he, too, was soon gone.

Knight Watch wore a ski mask over his face and sports equipment tightly strapped to his body for protection. The only item he wore that had some professional cartoon appeal was his cape. His mother had sewn that together for him. It looked awesome.

Dim was on his own now. He would not let any part of this circus prevent him from carrying out his plan. He attacked

Knight Watch with a battery of punches. We had seen this before. When Dim fought, he was like a runaway train.

If he were in a pool he might have been doing the breast stroke. It was hard to tell but from what could be seen one fist flew at Night Watch in round-house fashion, followed by another.

Knight Watch was skilled at Wing Chun and he met most of the punches with the back of his hands, using his body armor to absorb the shock.

After fifty or sixty repeated blows, Dim had slowed down considerably. His knuckles bled from hitting the hardened plastic of roller blade wrist protectors and the baseball shin guards Knight Watch had on his forearms.

Having conserved his energy, Knight Watch launched his offensive attack. He was now delivering several blows of his own at Dim. Many of them slaps really. They landed across Dim's face and one on top of his head for good measure.

It was a slap fight of grand proportions. Dim was too exhausted from punching so he had to slap back. The prize moment came when Dim could no longer keep his eyes open, his face was beet red from being slapped so profusely. He turned away and Knight Watch closed in for the kill.

It came in the form of a swift kick in the pants. When it hit Dim it was so powerful that it sent him falling into the garbage on the floor. His face landed next to a plastic bag labeled Poo-Protector.

Even Calagari held his nose at the very sight.

Dim was totally humiliated. He slipped around on the garbage trying to get up on his feet and crawled away into the night.

"Could I be of any more service to you citizen?" said Knight Watch.

As if this were not amazing enough, Knight Watch had said all without even the slightest trace of a stutter.

"No thank you, Vincent," said Calagari, in a whispered tone. "You are truly a Sedi warrior of cosmic proportions."

The challenge of facing three teens older than himself

and one with a bully's reputation at school hardly caused Vincent to stir, but how easily Penny D's uncle saw through his disguise completely unsettled him.

"But how, how, how, did, you, you, you, know?" said Vincent.

"I have a cape of my own, tucked away somewhere in my youth as well, young man," said Calagari. "Your identity is safe with me. Now go, and thank you."

"Cal, who are you talking to?" said Miss Novella.

"This young lad, he was out for a night run and fell," said Calagari aloud.

He helped the youngest boy who was still on the floor up to his feet.

The boy looked around nervously. Knight Watch was gone. So were the people he had called his friends.

"Now be careful, young man," said Calagari. "The path you choose tonight should be the one that will lead you back home, yes?"

The boy looked down. He was completely ashamed of himself. But he nodded that he understood, and off he went.

"Oh, Cal, you are so fatherly," said Miss Novella. "If only I had a father as wise as you, maybe things would have turned out differently."

Chapter 18
The Broken Heart Club

Once a year on this particular day all of the pie experts in town come out of their closets to dazzle each other with their crazy new recipes at the Terracotta Fall Festival of Pies.

Uncle Calagari had previously planned to enter one of his pies into the contest and compete for the prize money of a one hundred dollar gift certificate to Wallymarts Department Store. When Miss Novella came into the picture his attention went elsewhere and he failed to address the deadline.

The festival ran over a long weekend and just about everyone in town would attend. There were pies of all different concoctions on display for studying and tasting as well. To name a few, walnut broccoli crumb pie, sugar and beet with pineapple dressing pie and Greek yogurt pizza pie, were the favorites to win that year.

It was a good thing for the local pie experts that Uncle Calagari hadn't had the time to compete with his exploding pie. It would have made a very lasting impression on the judges indeed.

At this year's festival, Miss Novella and her gentleman suitor, the very odd looking gentleman known only as

Calagari, were all the rage.

In a small town like Terracotta, watching two people fall in love, no matter their age, was as addictive as watching an edgy soap opera on the internet.

From the moment they entered the festival grounds, all available eyes watched as Calagari and Miss Novella boarded a Ferris Wheel bucket, then slowly rode to the apex of the wheel. They appeared to be having fun the entire time, but certain eyewitness accounts of what happened next will differ.

There may have been something about the great height that gave Miss Novella a new perspective on her life (since this was not an activity she would have done on her own), but something changed that night.

Perhaps it was the thin air or the fact that she suddenly noticed all the little faces down below staring up at her, or that she missed what it was like to be feared and disliked, but Miss Novella suddenly became uncomfortable.

Being loved was out of her comfort zone and when she was with Calagari that was all that there was. In his presence, she felt warm and cared for, a feeling she was unaccustomed to. She was alive and she knew it. In either case, for reasons never explained, the Ferris Wheel suddenly came to a stop.

"Oh, Cal, I've had a wonderful weekend with you," said Miss Novella. "But I have some very bad news that I have to tell you. You see, I can't see you anymore."

"I am truly saddened to hear that Prudence," said Calagari. "Are you sure about this decision? One must not be rash about such things that one may regret one day."

"I've thought it over as long as I need to," said Miss Novella. "And it is not that I don't like you anymore. In fact, my feelings for you are quite the opposite. But you see, I have a certain reputation in this community. And well, it's because our views on politics are so radically different."

Miss Novella's strange point of view was suddenly reinforced by her delusion of herself as a pillar of respect in her community.

"People are starting to stare at us and the talk will soon follow," said Miss Novella.

It was obvious to Uncle Calagari that she was grasping at straws. She was looking for some reason, any reason why they couldn't be together, a reason why she shouldn't be happy, as if that were a special privilege or club that she was not allowed to enjoy or be part of.

"Even from up here I can see their little heads turning," said Miss Novella. "There. And there. And there."

She turned around and caught the people who were in the bucket right behind them whispering about her. They stopped as she glared back at them. This of course, made no difference to Calagari, he was above such things.

"I understand, Prudence," said Calagari. "You're principles are more important to you than the power of love."

"When you put it like that, Cal" said Miss Novella. "It sounds dirty."

Then true to form Miss Novella directed her attention elsewhere. It was most likely so that she would not have to deal with her feelings of loss. Because, she did in fact just lose a very important person in her life. Someone she would never have back again.

"Why aren't we moving?" said Miss Novella.

"Then I guess this is good bye, Prudence?" said Calagari.

"Oh, yes, good bye, Cal, it's been real," said Miss Novella, who then continued to study the mechanism in the gears below her.

Miss Novella sat back and looked out over the festival as the wheel began to move again. She oddly noticed that no one was looking back at her anymore. Everyone was going about their business. It was almost as if she were invisible again.

It puzzled her, but for only a minute. She took solace in this and didn't even notice that the Ferris Wheel had come to a complete stop at the bottom. The attendant was holding the tiny door open for her to disembark. It was only then that she realized she was completely alone.

It was bright and sunny in Terracotta that week. It would appear that all was right in the world. The Fall air had a slight breeze but there was still no need for a heavy jacket.

The school looked just as it had the week before as did the seventh grade classroom. However, there was one missing piece in this puzzle. And it was creating quite a stir.

It started as a happy surprise that morning until it fed on the fear of the growing anxiety in Miss Novella's classroom. That soon gave way to ignorant conjecture, and that turned into an all-out panic.

The students of Miss Novella's class sat at their seats looking nervous. Some of the students knew more than others and they were just bursting to share what little they knew with one another.

The late bell had rung a few minutes before and the silence was deafening. Miss Novella was still nowhere to be seen. This was the third day in a row that she had been AWOL.

She had been absent all week and this string of absences was so out-of-character for her, that the students didn't know what to make of it. The two substitute teachers had been a disaster so far, the whole week was a wash out. Chaos reigned. Penny S ruled. Malcolm pranked. Britney screamed. Little Paulie fainted. And Olivia daydreamed.

It was a strange week for sure. Penny D was also missing. She was presumed ill. Anthony confirmed that the change in weather often caused colds. No one knew whether he knew what he was talking about or not, but they went along with it anyway.

This in itself was not the cause of the uneasiness. There were extenuating issues, but the tales that were about to be told, would surely drive home the point.

Athena had pulled all of the pieces together from what she heard from her brother and from her classmates via digital networking. When Athena leaned forward, between two rows of desks, everyone around her knew that she had some juicy gossip to share. Or maybe even facts!

The ground work had already been laid so all she had to do was fill in the blanks and announce her conclusion to those students who didn't have the critical thinking skills she possessed. These were skills she had honed overseas where she grew up, skills that were no longer taught in the local school system.

The students already knew about Miss Novella's gentleman caller, but they didn't know what happened after her fateful night at the Fall Festival of Pies.

"What followed their breakup was even more bizarre," said Athena. "The EBTSOSW were involved from the very get-go."

"You mean the skirt chasers?" said Anthony. "That's what my pop calls them."

For a moment Athena fell out of character.

"No, I mean the EBTSOSW," said Athena. "Now show some respect, Anthony. You may become one some day."

Anthony hung his head again and suddenly felt that the spirit of Miss Novella were still in this room.

"It was no secret that every night for the past week, Miss Novella was secretly dating Penny D's uncle," said Athena. "And right after their horrible break up a few nights ago she was seen wandering the streets at some very late hours."

"I didn't know that," said Anthony.

"Big surprise there," said Penny S. "Go on."

"It was unclear where she was going and what she was up to," said Athena. "But it was also reported that she was being followed by stray cats."

Athena paused for dramatic purposes, but it did little good. Most of the children were still in the dark, they had no idea where this story was going.

Little Paulie unfolded a "Lost Pet" flier he had in his pocket. The entire class gasped at what appeared. It said that little Pookie had been missing for three days now and the owner was offering a hefty reward if he were found. This may have been nothing more than circumstantial evidence connecting the two, but when it came to conspiracy theories, it didn't have to make sense.

"Last night a concerned citizen was out walking his dog," said Athena, who paused again. You would think after the first long dramatic pause she learned something, but she hadn't.

"He spotted one of those hooded people wandering the streets," said Athena. "The ones we have been hearing about for so long now. So he called the police and reported it. The EBTSOSW intercepted the call and were first on the scene. Afraid they might lose him before the police arrived, they followed him, yet at a safe distance not to be detected. And you will never guess where he went?"

"It was Miss Novella, wasn't it?" said Olivia.

It was Olivia talking, so just about everyone ignored what she had to say.

"He went into, Miss Novella's house," said Athena. "When the police finally showed up, the neighbors explained what they witnessed and that they were concerned for her safety. The police knocked on her door and when Miss Novella answered she was dressed in,…the dark hooded robe."

"The horror!" said Anthony.

"Shut up, Anthony," said Penny S. "And, what else….?"

"The mystery didn't end there," said Athena. "There were cats everywhere in the house. And they weren't hers. When the door opened several ran on out. One neighbor recognized his pets and called out to them. Mrs. Santuccis' cat, Pookie was one of the many animals trapped in her home."

Athena looked over at Little Paulie when she said that.

"Needless to say she was arrested for pet-napping," said Athena. "It might have all been dismissed as a misunderstanding at the station house, but Miss Novella put up an argument that could only be described as downright psychotic in nature, said one police officer. Instead of letting her go, a psychiatrist was called in to evaluate her. Not surprisingly, his recommendation was to have her committed to a hospital for observation."

"I don't believe a word of it," said Penny S. "Dumbest story

I've ever heard. In a town as small as this one, why didn't I hear anything about this?"

Little Paulie could not contain himself any longer, his mother worked in the Emergency Room of the Terracotta Health Clinic and she was a witness to what Little Paulie was about to divulge.

So he suddenly made a sound much like a squeak, or a squeal, or a squeak-squeal. Actually it defied description. But the only thing that little Paulie's classmates knew for sure was that he had something to say and he was trying to do so.

"Spit it out you leprechaun," said Penny S. "What do you know?"

Little Paulie's face began to get beet red and when he started to speak he was inaudible.

"What, already?" said Britney, believing in her tiny mind that if you yelled at someone who had any trouble talking it would correct their problem.

"I, said," said Little Paulie who again was barely audible.

"Talk louder or I'm going to punch you," said Penny S.

"I, said, that Miss Novella, is in the hospital," screamed Little Paulie. "She is delirious and all she keeps on saying is that it was all because of the dreadful, the dreadful, I tell you. The DREADFUL!"

Little Paulie cupped his hands over his mouth, he couldn't believe he had said that as loudly as he had.

"I knew it," said Penny S. "She went too far this time. It was only a matter of time before something like this happened. Maybe now you all believe me about that snake and the spider? The girl is a witch."

Just about all the students of the seventh grade classroom wanted to disagree with Penny S, mostly because it was fun to watch her get mad. Additionally, they had no real beef with Penny D, who they hardly knew was there most of the time. But they couldn't come up with a reason why they should argue that point either.

Fact, Miss Novella was not at her desk. Fact, she hadn't been there for three days now. Fact, Athena's brother confirmed the police report. Fact, Pookie was found. Fact, little Paulie's mom confirmed Miss Novella's current location. And for some strange reason they couldn't come up with a rational way to explain why it had all happened. The only question that remained was, what should be done about it.

Malcolm and Harold remained indifferent to the story. They secretly wished to themselves that the stories were true and that Miss Novella would not return. The whole Penny D and her uncle involvement part made no difference to them at all and her current mental state was of even less interest to them. Malcolm felt that Miss Novella was unfit as his teacher, and Harold knew he was already much smarter than she.

The Homeroom interstitial was now over and the first period bell rang just as the rear door to the classroom opened and Penny D stepped inside.

"Whew, I made it," said Penny D.

Everyone in the class except Malcolm and Harold gasped when they saw her.

"Burn her at the stake!" said Penny S.

"What?" said Penny D, innocently.

"Mouth!" said Malcolm, staring Penny S down.

"Forget her," said Malcolm, his attention now on Penny D. "The monkeys are out of their cages again. That's all. And don't worry. I don't believe a word of it."

"A word of what?" said Penny D.

"The, stories," said Harold in a whispered tone.

"What stories?" said Penny D, but her question went completely ignored.

"Where you been, anyway?" said Malcolm.

"Actually I forgot I wasn't being home schooled anymore and from staying up so late completing a science project that I started last month, that I…" said Penny D.

"A World of Witchcraft project?" asked Britney.

"…that, I, slept, late," said Penny D. "And to answer your question, it was actually a project documenting the positive effect of soothing music on animals that have been traumatized by abandonment."

"You see, we found these baby ducks in our yard," Penny D continued. "Their mother had either abandoned them or, maybe she was the victim of a foul attack. But in either case, they were all alone in the world."

Suddenly the door at the front of the classroom opened and all heads turned to see who had entered. Low and behold there stood a gentleman in his forties with a round face and belly to match. His tie was too long for his shirt and he was smiling. He didn't look like a substitute teacher. He had that look in his eye like he did this full time.

"Hello students," said Mr. Proto. "My name is Mr. Proto. But please, don't hold that against me." Then he laughed to himself.

Athena, who was not a worrisome child, but fashioned herself concerned about almost everything, stood up slowly and raised her hand at the same time.

"Excuse me, Mr. Proto, sir," said Athena. "But could you please tell us what happened to Miss Novella? Some of us are, concerned."

"Short story," said Mr. Proto. "I don't know. See what I did there? But rest assured, I will be your new teacher until the completion of the school year. Shall we get on with the attendance and get acquainted? Of course we shall."

As Mr. Proto opened his seating chart and began to study it Penny D settled into her chair. She couldn't help but notice the odder than usual looks that she was getting from the students around her.

"It looks like we have two Penny's in the room," said Mr. Proto. "I'm always putting in my two cents."

He didn't wait for laughter this time. He probably knew he wasn't going to get any. He moved right along and assumed that sooner or later they would all come to their senses and find him hilarious.

"Penny Dreadful, your name comes first alphabetically so I will call you Penny, and Penny Social,..." said Mr. Proto.

Penny S stood up with the sole purpose of getting away with what she had been doing for her entire public education career.

"Hold on please, Mr. Proto sir," said Penny S. "But I was in this class first so I should be called Penny and that other girl should be called..."

"I'm sorry," said Mr. Proto loudly enough to drown out her whining. "There will be no calling out in my class. If you have something creative to add, you will raise your hand and I will be happy to call on you."

As Penny S sat down, her hand shot into the air.

"As I was saying," said Mr. Proto. "Penny Social, and I will assume that is you. I will call you Penny Squared."

Mr. Proto then chuckled to himself again. Only this time some of the students giggled along. But they stopped abruptly as soon as Penny S shot them a disapproving glance.

His jokes were painful all right, but let's face it, we all have our own ways of staying sane.

"Just a little math humor," said Mr. Proto. "I can call you both Penny. I will simply look at you, when I call your name and you, when I call your name. Simple. We all deserve the same respect."

"What an idiot," said Penny S under her breath.

"Attendance complete," said Mr. Proto. "Now have any of you ever heard of a little book called, Dr. Dolittle? He was a very special man, he could talk to animals."

"Saw the movie," said Britney.

"It was a funny thing," said Mr. Proto, looking at Britney. "When I got a tour of the school I noticed that the detention room was empty. Let's try to keep it that way, shall we?"

Britney shrunk in her chair.

Penny S pretended not to care and yawned to herself silently.

Olivia did something cute that only Malcolm noticed.

Little Paulie finally stopped shaking.

Athena closed one eye when she looked at Mr. Proto, as if this would dispel his facade and expose his real plan.

Anthony raised his hand and saw that Mr. Proto was looking up his name to call on him. When he found it he called on him, listened to his question, answered him and thanked Anthony for the question.

Vincent tapped out a secret code to Mr. Proto with the ring on his finger against the metal leg piping below his desk.

Mr. Proto snapped back a reply to Vincent with the spring ball point pen in his hand.

And probably, for the very first time in this class, Penny Dreadful smiled. She could tell they somehow knew one another.

Chapter 19
A Social Disorder

Britney looked at herself in the mirror of her home bathroom and didn't like what she saw. She had been told by Penny S that she had to bring an insulting gift to the party Penny D invited her to, her thirteenth birthday. She knew that it was supposed to make Penny D feel really bad when she got it so it had to be some really special piece of nastiness.

She resented Penny S for making her be a part of it. Stranger still, she actually believed that Penny S could make her do anything.

Although Britney was used to following orders blindly, she didn't want to do it. She knew she hated the girl, but didn't really know why. She knew she blamed her for any and all the miserable happenings that were going on in her life right now, and she also knew that Penny D had nothing to do with them.

She was so very angry all the time and didn't know what to do about it.

"Britney, what the hell are you doing in there," said her mother from perhaps several rooms away.

"Nothing," screamed Britney back at her blindly.

And then so softly, she said to herself, "I'm doing a whole lot of nothing."

Olivia waited until the very last second to determine what sort of gift she was going to bring to Penny D's birthday party. She knew what her assignment was and didn't want to do it either. Her solution to the problem was to put off even thinking about it.

She told herself that she would find something along the way and that would suffice. It was as if the universe would supply her with a gift. She took this approach with almost everything in her life and it often worked out, so why not now?

As Olivia left her home through the kitchen back door, she passed her mother's purse. She stopped, opened it up and looked inside.

Penny Social herself didn't know why she did the things she did, but she did know that they were considered wrong. They were considered wrong by her mother, her father, most of her teachers, and probably society in general. She didn't know that for sure but it sounded right.

Penny S came from an affluent and well-educated family. It puzzled their neighbors that they would choose to send her through the public education system. They could easily afford better. Few knew and a few suspected, but the reason was that Mr. Social needed something to constantly be at odds with. He set himself up with issues in his life to criticize and therefore something to complain about. He needed a fight to fight, so to speak. He lived for it.

By every definition of a man today, Mr. Social was successful. He had money, he had influence, he had contacts and he was not selfish with them when it came to his family. His daughter was given all the benefits and advantages a girl her age could ask for from their father except one. His attention. And as we all know, that equaled his love.

To meet this natural yearning for his attention Penny S had become what she was today, selfish, materialistic, egocentric and resentful. Some believe that bad people are born that way, and if that were true, it would not be in this case. She was a product of delusional parenting.

It was not that Penny S didn't know right from wrong, she most definitely did. She was far from ignorant. In fact she was quite bright. She could do her school work with great ease and accomplish straight A's. She was also outspoken and manipulative and knew how to get her way in school because she had brains.

Unfortunately she chose another route rather than to use them for good.

Penny S could read a crowd. Or a teacher as it were. She knew right away what she could get away with and what she couldn't. Most of the time it boiled down to almost anything.

She was raised a brat. Plain and simple. If there was any love to be had at home it came in the form of gifts. Sometimes lavish gifts from her father (like; an invitation to the recording of a famous singer's music video, and meeting the star as well).

Julius Kilowatt couldn't stand to be around her, but his manager had held up his contract and pointed to a line that said he was obligated to meet his fans. As unusual as it may sound in the world of entertainment, Julius was a young man of his word and chose to abide by his obligation to his contract.

He met with Penny S, talked with her, gave her free swag and he was so very glad to say goodbye to her so he would never have to see her ever again. Later that week he had his manager call his lawyer and add a line in his contract that said that a young woman named Penny Social was never allowed within one hundred feet of him ever again or he will quit his singing career.

Penny S, the seventh grade crowned princess of Terracotta Junior High School, the sparkle in Miss Novella's eye and class fashion setter, sat in her father's work shed and mixed rat poison into a small cake.

It was still a little fuzzy what exactly happened that day on the playground when Penny Dreadful came into her life and turned everything upside down. There were no credible witnesses to the events, but she knew that it was unsettling and that she didn't like it. That and the saliva on her clothes as well as the urine stain in her new pants made her very bitter.

Yes. This was about revenge. Why else would she make such a big scene about going to Penny D's birthday party? Even Olivia could tell that she didn't want to go.

Penny S tempted fate as she placed the rat poison cake in a box and wrapped it with red paper and a golden ribbon and bow. She looked at it and smiled. Her reflection stared back at her in the shiny ribbon.

She opened a card and wrote the following with the most exquisite hand writing you could imagine;

From one debutante to another, I know that you would never accept a gift from me on this joyous occasion, it would be so uncouth. So, I baked this treat for your pets to enjoy. Happy Birthday, from your friend.

She didn't even sign her name. As if by not committing her name to the card it would extinguish her from all responsibilities. And guilt.

Then in true crazy-person-like fashion, she spoke out loud to herself.

"It's party time," said Penny S, and placed the gift into her backpack.

Chapter 20
Party Games

Penny D was going to throw herself a birthday party. She had never done that before, she had never been invited to one before, and she had never seen one on TV or read about one in a contemporary book before. So what did she have to go on? Call it intuition, inspiration or sheer will power. That and what little advice she had gotten from her mother and father. One way or another she was determined to have a birthday party and make it as memorable as she could.

After all, how hard could it be? She had recently overheard a conversation between Britney and an unknown caller. She spoke loudly and clearly recapping the entire event. For all Penny D knew, since she didn't own a MyPhone, Britney may not have been talking to anyone at all and just pretending to talk to someone to get attention, but it sounded interesting all the same.

Britney told the unidentified caller how she had planned out a party for her mother and father's anniversary. She didn't know or probably care if Penny D was listening even though it was hard to ignore her, she spoke so loudly. Lack of courtesy aside, Penny D did find the entire ritual educational and she was sure she could reproduce it.

Filtering through the information that she had overheard, Penny D focused on the valuable parts and reduced the conversation to a simple mathematical equation.

Penny D subtracted the "crazy quotes and exaggerations" from the sentences and came up with the following formula; a comfortable location, plus exciting food, plus interesting music, plus party games, plus guests who want to be there, equals a good time by all party participants. Simple.

With this in mind, Penny D knew she already had the location covered. Both her parents agreed to allow her to invite her friends to the house. She planned on asking her Uncle Calagari if he could make the refreshments and they had a record player in the living room already where the party was going to be held. Penny D also knew some very smart word definition games and everyone who was invited had agreed to come. This was a near perfect plan as far as she could tell.

There was only one thing left to do; decorate.

When Penny D put her mind to something, even the smallest of projects, she directed all of her energy into it, to accomplish what she began. She learned from her father that no task was too big if she wanted it badly enough. Size meant nothing.

"Okay, let's get started," said Penny D. "Rebecca, you will be in charge of balloon inflation and mechanical reconstruction."

Rebecca saluted Penny D with the tip of her tail to her forehead.

"Check, darling," said Rebecca.

"Hawthorne, you'll be in charge of art direction," said Penny D.

"I got you covered, love," said Hawthorne.

"Bronte, I am leaving the streamer work for you," said Penny D. "Dig deep and give me something real creative."

"Wicked, baby!" said Bronte.

As it had been for all of Penny D's life as far back as she could remember, whenever she needed her Uncle, he would show up standing right next to her having never been called.

"And what will my assignment be, Penny dear?" said Uncle Calagari, who suddenly appeared from nowhere.

"Could you please be in charge of the refreshments, Uncle Calagari?" said Penny D.

The grown up militant attitude that she used to delegate orders to her pets suddenly vanished. To her uncle, she was a very mature twelve year old girl, and he always made her feel more mature than her years. He respected her decision and took what she said very seriously.

Alternately, Penny D could never boss him around. He was her father's only brother, her only uncle. Or at least he was the only one she felt comfortable talking to because she knew he would always drop what he was doing and listen to her. Yet, he brought out the little girl in her and she always spoke to him with a warm respectful and loving attitude.

"Capital idea," said Uncle Calagari. "I have a creative urge coming on even as we speak."

Bronte mumbled under his breath how Calagari got all the "pretty pleases" and sweet talk while they got the laws laid down for them by Penny D.

Her head turned away from Bronte, Rebecca mimicked him to herself. The shadow of her silly mimic could be seen on the wall behind Hawthorne who snickered at what he saw.

"Well, what are we all standing around for, let's get busy," said Penny D.

With almost unimaginable speed and skill all of Penny D's pets went to work for her.

For a python, who is two arms and two legs shy of a human, Rebecca managed to be more capable than most adults Penny D has met so far. She dragged into the room a bicycle pump with her tail and while holding a balloon onto the end of the air nozzle with her mouth, she pumps a balloon full of air.

She inflated one long thin balloon at a time then handed them off to Bronte who skillfully tied a knot at the end of the balloon opening. Soon there was a pile of balloons in the corner of the room in the most exciting of party colors; black, purple, green and a few white ones just for contrast.

With the party balloons all inflated, Rebecca proceeded to stage two; the mechanical reconstruction. She wrapped her body around a bunch of balloons and appeared to crush them, then squeezed them together. When she untied her knotted body from around the balloons, they emerged all twisted into a delightful party design.

The first completed balloon sculpture in a long line of them was a hang man's noose. Rebecca repeated the action and a monstrous bat emerged. She then made a witch on a broom stick and a skeleton that could stand in the corner of the room all by itself. The last of her creations was a balloon guillotine.

The advantage of having several legs was more than a blessing to Bronte. He was a master of multitasking. He loaded up four of his legs with thick rolls of paper streamers and ran up the side of the wall.

With an accuracy only associated with a theraphosidae he managed to stream the crepe paper across the ceiling from one corner of the room to the center. Then he artfully fills in between the streamed paper with web-like loops. When complete the entire ceiling appeared to be covered by a giant spider web.

Hawthorne could only carry one balloon sculpture in his mouth at a time as he ran up the shuttered windows. He leapt onto a wall sconce, then onto a stuffed animal head. He ran along the wall edging to attach one balloon sculpture to a different object in the room.

He placed a balloon witch's hat on top of the moose head, balloon battle weapons around each of the wall sconces and around the picture frames, he placed balloon silhouettes of ghostly apparitions.

On one trip back down the window shutters Hawthorne tipped over a lamp. The light from the lamp cast a shadow of a balloon monster onto a wall. The projected nightmarish shape hung appropriately behind the large comfy couch.

"Nice touch," said Penny D, unaware of the happy little accident.

Hawthorne took a bow and set about placing more balloons in front of other light sources. Fiendish shadows began to emerge on opposite walls.

Penny D collapsed on the couch, a bright and proud smile on her face. Her friends all stood back and admired their work as well. With one glance they all knew and silently agreed that they did one amazing job together. The room looked as though something very strange and beautiful were about to take place there.

All of the windows in the Dreadful Mansion were either shuttered or boarded up. Since there was no natural light illuminating the living room, nor any other room here, one could easily get disoriented in a place like this.

This was just one result of Natty's design: to create a timeless space in his home. "Do what makes you feel good. Keep it honest and happy and the result will always be perfect," was what Natty would say.

This was what Penny D was taught all her life. It was what she practiced as well. But the following few hours or minutes or days as it were, since time meant nothing here, was about to re-shape the very fabric of all she was taught, and to reveal to her the secret she was never told.

Let the party begin.

The doorbells rang repeatedly as if someone were pulling down on the chain from outside over and over again. Penny D jumped up to answer the door.

"That's them," said Penny D. "Places everyone."

And she clapped her hands twice.

Rebecca coiled up into a large woven basket in the corner, she pulled on the lid with her tail.

Hawthorne ran up the pendulum of the misshapen grandfather's clock, disappearing from view behind the half-sun half-moon face.

Bronte ran up the wall and between the paper webbing he created on the ceiling before settling himself in the center like a stuffed display.

"Really?" said Penny D with attitude to Bronte.

It would appear she was getting the hang of the new lingo that the other seventh graders were using.

"What?" said Bronte. "I want to watch. It's not like anyone will notice."

"Whatever," said Penny D.

Again she said it with that seventh-grader tone of voice, with a little bit of valley girl thrown in. Penny D didn't know that they didn't go together.

Uncle Calagari wound up the record player and set the needle onto the record. An eerie slow jazz recording, probably from the turn of the last century, whined out of the flower shaped speaker filling the large room.

Penny D ran to the front door but calmed herself down before opening it. Malcolm was standing in the doorway with an overnight bag thrown over his shoulder and a large wrapped gift under one arm. He was dressed differently from the way he was at school, he was wearing his fancy gold vest.

"I've been circling the block for thirty minutes," said Malcolm. "Am I late yet?"

"No," said Penny D. "Actually you're the first to arrive."

"Oh, snap!" said Malcolm. "I wanted to be fashionably late."

"I guess everyone did," said Penny D.

Malcolm walked right past Penny D (with her gift) into the living room. Clearly lacking the contemporary social skills of her peers, Penny D wondered to herself if showing a birthday girl her gift and then depriving her of it was correct or not. Committed to going with the flow, she closed the door and followed him in.

Malcolm spun around, he was mesmerized by the room.

"You know, when I had the chicken pox and a high fever, my bedroom looked just like this place," said Malcolm.

"Ah, thanks?" said Penny D.

Malcolm inspected one of the portraits on the wall. It

appeared to be looking right at him and smiling. He backed up a few steps and then moved to his right and then to his left. Penny D did the same. She figured that this was what they were supposed to do at parties, but she didn't know why.

"What is it with the eyes in that painting?" said Malcolm. "They keep following me."

"Oh," said Penny D, laughing to herself. "It's a very old painting technique. A clear glaze is painted over the oil painted eyes to give them a three dimensional look. An optical illusion, really. It makes it look like the eyes are actually watching you. In fact, it dates back to the early..."

"Sweet," said Malcolm, ending the explanation.

He was so impressed by the 3-D look of the eyes that he had cut her off without even thinking. He was not trying to be rude but, his mind was racing and he was thinking of how he could use this technique in a prank.

The doorbells rang again and Penny D ran to answer it.

It was Harold this time with his overnight bag.

"Sorry, I know I'm early but I wanted to be the first to arrive," said Harold.

"It sucks to be you," said Penny, making full use of her seventh grade lingo. "Malcolm beat you to it. Come on in anyway."

Harold clearly looked disappointed, but entered anyway. He showed Penny D a tiny wrapped gift as he entered the house as if it were a ticket to enter a movie theater.

"Don't worry, I brought a gift," said Harold.

"I wasn't," said Penny D.

He then put the gift back into his pocket rather than giving it to her. Penny D was as confused as she had been before and still unsure if this was the custom in this new culture. She didn't know if she enjoyed being part of it.

Why show someone their gift and then not give it to them? She shrugged her shoulders because she knew in her heart that these were two real friends and so she overlooked it, and closed the door.

The doorbells suddenly rang again. The fun part of the

party may be over with, Penny D thought to herself. She knew full well who must be right on the other side of the door.

When Penny D opened the door, Penny S was standing there chewing gum and looking like a cow might look eating hay. She also looked quite bored.

What looked even stranger to Penny D, was that Penny S had her backpack with her and it appeared quite full. She expected her to show up, if for no other reason than to find something to gossip about at school, but stay the night as well? That girl was an odd one indeed, she thought.

Britney stepped up behind her with a rather "creeped-out" look on her face.

"Hello," said Penny D, and nothing more.

Her modern seventh grade lingo escaped her.

"Are the animals back in their cages?" said Penny S. "Because if they're not we are out of here."

"They're, away," said Penny D.

As Penny S entered she took the gum out from her mouth and placed it into Penny D's hand. "Take care of that for me, will ya," said Penny S.

Britney handed Penny D a flower, or the flowering part of a weed, as it were. She obviously plucked it from a garden along the way. Some dirt still dangled from one of the long roots that hung below.

"Oh, you shouldn't have," said Penny D.

"I almost didn't," said Britney.

"Is that a zit?" said Penny D.

"No, it's a beauty mark!" said Britney, knowing full well that Penny D had just gotten the best of her, feeding her anger.

Britney shrunk her face into her chest as if that would make it easier to hide the pimples.

Olivia was the last to enter the Dreadful Mansion, her eyes wide with amazement. She just couldn't bring herself to do what Penny S had asked of her. Olivia was never a mean child, she was a lost child and she knew it. She also believed that she couldn't disobey Penny S, so she did the next best thing. She brought a gift that was neither an insult nor of any interest to Penny D.

She held out a "One-Dollar-Off" coupon for a car wash.

"My mother says that these always comes in handy," said Olivia successfully hiding her embarrassment.

"Thank you," said Penny D.

Penny D was unsure what to make of this. She didn't drive, let alone own a car. Could this have been part of the birthday rituals of the Junior High School students of this town? The only thing she knew for sure was that Olivia's gift was not intended to be an insult.

She followed her three new guests into the living room knowing all the while it was wrong to think to herself that it would have been just a grand party without two of them. She could have avoided it all by not inviting them but hadn't.

She also knew the only reason she caved in was because she thought that Malcolm would have backed out of the party if she hadn't invited Olivia. Then she and Harold would have been the only two humans at the party.

Perhaps her pets Bronte, Rebecca and Hawthorne would have been able to join them instead of pretending to be part of the furniture. That was not a bad scenario and she knew it. She also knew that it was all her own doing. She got exactly what she had asked for. So she was determined to make the best of it.

Harold was an easy read, he probably would have attended any party, if he were asked. He lacked social skills and was extremely self-conscious of just about everything he did, except playing video games.

Penny D now saw that Malcolm was a true friend indeed and would have come to the party as well, regardless of whether Olivia was coming or not. The size of the gift he had brought her clearly showed some level of appreciation and thought. Judging from the sloppy wrapping, he must have wrapped it himself. That showed sincerity and true character.

It didn't take Penny S long before the insults began. She stood in the center of the room and launched her attack.

"Who was your decorator, Frankenstein?" said Penny S.

"He was a scientist," said Penny D, "Why would he decorate a living room?"

"No, he was zombie, stupid," said Britney.

"He was a monster, can we leave it at that?" said Penny S.

"I'm going out on a limb here, but I am guessing you never read the book," said Penny D.

"A book?" said Britney. "I thought it was a cartoon."

Chapter 21
The Thirteenth Hour

The portraits on the walls of the living room said it all. Their once happy expressions had changed to sad and disgusted ones. Even Penny D looked up at them oddly. She couldn't ever remember seeing their faces look that way before.

You can't blame them (the portraits), really, it was not a very lively party. There was music coming from the wind up record player but practically no talking in the room at all. Penny S and Britney fell into the super-soft couch. It didn't act at all like the warm cuddle place that we had seen it become previously, it stood steadfast and couch-like. As if it didn't want anything to do with who was sitting on it.

They both began texting with their MyPhones as if it were a race. Britney held hers up from time to time to shoot something in the room, then tried to post it, most likely on her social networking page.

"Look what I wrote below this picture," said Britney to Penny S.

"Truth," said Penny S, then spoke aloud as if someone should attend to her immediate need. "Will someone kill the old fart music and turn on the TV."

"TV?" said Penny D. "Ah, we don't have one."

"Then let's go watch the one in your room."

"I don't have one in my room."

Olivia laughed out loud. Who knew she could do that?

"You are so funny," said Olivia. "I've got to remember that one. May I use it?"

"Ah, sure?" said Penny D.

"The next thing you're going to tell us is that you don't have a MyPhone," said Britney.

Penny S turned up the music on her MyPhone to something popular.

Penny D looked miserable. This was not how she had expected it to go at all. She always held to the outcome of her plans and those plans were that her birthday party turn out just grand. They always came true for her. Her dreams and wishes were always fulfilled. So, what had happened here?

Granted, she also knew there would be some adjustments for her going to a new school and for the first time in her life having made some new friends. But this was unbearable!

What was she doing wrong, she thought to herself? And what was her original wish? It was the same as it had always been, that everything turns out for the best for her. That was her promise to herself, so how could it be failing her now? Could this be the first in a long line of failures for her? Is this what it means to grow older?

Penny D thought hard. She had so many questions, many more than usual. She suddenly remembered that when she separated herself from the situation the solution to her challenge always came more quickly. This was no different than when she was hiding out the Girl's Wash Room, and she came to the same conclusion.

There was something out of balance here at the party and that was the cause. Now all she has to do was find out what it was. She directed her attention back to her guests and listened very carefully to their conversation.

She began with Olivia who was sitting on a leg rest

unaffected by her surroundings one way or the other. Malcolm was balancing next to her on the arm rest of the couch.

"Hello, Olivia," said Malcolm.

"Who are you?" said Olivia.

Malcolm was stumped. This was something he had not been expecting. They were in the same classes and in the same school since kindergarten. In first grade, he once found her crying on the playground at recess. When she told him she forgot her milk money that day he gave her his chocolate milk. She said thank you and he believed she meant it.

He had had a crush on her ever since. He'd felt a special unstated bond with her after that day and thought of himself as her knight in shining armor. Or court jester, as he more correctly fashioned himself. This had been his fantasy come true, to be at a party with her, until it had all come crashing down around him a moment ago. He could tell from the look on her face she really didn't know who he was at all, but Malcolm being Malcolm, shrugged it off and started from scratch.

"I'm your, butler, for this evening," said Malcolm.

Like a magician he slipped off the arm rest cover from under his butt and draped it over one arm like a towel, to appear as he imagined a butler to look. Or a waiter. Malcolm didn't really know the difference.

"No spit," said Olivia. "I have my own butler?"

"Yes, Madame Olivia," said Malcolm, then smiled.

Malcolm never realized how little it took to get Olivia interested in someone other than Penny S. He'd tried for years to make her laugh at his antics. He'd even convinced himself that he was doing it all for her, to get her attention and for no other reason, so that she would find him funny and smart and amazing. But it never happened. Not yet.

Not that anything he believed about her would have made a difference, Malcolm was a born clown. And he would have done all those crazy things anyway. They made him happy.

They looked comfortable, Penny D thought to herself. So she changed her focused to Harold.

Harold was a different person this evening. He felt free of the school room labels. Tonight he was asked over to his best friend's home for a birthday party, as he put it to himself. He knew for a fact that he had friends now. He was finally popular. He had even bought her a gift with the money he saved from his allowance. He was at the top of his game.

Harold had two older brothers. They were both more than ten years older than him. That made him the baby. He was the last in line for the throne in their house. Or as Harold referred to it, a position of authority that demanded respect from his parents.

They, his parents, were a hard working couple and by the time Harold came along they were too set in their ways to provide him with anything special like attention.

His two brothers both worked in a gas station. They both earned money and were revered as child prodigies. They left High School behind, and a higher education was no longer part of their future plans. They were comfortable sleeping in the basement, eating at home with mom still doing their laundry. The money they earned from their job went directly into the bank to save up for a new car one day.

Harold became the lost child who sat in front of the television or played video games much later than any child should be allowed to. He was so completely unseen by both parents and both older brothers, that Harold had no choice but to become a master of the digital universe. This gave him comfort.

He may have been a gaming champion, but the only people who knew it were several of his classmates, a boy in Japan of equal skill, a girl in Nepal with a similar skill and some unknown person on the internet who didn't wish to be identified. He would only play on line with Harold at three AM and went by the name of Apogee.

But tonight, with his new found confidence Harold felt compelled to start up a conversation with Britney. He believed that she thought of him as a brainy child who would most likely own a conglomerate computer company one day and that she would apply to for a secretary's position there when they were all grown up.

Harold decided he would give her the opportunity to become his friend now before he earned the billions of dollars one day that would turn him into a social recluse (not that he wasn't one of those at the moment).

"Where is your sleep-over bag?" said Harold.

Britney just laughed out loud, not even looking at Harold when she did so. Anger makes you do some very odd things.

Just when Penny D had begun to think that this was going nowhere, she noticed Rebecca, forever the romantic, slithering her tail out of the wicker basket. She was careful not to allow herself to be seen by anyone else, but little escaped Penny D when it came to her pets. Like all good friends, they were in perfect sync.

Rebecca's tail hugged the baseboard of the wall until it reached the record player. She knew that Penny D loved swing music and she also knew that if a record of said music were suddenly to play, she would drop what she was doing, or in this case not doing, and dance.

So, with lightning speed, Rebecca whipped her tail up and flipped off the record on the turntable, then slapped on a new record. Then she wound up the machine and set the needle in place.

From the very dawn of time it is well documented that music can change the mood of almost anyone who was listening. With that in mind, Rebecca felt that what this party needed was a good jazz swing record to liven things up.

As soon as those first few cords of music were played, Penny D did in fact begin to snap her fingers and tap her toe.

Soon Penny D was on the floor cuttin' the rug, dancing like a fool, and not caring who saw her or why. She did a Jitterbug / Lindy Hop mix. Yeah, Penny D knew how to swing!

Malcolm couldn't help but get caught up in that crazy music, his father was a record collector from way back. On summer nights when all the windows were open Malcolm could clearly hear one unusual music selection after another bellowing out of the garage.

It was there that Malcolm's mother had her husband store the four thousand plus records that he had been collecting, from his youth right up to the present. This was his father's, "Man Cave of Music," as he put it. Music was his passion.

Malcolm knew what was at stake here and he was inspired to join in. Penny D may have just recently become a friend of his, but she went to bat for him and he for her. She invited Olivia to her party for him, and only because he asked her to. No other reason. He knew that she could have said no, and that Olivia ran with a bad crowd. Actually, it was not a crowd, it was a company of two. So it was time for Malcolm to man up. Again.

It took but only a moment before he was in the middle of the living room dancing with Penny D. It was all free style. Completely improvisational.

Penny D and Malcolm were having the greatest time dancing to the rhythm of the music.

Music can change the way we feel and Penny D knew it. She concluded that it was not a "something" that was missing from her party, like a Television or a MyPhone, but the fun was what was missing!

She knew that sad music made us feel sad and happy music made us cheerful, and swing music made us want to swing. All except for Penny S and Britney, that is.

They quickly found their own water level to rise to. Rather than joining in and having fun, they took turns recording the dancing with their MyPhones and attempting to upload it onto their social network page again. Strangely, they couldn't get any wi-fi reception in the Dreadful Mansion at all. Hmmm, I wonder why?

Harold joined in the dancing and even did his own little interpretation of sorts. He knew nothing of rhythm, swing music, dance or what he was even doing, but he joined in anyway. This was perhaps the very first time in his entire life he had ever done this, but he knew it felt good.

The big surprise came when Olivia joined in to dance.

Penny D backed away and let her dance opposite Malcolm and whatever Harold was doing in the middle of the living room floor. It suddenly looked as though this party was on a roll. The joint was jumpin'.

But like all party-poopers, Penny S just couldn't let anyone have any fun unless she were involved and having more fun than anyone else there.

So when the jazz instrumentals came to an abrupt halt, everyone heard what Penny S intended for only Britney to hear, as silence hit the room.

"What does Olivia think she's doing?" said Penny S, then turned her attention to Olivia. "You're not allowed to have fun here."

The only other sound in the room was the needle skipping at the end of the song and the panting of Penny D, Olivia, Malcolm and Harold trying to catch their breaths.

"I'm working up an appetite," said Olivia without missing a beat. "Oh, butler, when will the party refreshments be served?"

Malcolm didn't even have the time to make up an answer before Uncle Calagari appeared right behind him with a tray of delicacies held out with one hand.

"Here you are, young lady and gentleman," said Uncle Calagari. "Try one, yes?"

Olivia carefully eyed the bite-sized crackers with jelly elegantly arranged atop them on the plate. She picked one up and tosseed it into her mouth. She immediately began to talk with her mouth full.

"Not bad at all," said Olivia. "What is this?"

Uncle Calagari held out a second plate of food to Britney. She carefully eyed it over with a neutral expression on her face that quickly turned brighter. There were tiny drum sticks on the plate glazed with a pineapple sauce and they looked delicious. Britney snapped one up and began to chew on it like a wolf who had starved through the winter.

"For you, young lady," said Uncle Calagari to Olivia, "well aged caviar. And for you...," turning back to Britney, "...New

Orleans style swamp chicken."

"Olivia?" said Penny S. "Like, you're eating fish eggs."

Her imitation valley girl accent made her comment sound all the more ridiculous.

Olivia stopped chewing for a moment and thought about what Penny S had said.

"Is that a bad thing?" said Olivia.

"Only for the fish," said Britney.

Then she laughed, and tiny bits of food shot out of her mouth.

"Penny S, try the chicken, it's sick," said Britney.

Penny D had been very quiet for most of this, she was taking it all in. She'd found the answer she was seeking and there was more to come. Under ordinary circumstances she may have kept her mouth shut but as the hostess of her own party she felt obligated to answer this one question.

"Swamp chicken, Britney," said Penny D.

"Chicken is chicken, yo," said Britney.

"My dear guest, you are eating boiled and glazed frog," said Uncle Calagari.

Britney had to stop and think, she was unsure if this were a malicious trick of some kind and she were the victim, or if there was a misunderstanding. She knew the drum stick came from an adult so the story had to be true. She began to choke and spit out the food on her plate.

Malcolm leaned over to Uncle Calagari, his hand held out in the kindest of gestures.

"And I thought I was the master pranksta," said Malcolm. "I see now I have so much to learn. Will you teach me?"

"Serves you right," said Penny S. "I'm not eating anything in this place."

Uncle Calagari leaned over to Harold with yet another tray of food.

"Have a chocolate covered strawberry, young man?" said Uncle Calagari.

"Will I?" said Harold.

With that, Harold stuffed five of the sweet treats into his

mouth.

Malcolm was feeling just about as good as he could and leapt to his feet. He picked up the gift box that he had brought with him and carried it over to Penny D. Oddly, it appears that Uncle Calagari is no longer in the room.

"Penny D, I can wait no longer," said Malcolm. "Open my gift first."

"Oh, good," said Penny S. "We're up to that part."

She readied her backpack, her fingers on the zipper.

Malcolm shot a disapproving glance at Penny S, but for only a moment. He then directed his attention back towards Penny D who was gently undoing the plastic tape holding the wrapping onto Malcolm's gift.

"Who taught you how to open gifts?" said Malcolm. "Tear it apart!"

There was a queer look on Penny D's face as if wondering if it was proper, then without thinking it through any further she tore into the wrapping and exposed a cardboard box. She opened the box and lifted out its contents. It was a plush rat doll that looked a lot like Hawthorne. The only difference was that it had a red bow on its head.

Hawthorne peeked out of the clock through a little door on the face and was excited by what he saw.

"Oh momma!" said Hawthorne.

Penny S and Britney had finally given up on entertaining themselves whispering to one another, shooting pictures with their MyPhones and failing to upload them to the internet. They found a new way to express themselves and their displeasure, by just rolling their eyes at everything that happens.

"Oh, sweet!" said Penny D. "It looks just like. . .well, not that I would know anything about what rats look like. Silly me. Thank you Malcolm."

Penny D gave Malcolm a big hug.

Malcolm turned to Olivia.

"Who's the man?" said Malcolm. "I'm the man."

"I thought you were the butler," said Olivia.

"Open mine next," said Harold with a mouth still full of

food. "Here."

Penny held up the tiny package, no bigger than a ten slice pack of gum. She wondered how many worms could fit in this box, and if there were worms in this box could they still be alive? Then a smile came across her face. Her faith in Harold grew by the second.

The wrapping slipped off of Harold's gift rather quickly and left Penny D holding a brightly colored butterfly pin. She pressed a tiny button disguised as the butterflies head and the wings began to flap as it played the tune, "Way Down Upon The Swanee River." Red, green and pink colored lights danced from within it.

Penny S and Britney smothered their laughter on the couch, while tears rolled up in their eyes.

Penny D shut off the musical pin and placed it in her pocket.

"Thank you, Harold," said Penny D. "I always wanted one of these, and never dared to buy one for myself."

"Why's that?" said Penny S, "They didn't have one in black and played a funeral march?"

She and Britney again began to giggle amongst themselves. Olivia was about to toss another cracker in her mouth but paused to giggle without knowing why. She then tossed back the cracker.

Penny D gave Harold a great big hug, and when she let go it looked as though Harold were going to cry.

"Thank you, Harold," said Penny D.

"How mushy could you get?" said Penny S.

"I guess this means the cake is next and we're done," said Britney.

Penny D was not expecting this kind of request. When she overheard Britney discuss how perfect her party turned out there was no mention of a cake.

"Cake," said Penny D. "What cake?"

"The birthday cake, Einstein," said Britney. "If there's no cake, then like what are we doing here? Let's blow this novelty stand."

"Wait!" said Harold. "What about the birthday games?"

Penny S and Britney stood and picked off the animal hairs from their clothing, and dropped them back onto the couch where they'd been sitting.

Malcolm puppeteered the rat doll he gave to Penny D, making it move as if it were alive. He made it leap onto Britney's shoulder.

"Squeak, squeak," said Malcolm.

Britney screamed out and Malcolm laughed.

Britney turned her anger towards Penny S.

"Why exactly are we here again?" said Britney. "And what is that smell?"

"Oh, ah, safety," said Malcolm, as if that made his flatulence socially acceptable.

Britney and Penny S held their noses and moved away from Malcolm.

Olivia was trying to peek out the front window between the closed up shutters.

"It got dark quickly," said Olivia. "I wonder if there is a storm coming."

"A storm?" said Penny D. "That means it is almost my birthday."

Malcolm and Harold ran to the window.

"You were born during a storm?" said Malcolm.

"That's the rumor," said Penny D. "Just past midnight."

"Midnight!" said Britney. "Not waiting, I'm out of here right now."

Penny S looked at her MyPhone, it said 11:59. Then she looked over at the grandfather's clock across the room. The hands showed that it was almost midnight as well.

"That's cra'y cra'y," said Penny S.

She shook her MyPhone as if it were a watch.

"It must be correct, my phone displays the same thing," said Harold. "Almost the witching hour."

"We have not been here that long, dimwit," said Britney.

The grandfather clock suddenly chimed very loudly. So loudly in fact that all conversation, what little there was, suddenly came to a halt. Malcolm counted the chimes on his fingers. Immediately after the twelfth chime he held up the rat doll in victory.

"That's twelve!" said Malcolm in his silly rat voice.

"Awe, that's cute," said Olivia.

"Happy Birthday, Penny Dreadful," is what both Malcolm and Harold were about to say when a thirteenth chime was heard. Then they all fell silent.

"What a bunch of freaks!" said Penny S just before all the lights went out.

Was it a mere moment in time or was it an eternity before the lights came back on? Penny D wasn't sure. Neither was Malcolm. Neither was Harold. Perhaps only Uncle Calagari knew for sure. But he never told.

The only thing that they knew for sure was that Uncle Calagari was suddenly in the room with them when the lights came back on. His arms were opened wide and a grin was proudly displayed on his face.

Oh, and one other thing. Penny Social, Britney Britannica and Olivia Smothers were gone. Not left the house gone, but disappeared gone.

"Congratulations, Penny, my dear niece," said Uncle Calagari. "I knew it all along. You are indeed one of us."

He reached out and shook her hand.

Chapter 22
Let the Goth Games Begin

Malcolm and Harold also shook Penny D's hand and congratulated her.

"Thank you," said Penny D. "Ah, thank you. Thank you, but where did the girls go? And what did you mean when you said, you're one of us?"

Uncle Calagari, being as courteous as he could began to answer his niece's question about the three missing girls in a low tone of voice. It didn't appear that he was at all worked up over them or that he even cared.

"Those three silly girls, you ask?" said Uncle Calagari. "They went away to where all the mean children go. Humph."

Then he spoke up with as much vim and vigor to his voice that he could muster.

"And as for you my dear little niece, you are a true Goth just like your father," said Uncle Calagari. "And me, of course. But that was never in dispute."

"Duh, like tell us something we didn't already know," said Malcolm.

Harold raised his hand.

"Ah, I have a question," said Harold. "What exactly is a

Goth?"

"It's a fashion statement and a bad attitude," said Malcolm. "That's what my mother says."

"Wait," said Penny D. "Hold on. Uncle, what do you mean, gone? Where did they go?"

Then Calagari's voice changed again and he answered her in as a nonchalant tone as he could.

"They were called away to the Gothic Kingdom, my dear," said Uncle Calagari politely. "Probably never to be seen or heard of ever again, blah, blah, blah."

It was like being on a roller coaster ride with him; he was acting like two different people. When Calagari addressed the issue at hand that Penny D felt was important, the missing girls, his voice dropped way way down, as if he were only humoring her with an answer. She never experienced a time like this. Penny D was more used to her Uncle encouraging her to ask questions about anything she didn't understand.

And then there was that rattling on he was doing about some imaginary place called the Gothic Kingdom that Penny S, Britney and the poor half-witted Olivia had been sent off to. What was going on here, Penny D wondered to herself?

Yet the second personality, the more vibrant version of the Uncle she thought she knew began to tell her a story about her life that she didn't know yet, one that she wanted to know more of.

"Let us consider your heritage, Penny dear," continued Uncle Calagari in a robust voice, "It is more than just a fashion statement, young Malcolm. It is a state of being, child."

Penny D had read about people with split personalities and bipolar disorders. She was determined to give her uncle as much respect as she could when he spoke, but she was also determined to get to the bottom of this mystery.

"But, this Gothic Kingdom?" said Penny D. "Wha. . .what is that?"

Malcolm had not really been following the story so far since it pertained to Penny S and Britney. He thought that it couldn't possibly bare any fruit of importance. Then he remembered that Olivia was with them. The conversation suddenly sounded like they could be in some danger. His wisdom kicked in and he became more concerned.

"Time out," said Malcolm. "Swamp chicken, missing children, Gothic Kingdom. Okay, I'm getting creeped out. I need to call my mom."

Malcolm took out his MyPhone and tapped in a number.

"That is a secret for me to keep, dear Penny," said Uncle Calagari. "And one for you to explore if you so desire. There is no need to talk about a place that you have never been to when you could experience it on your own. First hand. Yes."

"I'm concerned about my classmates, Uncle," said Penny D in a straight forward manner.

"Then if you are considering a rescue, you will need to make your decision quickly," said Uncle Calagari. "They don't appear too bright to me and there is no telling how long they could survive on their own."

Then Calagari laughed a bit too giddily to himself. As if he was enjoying every moment of this.

Harold was still working on those chocolate covered strawberries, stuffing them in his mouth like rocket fuel. He looked as though he was not paying attention at all to the conversation in the room, but in truth it was quite the opposite. He was taking it all in and he was lost in thought. It was as if he were watching a new video game unfold before him, memorizing the possibilities, the advantages and unlocking their secrets.

"Survive?" said Penny D. "You mean they could be in danger?"

Penny D was now thinking to herself that this may just be the answer to what she was looking for all along. This unknown place might divulge the true answers to her questions. Could this be a turning point in her life even. Not just a temporary solution, or a band aid remedy as she had come to expect. Something unusual was happening and she knew it. She couldn't put her finger on it yet but she wished with all her might for it to reveal itself.

It was as if the trunk at the foot of her bed had suddenly opened and all of those confusing questions jumped on out and were waiting for her.

"All I ever wanted to do was have a normal birthday party," said Penny D. "To fit in. How did it come to this?"

"Why you asked for it, Penny dear, this is your birthday wish come true," said Uncle Calagari. "You wanted to be normal, so tonight you will be just that. You will come to know who you really are by challenging yourself to prove you are a true Goth indeed. Find those little brats wherever they are hidden in the Gothic Kingdom because that is something only a true Goth could do."

Then his voice took a dive, probably just for dramatic purposes.

"And learn a little something about your unique heritage in the process," said Uncle Calagari. "Now tell me that, isn't exciting?"

"Okay, you got my attention," said Penny D. "I'm in."

The sweet little girl voice was gone. She suddenly sounded like an adult, not all corny and full of the serious false flattery of pretending she was self-important. Penny D sounded like a mature child of her years ready to accept the responsibility of the situation and take charge.

There was no reason for suspicion or any distrust between her and her uncle. She had known him and loved him for as long as she could remember.

"So how exactly do I get to this Gothic Kingdom?" said Penny D.

Bronte was the first to leap down in front of them and join in.

Rebecca sprang out of the woven basket and landed right next to Bronte, she coiled around Penny Ds' feet.

Hawthorne came running down the clock and sat up right next to Rebecca.

Malcolm was talking to his mother on the phone when he saw that the stories about Penny D's pets were true after all. She was a master of strange animals, he thought.

Harold reached out and stroked Rebecca as if she were a dog. She folded back to meet him face to face and smiled, then licked his face with her tiny thin tongue.

"If you're game, your pets here can lead you to a portal that will bring you to the other side," said Uncle Calagari. "But remember, each time you commit to a portal you will find yourself in a different part of the kingdom. And, if you are successful, to one of the missing brats. You may save them if you like, or not. I leave that to you."

This was getting way too intense for Malcolm to be talking to his mother on the phone.

"I changed my mind," said Malcolm. "Bye mom."

And with that he closed his MyPhone, his mother still talking away.

"I have a question, Master Pranksta?" said Malcolm.

"Yes, funny lad," said Uncle Calagari, pointing at him.

"Why even bother, sir?" said Malcolm. "It's not like they're worth it. Except maybe for Olivia, she has potential."

Uncle Calagari didn't have to answer, Penny D had known all along that this was her cue.

"Because, Malcolm," said Penny D, "we're not like them. You knew I would go all along, didn't you, Uncle?"

"If you are true to your heritage, and the daughter of the House of the Poisonberry, no, you didn't really have a choice," said Uncle Calagari.

Penny D took a moment to take that all in and reflect. It was as if her whole life had played out in one quick theatrical scene right in front of her. All her questions were about to be answered. That big fat elephant in her room that she had kept locked up in the trunk at the foot of the bed for so many years was just bursting to talk. All she had to do was the right thing all along and she had.

"Besides," said Penny D, "how else am I going to learn about why I am different?"

"Precisely!" said Uncle Calagari. "A challenge always brings out our true character. Remember Penny, your greatest power comes from being good. That is how your dreams become real. Are you ready for your journey?"

"You're not going alone," said Malcolm.

"What do you mean?" said Penny D.

"Because we're going with you," said Harold.

He took out his "Super X Boy" hat from a place no one was quite sure of and put it on.

Penny D wore a very proud look on her face. This may just be the amazing birthday she was wanting after all.

Rebecca hissed loudly and slithered up the oddly shaped stairs.

"Becka says to follow her," said Penny D.

"Let's move out!" said Harold.

He took the lead and ran after Rebecca. Against all odds and perhaps his own perception of himself (and reality), Harold climbed up the flat stairs leading to the second floor.

"I thought that was a painting," said Malcolm, running after Harold.

Penny D, Hawthorne and Bronte follow.

Natty and Lucinda suddenly appeared in the living room right next to Uncle Calagari.

"Nat, are you sure we should let her go?" said Lucinda.

"She isn't alone, Lucinda," said Natty. "She has her wits and her pets to keep her safe."

"Mostly nit-wits from what I gather, Natty," said Uncle Calagari.

"If we go with her, Lucinda, the Count will surely to be waiting," said Natty. "A lot can be said for the element of surprise."

"We can't stay here forever and the Count knows it," said Uncle Calagari. "Sooner or later we will all have to return."

"Then it will be up to Penny to find the family fortune," said Lucinda. "And restore our good name. Just think, Natty, you could go home again."

"I'm okay with that," said Natty.

Chapter 23
The Return to the Gothic Kingdom

What would have been thought impossible by either of Penny D's two house guests only moments before had now become their mission. Together, they were going to travel to an unknown place and rescue two very bad girls (and one very mixed up one).

Malcolm and Harold raced through the upstairs halls of the Dreadful Mansion with fearless abandon. Like a carnival fun house, the floor and walls of the hall moved and bent guiding them forever forward, as if they approved of the boys' destination.

The doors to other rooms along the way folded up and into the walls before they passed them, preventing Harold and Malcolm from entering the wrong chamber.

Finally, at the end of the hall, was a great wooden door with a patchwork of charcoal drawings nailed to it. Each image depicted an exaggerated humanoid figure, perhaps in excruciating pain, screaming for some sort of justice. Or were they just comically illustrated?

The door opened automatically for all of them to enter. Malcolm recoiled in horror as he looked around the room.

Strangely, it was not much different than his own room; it was just as cluttered with personal items but not at all as dirty. If he were asked why he didn't clean his room, he would tell you he had an irrational fear of vacuum cleaners.

"This can't be right," said Malcolm. "What horrible chamber is this?"

By now Penny D and all of her pets had caught up to them and had entered the room. She placed one gentle hand on Malcolm's shoulder.

"This is my bedroom," said Penny D.

"I like what you've done with the place," said Malcolm.

He was always quick with a save.

Rebecca dove under Penny D's bed and into the darkness. Her tail whipped around the room and knocked the metal mask that Penny D had created in metal shop off of her night stand and onto the floor. Bronte and Hawthorne scurried across the floor after Rebecca.

They brushed past the helmet. It spun like a top and then, it too disappeared under the bed with them.

"That's it," said Harold. "The portal. It's under your bed."

"Oh, please don't make me go under there," said Malcolm.

"Why not?" said Penny D.

"Dust bunnies, rotten candy and old underwear, that's why," said Malcolm, making an unusual face.

"Malcolm, I clean under my bed," said Penny D. "No underwear, I promise."

"Gangway!" said Harold.

And with that he dove head first across the floor and slipped under Penny D's bed and out of sight.

"Who was that?" said Malcolm.

"That was Harold Milquetoast, man of action," said Penny D.

Malcolm and Penny D glanced at each other one last time then rolled along the floor until they too, disappeared under the bed.

Behold, The Gothic Kingdom!

Not unlike the last time we were here, the buildings and landscape were still a wash of grey with only a hint of color here or there. It may have been the middle of the night, or just before dawn, it was hard to tell. Needless to say, it was dark.

What little could be seen of the streets was illuminated by the candle lit lanterns that hung above the old shops that lined the road.

Penny D, her friends and her pets suddenly fell out of a doorway and onto the cobblestones together in one tangled mess. They slowly unwound themselves and looked around at where they were. Except for Harold, he was wondering when they were.

It appeared they had have fallen onto an old European street, perhaps a few centuries ago. The houses and artisan shops were dark and foreboding and had traces of gothic architecture. It didn't resemble anything in Terracotta.

"Where are we?" said Malcolm.

Rebecca coiled herself into a noble pose, she looked comfortable and right at home.

"Young lady and gentlemen, welcome to the Gothic Kingdom," said Rebecca, and she bowed to them.

"The snake, I mean the python, it talked," said Malcolm. "It's finally happened, I'm cracking up."

Bronte leapt up onto Penny D's shoulder.

"Out here, we all speak the same lingo, kid," said Bronte. "Even Chinese and Swahili have a Brooklyn accent to my ear."

"Now that's just plain freaky," said Malcolm, pointing at Bronte.

Harold wasn't the least bit affected by his surroundings or the talking animals. He began to search through his pockets. He had other concerns.

"I wonder if my worm can talk?" said Harold.

Harold gently pulled a worm out of his pocket as if it was the last strand of spaghetti left in the pot.

"We certainly can," said the worm. "Now stop sticking us in your pockets, you moron."

"Oh, I'm sorry," said Harold to the worm. "I didn't know."

"Now put me down and go away," said the worm. "I have business to attend to."

"Business, what sort of business?" said Harold.

"I'm no ordinary worm, I'm a conqueror worm," said the worm. "I have armies to unite and lands to seize."

"Of course you do," said Harold and he placed the worm on the ground.

"Charge!" said the worm and he plowed head first into the earth between the cobblestones.

This place was as new to Penny D as it was to Malcolm and Harold. However, Harold found it down right interesting. He had wanted to talk with animals his whole life. This was an item on his bucket list realized.

Malcolm on the other hand was on the alert. The intrigue of getting here had been enough, but now he was having some second thoughts. He looked out into the darkness and suddenly noticed some movement on the streets. People, he first thought. Then he realized that they were girls, about his age. Six of them. Coming right at them.

"Don't look now but there are some really strange looking chicks coming this way," said Malcolm.

"Don't you mean girls?" said Penny D.

"I did," said Malcolm. "Pardon my French."

"You can speak French?" said Harold.

It was quite possible that Penny D and Malcolm were thinking the very same thing at this point, that the small band of Goth girls who were rapidly approaching them was just the beginning of what strange people and adventures lay ahead.

Not that any of this would throw Penny D, she had grown up in an unusual house with unusual parents, had unusual pets, and had been schooled at her home in an unusual way. The school she was now attending appeared far more alien to her than this place ever could.

As for Harold, there was absolutely no way of guessing what he was thinking. The arrival of the mysterious Goth girls was not as captivating to him. He was busy rubbing Hawthorne's belly, who just lay there wiggling his toes.

The small band of Goth girls (and by Goth girls I mean preteens dressed much the same way as Penny D), was walking down the center of the street headed right for her and her friends. One girl appeared to be leading the group, her eyes were fixed directly on Penny D.

"Are you the one called Dreadful?" said Daphne with great interest.

"I am," said Penny D. "But call me Penny. Who are you?"

"I am Daphne," she replied. "Daphne Deranged."

"And we are the Lost Girls," came another answer from the strange Goth girls behind her who all spoke at once.

"Welcome, Penny Dreadful," said Daphne. "We have heard so much about you."

Suddenly, Daphne appeared less intimidating. It was as if Penny D's reputation preceded her and Daphne felt unworthy of being in her presence. It was not jealousy or envy but a longing for the place that she knew Penny D had come from. Perhaps it was even a place familiar to her at one time in her life, a place she was no longer allowed to visit.

"You will need our assistance to find your friends," said Daphne.

"Oh, so you know about the three girls who mysteriously vanished from my home in the middle of my thirteenth birthday party when the clock struck thirteen?" said Penny D.

Daphne had no reply to the run on sentence.

"Actually, they are not our friends," said Malcolm.

"That's true," said Penny D. "In fact I don't really care for them too much. Would it be all right if we just call them my guests?"

"Except for Olivia," said Malcolm.

"Right, except for Olivia," said Penny D. "She was genuinely invited to my party and not really one of them. She just got mixed up with the wrong crowd. You know how it is?"

Rebecca and Bronte were right at home with the Goth girls. One girl was petting Rebecca and another was tickling the back of Bronte's head, as he danced up and down.

"I do," said Daphne, eager to be accepted by Penny D.

Then she thought again.

"No, I really don't," said Daphne. "Anyway, there are a few things you should know before you begin your journey here, Penny. First, you have but this one night to find your guests and return them to your world. For if they stay but a full night here they may never be able to return."

Daphne looked over at Harold who was now taking notes in his note pad.

"And that goes for these guests here as well," said Daphne.

"Oh, no!" said Penny D. "These are my friends."

Daphne looked further confused, but she was at least trying to understand her visitors. Another of the Goth girls had lost all interest in the conversation and was feeding Hawthorne a cracker.

"Then, what will become of them?" asked Penny D. "My guests I mean, if we can't find them and get them out of here by dawn?"

"Not to worry," said Daphne. "We will look after them. They can become one of us."

As if this were some kind of cue to trigger a group response, all of the Goth girls answered simultaneously.

"One of us," said the Goth girls.

"But what if they're just not into the whole Goth thing?" said Malcolm, using bunny ears around the word Goth when he said it.

"Let me just say this," said Daphne. "If you are going to spend the rest of your life here, you had better pick your friends wisely. There are far worse choices you could make for company than us."

Then a really creepy thing happened. The entire group of Goth girls all smiled at Penny D and Malcolm at the same time.

"Well played, Daphne Deranged ," said Malcolm. "You

are very persuasive."

"We're wasting time, give them the clue," said one of the girls.

"Yes, we are," said Daphne. "Thank you Voltera. We can help you only this much on your journey and provide you with just one clue. Listen carefully. Seek out the Drunken Gargoyle. If you are successful we will meet with you again."

"If?" said Malcolm. "I don't like if!"

"Good luck to you and your friends, Penny Dreadful," said Daphne. "You will need it."

"Wait," said Penny D. "That's it? That's the clue? What else ya got?"

"We are not allowed," said Voltera, shaking her head.

"There are rules here, Penny," said Daphne. "As you will soon find out."

As the Lost Girls turned and walked away, Penny D thought to herself that she may have gotten in over her head this time.

"Becka, can you explain?" said Penny D.

"No can do, rules," said Rebecca.

"Hawthorne?" said Penny D.

"See here sweet," said Hawthorne, "we have a little thing here called the Primate Directive. Sorry."

"It clearly states that it is forbidden for us to interfere in the affairs of your species," said Bronte. "You're on your own kid."

"I guess when serpents and vermin turn their backs on you, you're really in deep poop," said Malcolm.

Penny D was never one to back down from a challenge. She took a deep breath, closed her eyes and asked the burning question to herself; what was she supposed to do now?

It was as though Harold had heard her thoughts and answered them for her.

"It's this way," said Harold. "Follow me."

"How do you know that?" said Penny D.

Harold pointed across the street to an old wooden sign. It read, "The Drunken Gargoyle .2K." And with that he took off down a dark alley.

Penny D and Malcolm and her pets all followed Harold but not for lack of a better plan. They believed in their hearts that if anyone could make any sense out of this place it was a video gaming master.

"I want everyone to stay close," said Penny D.

She was feeling very responsible at this point. The pressure was on and she knew they were all here because of her.

"You can't lose me now," said Malcolm as he took hold of Penny D's hand.

When they found themselves about half way down the alley, Harold stopped short. It was as though he was expecting something unusual to happen.

"What now, a sleeping wino?" said Malcolm.

"Quiet," said Harold. "Listen."

There was the sound of a whiplash and the clumpedy-clump of horses' hoofs. Suddenly a horse drawn carriage turned clumsily into the alley that Penny D and her friends were wandering down.

The spoke wheels on either side of the carriage and the double set of horses stretched from one side of the alley to the other and there were no doors or recesses at either side to duck into. This left them no choice but to run or be trampled.

Harold was suddenly very pleased with himself.

"I knew I heard horses," said Harold.

"We should run now," said Malcolm.

"Wait," said Penny D. "Where are Rebecca, and Bronte, and Hawthorne?"

There was no time for anyone to answer her. There was only enough time to act. Malcolm pulled Penny D by the hand and she took Harold along with her. They resembled a drunken Chinese dragon of sorts trying to out run the reckless horse drawn carriage that was catching up behind them.

Penny D knew her mathematics well. She knew that if she was a train leaving her home town at fifty miles an hour and had a one hour lead, a train leaving her home town on the very same track speeding at one hundred miles an hour would eventually catch her.

She knew that the end of the alley was too far for them to reach so she looked around for cover but there wasn't any. However, there was a deep channel cut into the center of the cobblestone street. It was most likely there to catch the rain water and prevent it from flooding the streets. It was also just wide enough for her and her two friends to lie in and wait for the carriage to pass over them.

She knew it was risky but the train, I mean carriage was gaining on them.

Penny D slammed on her brakes and allowed inertia to do her job for her. The three of them collapsed onto the ground. Both boys screamed like little children at a Halloween party, scared by a friend who jumped out at them with a demon mask on, thinking that this was surely the end of them all.

"Roll into the center of the road!" Penny D shouted.

"I don't want to die," said Malcolm.

"We know," said Penny D. "Get into the ditch, now!"

No sooner had Malcolm, who was the last of them, rolled into the ditch, the horses passed on either side of them and the carriage bottom passed right over their faces. Although it had all happened in a fleeting moment, it would most likely be a moment that none of them would ever forget.

The carriage sped furiously down the alley and the driver never looked back. When it reached the cross street at the end of alley, it turned a sharp corner (not actually possible for a horse drawn carriage of that size traveling at that speed), but did so anyway. Just before it disappeared completely, a large wooden box tumbled off of the back of it and bounced across the cobblestones.

"That was righteous, Penny D," said Harold, not sure if he had used the term correctly.

Harold Milquetoast, a boy so easily scared of bullies, soured mayonnaise, glitter and clowns was not at all frightened by what had just happened. Instead, he'd become energized.

Malcolm, on the other hand, was starting to show signs of "extreme stress disorder." He knew this had been a very close call and he was not looking forward to the next one. And he believed that there would be one. After all, he was a prank-sta, not a cowboy.

He only enjoyed giving the impression that cruel and unusual things were happening to him. He'd never planned on really experiencing them himself.

Penny D remained calm. She was taught that everything happens for a reason so this had to be no different. There was something about this event that she was supposed to be a part of, or bear witness to.

"Is everyone alright?" said Penny D.

"Define, alright," said Malcolm.

"Alive," said Harold.

"Yes, I am alive," said Malcom. "And miraculously, I have not peed in my pants yet."

"TMI, Malcolm, but thank you for that update," said Penny D.

She was on her feet first and slowly approached the box that had fallen off the carriage. Harold was right behind her, but Malcolm kept his distance. He knew how this was going to end. He built many an exploding box in his time and more than once they had blown up in his face. He offered advice.

"Don't touch it," said Malcolm. "If you hear something moving inside, back away."

When Penny D and Harold were within arm's length of the box, the top opened up and a boy sprung out from inside. His eyes were closed tight and his fists were swinging fast and furiously into the air as if he were in the middle of a fight and still thought he was.

"Take that and that," said Dim. "Upper cut, round house, kidney jab, you dirty, stinking,..."

Breathing heavily from exhaustion and the lack of contact from his fists prompted Dim to open his eyes. Only then did he stop swinging.

"Yeah, you better run, punks," said Dim as he thumbed his nose at the imaginary foe he had pictured running for their lives'.

"Everyone runs from me," said Dim. "Just remember. You can run for now, but you can't hide forever. Cause when Dim finds ya, and he will, he's gonna give ya another bloody nose. He will."

It was true. Dim spoke of himself in the third person. He was confused.

Not only was Dim confused because he held to the belief that fighting was a solution to his problems, but also because he had learned nothing from his encounter with Malcolm in the cafeteria or from Calagari and Vincent in the park. Sadly, he didn't even know he wasn't in the little hamlet of Terracotta anymore. From the blank look on his face, he didn't care.

Malcolm recognized him immediately, he had taken a black eye from that guy standing up for his friends.

As soon as Harold saw that it was Dim in the wooden box, he lost all interest. This was his survival mechanism. Having dealt with his share of bullies in the past, he created this habit of completely ignoring them. More than once it had saved his life.

His keenly focused attention was elsewhere now. He suddenly became very excited and began to pull on Penny D's sleeve to get her attention.

"Hey, Penny D," said Harold, "It's this way."

"Wait," said Penny D. "This boy may need our help."

"Help?" said Dim. "From a girl? Okay. I'm hungry. Go make me a samich."

"Here we go again," said Malcolm.

Penny D was not under the table this time. She was right in front of him, Dim, and was not going to be talked to that way.

"I'm not your maid," said Penny D, folding her arms. "I was just trying to be neighborly."

"And so you were, Miss Dreadful," called out a young voice from down the street.

They had two more visitors. Street urchins, boys really, about their age, were walking right toward them.

"We can take it from here," said one of the ragged boys,

who was accompanied by another boy dressed not quite as nicely.

At first glance the Gothic Kingdom had appeared to be deserted, now everywhere they went the visitors ran into some of the locals.

As the two boys approached, Penny D and her friends wondered if all the people here were teenagers and if there weren't any adults.

The leader of the two boys wore a hat and the way he wore it made him look more street-wise than his age should have allowed. The other lad looked just as astute, his lips were constantly pursed to prove it. Both were thin and looked as though they hadn't eaten today.

"Don't tell me, let me guess." said Penny D as she pointed toward Dim who was still standing in the open box. "He's a bad boy and you guys are here to collect him?"

"D'artanion," said D'artanion. "At your service, Miss. Dreadful."

He took off his hat to bow to Penny D.

"Wait, I get it," said Malcolm. "You're the Lost Boys, right?"

"Not quite," said D'artanion.

He gave Malcolm an odd glance as if he was trying to figure him out. Then he folded his arms and gave Dim a good look over as well.

"Some things never change, eh?" said D'artanion. "Miss Dreadful, you have more pressing matters to attend to, do you not? Be on your way, and good luck to you."

"Thank you, D'artanion," said Penny D. "He's all yours."

Malcolm and Penny D gave Dim one last parting glance.

"Take a good look around," said Malcolm to Dim. "Something tells me you may be here for a while."

And with that he gave D'artanion a thumbs-up.

"Lead on, Harold," said Penny D.

"Hey, what about my samich?" said Dim.

Chapter 24
The Carnival Of Lost Souls

Harold was off and running again. Penny D and Malcolm were doing their best to keep up with him. As inconceivable as it was, they were thoroughly convinced that Harold actually knew where he was going. But how could he? This was a first timer for all three of them. If there were any other clues present, then both Penny D and Malcolm had missed them.

The streets were all deserted as they had have come to expect. In fact, it was even more deserted than before, now that Penny D's three pets had also disappeared. As they ran alongside of Harold, Penny and Malcolm could hear their own breathing and the patter of their feet on the cobblestone's echoing off of the closed shops and boarded up houses.

They heard every day noises coming from here and there, but it was those darn additional wood creaking sounds and tapping against glass or metal sounds, that made them nervous. There was no breeze, so what exactly was causing them? They were not sure. There was a clicking sound that bothered Malcolm most of all. It reminded him of a scary campfire story he used to tell his younger cousins about a man with two metal clawed-hands.

More comically, there was a squeaky sound coming from somewhere overhead that reminded Penny D of an octopus squeeze toy she'd had as a child. Nothing appeared to bother Harold. He was in his own world, which may or may not have been the Gothic Kingdom.

Then a new and alarming sound was added to the orchestra. It was coming from Malcolm. It was his heavy breathing. He was having some very serious thoughts about being here and his labored breathing made it clear.

Malcolm knew he hadn't had the best reputation for being a stellar student in school or a model child at home. He was thinking about D'artanion and his friend, the kid with the pursed lips. He was wondering if they knew about him. Because if they knew about him what he knew about himself then he knew they would be coming for him next.

This was not the kind of place he wanted to find himself stuck in for the rest of his life or even another ten minutes if he could help it.

He tried not to think about these things, but he knew who he was and what he spent his entire professional elementary school career doing. This gave him much cause for concern. But then again, there was Penny D. She was fearless. From day one when he'd tried to prank her in class just minutes after she arrived. He failed and she turned the tables on him for good. She'd immediately earned his admiration.

Maybe it wasn't his school history or the scary place he was in at this moment that was keeping him on edge. Maybe it was the fact that nothing here made any sense to him, and try as he might, all he could think of were questions.

Like, how was it that Harold, who in a normal world, couldn't text and chew gum at the same time had become the leader of this little expedition? That really bothered him. Or was it that band of Goth girls, who were they really and where had they come from? (The leader of which he found strangely attractive and he couldn't understand that either.)

He started to imagine himself in Goth-style clothing, or

worse yet a Goth-style prison. He became very attached to his fancy vest. He only took it out on special occasions. It was anything but Goth looking. If he had to stay here would he have to give it up? Would he have to dress as they did?

There was only one thing that Malcolm knew for sure and that was that Penny D was his friend and she needed his help. Focus Malcolm, focus!

"Penny D," said Malcolm. "I need to rest a moment."

"Are you all right?" said Penny D. "You don't look so, I mean, you look okay."

She could read the look on his face and knew what was on his mind. She smiled back at him with a confident look on her face. She was on a mission and determined to locate the girls who had done her wrong (and the one girl who didn't know the difference between a pickle and a lime, if you could imagine?)

"I won't let anything happen to you," said Penny D.

Courage swelled up inside of Malcolm, just hearing those words come from Penny D changed his entire attitude.

"And I will not let you down," said Malcolm. "I'm okay now."

She took his hand and he knew it was all going to be all right from then on. He, too, was on a mission. He was going to save Olivia.

Harold was also on a mission, or so Penny D and Malcolm figured. Suddenly he came to a halt at a store front. He pointed to two stone gargoyles at either side of the stone steps leading up to the front door of a tavern. One gargoyle was poised and alert, while the other was asleep.

"I give you, The Drunken Gargoyle," said Harold, waiting for applause but there weren't any.

Although both gargoyles were stone, there was a strange snoring sound emanating from one of them.

"What is that, in his arms?" said Penny D.

There was a rolled up parchment paper closely cuddled in the arms of the sleeping stone figure.

"Allow, me," said Harold.

With the precision of a surgeon, Harold carefully slipped the paper from between the gargoyles arms without waking him.

"Harold, he's made of stone," said Malcolm confidently.

"Still, that is no reason to wake him," said Harold.

"Let's see?" said Penny D.

Harold handed Penny D the parchment. She unrolled it and began to read it in a hushed tone.

"Why are you whispering?" said Malcolm. "He's made of stone."

"Shush, infidel," said Harold in a play-along character voice. "Proceed, young wench."

"Thank you my lord," said Penny D in a similar character voice.

When Penny D began to read the parchment again, she was careful to stay in character;

Welcome to the Carnival of Souls.
Be sure to leave before the bell tolls.
If you feed your desire, you just may expire.
So choose to be smart and proceed with your heart,
or the price you will pay is forever a stay,
in this world until you get old.

"Can we go home now?" said Malcolm.

"Olivia," said Penny D.

"Right," said Malcolm.

"It all makes perfect sense," said Harold, as he scribbled in his note pad.

"It all makes perfect sense, to whom?" said Malcolm.

"We go inside here," said Harold plainly.

"That's what you got out of that?" said Malcolm.

"Didn't you?" said Harold.

"Who is this guy?" said Malcolm.

"We should keep moving," said Penny D.

Once at the top of the steps, they pushed the door open. Penny D, Malcolm and Harold huddled together and peered into the darkness of the tavern.

"I don't see anything," said Malcolm. "Harold, go in and feel around."

"Okay," said Harold.

"Harold, stay put," said Penny D.

"Okay," said Harold.

"If there are any risks involved," said Penny D. "Well, it is my party."

"No, we go in together then," said Malcolm. "Ready?'

They all started to move in together but soon found that they were no longer walking, they were crawling on their knees, then resting on their bellies.

A dull light came up and Penny D, Malcolm and Harold found themselves peeking under a carnival tent wall.

Penny D had read about carnivals many times in her books, so she immediately recognized it. Harold had seen imaginative artists' renditions of them in video games, so he, too, had an idea of what lay ahead. But Malcolm had only the smallest idea of what this was about since his only reference to a carnival was from some badly animated cartoon shows.

This old time carnival was well lit by the string of lanterns that hung from poles every few feet. Canvas dividers hung from ropes and separated the attractions that local residents would pay a nickel to witness. Lavish and colorful designs were painted on the canvas walls depicting what great marvel they would see once inside.

Although the carnival looked as deserted as the streets outside, there was nothing in the Gothic Kingdom that turned out to be what it appeared to be at first glance. So this should be no different, thought Penny D.

Penny D, Malcolm and Harold climbed to their feet and brushed off the sawdust from the floor that had gotten on their clothing.

"How did we...," said Malcolm.

"Just roll with it," said Penny D. "We're running out of time. We should spread out. Harold, you love animals, you check out the Snake Charmer's tent. Malcolm?"

"The Mad Magician," said Malcolm. "I'm on it."

"I guess I'll start with the Freak show," said Penny D. "We meet back here in ten minutes. Good luck."

As her friends wandered off Penny D looked around for her pets again, but they were still gone. This only reinforced the notion that they were truly on their own.

"I know, rules," Penny D muttered to herself.

She stepped through the colorfully painted tent flap and entered the Freak Show.

Each of the "freaks" as they were so labeled, were separated by another canvas wall. So the first "freak" that Penny D came up to had his own separate booth.

There was not much to it really, not at all what Penny D would have expected. All she saw was a man sitting on a high chair at a tiny table. In front of him was an old fashion adding machine set upon it and the man was busy calculating numbers. If she'd had to guess she would say that he may have been an accountant.

"Okay, I give up," said Penny D. "Where's the freak?"

"That wasn't very nice!" whined the Accountant. "And hardly imaginative at all. Isn't it bad enough I'm put on display like this? But to endure comments like that thrown at me day in and day out? You should be ashamed of yourself, little girl."

"Oh, no," said Penny D apologetically. "I truly didn't think that you were a freak. What I meant was, well, the sign said that there were freaks in here and so I had no idea what to expect."

"Like I've never heard that one before," said the Accountant. "Just move on, you make me sick."

It was not hard to tell that he was one unhappy camper. Perhaps it was his job, Penny D thought to herself. And if that were so, why didn't he get a new one; one that would make him happy?

She would never volunteer such a thing to an adult. Not only because it was rude, but also because she knew she was a child and her perspective was colored by her age. Like most adults, he probably believed that children should be seen and not heard and that they couldn't possibly understand that adults have no choice but to do what they did no matter how miserable they were doing it.

She could tell that he was set in his ways and would never ever entertain the notion that happiness was an option. Regardless, she believed that he would be happier if he had a job that excited him; one that he would be eager to come to every day. One that made him smile.

As Penny D slipped between the canvas flaps she found herself in a post office, or part of one anyway. The office furniture appeared to be growing right out of the painted canvas wall. There was a single postal worker standing next to a row of pigeon holes and filing in one letter at a time into their correct box by hand.

Penny D watched quietly, having learned from her previous experience with a "freak," not to disturb them when they were concentrating.

"You're making me ner---vous," sang the Postal Worker.

"I'm sorry," said Penny D. "I didn't want to disturb you. I was waiting for you to take a break."

"Lunch isn't till 1400 hours," said the Postal Worker.

"Then perhaps, may I just like to ask you one question please?" said Penny D. "Did you happen to see three young girls about my age come through here recently?"

"You're talking to me," the Postal Worker continued to sing-song his reply.

Penny D saw that she had agitated him. When she was just about to leave he snapped an answer at her.

"Do you have any idea what would happen if I put just one of these letters in the wrong box?" said the Postal Worker. "Huh? Huh? Huh? Of course you don't, how could you? You're just a stupid little girl."

"I see no reason for name calling," said Penny D defensively.

"You don't?" said the Postal Worked. "Well isn't that too bad. Huh?"

The Postal Worker suddenly stopped what he was doing. He looked confused, then disoriented. Sweat beaded up on his brow then ran down across his eyelashes.

"That's, just, great!" said the Postal Worker, throwing down his hands full of letters. "I lost my place. I don't know what to do. What should I do now?"

Penny D threw up her arms and walked through the open tent flap and onto the next booth.

"How very strange," said the Postal Worker to himself. "I am suddenly thinking about all that military training I've had in Special Ops and as a Navy Seal. Blue wire. Red wire. Code orange. Yes, Mr. President. On your command, sir. Semper fi!"

Harold was sitting at a little café sipping a hot chocolate. The canvas wall behind him had a lovely painting of Paris, the Eiffel Tower was in the center. In the seat across from him was a very large snake.

Like Rebecca, the snake had an unusual look on its face as if it too could emote.

"Would you like a bissssscuit," asked the Snake Charmer, "...to go with that hot chocolate?"

"I don't mind if I do," said Harold.

"I love your hat," said the Snake Charmer. "It makesssss you look so very mature."

"Why thank you," said Harold. "I got it with the video game of the same name. It is my current fav."

"You look awfully ssssmart to me," said the Snake Charmer. "I'll bet you do very well in your ssssstudies."

"As a matter of fact, I do," said Harold. "Sssstraight A's. My homework gets copied by more students than any other nerd in the class."

"Sssstraight A's?" said the Snake Charmer. "No kidding?"

The Snake Charmer licked its lips more than once. Its eyes rolled in its head. It wondered what Harold would taste like.

Rebecca suddenly rose up next to Harold. She coiled around him but directed her attention to the Snake Charmer.

"I beg your pardon," said Rebecca. "But I need to inform

this young gentlemen of the most urgent news."

"Oh, not at all," said the Snake Charmer. "But please, why not join us my dear lady?"

"I don't mind if I do," said Rebecca.

"Tea?" said the Snake Charmer.

Rebecca held up her cup with the tip of her tail whilst the Snake Charmer filled it from the kettle it held up with its own.

"Rebecca, didn't you say that you have some urgent news for me?" said Harold.

"Oh, yes," said Rebecca. "Malcolm is in trouble."

The Snake Charmer offered Rebecca a biscuit.

"Are those shortbread?" said Rebecca.

"My grandmother made them jussssst this morning," said the Snake Charmer.

"Malcolm?" said Harold. "In trouble? Where? What happened?"

"These are delicious," said Rebecca. "You simply must provide me with the recipe."

"Rebecca?" said Harold.

He was beginning to get frantic. He realized that he had dropped the ball and now Malcolm may need him.

"The magician's tent, darling," said Rebecca, accidentally spitting out the shortbread crumbs at Harold. "Now stop interrupting your elders."

"Nice to have met you," said Harold to the Snake Charmer. "But duty calls."

And with that Harold ran out of the Snake Charmer's tent.

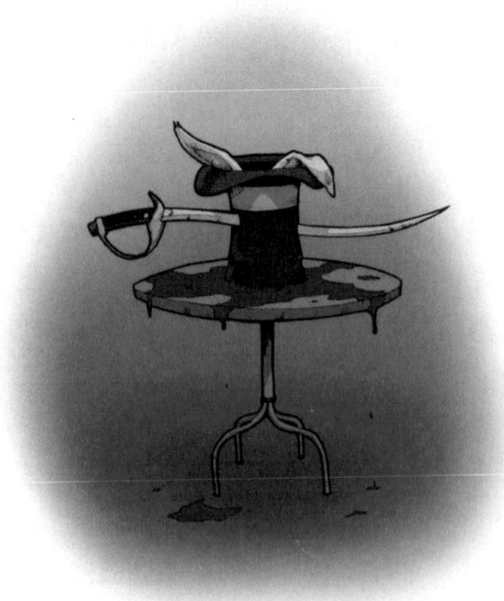

Chapter 25
The Mad Magician

Penny D found herself all alone wandering around in a dimly lit warehouse. It was filled with the stage show gadgets and showmanship trickery contraptions of the man only known as "The Mad Magician."

She cautiously looked over each show-stopping, applaud-raising mechanical gimmick with a careful eye. She was never a big fan of magic. She was too cool-headed and could never get caught up in it. She knew it wasn't real. So without the distraction of accepting the impossible, that magic actually happened, Penny D often found herself figuring out how the magic tricks were done. Sometimes before they were even finished.

Once her aunt on her mother's side of the family invited her over to her cousin's birthday party. They had a magician there. He did some magic tricks with his hat, his scarf, his little magic box and had amazed the other kids, but not Penny D. She had been clearly unimpressed. When she was asked why by the other children, she told them the truth.

"The Rabbit was in the hat all along, the scarf had an inside sleeve where the ribbon was tucked into, and the magic box had a mirror inside that reflected the side of the box and made it only appear empty," said Penny D.

Her cousin cried because she felt that Penny D had ruined her birthday and her aunt had a fit because she had to pay the magician anyway. Needless to say that was the last time she had been asked to attend any of her cousins' birthday parties.

Admittedly, Penny D hadn't done it to be mean in any way, she simply felt obligated to be honest when asked.

But this time it was different. The normal rules of physics didn't apply in The Gothic Kingdom. In the short time she'd been here she had witnessed several things happen that couldn't possibly happen in the world she had come from; the world that she was born into, the world she was told was real. Although she was now rethinking that label.

Curiously she looked over the water torture booth trick, the saw-the-lady-in-half table trick, the bear-trap chair escape trick, the welded shut milk container escape trick and the upside down straight jacket with matching trousers trick that hung from the rafters.

Penny D was not intimidated or frightened by what she saw or by where she was, but not to upset any unknown warehouse inhabitants, she called out in guarded whisper.

"Malcolm?" said Penny D. "Are you in here?"

A bright light much like a spotlight came on with a heavy pop. It panned across a stage backed with a red velvet curtain. It fixed itself on a man dressed in black with his back to her. When he turned around Penny D could see that he was wearing a black tuxedo and a harlequin mask; one half of his face a frown while the other half a smile. This must be the Mad Magician, she thought.

"I want to thank you all for coming here tonight," said the Mad Magician. "But before I begin the show, I would like to introduce to you a very special celebrity in our audience. Penny Dreadful, please stand up and take a bow."

There was a sudden round of applause from somewhere unknown and the spotlight swung over to Penny D who was now sitting in an audience populated by lifeless wooden mannequins. Each wooden face had a carved expression on it. Some were laughing, some crying, some in pure hysteria and others in surprise.

Caught so unexpectedly, Penny D smiled and responded with a Queen's wave.

"Ah, thank you?" said Penny D.

She no longer expecting an answer from Malcolm, now that she found herself as part of the show. She suddenly got one anyway in the form of a muffled reply.

She heard him. She was sure of it. She heard Malcolm. He was there, but where?

The Mad Magician held his sides and pretended to laugh along with his audience.

"I'm sorry, but your little friend is all tied up at the moment," said the Mad Magician. "So just sit back and enjoy the show."

Harold stumbled through the row of mannequins on his way towards Penny D. He removed the one seated next to her to sit down.

"Harold," said Penny D, "I know that Malcolm's here. I heard him but I can't find him."

Harold scanned the stage and pointed to a large wicker basket on casters. It glided across the stage and was stopped short by the foot of the Mad Magician when it reached him.

"He's in there," said Harold.

There was a tiny wicker panel on the front side of the wicker basket. It slid open and Malcolm's hand reached out of it. He waved.

"Help me. Penny!" said Malcolm.

"Ladies and Gentlemen, I would like to draw your attention to the ordinary wicker basket that I have here on stage under foot," said the Mad Magician. "And, to the nasty little boy who is trapped inside."

The Mad Magician bent over and knocked twice on top of the wicker basket.

"Knock, knock," said the Mad Magician. "Is there anyone home?"

"Let me out of here, you psycho," said Malcolm.

Again the sound of laughter filled the auditorium.

"Kids today, they say the sweetest things," said the Mad Magician.

He then held up several steel swords, different shapes and sizes but all very, very sharp.

"He's a real cut-up, this little fellow," said the Mad Magician, as he clapped the steel swords together proving them real. "But let us get back to business. In just a moment I will penetrate this ordinary wicker basket from every known angle with these ordinary dangerous weapons."

"No!" said Penny D. "You can't, he'll be hurt."

"Killed, actually," said Harold.

"Harold, we have to save him" said Penny D.

"Here we go," said the Mad Magician.

With marksman-like accuracy and lightning speed, the Mad Magician quickly slid four of the swords through the wicker basket until they come out the opposite side.

Malcolm could clearly be heard moaning through the laughter in the auditorium.

"Stop it!" Penny D shouted. "You'll hurt him."

"Harold!" said Malcolm. "Get me out of here. Where the heck are you guys?"

Penny D and Harold rushed through the isle of mannequins to come to Malcolm's rescue. But it appeared that the mannequins now had a mind all their own. They flipped and they flopped as the teens passed them, as if intentionally getting in their way.

Harold was tripped by one of the mannequins and landed face first across its raised arms. Without missing a beat he waved his arms in a swimming motion and managed to body surf over the tops of the mannequins safely to the bottom of the bleachers.

Penny D sprang up onto the shoulders of one mannequin and like a dingo dog she descended as quickly as Harold had, as if skipping from one stone to another across a flooded road.

From the looks of the wicker basket rocking back and forth, Malcolm was panicking.

"I, still, hear, you," called out the Mad Magician. "What is it you say, you want some more?"

The Mad Magician shoved three more swords through the ordinary wicker basket from three other angles. It appeared as though no one could possibly survive this harsh sort of treatment.

Malcolm screamed in pain.

The Mad Magician laughed again just before sending one more sword straight downward through the top of the basket until it came out of the bottom and stabbed the stage floor.

When Penny D and Harold climbed up onto the stage, the Mad Magician raised his arms and disappeared in a green cloud of swirling smoke.

"Malcolm," said Penny D. "Hold on. We are here for you."

Penny D rapidly pulled out a few swords from the top of the ordinary wicker basket and dropped them onto the stage. Harold undid the latch and opened the lid. They both frightfully looked inside expecting the worst.

"Oh, so that's how they do that," said Harold calmly.

Malcolm sprang out of the basket and began to check his body for holes. The look on his face suggested that he had expected to find at least one.

"Malcolm, are you all right?" said Penny D.

"I don't know," said Malcolm frantically. "I'm not sure. Am I dead? I don't think so."

Malcolm looked around for the Mad Magician.

"Where did he go?" said Malcolm. "I've got a trick of my own to show him."

Penny D took Malcolm into her arms and hugged him.

"He's gone," said Penny D. "Forget about him. We have to stay focused. We can't forget why we are here. Be the bigger man and let it go."

Not unlike the first time they had met, Malcolm felt a little embarrassed and reassured at the same time by Penny D.

What she was saying was that it was okay to be scared and more noble to forgive.

"Right," said Malcolm. "I'm cool."

And Malcolm was.

"Have you seen any of the girls yet?" said Penny D.

"No, have you?" said Malcolm.

As if on cue, Olivia's voice pierced the air and answered their call.

"Yoo-hoo, I'm over here you guys," said Olivia.

With a life all its own, the spotlight swung wildly across stage and onto Olivia whose wrists and ankles were tied to a carnival wheel. Stranger still, she was dressed in a black and white magician's assistant outfit.

"Hello Penny D, this is some wacky nightmare I'm having, huh?" said Olivia. "I kind of wish it would end now."

"Olivia, are you all right?" said Malcolm, as he ran over to her.

"Oh, hello Butler," said Olivia. "I'll be fine as soon as this nightmare ends."

"Nice outfit, O," added Malcolm with a wink.

"Do you really like it?" said Olivia. "I'm not crazy about the color, and I think the skirt is too short."

"Oh, no, it's just the right length," said Malcolm.

"Thank you Butler," said Olivia. "That was sweet." And she smiled at him.

A cloud of orange smoke suddenly spun into a vortex and the Mad Magician appeared behind the carnival wheel. He laughed (wildly as most mad people do) and then he spun the wheel that Olivia was fastened to.

Malcolm raced around to the back of the wheel and just as he reached it, the Mad Magician disappeared again in a purple cloud of smoke. Malcolm punched wildly into the smoke but to no avail.

"If you're going to help me, please hurry," said Olivia. "I think I'm going to hurl."

Penny D and Harold joined Malcolm to look over the mechanism behind the wheel to see if they could stop it from spinning.

It was a mass of old wooden gears, cams and pistons, all spinning at high speed.

"This makes no sense," said Penny D. "What are all these gears for?"

"Don't worry Olivia, we'll get you down," said Malcolm.

"I hope so, my lunch is on its way up," said Olivia.

The Mad Magician reappeared on the opposite side of the stage from a black cloud of smoke. He was holding up several sharp throwing knives.

"And for my next trick, ladies and gentlemen, I will toss these razor sharp knives at my beautiful assistant," said the Mad Magician. "And quite possibly never even hit her."

"Over my dead body, you maniac," said Malcolm.

"That is so brave," swooned Olivia.

"I need something to stick into the gears," said Penny D.

The Mad Magician threw four knives at the wheel.

"Harold, look out!" said Penny D.

Four thuds were heard one after the other. The four throwing knives hit something on the spinning wheel, perhaps missing Olivia. But it was hard to say, she was spinning so fast.

"Ha-ha, missed me," said Olivia.

Penny D and Harold let out their breath with a sigh of relief.

"Olivia, don't encourage him," said Malcolm.

One of the knives fell from the spinning wheel and landed at Harold's feet. He reached down and picked it up.

"Penny D, stand aside," said Harold.

Harold closed his eyes and stabbed the knife into the gears of the mechanism behind the spinning wheel. As unbelievable as this may sound, since the gears were made of wood, sparks flew. What followed was a squealing metal sound just like the brakes of a locomotive coming to a halt. The spinning wheel came to a full stop. Olivia was left upside down.

The Mad Magician tossed three more knives at the wheel.

Malcolm stepped in front of Olivia using his body as a shield. The sound of the knives hitting their mark was heard again. Olivia screamed in agony and so did Malcolm.

When Olivia and Malcolm opened their eyes they saw that the knives had passed between Malcolm's outstretched arms and missed Olivia's body as well. They remained stuck in the wooden wheel on either side of Olivia.

However, one side of Malcolm's fancy vest was tattered, a knife had passed right through it. At first he appeared unscathed, but then the blood began to run.

"My fancy vest!" said Malcolm. "Oh, you are so going to pay for this!"

"Oooopps," was all that the Mad Magician said.

Malcolm turned to unfasten the leather belts that held Olivia to the wheel and she fell down on top of him. He got her up to her feet but her knees responded like a Gell-O dessert. She wobbled around the stage for a few moments. She shook it off and noticed Malcolm's torn vest.

"Malcolm, you're bleeding," said Olivia.

"She said my name," thought Malcolm.

Penny D pulled out her handkerchief and held it to Malcolm's side.

The Mad Magician laughed again and disappeared in a cloud of blue puffy smoke.

From out of nowhere, Hawthorne whistled discreetly to get their attention. He was just off stage and nonchalantly pointing to the inside of the steamer trunk with his tail. He pretended to cough, but he was really talking; sending Malcolm and Olivia a message.

"Quick, get, in," coughed Hawthorne.

"Malcolm, take Olivia and go to Hawthorne," said Penny D. "Run!"

Malcolm shot one last glance in the direction of the Mad Magician, knowing there was some unfinished business here, then he took Olivia by the arm and ran for the trunk.

Both Malcolm and Olivia jumped into the trunk and disappeared inside completely. Hawthorne leapt in after them and the lid on the trunk magically slammed shut. Several locks snapped together from around all sides.

A cloud of pink smoke suddenly appeared behind the

steamer trunk. The Mad Magician stepped out of the smoke and held up a very large wooden mallet. He brought it down on top of the steamer trunk, and smashed it to splinters.

Malcolm, Olivia and Hawthorne had disappeared.

Chapter 26
The Faust Theater

The Dreadful living room appeared much the way it had when we saw it last. That unusual sofa, the centerpiece of the room, suddenly split in half and from between the two large cushions Malcolm and Olivia sprang out as if it had given birth to them.

Although Olivia's magician's assistant's outfit was gone and her own clothes were in their place, Malcolm's fancy vest was still tattered and blood dripped from his side.

The crazy nightmare was over. Malcolm took a deep breath and sighed with relief but Olivia still held her hands over her eyes.

"Is it over yet?" said Olivia. "Tell me when it's over."

"Yes, it's over," said Malcolm. "You can open your eyes."

"Are you sure? I didn't like that dream"

"Yes. I know. Neither did I."

"Where are we now?"

"We're back in Penny's house now."

"Penny S or Penny D?"

"We left from Penny D's...Penny D's house. We're in the middle of her creepy living room. Would you like me to describe it to you?"

"No, I can see it for myself."

Olivia slowly opened her eyes and looked around. The portraits on the wall appeared different than when she'd first come in. They were all smiling now.

"It was all just a bad dream, right?" said Olivia. "None of it was real, right? None of it really happened?"

"Yes, just a bad dream'" said Malcolm.

He held one hand to his side to cover the torn vest and the blood soaked fabric. He felt inspired or perhaps just down right curious how far he could take this gag.

"However, we're in the middle of the good dream now," said Malcolm.

"We are?" said Olivia. "Are you sure?"

"Oh, I'm sure," said Malcolm. "And this is the part where you kiss me for saving your life."

"It is?" said Olivia. "Okay."

Malcolm turned his head and pointed to his cheek.

Olivia closed in and just before she kissed him, she paused long enough for Malcolm to wonder to himself what was holding it up. Right after he turned to look at her, she closed in further and gave him one swift kiss on the lips.

Olivia quickly held up a finger, and pointed it right at Malcolm's face. There was suddenly an awareness in her eyes that Malcolm had never seen before. It was a fair bet that few had.

"You better not tell Penny S," scolded Olivia. "Okay?"

"But how could I?" said Malcolm. "This never happened. It's all a dream, remember?

"Oh, yeah, right," said Olivia.

"Besides, what happens in the Kingdom stays in the Kingdom," said Malcolm.

Uncle Calagari was suddenly at their side dressed in a World War II medic outfit, pith helmet included.

"I apologize for the intrusion, soldier," said Uncle Calagari, and he saluted him. "I should have a look at that side, yes?" said Uncle Calagari. "I am sure it is but a graze, but if I don't have you all patched up, I fear your mother may forbid you from attending any more happy birthday parties with us."

"You were hurt!" said Olivia. "Then the dream was real. And that means that the kiss was..."

Malcolm was suddenly stumped. He looked to the Master Pranksta for help.

"All of our dreams are real, young Olivia," said Uncle Calagari. "It is from our dreams, that our reality is born. That is why we must be careful what we dream. So tell me, what dreams do you have?"

Olivia began to blush.

Delighted with himself beyond measure, Malcolm looked around the room and couldn't help but notice that one portrait on the wall was painted mid-wink, apparently, right at him.

***

"Welcome to the Faust Theater," is what the sign read that hung above an archway at the end of a cobblestone path. Penny D and Harold skipped down a long row of steps, then stepped up onto a stage. It was all very Greek amphitheatrical.

They heard a soft flute play a little tune and knew something was about to begin, so they stood quietly in the wings.

A stage light came up on a make-shift library from the darkness. Unusually tall stacks of books surrounded a few distorted chairs circling a podium.

Britney was seated on stage all dressed in black, her hair dyed black as well. Seated on either side of her were two Goth girls, Lilith and Dragma. There were two Goth boys seated behind them.

Even through the dark eye shadow and pale skin they could see that Britney was at her wit's end, she was pulling at her hair with two fingers. Something continued to agitate her.

"Everyone's attention, please," said Lilith, clapping her hands twice. "Dragma would like to share her emotions with us tonight."

"Oh no, not another poem," said Britney. "I can't stand to hear anymore complaining." She cupped her ears.

"If you don't mind?" said Lilith.

"Thank you, Lilith," said Dragma. "To begin with, I digress. My heart was broken yet again last week, so I recorded this to properly embrace the pain."

Dragma suddenly slid across the center of the stage and into a spotlight. She covered her eyes with one arm, preparing to overdramatize every line she was about to deliver.

"Innocent!" said Dragma. "My immortal. A perfect storm. One fragile heart destroyed in its prime. Men. Disdain. To blame. Oh, the shame."

Britney was seething with anger (no surprise there).

"Crazy people, crazy poems," said Britney. "This junk doesn't even rhyme. Haven't you ever heard of Dr. Shmoose?"

Britney suddenly slid out of the darkness and into the same spotlight where Dragma was. She hip checked her and sent her flying out of the way and back into the darkness.

"Me me me," said Britney, mocking Dragma. "Me me, me me, me me. It's all about me. Hello? Buy a clue."

Penny D helped Dragma up to her feet and brushed the lint off her long black skirt. There were tears in Dragma's eyes.

"I am mocked," said Dragma. "And I deserve it."

She cried to herself.

"Don't tell me," said Britney. "Like, let me guess. Like, a boy told you that you were like, beautiful, and other things you wanted to hear? Then he like, dumped you right? Well guess what? Like you deserve it."

Then adding insult to injury as only Britney could she used her fingers to form the letter "L" up over her forehead, and stuck her tongue out at Dragma for good measure.

Lilith gently stepped into the circle of light from the darkness. Britney, with all of her big talk, was suddenly taken aback. It was as if, for the first time, she had truly been challenged without all the bravado.

Lilith took a pragmatic pose and began a story slam.

"All she wanted was a little love and attention, she said," said Lilith. "But there was none to be had at home, she was told. It was her little brother's fault, she thought. Why did he have to be born, she questioned. After all, they shared a different father, she overheard. To keep it a secret, she was warned. She couldn't, she said. Unfair, why me, she thought. It was not my doing, she argued. A grudge held between them, she felt. And did it on spite, she did."

She pointed her finger menacingly at Britney.

"Her destiny," said Lilith. "Loneliness. An isolated life."

The walls of books shuffled together and began to surround Britney. The pages flipped open as if hit by a great wind. They appeared to multiply at the same time preventing Britney from leaving the circle.

"A prison, self-made," said Lilith.

"But why me?" said Britney. "What did I do?"

"It is what you didn't do," said Lilith. "You didn't forgive."

Britney's eyes became big and round like saucers. She stared into space.

Lilith hung her head to rest. The spotlight on her faded until she too was gone.

Penny D and Harold applauded lightly before they walked up to Britney. Harold waved his hand in front of her face a few times. Britney didn't move.

"Harold, maybe you'd better take her home, before it's too late for you both," said Penny D.

"And leave you here all alone?" said Harold. "If I did that..."

"I know, I know," said Penny D. "I would have to find Penny S all by myself."

"I won't leave you with nothing to go on," said Harold.

Penny D looked around as if seeking an answer. Then, she saw one.

"Look here," said Penny D. "Maybe the titles of these books are clues?"

Harold picked up a few books and began to read off some of the titles.

"But, these are children's books, I think," said Harold. "The Little Engine That Couldn't do a Darn Thing,' and, 'Thomas, the Runaway Train'. Wait. Why would anyone want to read these to children?"

"Maybe not those, but this one is called, 'A Penny saved, is a Penny Found in Time," said Penny D. "That kind of makes sense."

Rebecca appeared from nowhere balancing a book atop her head.

"You may want to read this one as well, darling," said Rebecca, handing the book over to Harold.

"A Penny Wise Would Stay Away from Castle Longtooth," said Harold. "It sounds like an invitation to me."

"Okay, so I know she's alive and where she is, but I still don't know how to get there," said Penny D.

It was Bronte's turn to appear from nowhere. He hopped up on Penny D's shoulder.

"It's at the end of Penny Lane, of course," said Bronte.

Penny D gave Bronte an affectionate pat on the head.

"Like always, you show up at just the right time," said Penny D. "You guys better get going.

I'll be okay from here. Make sure Harold and Britney get home safe, will ya?"

Harold led the traumatized Britney by the arm off to another part of the stage.

"Thank you, Penny D," said Harold, "for the very best birthday party that I have ever attended."

Harold bowed and Britney curtsied.

Rebecca coiled around a large wooden lever and pulled it to one side.

A trap door opened in the stage below Harold and Britney, who fell right through it. Rebecca slithered across the stage and down into the opening as well. Once they were all gone, the trap door closed back up as if it had never been there.

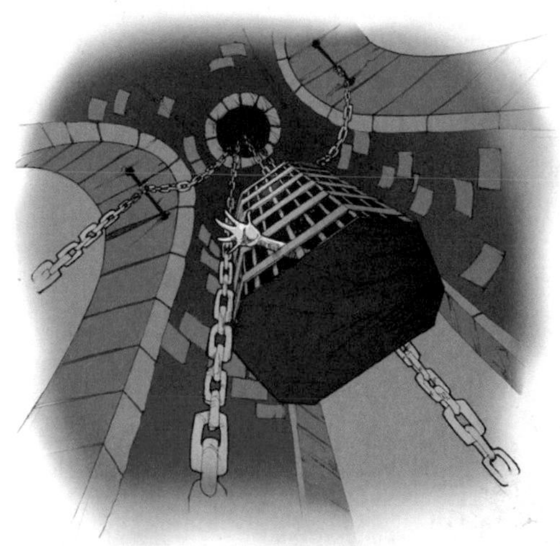

Chapter 27
Castle Longtooth

The antique wooden cabinets in the Dreadful Mansion's kitchen looked much the way they had when Penny D and her mom had had their heart to heart talk. Opposite the food preparation table was an unusually large sink, both in length and in depth.

Underneath the sink were the two false cabinet panels that most kitchens have, only these had no handles because they were just panels.

Those same two false wooden panels suddenly fell open and Harold and Britney came sliding out as if they had come down a sliding pond. They spun around in the center of the room as if they were in the middle of a frozen lake because Uncle Calagari knew how to wax a floor to perfection.

It was hard to tell if Britney was more overjoyed to be back in semi-normal surroundings or because she was dressed in her own low rider jeans and belly shirt. The one thing that could be seen for sure was, that she was not herself. She started to do and say things that were not at all akin to her previous self-centered acquired nature.

"Harold, you saved me!" said Britney. "That was the most

selfless act I have ever had any part of. Thank you, thank you, thank you!"

Then most unexpectedly, Britney grabbed Harold around the neck and hugged him. She thought about kissing his cheek, but didn't. Then in true Britney fashion, she started to hate herself for thinking so.

Harold's face got beet red. He hadn't seen that coming. But it was welcome none the less.

Malcolm and Olivia walked into the kitchen with perhaps the worst timing Britney could ever want anyone to have.

"Oh, gross," said Olivia. "Get a booth at the fair, you two."

Malcolm gave Harold two thumbs up.

"Nuh-uh!" said Britney and let go of Harold at once. "This is not what you think."

"It never is," said Malcolm.

"If either of you ever repeat anything that you did not see here just now I will make your life a living nightmare at school," said Britney. "Get it?"

"And, how is that different than what you do to us now?" said Malcolm.

***

Penny Dreadful never felt alone, no matter where she went.

Loneliness was a feeling she was taught, that could only occur if you suddenly lost your mind and forgot who your closest loved ones were. In times like these when it may have appeared that Penny D was alone, she would stop and look into the locket she hung around her neck.

Inside it were tiny pictures of her mother, her father and her uncle sitting on that unusual sofa in the middle of their living room. No, Penny D was not alone. She had her memories and that was something that no one could possibly take from her.

In this case, she actually did have company. Bronte had not slipped away with Hawthorne and Rebecca as he had earlier. He was perched up on her shoulder determined to see this journey through to the end with her.

Together Penny D and Bronte walked under a huge gothic arch at the entrance to the great Castle Longtooth before them. Even in the state of disrepair that it was, it was both captivating and intimidating.

"Castle Longtooth," said Bronte. "I knows it well. I used to hang out here a lot during my rebel youth. Those were some wild times we had. I never told you about the pranks we used to play on old Longtooth back then. I couldn't. It was a family rule; leave Penny out of our past until we are sure she is Goth like us."

"Hmmm," said Penny D. "What do you mean by pranks?"

"Well, hee hee," said Bronte, unable to stop his snickering. "Some pals of mine used to spin a web across his toilet seat. And, and, and then there was the time we left a flaming paper bag of bat guano on his door step. We pulled on the doorbell chain and ran."

Penny D stopped and suddenly reverted back to the newly anointed seventh grader that she was rapidly becoming.

"Really?" said Penny D. "How mature."

"Yeah, good times," said Bronte. "Good times. But I'm sure he's forgotten all about that by now," then he hung his head in pretend shame.

"You don't have to come with me, Bronte," said Penny D. "I'm not afraid to do this on my own."

"Just you try and leave me behind," said Bronte. "We're a team you and I, like a superhero and her trusted sidekick. We need superhero names. How about, "Goth Girl and Bronte the Magnificent?"

Penny D was used to his never-ending chatter. She would listen for as long as she could then simply tune him out. Eventually he would realize that she were not paying attention to him and he would fall asleep.

However here, in the Gothic Kingdom, there was an energy all its own. Something was keeping him going. Although she would not have admitted it, she was very glad to have him along with her.

Penny D and Bronte walked across a narrow drawbridge and under a heavy wooden gate. Bronte became even more agitated as they moved closer into the castle.

"The tunnel ahead leads into the center of the castle," said Bronte. "That's a good place to start."

They heard the howl of what could have been a wolf echo off the walls of the castle. It had come from a forest behind the castle.

"That could be him," said Bronte. "He's a shape-shifter and probably out for a late night snack."

"T.M.I., Bronte," said Penny D. "Let's just do what we came for and go home."

"I'm just say'n," said Bronte.

"You know I dislike that expression," said Penny D.

"Here we go again," said Bronte, knowing full well that a lecture was on the way.

"It's like saying that nobody is allowed to have an opinion unless you attach yourself to it," said Penny D. "Not everything is about you. And at the same time, you are making a statement and not owning up to it. Take responsibility for what you have to say, gosh darn it."

She was back to her usual self. Her own lingo included. They stopped for a moment to look each other in the eyes. Her two into his many.

Bronte knew he was wrong but it didn't matter to him. He liked to hear himself talk and so he did. He talked incessantly and continuously whether Penny D or no one at all were listening.

The long day had finally taken its toll on her. As Bronte began talking again, Penny D began to feel a bit lost. When times like these came around, she was taught to close her eyes and focus her energy on what she wanted to have happen, rather than just waiting for something or anything to happen on its own. And so she did.

Her Uncle Calagari was most adamant on this point. He said that she should never leave her wishes on default settings. Because if she did, she could receive almost anything except what she wanted and needed to have happen at a given time.

This was a most interesting and educational place to visit for one night, Penny D was thinking to herself, but she was ready to go home now. Determined to keep to her true self and do what was right, Penny D conjured up a very clear picture in her mind of finding Penny S and bringing her back home with her. And at the end of the little scenario that played out in her head, she smiled to herself because she knew it was now a done deal.

When she opened her eyes something new caught her attention.

"Listen," said Penny D.

"I don't hear nothing," said Bronte.

"That's because you keep talking," said Penny D. "Shush!"

"Oh, excuse me," said Bronte. "Bronte must be quiet now. Bronte not allowed to talk. Bronte is so..."

Penny D pinched his pincers together with her hand. Bronte's many eyes bulged, but at least he was quiet.

They both could heard a very faint echo coming from deep within the castle. Faint but audible. As they walked father and listened more closely it became more clear. It was Penny S.

"Help!" said Penny S. "Someone? Anyone? Help me please. I don't want to die here."

Penny D let go of Bronte's pincers.

"She must be just up ahead," said Penny D. "Let's hurry."

"And it won't be too hard to find her," said Bronte. "Just follow the annoying voice."

As they entered the tunnel under the castle Bronte made one last pitch at bringing Penny D to what he called "her senses." It was a good thing that Penny D had not been looking at Bronte, for if she had she would have noticed that he was sweating profusely. And if you have ever seen a tarantula sweat before, you would know it is not a pretty sight.

"You know, Penny darling, it's not too late," said Bronte. "We could still have a great party with five teenagers. Right?"

His advice fell on deaf ears. Without skipping a beat, Penny D sang her reply right back at him.

"Not, leaving, her," sung Penny D.

As Penny D and Bronte entered the open chamber in the center of Castle Longtooth Bronte leaped off of Penny D's shoulder and readied himself for attack. He shifted to the right, then he shifted to the left anticipating where his enemy might be coming at him from. In short, he was very nervous.

Penny D's attention was elsewhere. Her gaze was drawn upwards to the tiny cage suspended from the ceiling of the chamber by a chain. Inside the cage was Penny S.

The entire chamber was ablaze with torches hung from the walls. There were only two openings in this chamber, the one that Penny D and Bronte just arrived from and the two wooden doors at the furthest end.

Battle armaments decorated the walls as did chains with some skeletal remains still shackled to them. They were possibly some unfortunate souls who had a difference of opinion with the Count, Penny D thought, but she didn't know for sure. She also thought that she didn't want to find out.

The acoustics in the chamber were amazingly clear, even a whisper from Penny S high above them, could easily be heard from below. She began to mumble to herself as soon as she saw Penny D, perhaps not knowing or even caring if she could hear her.

Penny S was dressed in a peasant outfit from perhaps the 1600's. As much as she hated how humiliating she looked, Bronte was thinking, how fitting.

"It's about time you showed up," said Penny S.

She felt completely helpless but she didn't want Penny D to know it. So like any hunted or cornered animal she used the only weapon she had to defend herself, her mouth. This girl had a tongue that could clip a hedge and make her apology sound like it were your fault that she had gotten into this mess in the first place.

"Look, Goth Girl, you made your stupid point, okay," said Penny S. "If I ever come to another one of your birthday parties again, and there is no chance of that, I'll be polite, okay? Now get me down from here!"

Penny D was still unaccustomed to this very strange place. It was not that she was unaccustomed to a place where odd and unusual things could and did happen all the time, she wasn't.

What she was unaccustomed to was all the snickering, lying, cheating and name calling that she had witnessed every day in school since she had begun to attend it. And it was a bit of a let down to her that the Gothic Kingdom, a place where she now knew her family hailed from, practiced many of these same rituals.

Growing up and facing the world was hard to do for a teenager, or so it was stated in many of the stories from the books in the Dreadful Library. But Penny D was never quite sure what was meant by that. She enjoyed her family. So she shrugged it off as nothing more than a bi-product of a story that took place at another time and in another place.

In light of what she had been forced to participate in over the last few weeks, Penny D was starting to reconsider her conclusion. And so, she thought, there was more to growing up than met the eye.

It was her thirteenth birthday, she thought. She was a young lady now and by her own reckoning, it was time to face the music.

"How exactly did you get yourself up there?" said Penny D.

"How should I know?" said Penny S. "It's not my fault you live in a freak'n haunted house. I mean, just look at these clothes. Who designed this, Oliver Twisted?"

"You read Oliver Twist?" said Penny D. "I loved that book."

"It was a book?" said Penny S. "I meant the cartoon."

"It was a book first," said Penny D. "Then, I think they made the stage play. I'm not sure really what came next. When was the cartoon made?"

"Like I care?" said Penny S. "Get, me, down, from, here!"

There was a strange quiet for a moment or two as Penny

S's voice just echoed around the chamber.

"You still want to risk your neck to save that?" said Bronte.

"I'm regretting this even as I say it," said Penny D. "Yes, I do. I can't leave her here."

Bronte fell over. If he were a dog you would have imagined he was playing dead. But since he were an over-sized theraphosidae, we should just assume that he was exasperated by Penny D's answer and decided to pretend to faint.

"The only problem is, I don't know how I can get up there to let her out," said Penny D. "And bring her down. And get her to shut up long enough to get her home. And…"

"I get the point," said Bronte. "You don't. But I do. It's time to break a few more rules."

Bronte flipped over and landed back on his feet. He cracked his knuckles and hit the ground running right over to the chamber wall. Then, true to his closest cousins, the arachnids, he began to scale the walls.

"I'm waiting," said Penny S. "Sheesh, how long is this going to take?"

Penny D always knew that when Bronte had a plan in mind it would be best to simply stay out of his way.

"Hold tight," said Penny D to Penny S. "We're working on a plan."

Penny S was lying on her back tossing her slipper up into the air and catching it to pass the time.

"We?" said Penny S.

She flipped over on to her stomach and looked down at Penny D through the bars.

"You and who else, your invisible friend?" said Penny S.

Penny S was in her element, so to speak. She had a stranger doing her bidding. She felt completely at home firing away one order or insult after another. She didn't see anyone come in with Penny D, Bronte had already leapt off her shoulder. So her best guess was that Penny D was just shooting off her mouth making up bizarre things again that didn't make any sense, to her at least.

Bronte, on the other hand was on a mission. His plan was

simple; he was going to climb across the ceiling until he got to the chain that suspended the cage that Penny S was locked inside of. He would spin down the chain like it were a pole at a firehouse and open the cage so that Penny S could escape.

This Bronte had known from the very moment he'd entered the chamber. What he didn't know was if he had enough time to pull off his plan and exit the castle with both Penny's before the Count returned home. And that made him very, very nervous indeed.

Bronte landed on top of the cage with a great big thud. Penny S immediately leaped to her feet and started to create the worst possible scenarios she could; like that the cage was about to fall or that some new unknown creature were about to eat her alive.

From one end of the cage, peeking down from above was Bronte in all his glory. If you have never seen a theraphosidae smile, then you have really missed out on something. As soon as Penny S saw him, she turned three shades of white.

"Oh!," said Penny S. "Hurry up Goth chick, I'm being attacked by spiders."

"Correction," said Bronte. "You are being saved by a tarantula."

"Now I'm being attacked by a talking spider," said Penny S. "Do something, Goth girl."

Bronte was not phased by her stupid comment, after all, who couldn't tell the difference between an arachnid and a theraphosidae? So he slid down the bars and stuck his long pincers into the keyhole of the lock. He wiggled them around and the deadbolt slid back and the door slowly swung open.

"There, now you're free," said Bronte. "But if you want me to get you down from here, you'll have to talk nice to me."

It would appear that Bronte had an ulterior motive after all.

"Penny, Penny, Penny, Penny, do something," said Penny S. "He's getting closer."

"What do you want me to do," said Penny D. "I can't

climb walls. Besides, he's not going to hurt you, he's just being obnoxious."

Bronte leapt inside the cage and took one slow ponderous step closer to Penny S. She began to sweat, shiver and finally curled up into a little ball in the corner of the cage.

"What did I ever do to deserve this?" said Penny S asking herself. "What, what, what, what, what?"

"I don't know, but I would bet there was plenty," said Bronte.

"Conscience," said Penny S. "Is that you?"

Bronte being the opportunist that he was, seized the moment and ran with it.

"Why, yes, it is I, your conscience," said Bronte in a higher voice than normal.

"What is it you want from me?" said Penny S.

"You have been a very bad little girl and you deserve to become theraphosidae food," said Bronte.

"What is a theraphosidae?" said Penny S.

"A tarantula, stupid," said Bronte.

"Is that like a spider?" said Penny S.

"Yes, but a lot worse," said Bronte.

Penny D had reached the end of her patience. She was never a person to hurry or rush, she knew that to hurry you would cause stress and stress was probably the worst thing that anyone could ever have in his life. She also knew why she'd come here and was ready to have the day come to an end.

She stomped her foot down hard on the tiled floor and it echoed clear around the chamber. What came next was channeled from deep inside her.

"Bronte!" said Penny D in a very serious tone. "Stop scaring her!"

"But, Penny, it's fun," Bronte pleaded. "Besides, she insulted me. If she wants to be saved, she has to apologize."

Penny D was baffled as to why Bronte who, she had known since he was an egg was being so childish. In theraphosidae years he was middle aged and he should have been past all of this.

Then a new idea hit her. It was this place. Maybe, it brought out the side of you that summoned you here in the first place, thought Penny D. The three girls from school were the first example to come to mind. And Bronte had said he traveled back here when she was asleep in her bed at night, perhaps even more often than he was willing to admit. Then another example came to mind.

There was also that boy, Dim. She recognized him from school, but he was in a higher grade and so she had never had the displeasure of making his acquaintance until today (and under the worst circumstances she might add).

She had overheard stories that proved he was not the kind of boy she would ever get along with. She'd even heard Vincent say that he was "of the violent kind" once. She had no reason to doubt it. Vincent was a quiet and studious boy, he sounded honest when he answered questions in class and ignored the snickering that followed when he struggled to control his stuttering.

Since Penny D had come here to the Gothic Kingdom, there had been subtle but noticeable changes coming over her trusted pets. In the Goth world things were played by a different set of rules all together.

She could tell that Bronte was not going to listen to her now and although she was sure he would not hurt Penny S, she had to change her strategy fast or they would never get out of there.

Penny D could not put her finger on it, but here in the Gothic Kingdom there seemed to be a test of one's pride that came with living here. It was as if they had to live up to some expectation or another. She didn't believe in such things. She knew they were all part of the ego, a false sense of self worth, and formulated that this place was a Limburgatory. It attracted those who felt compelled to repeat their misguided actions. Here they could play them over and over again. Perhaps until they learned some kind of lesson.

Realizing that, she figured that Penny S had better wise up

and wise up fast.

"Penny, listen!" said Penny D desperately. "Bronte is the only one who can save you now. Just apologize to him. It's a good thing. Then we can all go home."

"No way!" said Penny S. "I'd rather die here than apologize to a bug."

It was a stalemate.

Bronte laughed.

Penny S whimpered.

Until, the singing began.

Chapter 28
The Count and his Brides

The singing was muffled, as if it came from behind closed doors, but its piercing echo came at the two teens and one large theraphosidae from all sides. They were women singing, opera perhaps. Maybe even in German.

"Hear that, stupid head?" said Bronte. "Those are the brides of the evil Count Longtooth. They ain't just whistling Dixie, they would be calling him for dinner. And that is most likely you."

From years of emotional neglect, Penny S had learned how to pull herself together when necessary. She rolled out of her fetal position and began to take the strange English speaking creature seriously. Well, not completely seriously, she still swung her sarcasm around like a bullwhip.

"Yeah, right," said Penny S. "Like I believe that those are real cannibals, and coming from a fat spider no less?"

"I'm not fat, I have a large exoskeleton," said Bronte.

Bronte squeezed his head and front legs between the bars.

"Penny, can we please leave her here?" said Bronte.

The double set of doors at the far end of the chamber

slowly opened all by themselves. One of Count Longtooth's brides floated through the doorway and into the chamber. Not flying really, just hovering, a few inches above the tiled floor.

Although she was human-like, she, or it, was anything but human. Her appendages were far too long for her to be a human. Her skin was far too white and her body was barely clothed with a silky fabric that danced in the gentle air that rushed through the chamber.

She was almost translucent. You could practically see her organs beating, breathing and digesting within her. Her muscles strained up and down her long neck as she sang.

"Oh, poop," said Bronte.

And with that a heap of thick webbing spilled out of his bottom.

"See," said Penny S. "Webbing! I knew you were a spider."

"Is that what that is," said Bronte. "Who knew?"

"This can't be good," said Penny D. "What is taking you two so long?"

The second of the Count's brides levitated into the chamber from beyond the doors at its far end.

Penny S suddenly realized that this little temper tantrum had gone on for too long.

"Okay, Mr. Spider," said Penny S. "I'm ready to be saved now. I'm sorry. See, I said it. Now get me down now. Hurry, hurry, hurry, hurry."

"Now you're ready to be saved?" said Bronte. "Are you sure you wouldn't want to wait a little longer? You know, like to find out what's on the dinner menu?"

"No, I'm ready now, Mr. Ugly Bug," said Penny S. "I don't want them to suck my blood or anything. Please, please, please, please."

"Okay, already," said Bronte.

"Please, please, please, please," continued Penny S.

"Will you shut your pie hole?" said Bronte. "I'm trying to think."

If you have ever seen a theraphosidae, er, I mean, a spider

think, it is quite an amazing thing. His many eyes began to blink out of sequence and his legs began to quiver.

Bronte was considering his new found talent, the wind velocity and the weight of the package that he was entrusted to deliver to the ground thirty seven feet below. He thought to himself that if all of his calculations were correct he should be able to deliver this brat to the ground below with at most only one broken leg- but alive!

This was a chance he was willing to take. Enough thinking, he thought to himself. It was a time for action.

"Okay, do exactly what I tell you to do," said Bronte.

"Yeah, sure, whatever," said Penny S. "Let's go, go, go!"

Bronte released another blob of thick webby fluid that stuck firmly to the floor of the cage. It made the strangest squishy sound when it hit.

"Oh, that is so nasty," said Penny S. "How many more times are you going to do that?"

"We're just getting started, sister," said Bronte.

He then leapt into Penny D's outstretched arms, her head tilted back and away from him.

A third siren bride drifted into the chamber next to the other two.

"Whatever you are planning, Bronte, do it now," said Penny D. "They're multiplying."

"Okay, vamp food, jump," said Bronte.

"What?" said Penny S. "That's your plan? Goth girl, the bug wants me to commit suicide. What kind of stupid plan is that?"

Bronte began a tug-of-war between him and Penny S. She quickly spun off balance and tumbled out through the open cage door, with Bronte clinging to her rope belt.

Penny S screamed all the way down as she watched the ground race toward her. Just before she hit it, the web tightened and pulled her back upwards toward the cage.

It was a bungee cord effect. The web saved her life, although this same action was repeated a few times before Penny D was able to grab hold of them both and put a stop to it. All the while Penny S was screaming.

Once safely on the ground, Bronte climbed up onto Penny D's shoulder and slapped Penny S across the face, finally shutting her up.

"So, you are a spider after all," said Penny D.

"It would appear so," said Bronte. "Why didn't my family tell me?"

"Welcome to my world," said Penny D.

Even though Penny S was a bit rattled and dizzy from the near-death, life-saving experience, she managed to pat Bronte on the head. This may have been her only way of thanking him. Bronte didn't ask, so we may never know.

"It's time to blow this opera house," said Penny D.

"I'm with you, little sister," said Bronte.

Before they could even move in their tracks, the ground began to rumble.

The floor of the chamber heaved open and exploded apart sending tiles everywhere. As soon as the dust cleared, standing in the center of the mess was the master of the castle, the lord of the House of Longtooth, the Count himself.

"Too late," said Bronte.

Chapter 29
A Duel to the Death

The Count was looking a little long in the tooth. His cloak and cape were badly tattered. His skin was more wrinkled, as if that were even possible. He hardly resembled the terrifying and powerful Count that had terrorized the local town a little more than a decade before.

Penny D knew nothing of this but Bronte had kept at least one of his many eyes on the fall of the House of Longtooth over the years. He claimed that he no longer feared him but that was because he was able to keep a safe distance away.

Today, Bronte was thinking differently. Today he was regretting his decision to allow his ego to get the best of him and procrastinating his escape from this dreaded place with both Penny D and that other creature before the Count had returned.

"It wasn't my fault," is what he would say if asked, and he was only half correct. This place made him feel different when he was here. It was a phenomenon for sure. He knew even Penny D had witnessed it.

But there was so much more to the story than that. What Penny D didn't know was that the townspeople had banned together against the Count since her mother and father had had their altercation with him. Natty had shown them how to turn the tables on him and they had utilized all that Natty had recommended.

The Count lived practically as a recluse. That is, with the exception of his three strange wives. But they didn't talk much, they were too busy singing.

There was a brief war that went on for a while. The Count would steal a sheep for dinner and the townspeople would set traps for him. Although he was often caught like a rat in a maze that had no exit, he would eventually escape and retreat to his castle. It was so huge and had so many places to hide, that they never even bothered to try to find him there.

They simply laid their traps and let engineering do the job for them.

More often than not the Count would have to remove a bear trap from his leg, or a noose knotted tightly around his neck, all the result of a trap successfully sprung. You see, Natty had left the townspeople with numerous detailed trap diagrams for them to build and set for the Count. And they had all worked.

At one time it had appeared that the Count was indestructible to the townspeople. This was the cause of their vexation and their misery. However, Natty was schooled in the laws of physics. He taught them that for everything that existed, no matter how evil it appeared, there was a solution to eliminate it.

The formula he had taught them was that for every creation that exists, there was an equal and opposite recreation. Thus, a solution to every problem, a cure for every illness, and therefore a way to eliminate a skin-walker who suddenly appeared in their backyard.

As for the Count, it was not so much the pain of the traps that deterred him from retaliation on the townspeople, he thrived on pain. It was the nuisance. They outnumbered him too greatly and they also baited him with sickly livestock: a delicacy he couldn't turn down. He should have detected the trap, but when tempted he resorted to his lower self because he was an animal after all and fell for their tomfoolery. The result was always a near capture, followed by a lot more pain.

The townspeople formed a covenant to protect themselves from the Count and other creatures like him. Although they couldn't transform themselves into tiny animals and hide to listen to the plans from their enemy, it was their darned unity that drove the Count away (that and, he was getting older).

Eventually he'd given up. It wasn't worth the fight. The townspeople would lose a chicken here and there, and he would pay the price for having stolen it. He would have to attend to a severed bone in his arm, rib or skull.

He healed with remarkable speed but could only do so at night. The night was all the time he had to do his dirty work. The townspeople had all day to plan and set traps in his own castle against him.

Soon he'd become a mockery. Even the teenagers like Bronte and his cohorts had started to play pranks on him just for laughs. The once great skin-walker had been reduced to a laughing stock.

He was full of regrets. There wasn't a single day that would pass that he didn't plot his revenge upon the one family who had revealed to the masses just how easily they could overthrow him. All they'd had to do was lose their fear and allow common sense to direct their actions.

There was no telling where he had picked up the three brides that shared his castle. Perhaps he had nothing to do with finding them at all. We know how similar people attract one another, so they may have come to him. They did serve one particular purpose for the Count, their singing drove away the townspeople and allowed him to live in his misery alone.

But not tonight.

Tonight the future was looking awfully bright for the Count. Patience had its rewards.

It was not that the Count had lost his evil deadliness, no, he was just as dangerous as he had been a decade before. What he'd lost was his will to execute bad deeds on a daily basis. His mortality had been catching up with him. Until tonight. Tonight, he felt young again.

"Good evening, Miss Dreadful," said the Count. "Count Longtooth, at your service."

Then he bowed to Penny D as if this made everything proper.

"I have been waiting a very, very long time for you to return."

And then he smiled, broken and rotted teeth and all.

Penny D was all fed up. She hadn't even a hint of what was about to transpire but she was fed up all the same. The simple fact that everyone she ran into in the Gothic Kingdom knew her and had been expecting her, was racking her nerves.

"Why was I the last to be told?" said Penny D. "Is there anything else I should know? Like, I have some special powers that I have yet to discover, or that some of my friends are really fish from Venus, or that I can talk with inanimate objects? Please, tell me now and let's get this over with already."

The Count had no idea what she was babbling about. And to tell the truth she wasn't what he had expected at all. She was not quiet and reserved like her mother or apparently very bright like her father. He felt that she was off track. A disappointment.

He'd waited all these years to exact his revenge on her family, on her, and was not about to blow that simply because she was a young teenager who could shoot off her mouth at him.

"But,..." said the Count. "Where else would you be on your thirteenth birthday, daughter of Natty Dreadful, from the house of the Dreadful Poisonberrys?"

To the Count this all made sense. Then he laughed to himself to punctuate his comment.

"I've never actually heard it put that way," said Penny D.

"But to tell you the truth, I was having this really cool birthday party for the first time in my life."

"Don't flatter yourself," said Penny S in a droll voice. "It wasn't that cool."

"Zip it, mouth," said Bronte.

Bronte leapt onto Penny S' shoulders and spun a web around her head.

"Ah, Bronte," said the Count. "I had almost forgotten about you waiting for her return. I still get a rash on rainy nights and, well, that reminds me of you."

The Count suddenly felt uncomfortable disclosing this information in front of two young girls or perhaps he realized that he was straying from the topic.

"Go, on..." said Bronte.

With a flap of his cape, the Count's arm began to transform into a large crab claw.

Neither Penny D nor Penny S had ever seen something like that before. Right in front of them totally beyond their expectation this creepy old man transformed his arm.

With that the Counts mood dramatically changed and without even looking, he pinched and severed the rusty chain that was fastened to the wall.

The cage that Penny S had been held captive in suddenly began to fall from above. Penny D pulled Penny S by her arm clear from the descending metal box. The door of the cage swung wide open just before it hit the ground smashing the tiles of the floor.

It landed right over Bronte missing him by inches on every side. He was still alive, but imprisoned.

"That was a mean thing to do," said Penny D.

"Yes," said the Count, with no expression at all. "It was. But don't worry, your turn is coming up. I'm just getting started."

"Penny, run," said Bronte, in as quiet a voice as he could whisper.

But she didn't. She was her parents' daughter and fear was not part of her upbringing.

Penny S, on the other hand, was all full of fear. She wisely began to back away and considered running, but her legs wouldn't listen to what her head was telling them to do.

The Count's siren brides began to close in on Penny S and started to sing again. She pulled at the webbing that was stuck across her mouth and removed it from her head.

"No, no, no," said Penny S. "Not opera."

She was gone. She was as confused as one could be at her age before she had even come in here. So instead of thinking about how to escape with her life all she could focus on was how much she hated opera. German opera in particular.

Her father used to play it when she was a baby and for many years after until she was ready for grade school. He'd called it enrichment, she'd called it child abuse. She often told him how much she hated it, but he was not the type of parent who listened to his offspring.

Bronte was starting to regret all the time he'd wasted terrorizing Penny S. His best friend in the world was in trouble and he felt that it was all his fault. He would gladly lay down his life to save her, but this could not be done. He was in a self-made prison. He'd chosen to prolong the rescue of Penny S and now he was paying the price for it.

He'd often heard Penny D say that wisdom was the only means by which one could derive a positive solution to any problem. With that in mind, he closed all of his eyes and concentrated.

"Okay, think, Bronte, think," said Bronte. "Harder! If I break the Primate Directive twice in one night I could go to Gothic prison for a very, very long time. But how different is that from where I am right now? And in the clink, I get free food and a potty break. In here, I'm watching my best friend in the whole world about to become Swiss cheese and I will most definitely end up the same way. But, what can I do?"

One of Bronte's eyes caught a glint of light from a shiny metal sword hanging up on the wall. It was part of a coat of arms.

He turned around and squeezed his butt between the

cage bars. He dispensed a steady flow of webbing to the adjacent wall and hit the sword solid.

"What is that odor?" said the Count.

"You're the one with the animal fetish, so I guess it was you," said Penny D.

"No, it smells like guano, but there is something else in there," said the Count, unaware he was being made fun of.

"And now the part that is going to hurt for a very long time," Bronte thought to himself.

With all his might he reeled in the webbing, pulling the sword off the wall and across the tiled floor. He dragged it just far enough so that it stopped right in front of Penny D.

Without missing a beat, Penny D flipped the sword up into the air with her toe and caught it in her hand. She then pointed the cutlass directly at the Count.

"Leave, my, friends, alone!" said Penny D.

"Oh, you must be kidding me," said the Count.

Again, with a wave of his cape the Count transformed his hands into two long three-toed sloth paws. He slowly, invitingly, presented one long claw to Penny D.

"Come a little closer, my dear," said the Count. "And say that again."

Like greased lightning Penny D parried forward and sliced off one of the Counts long sloth claws.

The Count recoiled, he was not only surprised but down right infuriated. Not even Natty had gotten the best of him so early in their duel.

"Why, you little brat!" said the Count. "Do you have any idea how long it took me to grow that? It looks as though the head doesn't roll very far from the guillotine after all."

By now Penny D knew exactly just how far she had gotten herself into this mess. She knew she was up against ridiculous odds and that reasoning time was over. She knew what a skin-walker was and what they were capable of doing. She knew that her only chance for survival depended upon her ability to fend off the Count long enough for help to arrive (assuming that there was some help to arrive and they would arrive in time).

Earlier that day she had witnessed some very unusual transformations. No, not the physical kind, but the metaphysical kind. She'd watched her new friend Harold transform from a seventh grade class nerd into a "man of action." She thought this was a good idea and that she should do the same.

"Penny S, run for help," said Penny D.

But Penny S didn't move. She just stood there with her hands cupped over her ears.

Penny D slashed forward again and chopped off another of the Count's long sloth claws.

"Fine," said the Count. "I was going to go easy on you and kill you quickly being that you're children and all. But as far as I am concerned, play time is over."

The Count crouched down, his cape billowing behind him. Penny D had no idea where that sudden gust of wind had come from but she was sure of one thing- it made the Count look quite dramatic.

His hind legs transformed into those of a goat, and the Count launched at Penny D with his long sloth paws pointed right at her.

Penny D completely dodged his first attack and swiftly retaliated by smacking his behind with the flat side of her sword.

It may have been her height and her low center of gravity that made her appear faster on her feet than the Count expected, but he wasn't sure. He was very tall and clearly out of practice while Penny D was in her very best form.

The Count crashed into a candelabra, and wax candles scattered the floor. He was soon back on his own human feet and preparing himself for another attack.

"We both know how this is going to end," said the Count. "So stop being an impetuous child, little girl, and let me kill you."

"Okay," said Penny D.

She dropped her sword to her side and plainly walked

towards to the Count. It suddenly dawned on her why the townspeople were no longer afraid of him. He was stupid.

Penny D was not about to give in.

To throw him off balance, she switched her sword fighting form to samurai style. Her attack came suddenly and straight on like a dart seeking the bull's eye of a target.

The Count had just enough time to use his cape as a distraction and dodge the tip of her sword as it slashed through his tattered cape and grazed him. Strangely, this upset her.

The Count looked down at where she had struck him, blood dripped from his side.

Unfortunately, this may have been a turning point for Penny D, she may have found out that she had no real killer instinct after all. Her goal was and still is, to get herself and her friends out of the castle alive. Nothing more.

She was still unafraid, but the stress had finally gotten to her. Fully aware that her back was firmly against a wall she did what any one would do; she turned the blame on someone else.

"Penny S!" said Penny D. "Why are you still here? I told you to go get help."

Even before the words came out of her mouth Penny D realized what she had done. She was blaming another for her own well intentioned actions. Further, she let the Count know that she couldn't kill him even if she wanted to. It was simply not in her nature.

The Count took it all in. He was a true artist when it came to luring his enemy into a false sense of security.

Penny D had finally come to realize that she was completely alone. It was time to either sit down and die, or to die trying to live. She mustered up all of the courage any thirteen year old girl could have and attacked the Count again.

This time the Count was way ahead of her. He transformed his legs into those of a kangaroo and sprung out of her way. He met her attacks defensively but never offensively. He was incubating a plan that he knew would work. He started to laugh at her, but this only made her fight harder.

"Why don't you pick on someone your own size?" lashed out Penny D. "Or someone half as ugly, if you can find one?"

Once or twice she felt that she had him on the run, he kept missing her head and face by several inches with his claws. Little did she know that he was doing this on purpose. Then, he didn't miss.

As Penny D backed away from their last exchange she realized that she was grazed over her forehead, on her arm and on one of her legs. She came to a very quick conclusion that he was baiting her; just toying with her all along. She knew she would have to end this soon if she were to live to tell this story.

Haymaking with a sword, that is, swinging it wildly, is never a good idea. It usually means that the swords' person is at their wit's end and / or just completely tuckered out. But in this case, while the Count was focusing on his next attack (to maim his victim); he found himself at even odds with the half-size powerhouse that Penny Dreadful was.

Her sword was moving faster than the human eye could see. She used the stone wall to her left and the floor below to bounce her sword off of. This helped her to redirect her attack instantaneously without projecting a direction for the Count to defend against.

For once she really did have him on the run and she knew it. But she needed a new playing field to prevent the Count from compensating. If she'd had more clutter to hide behind, she could have found a moment to rest, if even for a short time. This was all she would need to throw him off, maybe even scare him away, she thought to herself-wrongly.

Penny D ran up a narrow stone stairway to the next level. It overlooked the chamber below.

Bronte cheerd her on from inside the cage.

"Go Penny, go Penny!" said Bronte. "You got the moves, he's gonna lose. Go Penny, go Penny!"

Penny D stood at the top level and looked over her battle-ground. She knew the Count would either be leaping up the steps after her or come flying over the balcony any second now.

As expected, the Count spread out his cape and like a magnet drawn to another magnet, he was suddenly pulled to the wall of the chamber. Like a catfish in a glass tank he hugged the stone wall and slithered upwards at an alarming rate. Then with a single bound he cleared the railing and landed onto the stone floor of the second level.

Falling forward onto his hands, the Counts' cloak rushed forward and his hands transformed into the hooves of a rhinoceros. His shoulders swelled and the entire front half of his body followed suit.

Penny D sensed what was coming and swiftly ran behind a natural stone column just as the Count hit it head on with his new mighty front horns.

Most of the wall shattered and Penny D was pushed by the blow onto the ground. She rolled onto her back and then up onto her feet. She used the dust from the debris as good cloud cover for a final escape.

She tossed her sword over the side of the railing and climbed down a rope that was hanging over the edge of the second level to the ground below. Her hands slipped from the rope and she fell but a few feet to the ground. It was just enough of a fall for her to twist her ankle when she landed.

Penny D tried to get up, but failed. Her stockings were torn and her blouse all bloodied. She was a mess.

She located her sword and tried to reach for it. Just before her fingers touched the handle a massive gorilla's foot landed on top of it. With his opposable thumbs, the Count gripped the sword and tossed it clear out of her reach.

The cape of the Count deflated back into the form of the human underneath it. His hands were transformed again into mighty sloth claws.

"No, Penny, get up, run," was all Bronte could whisper to himself.

Penny S answered Bronte, her voice barely audible even to herself. She may have even been in a state of shock, (or denial, or apathy) when she said what she said, "Just give up.

There's no point. You can't win."

"Bravo!" said the Count.

Never one to surrender a chance to mock his victim, to rub salt in the wound so to speak, the Count held out his sloth-like paws and pretended to applaud.

"I would applaud you, but as you see…I can't," said the Count. "But as for our encore performance, I will finally rid this world of the last of the Dreadful clan. It is time for your final curtain, my dear."

True to the evil being that he was, the Count raised his one clawed paw into the air in preparation to strike. He loved the drama and the attention his siren brides gave him. They'd even stopped singing for this.

They were waiting to swarm around Penny D as soon as he struck her down for good.

Penny D, never once looked away, she focused her eyes on the Count. She looked over his screwed up face and clenches her shaking fists as she held them out in front of her.

She slowly stood up on her wobbly legs. Her teeth were clenched so tightly it was a wonder she could even utter a word at all.

"Bring it on," said Penny D as tears swelled up in her eyes. "You dental nightmare!"

"Good bye," said Count Longtooth in a very soft voice.

The butterfly pin that Harold had given Penny D for her birthday suddenly slipped out of her torn pocket and hit the ground. The sound and light mechanism was activated and the rest was history. The musical tune of, "Way Down Upon The Swanee River" began to echo around the chamber. The magnificent acoustics of this chamber had once again proven to be a credit to the architect who had designed it.

The colorful lights of red, green, orange and yellow distracted the Count as his final blow came down at Penny D missing her completely.

The colors danced across his face, blinding him. Finally, there was some natural color in this place!

"My eyes," screamed the Count. "I can't see. Make it stop."

Penny D unclenched her fist and picked up the pin. She held it out at the Count, the colors decorating his face like a holiday ornament.

Bronte was beyond himself. He was so full of excitement he began to dance around the cage singing as well.

"You did it, you did it, Penny!" said Bronte. "Way, down upon the Swanee River, far, far away..."

The Count appeared immobilized.

His siren brides covered their ears.

"Southern music," wailed the Brides.

As quickly as they had come in, the Count's siren Brides drifted away. Then disappeared from the chamber entirely.

Penny S was still unable to comprehend what had happened. A moment ago she were wishing Penny D to simply give up and die.

Her anger spent, Penny D was a lot calmer now.

"The gift that keeps giving," said Penny D. "You came to my rescue after all. Thank you Harold."

She put the pin on.

The Count screamed one last time as his body began to crack and disintegrate.

"This is not, the end, Dreadful," said the Count. "I will, be, bacccckkkkk..."

"That's what all evil people say," said Penny D. "But I'm pretty sure you're a done deal."

When all that was left of the Count was a smoldering pile of ashes, Penny D shut off the pin. She walked over to Bronte who was still trapped in the cage.

"It's time to go home, my friend," said Penny D and smiled at Bronte through her bloodied teeth.

Chapter 30
The Return of the Lost Girls

As the two Pennys, D and S, and Bronte traveled down the long tunnel underneath Castle Longtooth, Penny D felt that her victory over the Count was bitter-sweet. On the one hand, she had accomplished what she'd set out to do; she saved Penny S. But on the other hand she never meant the Count any harm nor had she ever seen a skin-walker dissolve before. It was not pleasant.

She knew in her heart that she hadn't done anything harmful to him directly, therefore what befell him was his own doing (and maybe Harold had more than just a little to do with it).

Bronte on the other hand was in great spirits. Whatever it was that had possessed him just a short while ago, that which made him procrastinate rather than assist Penny D on her mission, was over with. He was back to normal, and he simply couldn't shut up. He was pumped.

"And also, you know, this is just like that TV show I was watching," said Bronte. "At the very end of their great adventure together, the lad and his faithful pet walked into the sunset."

One utter of the word TV and Penny S snapped out of her depression-coma.

"You watch TV?" said Penny S. "I thought you didn't have a television in your house?"

"I said I don't have a TV," said Penny D. "Bronte does what he pleases."

"I don't believe it," said Penny S, "The bug has more privileges than you do."

Bronte drifted from one subject to the next until they came to the entrance of the castle. Waiting for them there under the great arch were the Lost Girls, looking no less forlorn than when she'd first met them.

"Oh, great," said Penny S. "Those crazy Goth chicks again."

She circled her temple with one finger.

The Lost Girls circled Penny D, Bronte and their guest. They may have been delighted, it was hard to say what the broken smiles on their faces meant.

"We knew you would succeed, Penny Dreadful of the Poisonberries," said Daphne.

Then she almost made a complete smile, but the moment didn't last long.

"Congratulations," said Daphne blankly.

Surprisingly, all the girls applauded, but ever so lightly. That, too, came to a quick end.

"Thank you, everyone," said Penny D. "Then you knew more than I. Not that anyone around here doesn't."

"Are you then ready, the one called Social?" said Daphne.

"Say what?" said Penny S. "What does that mean? Are you ready? You mean ready to go home? Heck, yeah!"

"No, to become, one of us?" said Nellie Deranged, the younger sister of Daphne.

Penny S turned white and dressed in her peasant outfit she suddenly looked like she fit right in. Her breathing labored again and she looked like she was finally about to cry.

"Sounds good to me," said Bronte. "Let's get going Penny."

"Wait," said Penny D. "But I found her in time, didn't I? I must have."

"Does it really matter?" said Daphne. "She stays with us, Penny Dreadful. She is not your friend. No one will miss her and it's not like she learned anything from her experience anyway."

Through teary eyes Penny S spoke her case.

"That's not true," said Penny S. "I have. I swear it."

Her mind raced. She knew that this was her do-or-die trying moment.

"I learned, um, don't make fun of Goths," said Penny S. "Um, don't eat boiled frogs, um, vampires don't brush their teeth,...Penny, don't let them take me. I can be your best friend, honest!"

"Don't push it, little sister," said Penny D, without getting caught up in the drama.

Then she began to reflect. If there was a way for her to take Penny S back, she would. And so she made up her mind that there was and saw it as fact. She would take Penny S back with her. That was why she had come and she will not leave there without her. From that moment, it was in her mind as done.

Meanwhile, through sobs of bitter anger and regret, Penny S suddenly became human.

"When you get back home without me," said Penny S to Penny D. "There is a gift in my backpack for your snake. Don't let him eat it. It's filled with rat poison."

Bronte found this to be the most hilarious thing he had ever heard. The way he rolled around and flipped in the air you would think he'd heard the funniest joke ever told.

"Bronte...," said Penny D.

"Like Rebecca is so stupid she would eat anything that came from you!" said Bronte.

"I'm sorry, Daphne," said Penny D. "I appreciate what you did for us and all that, but I can't let her stay here. For one thing, she doesn't belong."

"Neither did we," said Nellie.

Then a strange little smile crossed all of their faces. This one stayed.

"We are so lonely here, my little sister," said Daphne. "We were hoping for a new playmate. Will you at least promise to come back and visit us?"

"I didn't know that I could," said Penny D.

"You can," said Daphne. "All the time. You are of both worlds, Penny Dreadful. You are a Dreadling. Didn't you know?"

"I do now," said Penny D. "And I will be back. You can bet on it. I promise."

"And Penny always keeps her word," said Bronte, then he shot a nasty look over at Penny S.

The Lost Girls exchanged hugs with Penny Dreadful and Penny S as well, but no one was sure why.

"Follow me, clueless," said Bronte to Penny S.

A sewer hole cover unscrewed itself and rolled away in a circle like a coin thrown onto a table until it stopped spinning. Bronte leapt down into the open sewer hole and Penny S did the same without any hesitation.

"Mission accomplished," said Penny D.

She slapped her hands together twice as if cleaning them off.

"We dislike farewells," said Daphne. "So we will just leave."

And with that they, the Lost Girls, turned and walked away.

Just off to Penny D's right, perched up on stone pedestal was a large stone lion. Posed in mid-roar, it suddenly belched (accompanied by the proper sound of one), and the lion spit up the metal mask that Penny D had created in her shop class. It had made its way here to the Gothic Kingdom after all and slid across the ground stopping right at her feet.

"My mask," said Penny D. "What's that doing here?"

Then she remembered back when with all the commotion of following Rebecca, Bronte and Hawthorne through her home and into her bed room, the mask had been knocked off her night stand and must have slipped under the bed with them.

This was no accident, she thought to herself. Penny D didn't believe in such things. The mask came to her at this very time and place for a reason. She didn't know why, but she felt compelled to pick it up and put it on.

Once she looked out through the dark green visor glass of the eye ports, it all became crystal clear. This was what she had been meant to see.

Through the dark green visor glass, Penny D saw the landscape of the Gothic Kingdom in multiple shades of emerald. But when she turned around to look at Castle Longtooth she saw something else.

It was just as it had been in shop class on the day she first completed the mask, when she had gotten a very unusual surprise. When Mr. Kindle had smiled at her, he revealed his one golden tooth. The unique properties of the golden luster transcended the green filter of the visor glass.

This time around Penny D saw something similar, exactly what her family had expected her to see.

Her family fortune was hidden right here before her eyes, covered by a layer of dirt and grime. It was probably hidden by her father and her uncle to prevent the Count from finding it more than a decade ago. It was gold! And all the dirt and grime in this world could not hide it when seen through the dark green visor glass.

The gold lay hidden in the walls in unusual ways, a nugget here, a nugget there. It was cast into an unused chain link that dangled from the wall. It was also made into several bolts on a broken wagon wheel, screwed into the hinges on the sign that pointed the way to town, and hammered into the metal collar around the stone lion's neck.

It was in bits and pieces everywhere! The drainage pipe was made of gold, and the coat of arms hanging on the wall outside the tunnel they'd just come through was made of gold. Gold was cast in the form of a rooster on top of the weather vane and fashioned onto the mending that wrapped around an old broom.

It was the Poisoinberry Fortune! She had found it.

"Cool beans," said Penny Dreadful.

Chapter 31
There's No Place Like Home

The bells above the front door inside the Dreadful Mansion started to ring and the door itself swung open. Penny S was standing on the other side and came racing in as if she were magically pushed by some invisible force from outside. She rubbed her behind and glanced back at the door as it closed. Perhaps the kick was real and not as imaginary as it seemed. We will never know for sure.

Penny S was dressed in the same clothes she was last seen in while she was here, most unenjoyably attending Penny D's thirteenth birthday party.

Aside from that, there appeared very little change about her. Now that she was back in the normal world, she didn't want anyone to know that she'd almost had the teenage equivalent of a nervous breakdown while she was in the Gothic Kingdom.

"Penny S!" said Britney, leaping off the couch. "You're back. Thank heavens you're all right."

"We sadly gave you up for dead," said Olivia.

"When we factored in the particulars of what happens to bad girls who go to that place that you just came from, that is," said Harold. "We figured that your return was most unlikely."

"Britney and I were discussing how to divide up your Julius Kilowatt collection," said Olivia.

"But only if you were dead or never to return," said Britney. "But you're not and you did. So that point is moot. Right, Olivia?"

Never one to filter anything she said, Olivia spoke the truth, as Harold just had.

"I guess so," said Olivia.

"So, where did Penny D find you anyway?" said Malcolm.

Penny S was back now. And never one to learn the full lesson of her mistakes, the old Penny S and all that, that implied, suddenly kicked in.

"Like it matters, meat head?" said Penny S. "I just want to get out of this creepy place before the lights go out again."

She could have just left, and in a hurry at that, but once again Penny S had to prove that bad habits were hard to break. She started for the front door then paused.

There was something more on her mind and her ego (or her pride, or her self-loathing), just couldn't let her step through that doorway to the outside world where she would be home free without dishing out one last insult.

"You know," started Penny S. "If I never came to this stupid party in the first place..."

With perfect timing that only coincidence could deliver, the lights in the room suddenly went out.

The screaming from Britney and Penny S could probably have been heard clear down the road to Terracotta Junior High School. One of them, most likely Penny S, managed to open the front door and bolted like lightning down the path and out of sight. Britney was a close second and it was a good thing that she was not standing in front of Penny S at the time, the result would not have been pretty.

When the lights came back on, Olivia was standing there at the open front door all by herself. She was patting Bronte on the head who had been toying with the light switch and snickering to himself. It looked like he had pulled a fast one.

"That was a funny little thing you did there," said Olivia.

Then she held up her cellphone and mouthed the words "call me" to Malcolm as if Harold couldn't read her lips from just a few feet away. She waved to Harold and left the Dreadful Mansion.

Malcolm was still in mid wave after the front door closed shut. His open palm had Olivia's phone number clearly written on it.

Accompanied by a very loud "bong," from the grandfather's clock, the walls of the living room appeared to shift. Uncle Calagari and Penny D stepped into the room together. She still had her metal mask in her hand.

Penny D had already changed her clothes into a new very Goth looking outfit, and where she had suffered her injuries, she was bandaged neatly. Uncle Calagari was also looking quite dapper. But the look on his face clearly said that he knew he would have to answer for a very bad call on his part, the call that sent Penny D back to the Gothic Kingdom alone and unprotected by an adult.

Her mother and her father were suddenly gathered around the three children.

"How do you guys keep doing that?" said Malcolm.

"I'm sure I don't know what you mean," said Uncle Calagari.

Then he winked at Malcolm.

"Penny dear, I trust you see now why we couldn't tell you about your special heritage?" said Natty.

"We needed to see if you were a true Goth like your father or, if you were like me?" said Lucinda. "Now that we know for sure, there is so much to tell you. That and, rest assure that we will never keep any secret from you ever again."

"There was never a doubt in my mind," said Uncle Calagari. "I knew it from the very start."

"We also knew you were confused and we didn't want to make it any worse for you than it had to be," said Natty. "That and the most important reason; we didn't want to fill your head with ideas of failure. Only the belief that you can succeed at anything you put your mind to."

"That was why we chose to home school you; to extinguish the doubt before it manifested," said Lucinda. "But, it would appear we didn't account for everything. The reports we were receiving from the other side must have been exaggerations."

Natty glanced over at Rebecca and Bronte and Hawthorne.

"We put you in harm's way, didn't we?" said Natty. "We are sorry for that. The best intentions aside, I feel as though we ultimately failed you as parents."

"Oh, forget it," said Penny D, waving it off as if it were nothing. "I'm fine."

She held up both her hands, thumbs and pinkies stuck out, then made a face. Yes, their little seventh grader was back.

"Is it true that I can travel back and forth between here and the Gothic Kingdom?" said Penny D.

"Quite true," said Lucinda. "You have family there that you have yet to meet. We can visit them together, if you like?"

"Suddenly I don't feel so bad about being different," said Penny D.

"Being different, Penny," said Natty, "is the very best part about being."

It was written all over Penny D's face, she was overjoyed about being.

"Group hug," said Malcolm, and he and Harold joined in.

"It may not be easy being Dreadful," said Penny D, "but it sure is a lot of fun. Oh, I almost forgot. Have I got a surprise for you."

Then she winked at them.

Uncle Calagari stood behind an old-fashion picture camera. He held up a flash tray with one hand and a squeeze bulb with the other.

"Let us get a picture to properly commemorate the occasion, yes," said Uncle Calagari.

Penny D posed with one arm around each of her two

best friends, Malcolm and Harold. Rebecca, Hawthorne and Bronte cuddled up next to and between them.

"You guys are the coolest friends a Dreadling could ever have," said Penny D.

"What she said," said Malcolm.

"Now hold very still," said Uncle Calagari. "This could take a few moments."

"Why not just use your MyPhone?" said Malcolm through his smiling clenched teeth. "Oh, right. I forgot where I was."

Penny D had something on her mind and decided to share it. She asked it through her smiling clenched teeth.

"So, Malcolm, did you get a date with Olivia?" said Penny D.

"Spot on," said Malcolm. "However, there's no telling if she will remember any of this by tomorrow."

Harold joined in, but he had trouble keeping his lips from moving as he talks.

"Britney told me that I was her hero," said Harold. "But I still don't like her. Should I pursue a relationship?"

Without any rehearsal, both Penny D and Malcolm answered Harold at the same time.

"No!" said Penny D and Malcolm.

A huge flash of light and a cloud of smoke filled the room. With big smiles on their faces, Penny D, Harold and Malcolm laughed as they rubbed their eyes to extinguish the bright spots that floated in the air.

"Let's start up this party all over again," said Penny D.

"Aight," said Malcolm.

"Is there really no cake, or were you just kidding?" said Harold, in a concerned tone.

"Give me a few minutes, I will see what I can do," said Uncle Calagari.

At that very same time, outside the Dreadful Mansion, a small group of children were walking past the front gate. As their mother continued on, they stopped to stare, point and whisper about what they saw and imagined what must have been going on inside that creepy old house right then.

Suddenly Olivia ran past them, up the front path, looking over her shoulder as if she was being followed. When she was sure that she hadn't been she pulled on the chain that rang the front door bells.

The children who were watching her became agitated and called out to their mother. She came running back and took them by the hand. But before she left, she called out to Olivia.

"Where are you going, young lady?" demanded the children's mother. "Come away from there before they answer the door."

Olivia turned around to face them, she held up both hands, thumbs and pinkies stuck out.

"Sleep-over, par-ty!" said Olivia, just before the front door opened and she disappeared inside.

Chapter 32
One Of Us

Nearly an entire school term had passed since Penny Dreadful and her friends had their very first great adventure in the Gothic Kingdom. She hardly noticed the time though. She was too busy concentrating on school work, making new friends and learning from her Uncle Calagari all there was to know about the twin world that she now knew she was a part of.

On Sunday afternoons, they would travel there together and visit her relatives, her old friends and make some new ones in the process.

She and D'artanion became close friends and found all sorts of mischief to get into, but that's another story. For now it would suffice to say that Penny D no longer felt isolated and lonely. She felt part of something.

For the first time in her life she was looking forward to spending the Summer in Terracotta. Outside of her house that is. And with Malcolm, Harold and Olivia as well.

However, Olivia would only be available on Tuesdays, Thursdays, Saturdays and every other Sunday. She had to spend her Mondays, Wednesdays, Fridays and every opposing Sunday with Penny S and Britney, and while in their company she was forbidden to speak about or refer to Penny D in any way, shape or form.

How odd it was that they all occupied the same classroom at the same time, yet Penny S and Britney ignored Penny D completely (like, really completely, as if she were a ghost or invisible or something).

For example, if Penny D were in the middle of answering a question in class, Penny S would begin to whisper to those around her and distract who she could away from her. Or worse yet, talk over her.

Mr. Proto did what he could to derail the crazy train that Penny S was riding, but there was only so much fixing a teacher could do. He didn't live with her, nor did he raise her.

Her parents were no help either. As long as she got good grades, and she did, they were fine with her and all the mischief she could conjure up.

Once, Mr. Proto had her father called into the principal's office for a stern warning about Penny S and her disruptive behavior. By the end of the meeting, the principal practically kissed his rear end as he left his office. Why? Because the little donation check he had left behind did more than compensate for any hassle she may have caused. That's why.

Yes, Penny S was still a problem. This was her own little passive aggressive way of absorbing attention from all the wrong people, places and events that she could. She simply couldn't get enough of it. She was an attention sponge.

So generally speaking, Penny S continued to be as obnoxious as usual and Penny D was fine with this.

The school as a whole became tolerant of the little Goth girl and generally ignored her. She was no longer the subject of their daily digital social media gossip. She eventually became, one-of-them. A teenager.

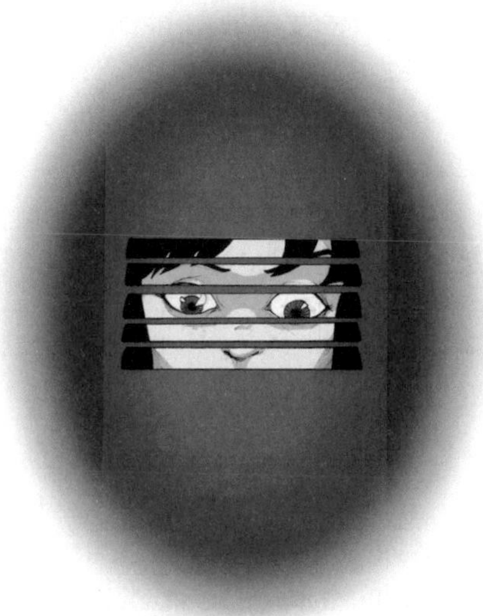

Epilogue

On the last day of the last week of the last month of school, Penny D was paid a visit by an old friend who showed up in of all places, her school locker.

It was not that she (the visitor), was hiding in there or the victim of a cruel prank but she chose this space to exit from the Gothic Kingdom in order to find Penny D as quickly as possible. It was Nellie Deranged, and as you may remember, she was the younger sister of Daphne, the leader of the Lost Girls.

It began as a day just like any other day as Penny D opened her locker without looking. She had gotten into the habit of opening the combination lock with one hand without ever looking at the dial. She was too busy using her other hand to hold up a book. She felt compelled to finish reading the chapter she'd started reading in her last class even though the lessons for the semester were considered over.

By the end of the school year, she, Malcolm and Harold had become such good friends that they sat next to each other in every class, spent every lunch period together and walked through the halls together as well. They were so comfortable together there were times when they didn't talk at all. Penny D would read a book, Malcolm would watch a cartoon on his MyPhone and Harold would play a video game on his GameJoy.

But not today. Malcolm and Harold were, somewhere else (most probably in the Boys' Wash Room). Today two of her newest friends, Vincent and Athena, were with her. And little did they know, they were about to witness first hand what Harold had labeled as a "D Manifestation."

They were not always friends you know, that is, Penny D, Vincent and Athena. It wasn't until she'd returned from the Gothic Kingdom that they had become better acquainted.

It had happened one winter month when they, Vincent and Athena, on separate days, migrated from another lunch table to theirs, the one where Penny D, Malcolm and Harold sat. Call it curiosity or the power of attraction, but Vincent for one, felt a higher calling at this table. He was also far enough away from Penny S, that he could no longer hear her ridiculing his stutter.

Penny S, would imitate him in such a way that she could easily defend her actions if challenged. Once the room monitor asked her what she was doing, knowing full well that she was mocking Vincent. She answered, "I am practicing my Dorky Pig impression".

They all knew the colorful cartoon character Dorky Pig. He was a staple animated figure from the heydays of cinema. The room monitor suddenly forgot that Vincent was a real person with a speech impediment, who had real feelings and laughed along with Penny S and her friends. After all, she did have the impression down pat.

Not long after Vincent joined their group, Athena gravitated to their table as well. She came at first as a spy. The school president, a ninth grader whom she had a minor crush on, wanted to find out what all the gossip was that revolved around this little Goth girl.

He'd asked Athena to go incognito and do reconnaissance for him. She'd gladly agreed, but after spending only one day at the little Goth girl's table, she either forgot to report back to him or changed her mind completely.

(Or perhaps it was just friendship that changed Athena's mind. You decide for yourself).

She immediately found Penny D a likeable person when she learned that ancient culture was just one of her favorite subjects. And she was further impressed that Penny D knew the origin of her name and what it meant.

"How could anyone who had an appreciation for Greek culture be bad?" Athena thought to herself.

When she asked Penny D about her name, meaning the Dreadful part, Penny D thought she was talking about her first name. So she told her the layman version of the origin of her name, leaving out the Gothic Kingdom and skin-walker parts. What she did tell Athena was how a one cent piece became the symbol of her parents' love for one another. Thus Penny, should be the name of their first born child.

Athena found the story romantic and they bonded. However, she was forever the pragmatist and pointed out a loop hole in the story as she saw it.

"Well, then it was a good thing you didn't turn out to be a boy." said Athena.

"But they didn't want a boy," said Penny D. "They wanted a girl. Me. And they got it. Me, that is."

"It's not like we get a choice," said Athena, then snickered to herself.

"I'm sure you're wrong," said Penny D. "Both my mother and father decided very early on that they wanted a girl and that was that."

"Wait, you're confused, medical science says...," started Athena.

"No she isn't, just go with it," said Malcolm, cutting in without ever even looking up from his Dorky Pig cartoon.

"That's ridiculous, I just read in the American Medical Journal, a conclusive report...," Athena started again.

"No, it's wrong," said Harold. "This is just one of the many medical fallacies I intend on disproving once I get into med school. I plan on writing my thesis on it."

"There are more things in Heaven and Earth, Athena, than are dreamt of in your medical journals," said Vincent.

They all laughed but not at Athena's expense. It was a release of their pent up anticipation. Penny D had been coaching Vincent on reviewing and focusing on his sentences before he spoke them. She asked him to imagine himself speaking cleanly and clearly without any stuttering. When he followed this meditation, he almost always spoke without a stutter. It was a work-in-progress and his friends cheered him on.

But stutter issues aside, Athena was going to argue her point anyway. And that was how Athena became part of the group.

Vincent and Athena blossomed into an old married couple. They bickered, they agreed, they bickered again and agreed again. But on this special day, a day that will be remembered and discussed for years to come, they were following Penny D down the hall to her locker and stopped their typical teen bickering just long enough to witness what could only be described as a young girl stuffed inside of Penny D's locker like a chef would stuff a turkey.

Vincent was the first to see this oddity, and paused just long enough for Athena to realize her argument was being ignored. When she, too, saw what Vincent saw, they both tugged on Penny D's blouse sleeve. Then pointed. Yes, it was that weird.

"Penny D, there is a girl in your locker," said Athena.

She had heard the stories from Malcolm and Harold about how all that is normal in the world began to change when you hung out with Penny D. She and Vincent had been experiencing it every day without knowing it. Good luck always appeared to follow them when they were with her.

It came in the form of simple things like; they always caught the school bus on time together or, they found lost personal items that they'd given up on or, there was just enough dessert for them in the school cafeteria even though they were last on line.

They were living the magic everyday they were with her and hadn't realized it fully. They called her lucky and it was all considered coincidence. They threw around that word as most teenagers do without knowing the full implication of its meaning.

They were taught to believe that, coincidence, meant "chance," or an unusual "happening" that should not or could not have happened but did.

This was a hard concept to wrap their minds around. As were the stories that came from Malcolm. He would jump up and down when such an occurrence took place, point to it and say "See! I told, ya."

Malcolm did have a reputation for making things up and playing pranks on people, but true to form it was always there staring them in the face and they had never paid it any mind. Until now.

Athena and Vincent's first live dose of the inexplicable and undeniable things that happened around Penny D, that could not be explained away easily, came in the form of a human body, a friend of hers, that showed up in her locker at school.

There was no way she could have gotten in there by herself and locked the door behind her. She didn't look hurt or bothered by the fact that she was in the locker at all. She was instead focused on Penny D, and there was something on her mind for sure.

"Hello Nellie," said Penny D as if nothing was wrong.

But Nellie looked different than the last time she had seen her in the Gothic Kingdom. She was not dressed in her Goth clothing, but something entirely new. In fact her whole look, her make up and her attitude were different.

To be more descriptive, she was dressed in old work clothes. She had a small metal tank hanging over her shoulder and a tool belt around her waist.

Once she had squeezed herself out of the locker, it was evident that she was dressed, or prepared for some place other than the Gothic Kingdom. On her back she had a leather backpack, with glass tubes uniformly poking out from the top, some containing a liquid and some a powder.

Around her head she sported brass goggles that had an assortment of glass lenses ready to flip down over her eyes. On her feet were some pretty tough looking boots with metal toes. She was not at all the Goth girl she had been before. She was all "steampunk" now!

But what was most disturbing was the sheer terror in Nellie's voice when she finally spoke and the true horror in her eyes that refused to blink.

"It grows, Penny Dreadful of the Poisonberries," said Nellie with a quiver in her voice.

In a worrisome fashion she pulled at her fingers that stuck out through the fingerless canvas gloves she wore.

"Bigger and bigger every day, stronger still when fed," said Nellie. "It must be stopped. It has to be stopped before it consumes us all. We are at our wit's end. That was why I was sent to collect you. We need your help. You helped us before, so you must help us again, Penny Dreadful. Will you? Will you come with me, please?"

"The girl is delirious," said Athena. "Slap her till she starts making sense."

"What, no!" said Penny D. "Nellie, I don't understand. What grows stronger? What are you talking about? Are my friends all right? Is D'artanian ill?"

"We are all in great danger," said Nellie. "All of us. And it is the Boilermaker, who threatens us!"

Then her mood changed as if she had suddenly realized something she hadn't wanted to admit to herself, until now.

"Although, it may already be too late," said Nellie.

THE END

About the Author
Carl Philip Paolino

Carl Philip Paolino is a thirty year veteran of the entertainment industry. As a producer, director, screenwriter and production designer, his credits include feature films, television series, music videos, Broadway shows and television commercials. His most recent animated film project, "The Halloween Pranksta," was co-produced by and starred Mark Hamill. As an author, his first Young Adult novel was, "Penny Dreadful and the Poisonberry Fortune." "Penny Dreadful and the Steampunk Ziggurat," is the second book in this series (available August 2015). His Young Adult literary works also include, "The Secret of the Cybersapiens."

Editors

Teel James Glenn

Teel James Glenn is a noted author living in New Jersey. He is a winner of the 2012 Pulp Ark 'Best Author of the Year,' Epic ebook award finalist, P&E winner 'Best Thriller Novel', "Best Steampunk Short", and a Multiple finalist in the "Best Fantasy short stories" Collection.

Emily R. Villany

On the short list of things Emily Villany loves, books (and the words in them) hold an extremely high rank! When she's not neck-deep in a novel or office-managing Wondersauce (a digital agency in Manhattan), you can find her either brunching with her parents and friends, or curled up on the couch with her loving boyfriend Fletcher and two of the roundest, most orange kittens you've never seen.

Cover and Chapter Artist

Zach Brunner

Zach Brunner is a New York-based illustrator. After graduating from School of Visual Arts with a degree in Film, he moved on to illustration, working on comics, children's books, animated films, and commercial storyboards. Most Notably, Zach has illustrated a graphic novel written by award-winning writer Jim Krueger, titled "The High Cost of Happily Ever After," now available on Amazon. He has been working at Mercedes- Benz's in-house Ad Agency, Torque Creative, storyboarding print campaigns and television spots. He also illustrated the cover and interior Illustrations for, "The Secret of the Cybersapiens."

Graphic Designer

Stacia Murphy

Stacia has always been an active and inspired artist whether it is with a computer, paint or thread. During her college education at Fordham University at Lincoln Center studying visual art, she discovered the beauty of typography and has been hooked on graphic design ever since.